THE CROC ATE MY HOMEWORK

THE CROC ATE MY HOMEWORK

Stephan T. Pastis

Andrews McMeel
Publishing®

Kansas City • Sydney • London

WHY DO YOU PUT UP WITH THAT STUPID RAT?? HE PLAYS YOU FOR A SUCKER! STAND UP FOR YOURSELF!!!
NO, PIG, YOU MUST LOVE RAT. HE IS YOUR FRIEND, AND HE CARES ABOUT YOU.
WHY DO YOU CARE SO MUCH ABOUT THE OTHER ZEBRAS?... YOU NEED TO LOOK OUT FOR NUMBER ONE!!
NO, NO.... YOU MUST LOVE YOUR FELLOW ZEBRAS... ...THEY DEPEND ON YOU FOR THEIR EXISTENCE.

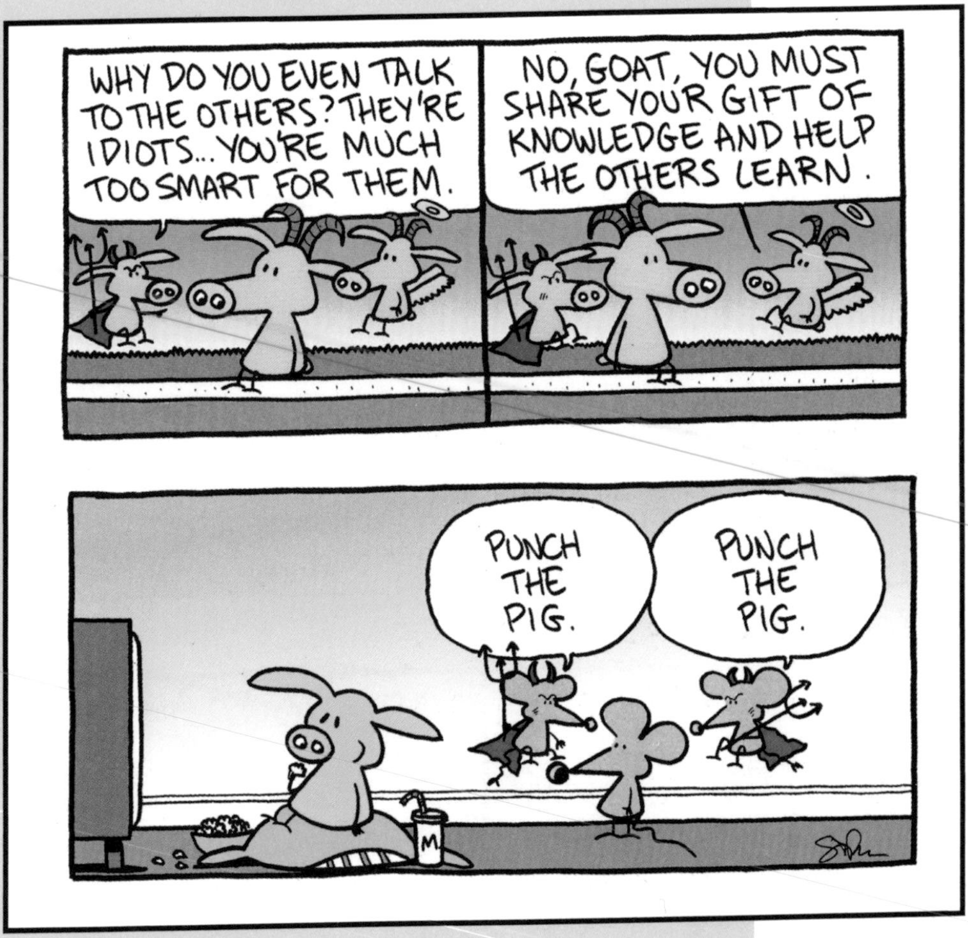
WHY DO YOU EVEN TALK TO THE OTHERS? THEY'RE IDIOTS... YOU'RE MUCH TOO SMART FOR THEM.
NO, GOAT, YOU MUST SHARE YOUR GIFT OF KNOWLEDGE AND HELP THE OTHERS LEARN.
PUNCH THE PIG.
PUNCH THE PIG.
M

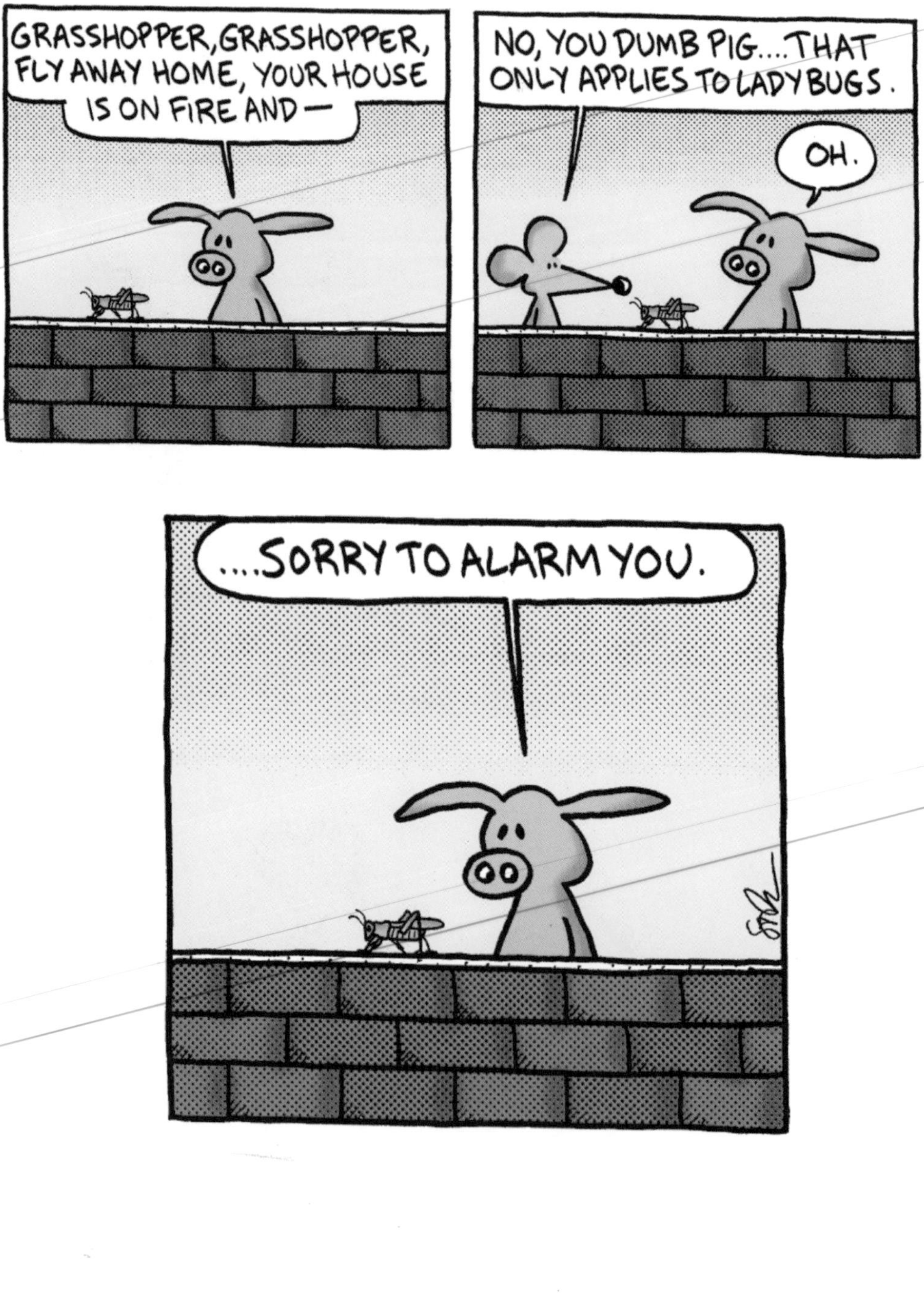
GRASSHOPPER, GRASSHOPPER, FLY AWAY HOME, YOUR HOUSE IS ON FIRE AND—
NO, YOU DUMB PIG.... THAT ONLY APPLIES TO LADYBUGS.
OH.
....SORRY TO ALARM YOU.

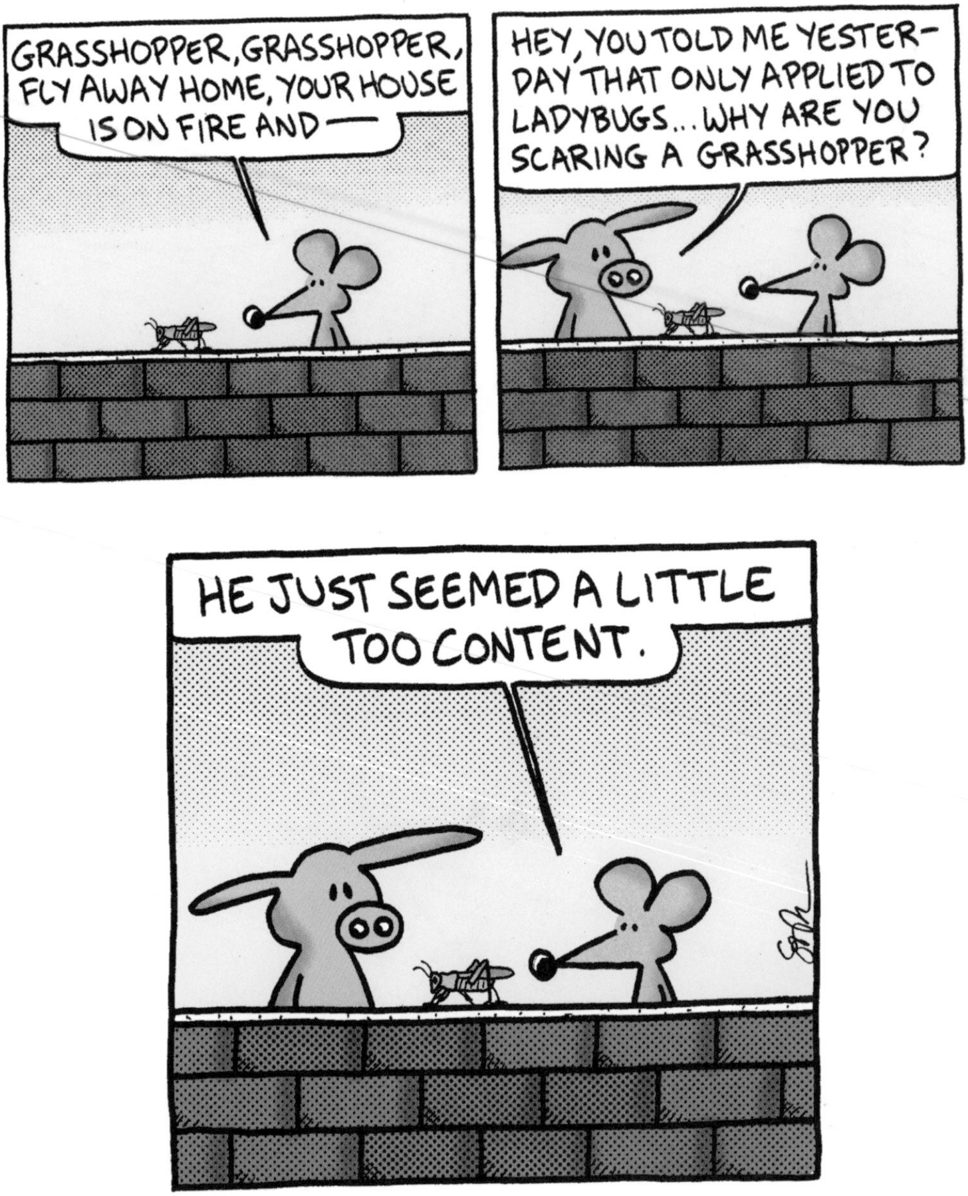
GRASSHOPPER, GRASSHOPPER, FLY AWAY HOME, YOUR HOUSE IS ON FIRE AND —
HEY, YOU TOLD ME YESTERDAY THAT ONLY APPLIED TO LADYBUGS... WHY ARE YOU SCARING A GRASSHOPPER?
HE JUST SEEMED A LITTLE TOO CONTENT.

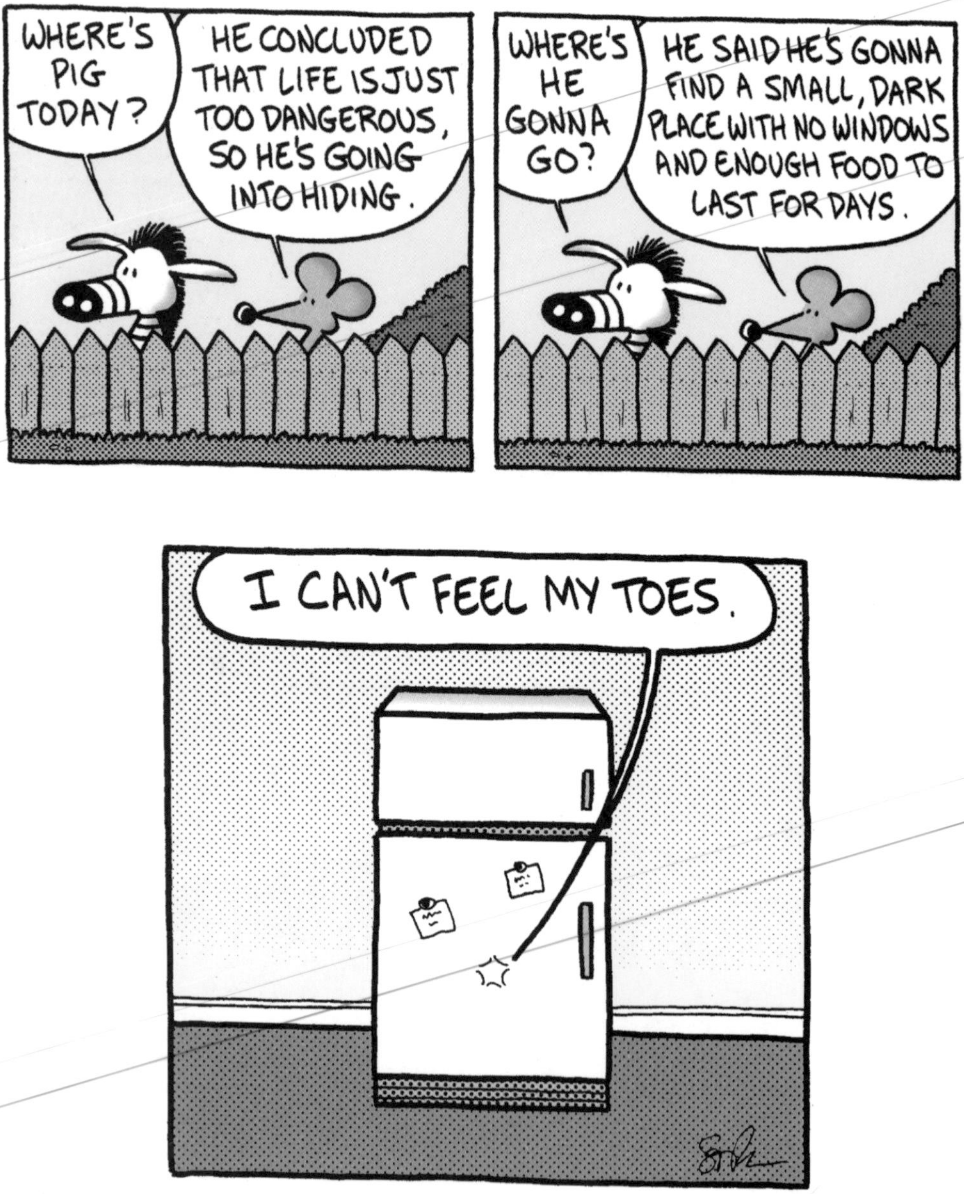
WHERE'S PIG TODAY?
HE CONCLUDED THAT LIFE IS JUST TOO DANGEROUS, SO HE'S GOING INTO HIDING.
WHERE'S HE GONNA GO?
HE SAID HE'S GONNA FIND A SMALL, DARK PLACE WITH NO WINDOWS AND ENOUGH FOOD TO LAST FOR DAYS.
I CAN'T FEEL MY TOES.

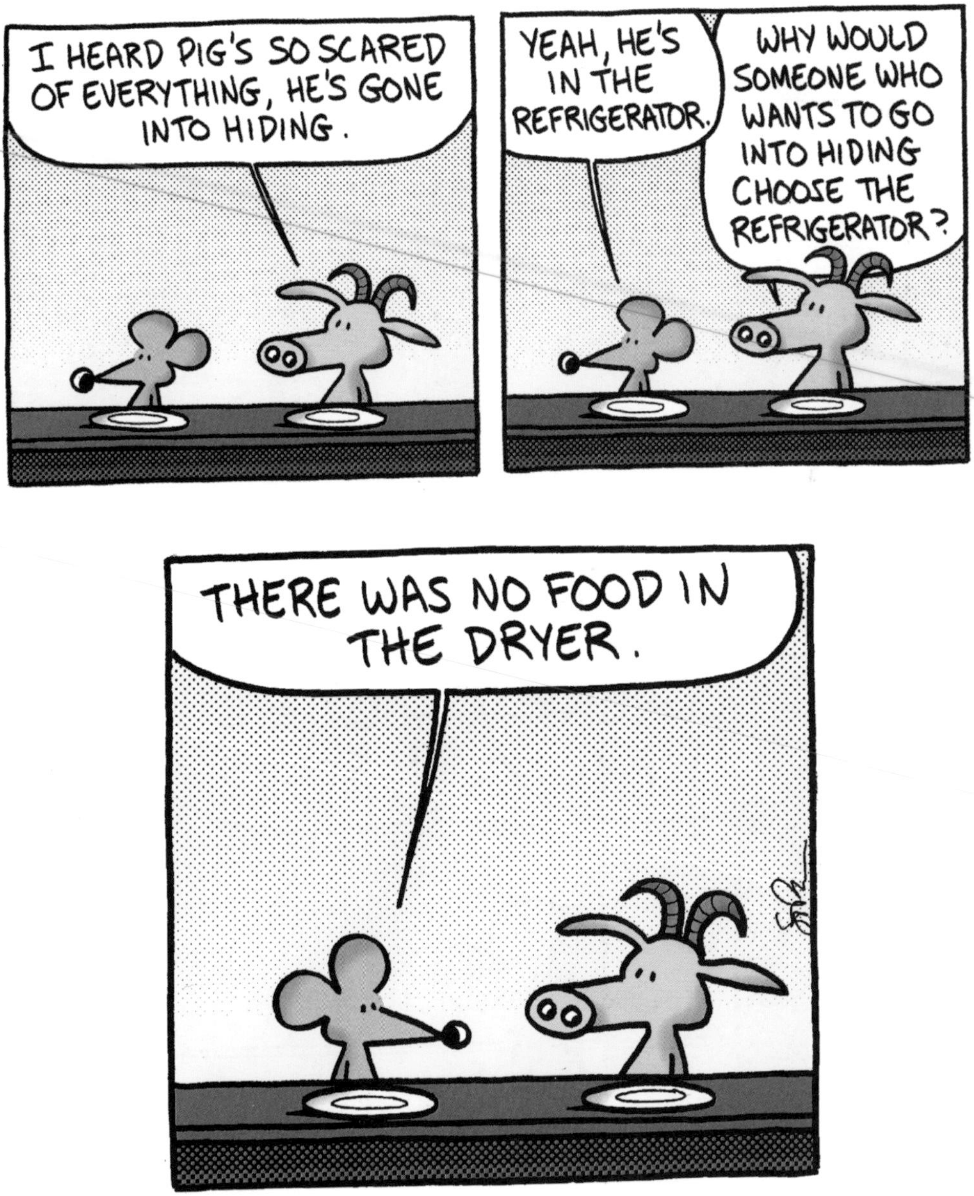
I HEARD PIG'S SO SCARED OF EVERYTHING, HE'S GONE INTO HIDING.
YEAH, HE'S IN THE REFRIGERATOR.
WHY WOULD SOMEONE WHO WANTS TO GO INTO HIDING CHOOSE THE REFRIGERATOR?
THERE WAS NO FOOD IN THE DRYER.

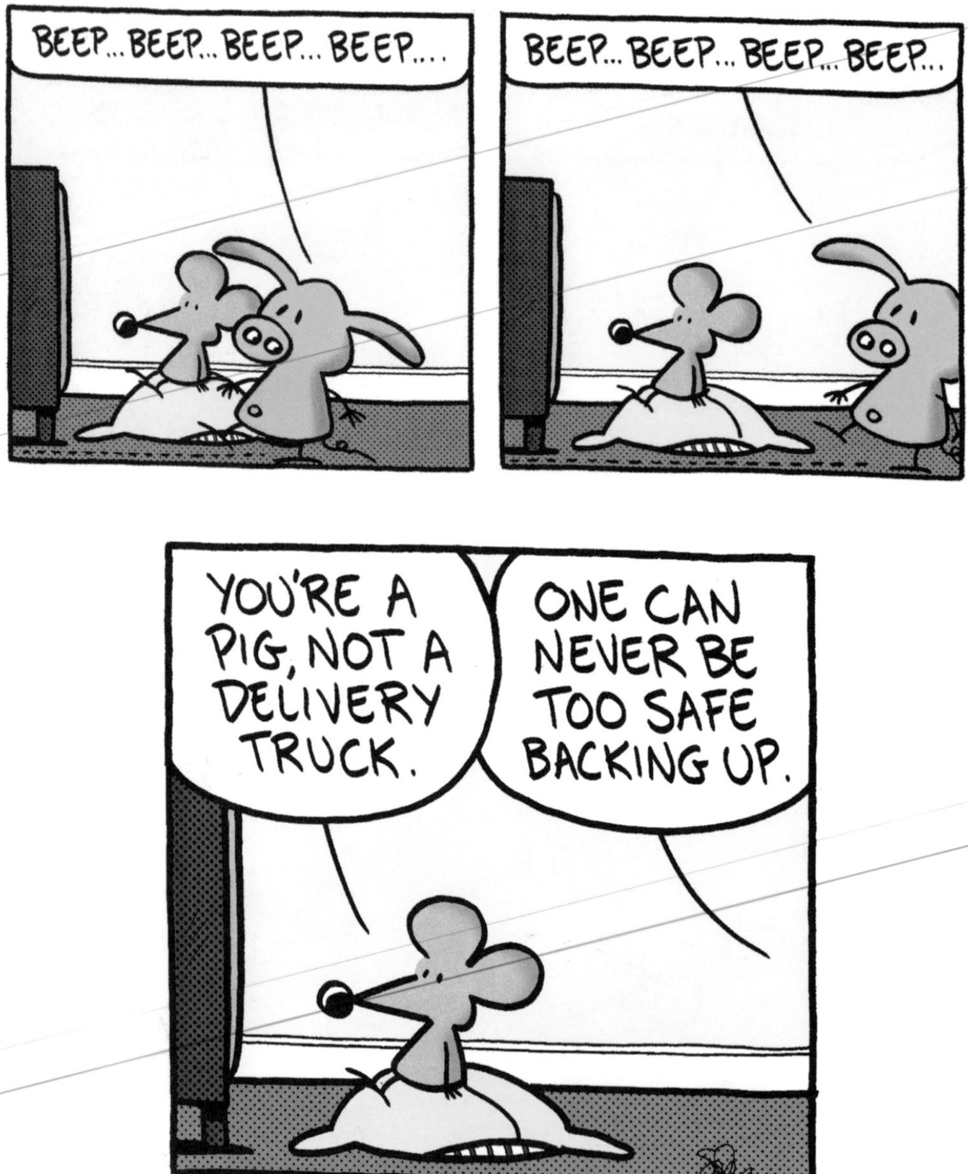
BEEP... BEEP... BEEP... BEEP....
BEEP... BEEP... BEEP... BEEP...
YOU'RE A PIG, NOT A DELIVERY TRUCK.
ONE CAN NEVER BE TOO SAFE BACKING UP.

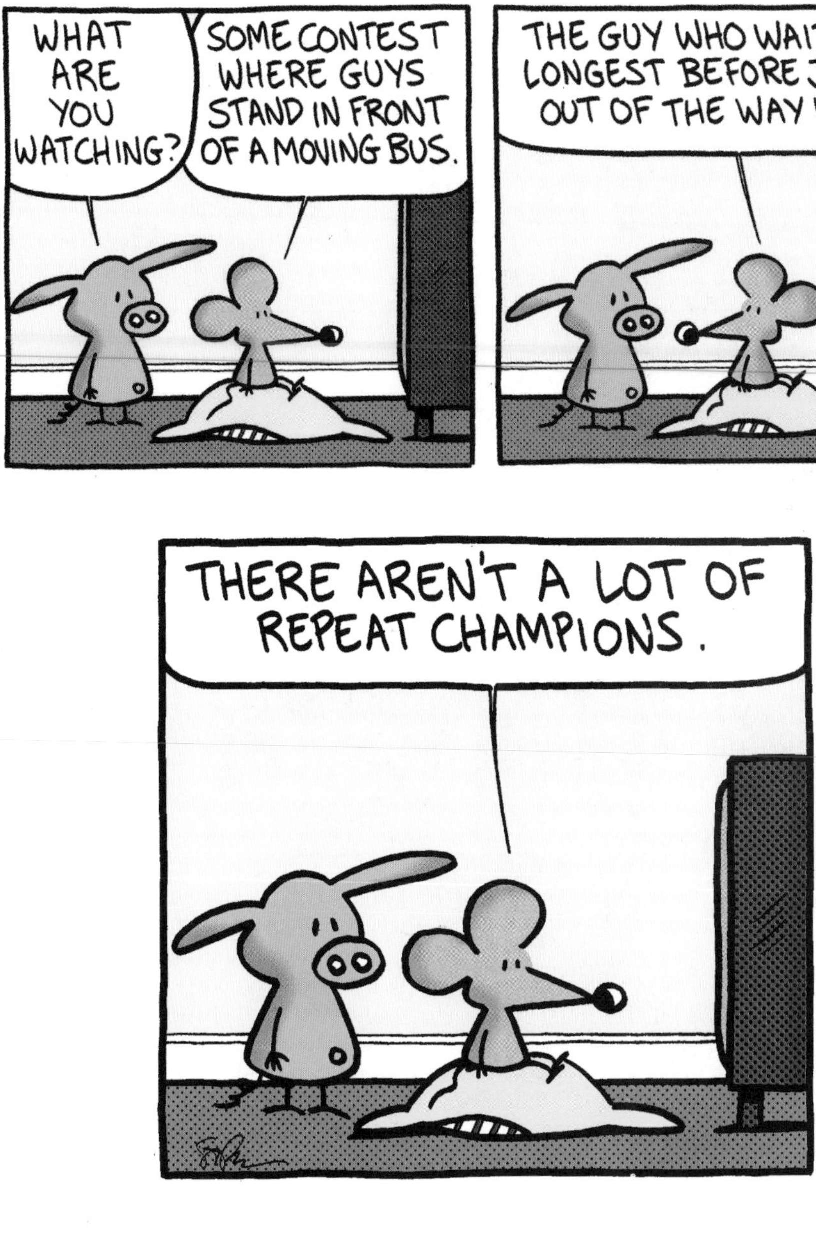
WHAT ARE YOU WATCHING?
SOME CONTEST WHERE GUYS STAND IN FRONT OF A MOVING BUS.
THE GUY WHO WAITS THE LONGEST BEFORE JUMPING OUT OF THE WAY WINS.
THERE AREN'T A LOT OF REPEAT CHAMPIONS.

THIS IS MY NEW FRIEND, FROLO, THE COMEBACK CLOWN.

FROLO REBOUNDS FROM EVERYTHING.

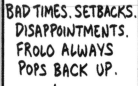

PUSH

SPROING!

BAD TIMES. SETBACKS. DISAPPOINTMENTS. FROLO ALWAYS POPS BACK UP.

PUSH

SPROING!

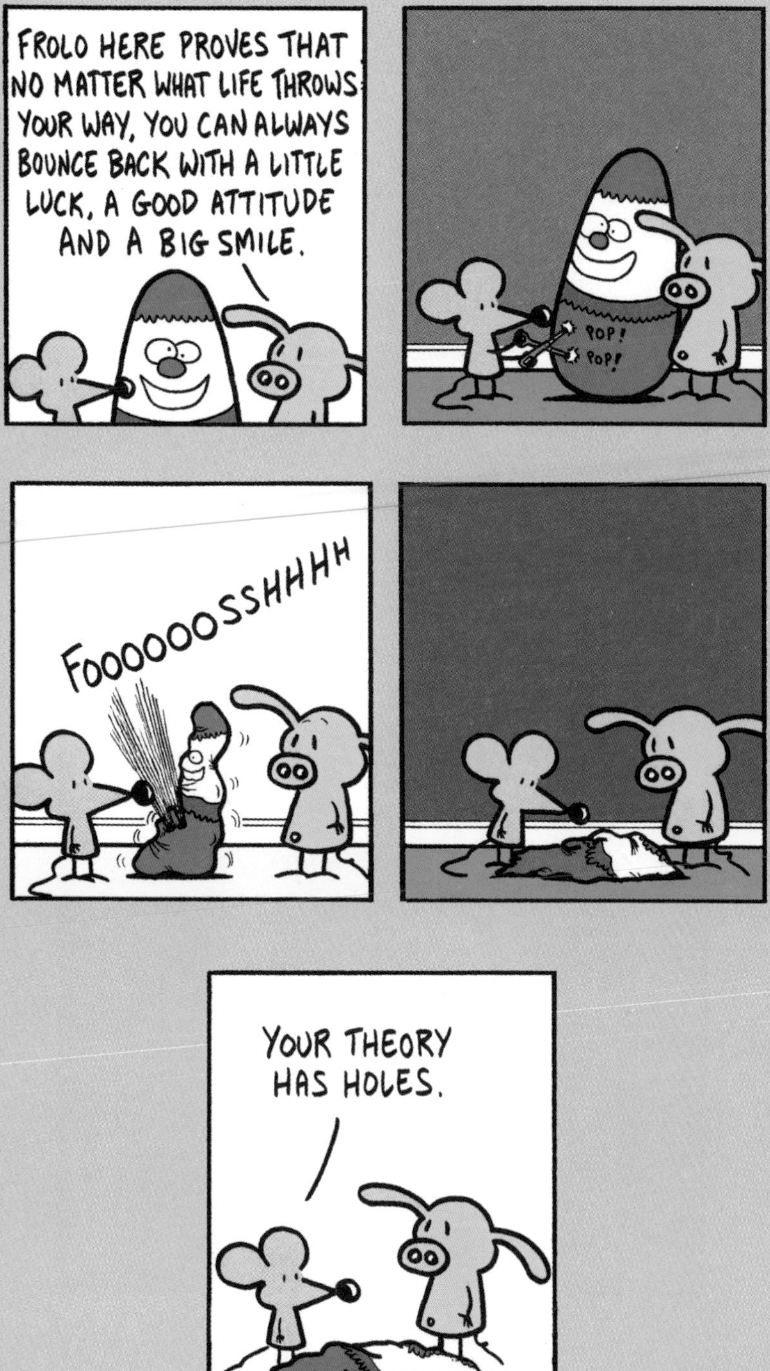
FROLO HERE PROVES THAT NO MATTER WHAT LIFE THROWS YOUR WAY, YOU CAN ALWAYS BOUNCE BACK WITH A LITTLE LUCK, A GOOD ATTITUDE AND A BIG SMILE.
POP!
POP!
FOOOOOOSSHHHH
YOUR THEORY HAS HOLES.

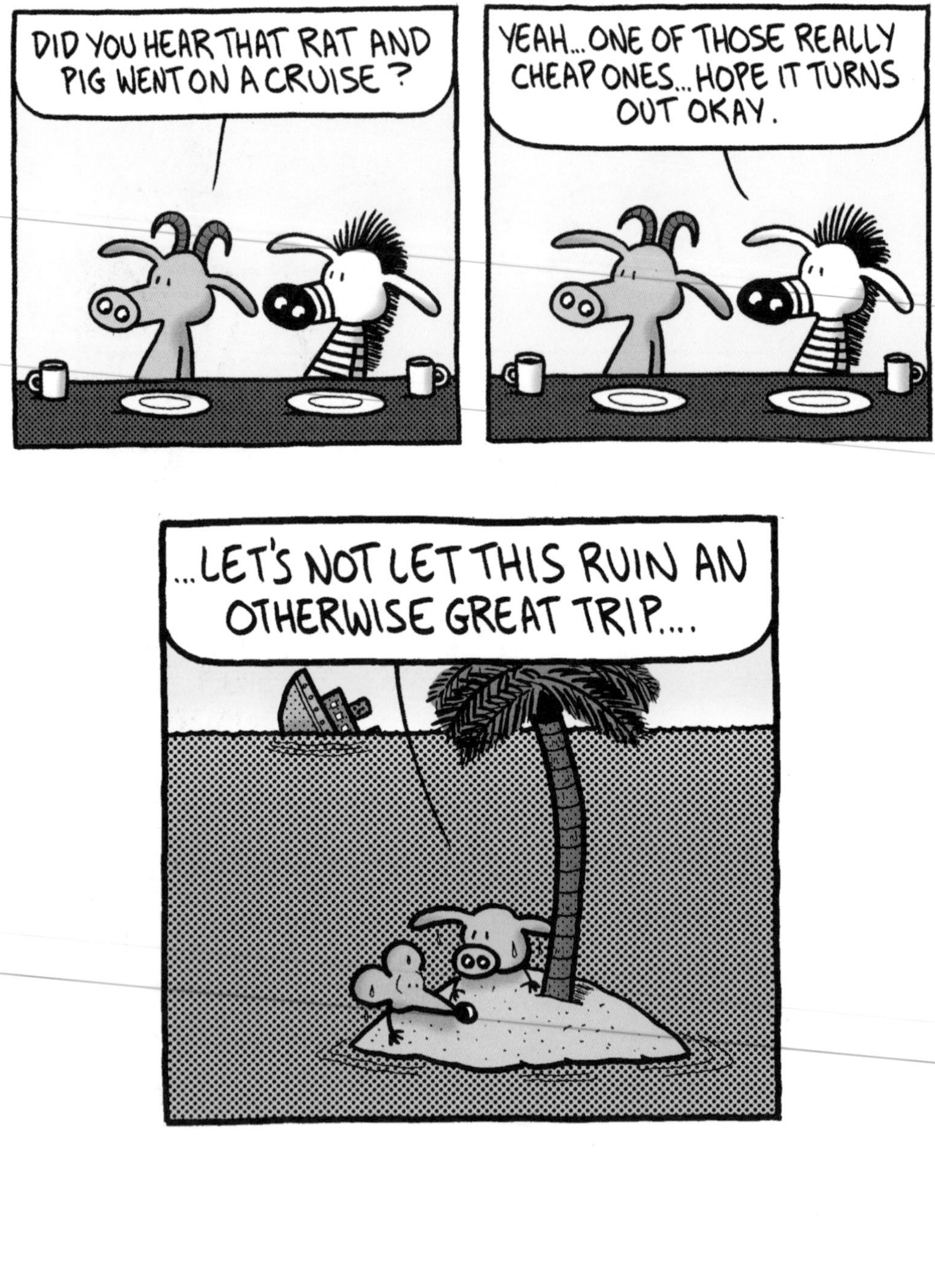
DID YOU HEAR THAT RAT AND PIG WENT ON A CRUISE?
YEAH... ONE OF THOSE REALLY CHEAP ONES... HOPE IT TURNS OUT OKAY.
...LET'S NOT LET THIS RUIN AN OTHERWISE GREAT TRIP....

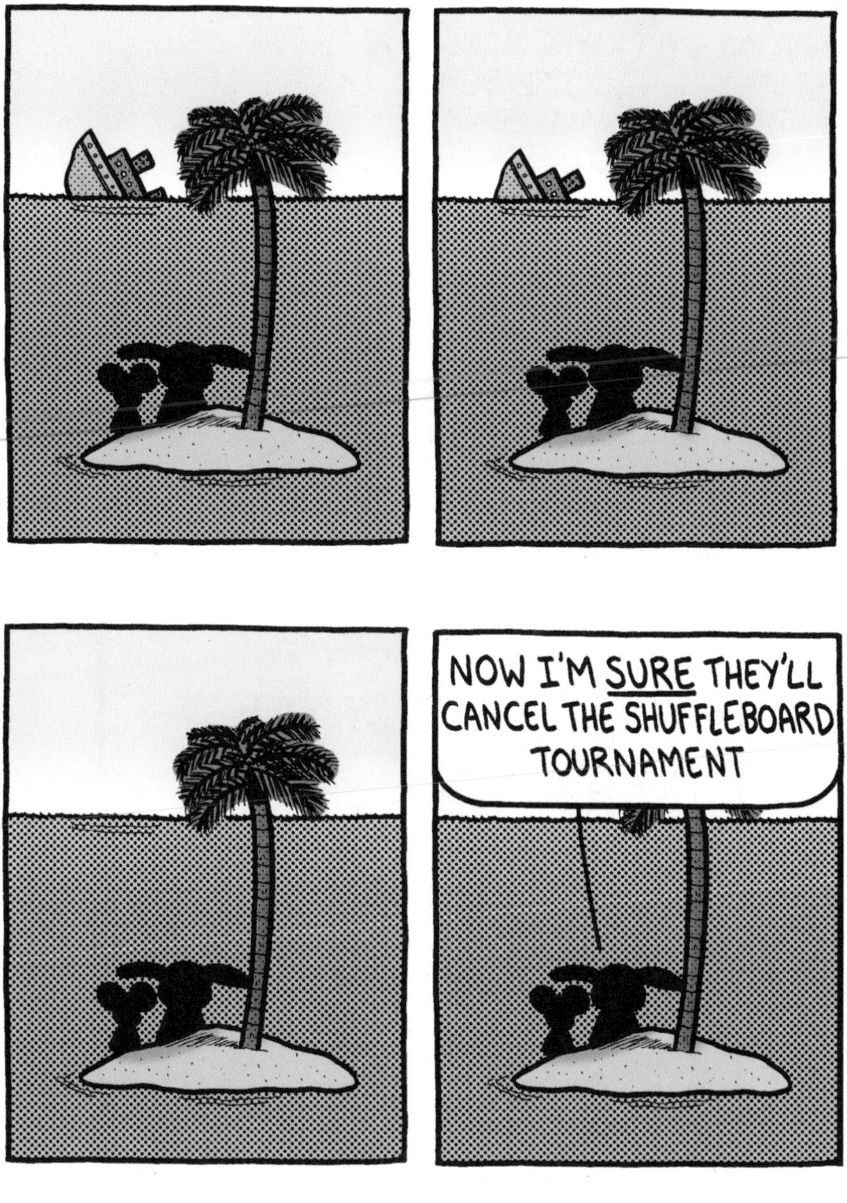
NOW I'M SURE THEY'LL CANCEL THE SHUFFLEBOARD TOURNAMENT

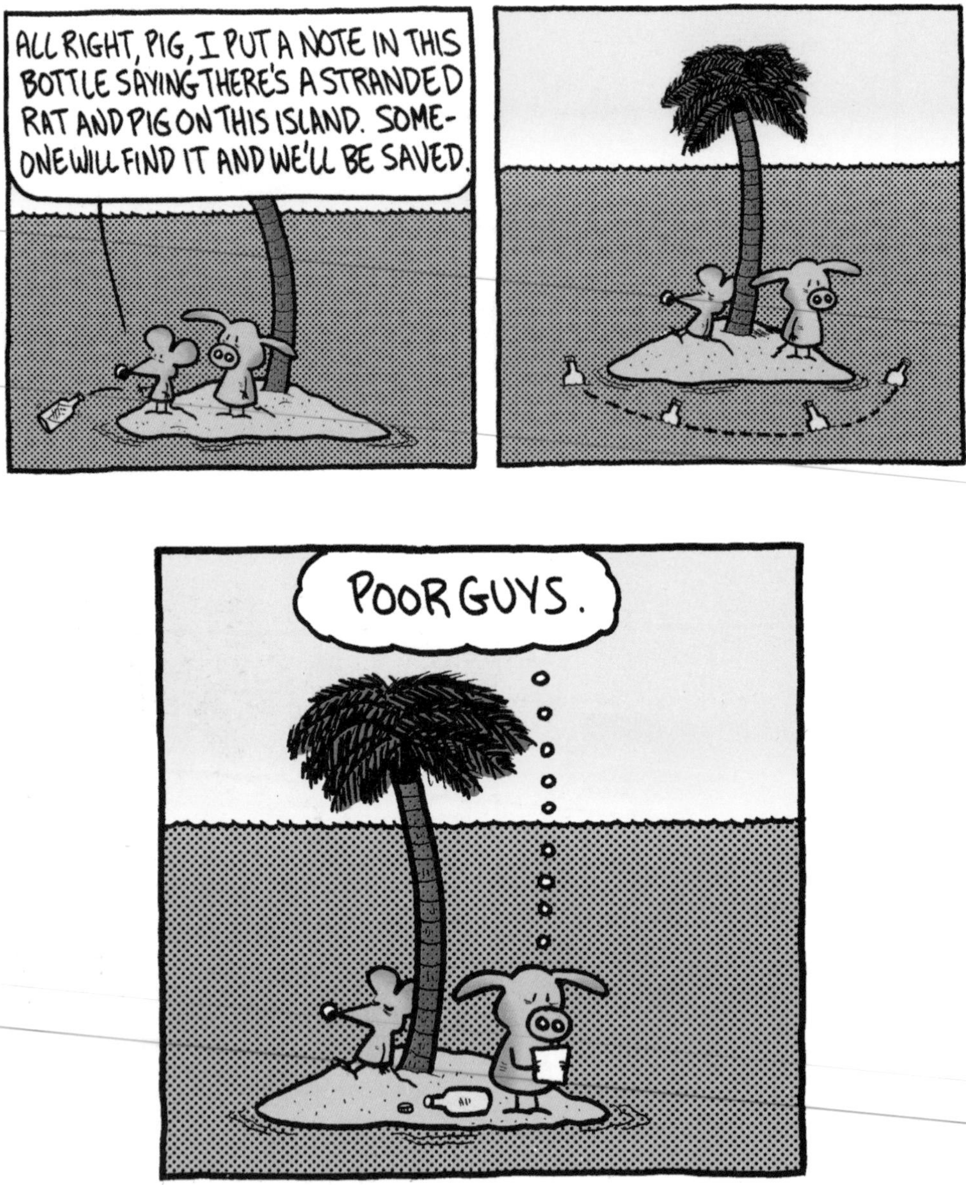
ALL RIGHT, PIG, I PUT A NOTE IN THIS BOTTLE SAYING THERE'S A STRANDED RAT AND PIG ON THIS ISLAND. SOMEONE WILL FIND IT AND WE'LL BE SAVED.
POOR GUYS.

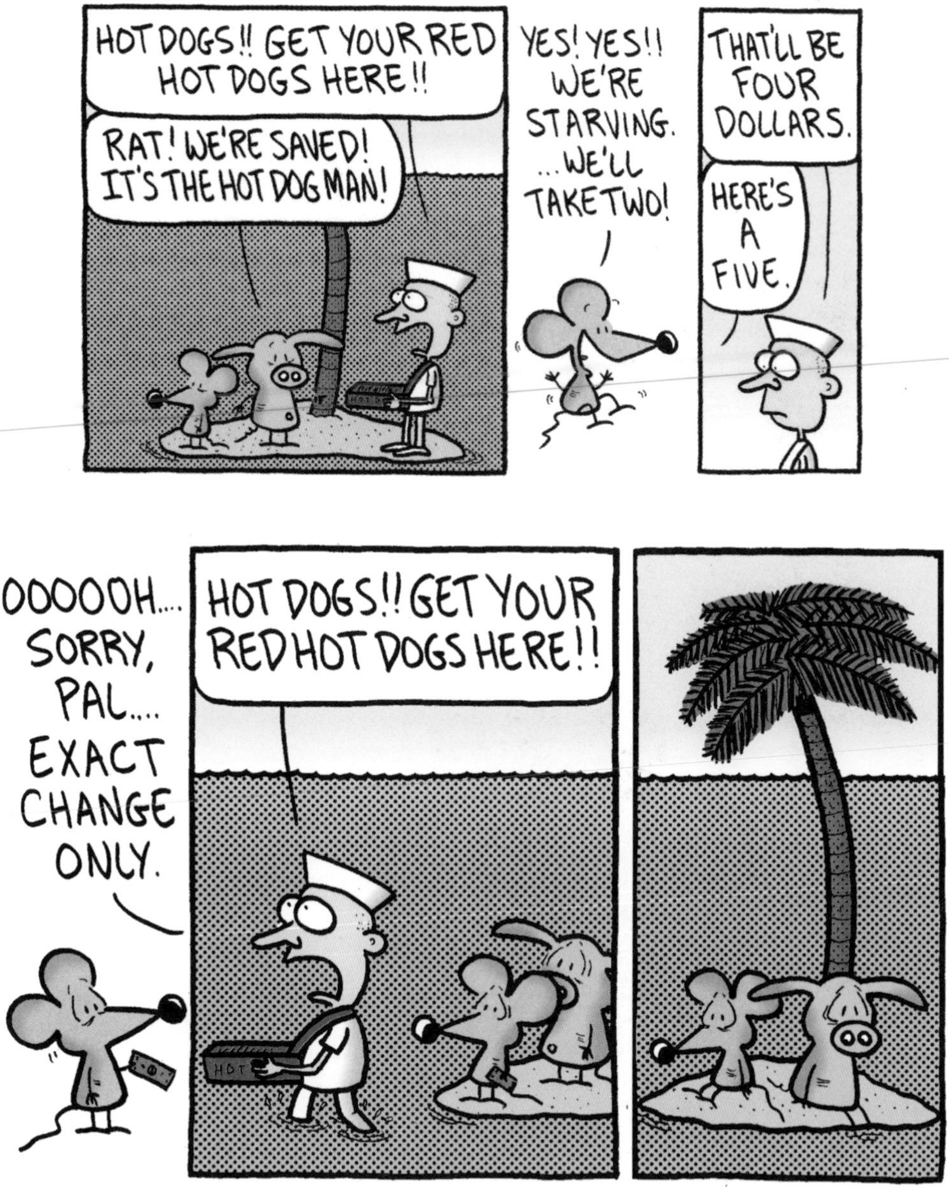
HOT DOGS!! GET YOUR RED HOT DOGS HERE!!
RAT! WE'RE SAVED! IT'S THE HOT DOG MAN!
YES! YES!! WE'RE STARVING. ...WE'LL TAKE TWO!
THAT'LL BE FOUR DOLLARS.
HERE'S A FIVE.
OOOOOH.... SORRY, PAL.... EXACT CHANGE ONLY.
HOT DOGS!! GET YOUR RED HOT DOGS HERE!!

THE CROCODILE IN THE SERENGETI KNOWS THE ZEBRA'S ROUTINE...HIS PATTERNS...HIS DAILY MIGRATION.

SO HE PICKS A CAREFULLY CONCEALED SPOT ALONG THAT ROUTE AND LIES IN WAIT...POISED FOR THE DEADLY SURPRISE ATTACK.

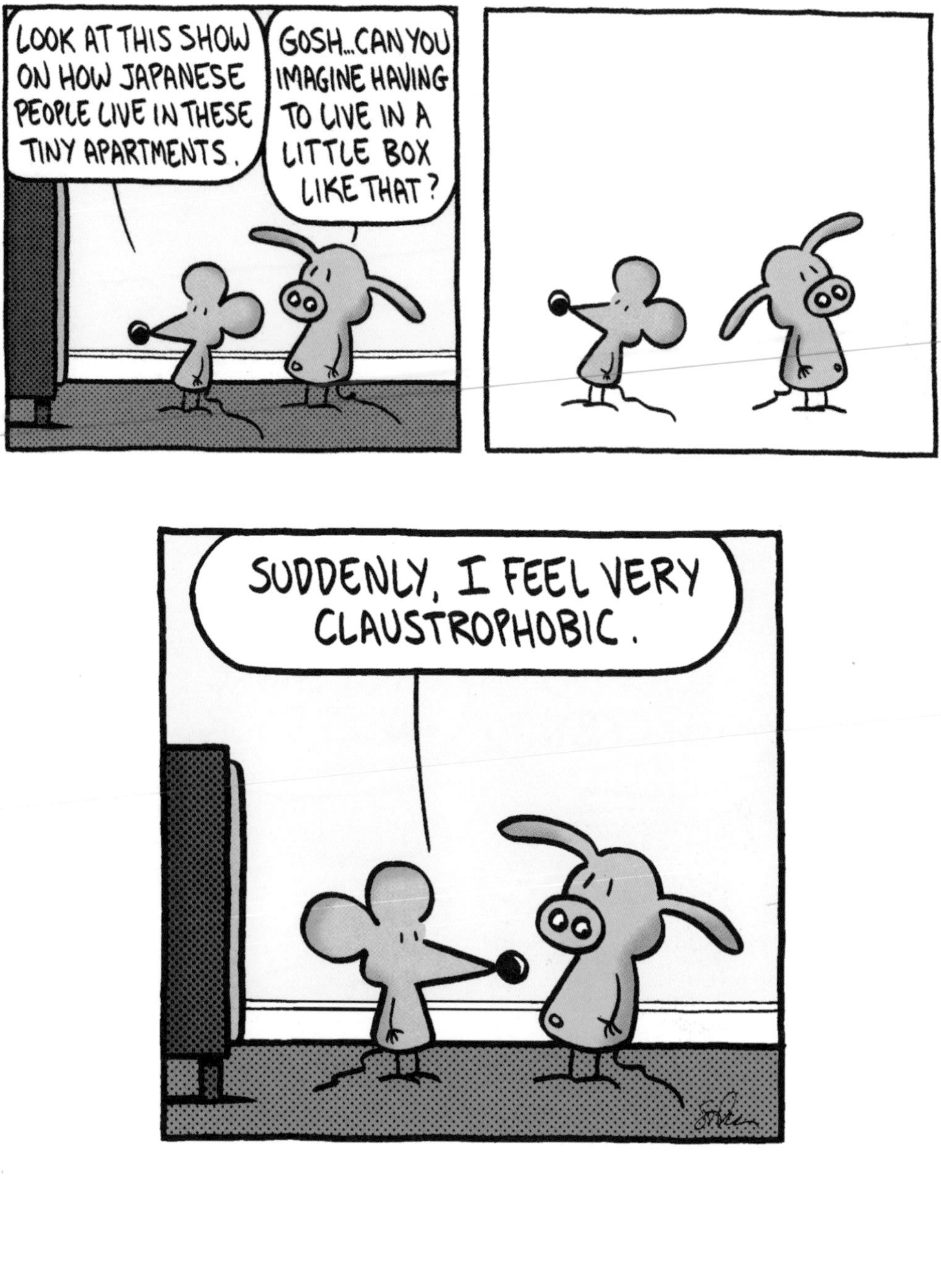
LOOK AT THIS SHOW ON HOW JAPANESE PEOPLE LIVE IN THESE TINY APARTMENTS.
GOSH... CAN YOU IMAGINE HAVING TO LIVE IN A LITTLE BOX LIKE THAT?
SUDDENLY, I FEEL VERY CLAUSTROPHOBIC.

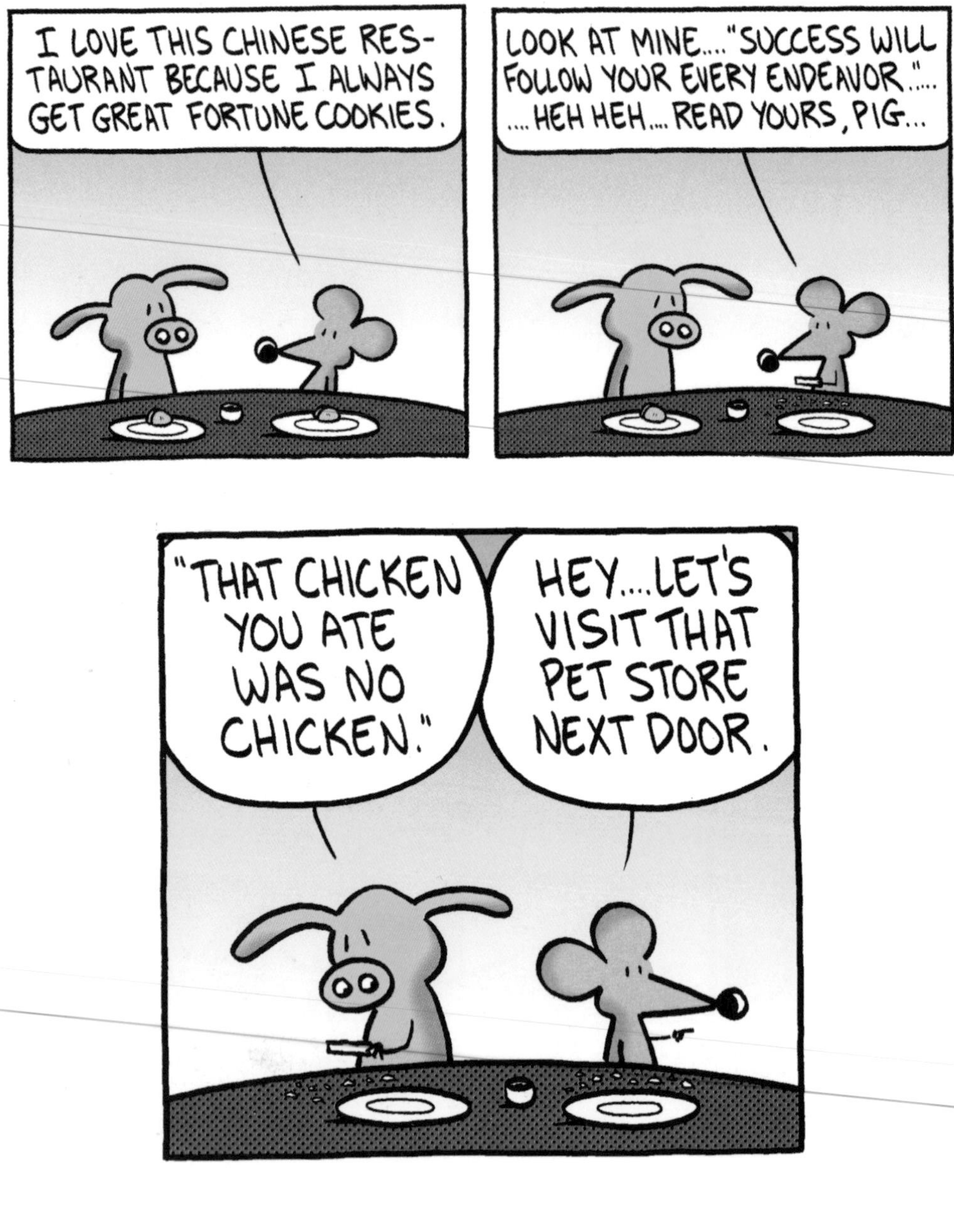
I LOVE THIS CHINESE RESTAURANT BECAUSE I ALWAYS GET GREAT FORTUNE COOKIES.
LOOK AT MINE...."SUCCESS WILL FOLLOW YOUR EVERY ENDEAVOR."..... ....HEH HEH.... READ YOURS, PIG...
"THAT CHICKEN YOU ATE WAS NO CHICKEN."
HEY....LET'S VISIT THAT PET STORE NEXT DOOR.

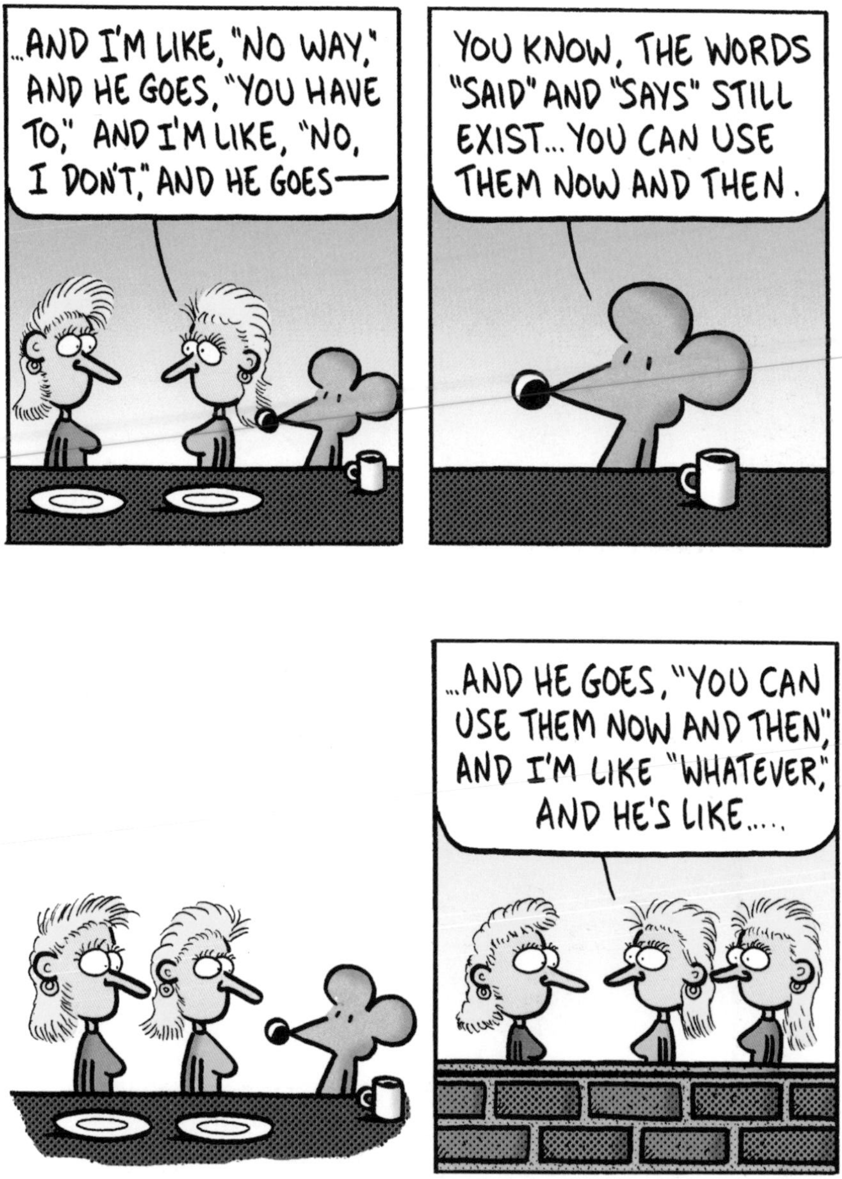
...AND I'M LIKE, "NO WAY," AND HE GOES, "YOU HAVE TO," AND I'M LIKE, "NO, I DON'T," AND HE GOES—
YOU KNOW, THE WORDS "SAID" AND "SAYS" STILL EXIST... YOU CAN USE THEM NOW AND THEN.
...AND HE GOES, "YOU CAN USE THEM NOW AND THEN," AND I'M LIKE "WHATEVER," AND HE'S LIKE.....

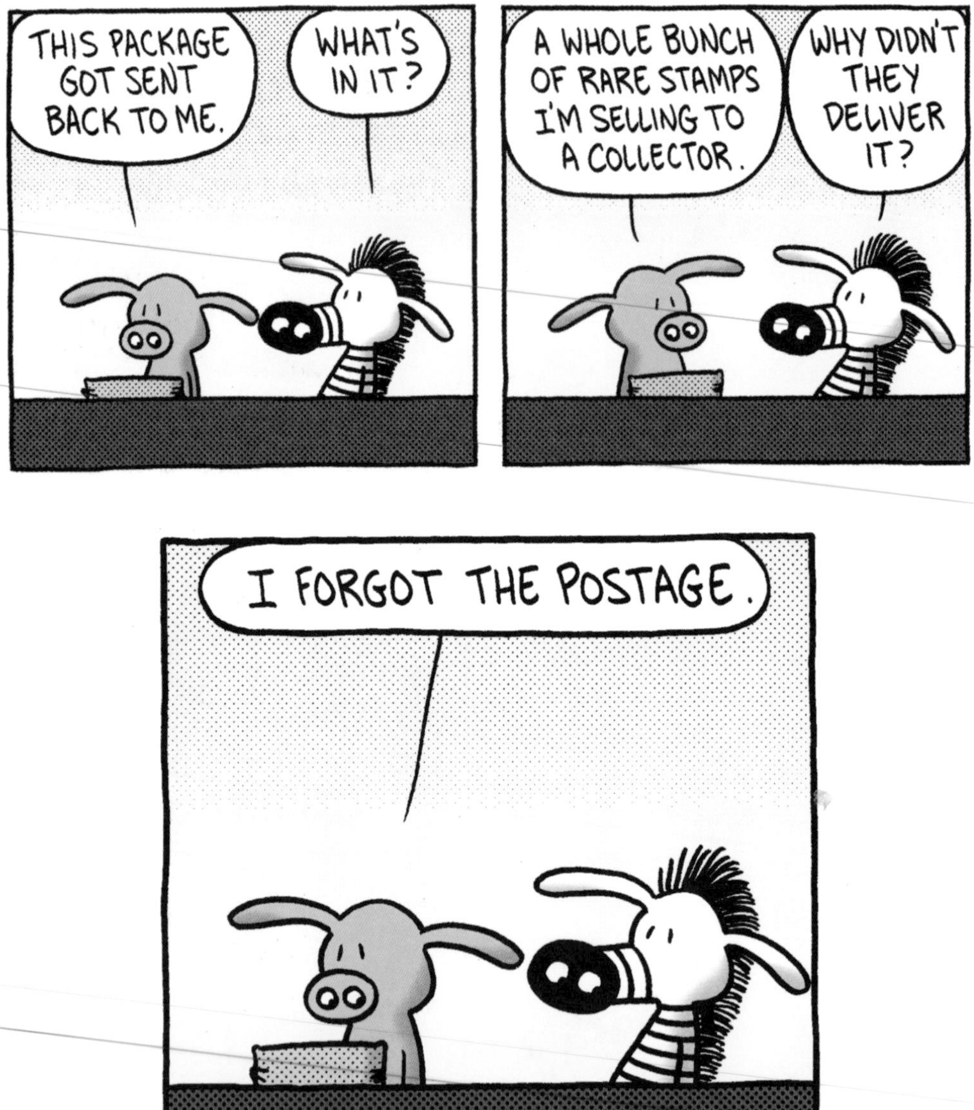
THIS PACKAGE GOT SENT BACK TO ME.
WHAT'S IN IT?
A WHOLE BUNCH OF RARE STAMPS I'M SELLING TO A COLLECTOR.
WHY DIDN'T THEY DELIVER IT?
I FORGOT THE POSTAGE.

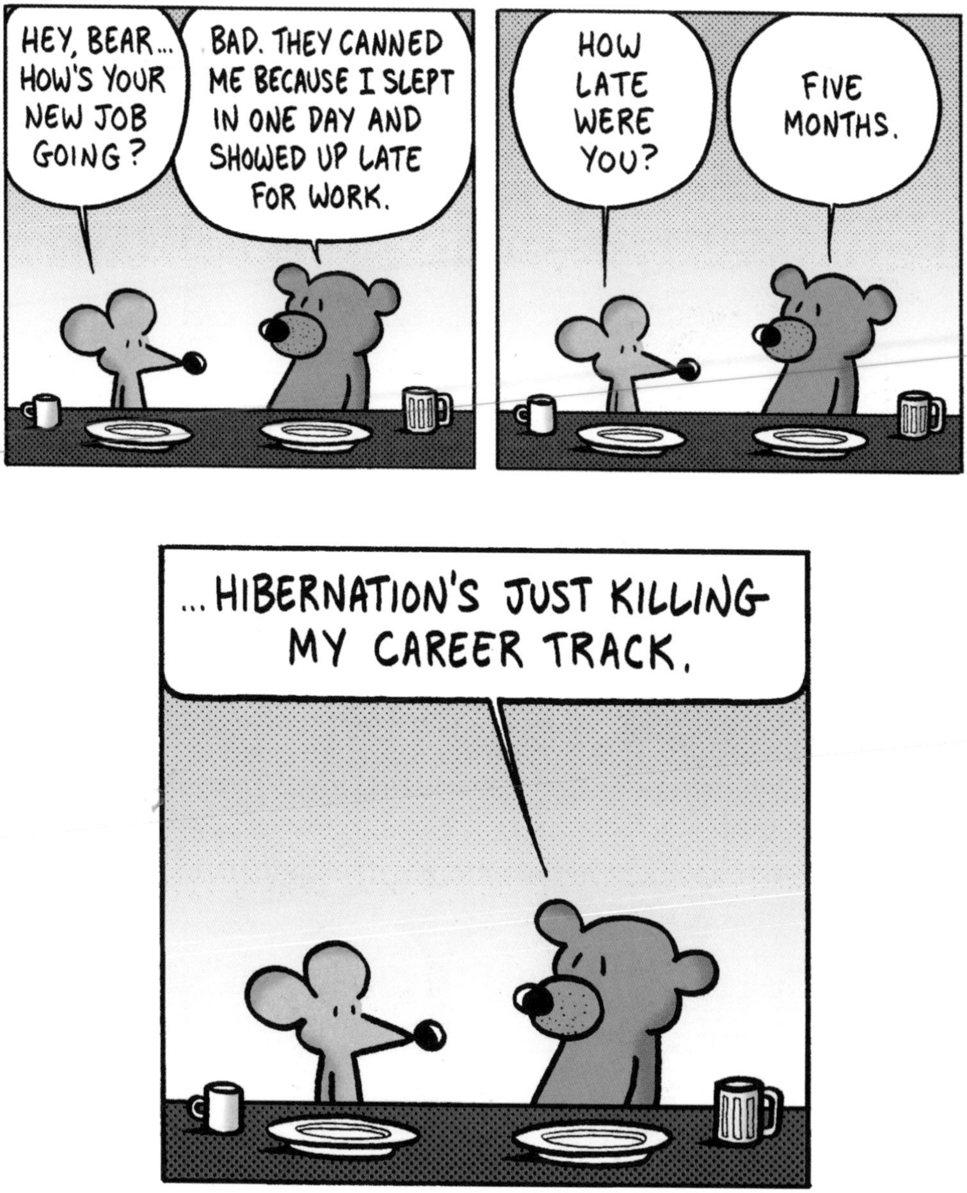
HEY, BEAR... HOW'S YOUR NEW JOB GOING?
BAD. THEY CANNED ME BECAUSE I SLEPT IN ONE DAY AND SHOWED UP LATE FOR WORK.
HOW LATE WERE YOU?
FIVE MONTHS.
...HIBERNATION'S JUST KILLING MY CAREER TRACK.

DING DONG DING DONG DING DONG
TRICK OR TREAT!
HI, RAT.
HI, PIG.
HI!
HI!

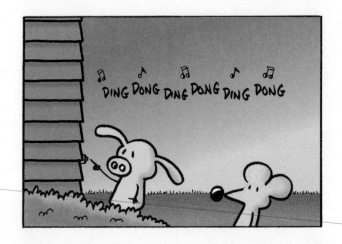

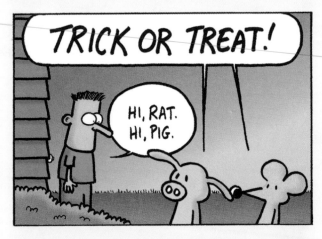

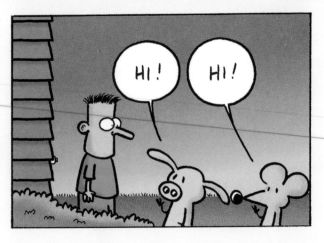

HEY, GUYS, NOT TO BE A JERK ABOUT IT, BUT I HATE IT WHEN I GET TRICK-OR-TREATERS WHO DON'T EVEN BOTHER TO WEAR A COSTUME... SORRY ABOUT THAT, BUT I JUST CAN'T GIVE YOU ANY CANDY........SEE YA.......
....YOU STUPID MORON....I TOLD YOU THIS WAS A BAD IDEA....
....AND I WORKED SO HARD ON THESE.....

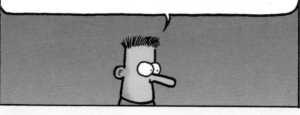

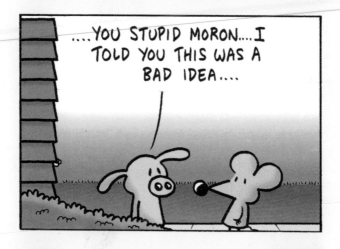

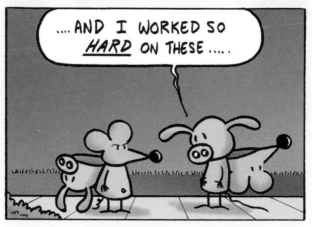

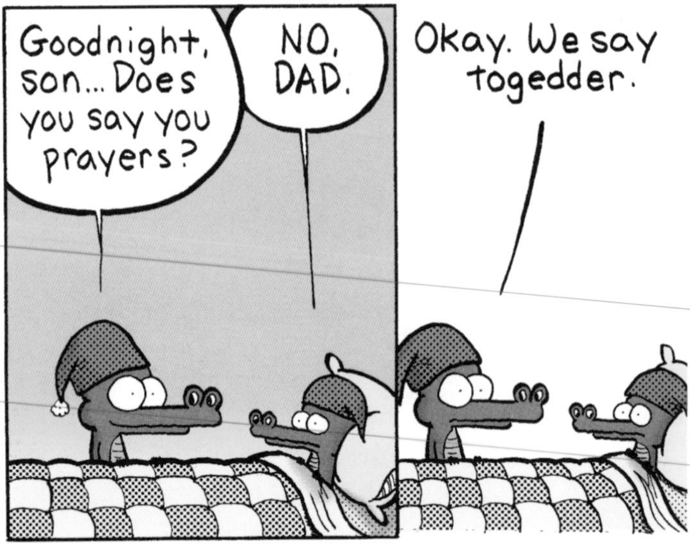
Goodnight, son... Does you say you prayers?
NO, DAD.
Okay. We say togedder.

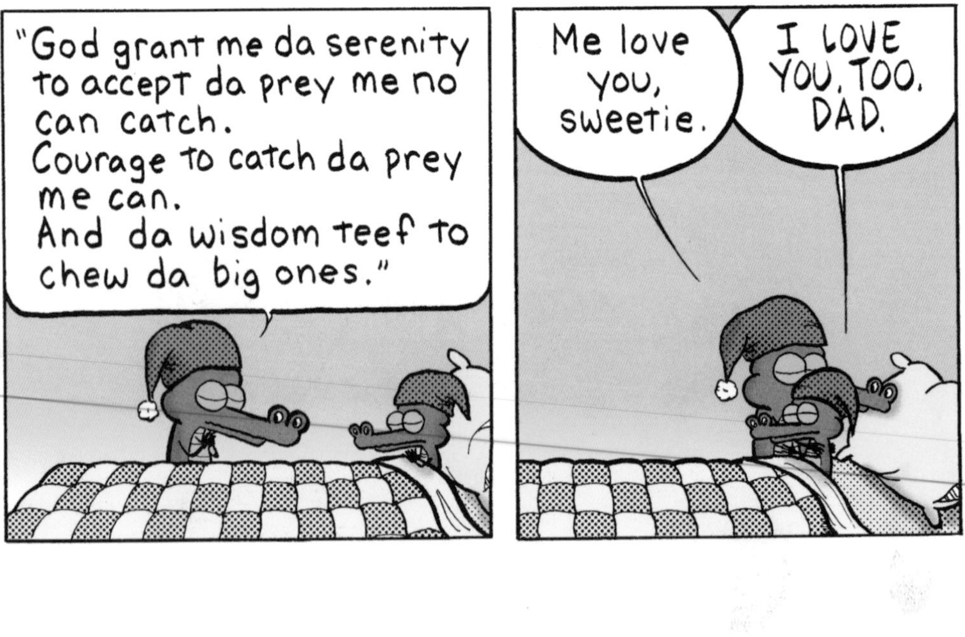
"God grant me da serenity to accept da prey me no can catch. Courage to catch da prey me can. And da wisdom teef to chew da big ones."
Me love you, sweetie.
I LOVE YOU, TOO, DAD.

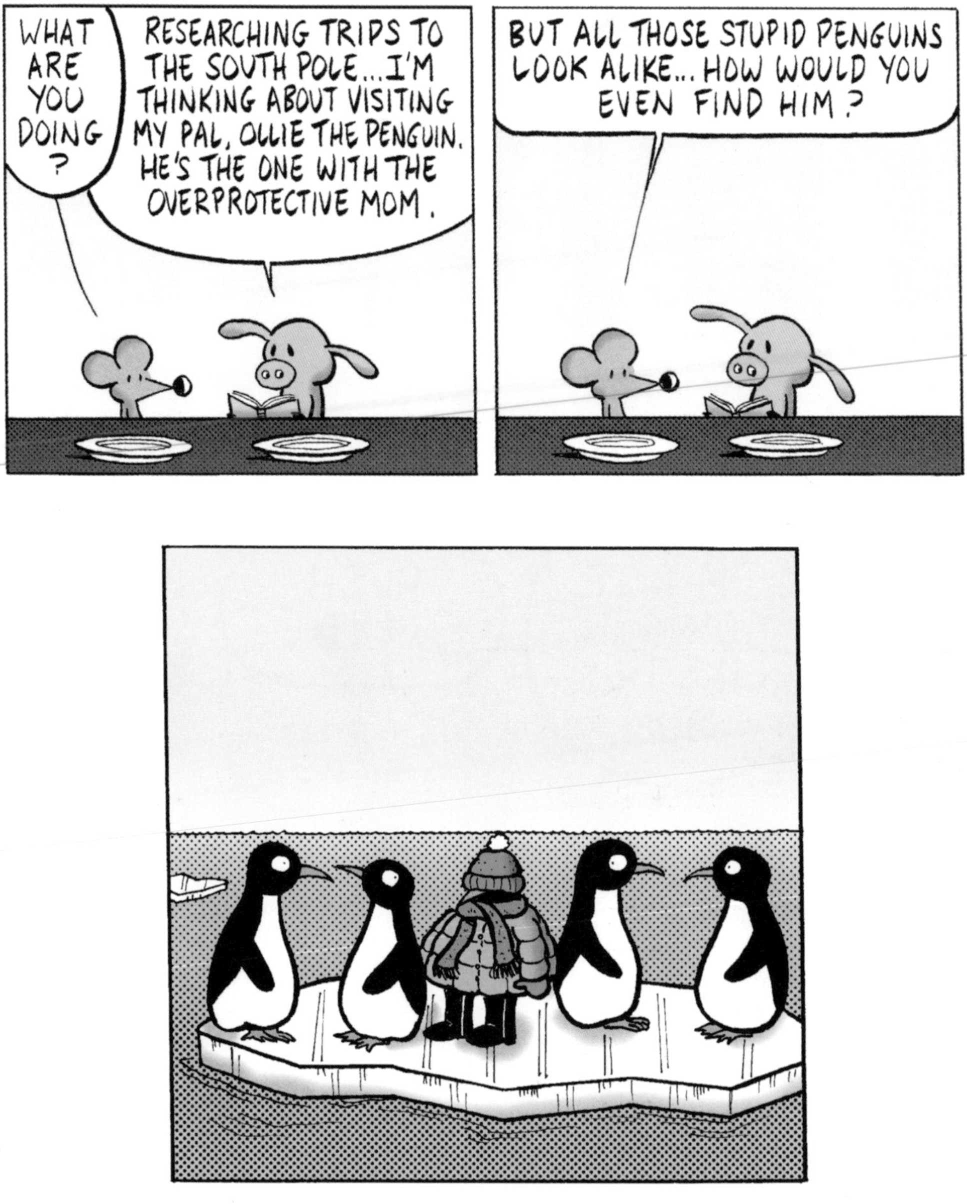
WHAT ARE YOU DOING?
RESEARCHING TRIPS TO THE SOUTH POLE... I'M THINKING ABOUT VISITING MY PAL, OLLIE THE PENGUIN. HE'S THE ONE WITH THE OVERPROTECTIVE MOM.
BUT ALL THOSE STUPID PENGUINS LOOK ALIKE... HOW WOULD YOU EVEN FIND HIM?

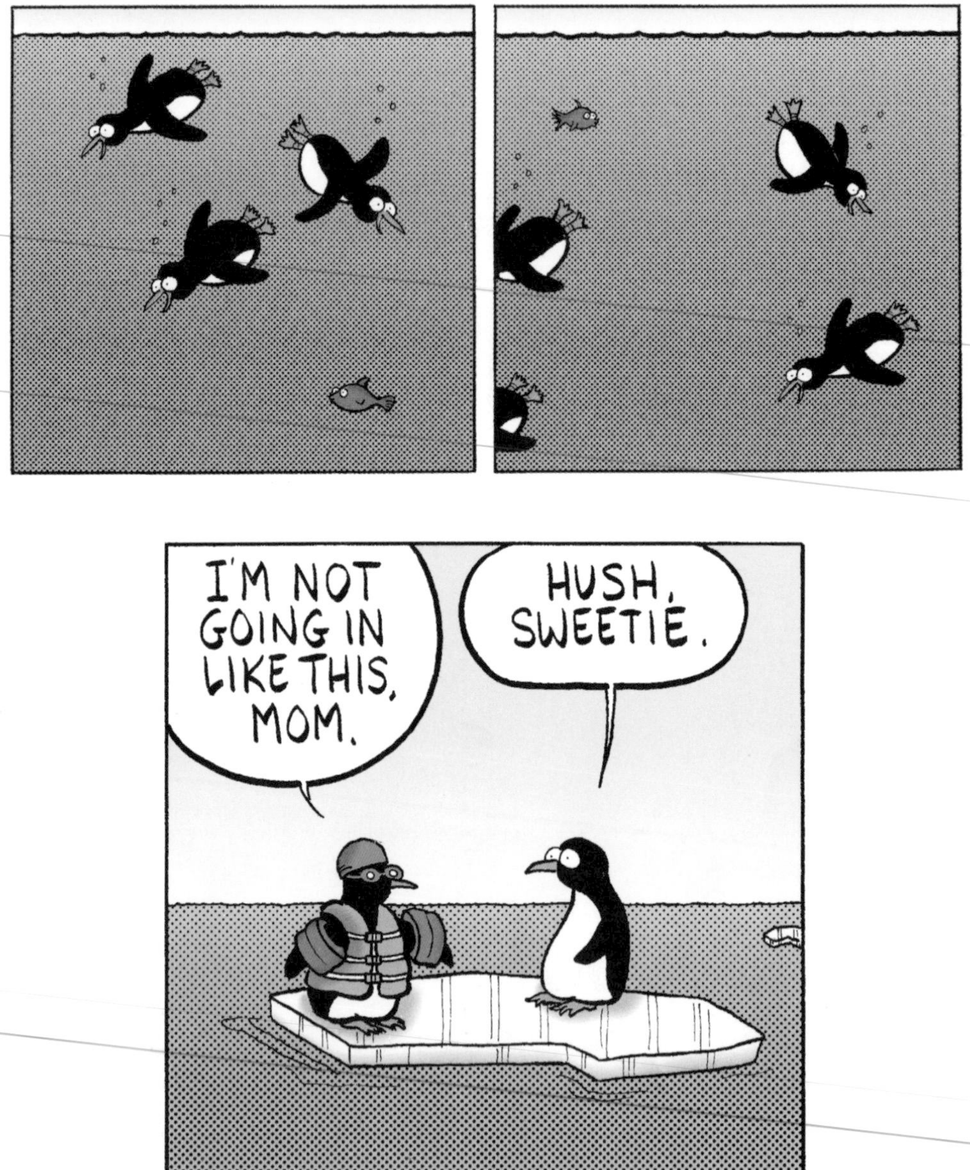
I'M NOT GOING IN LIKE THIS, MOM.
HUSH, SWEETIE.

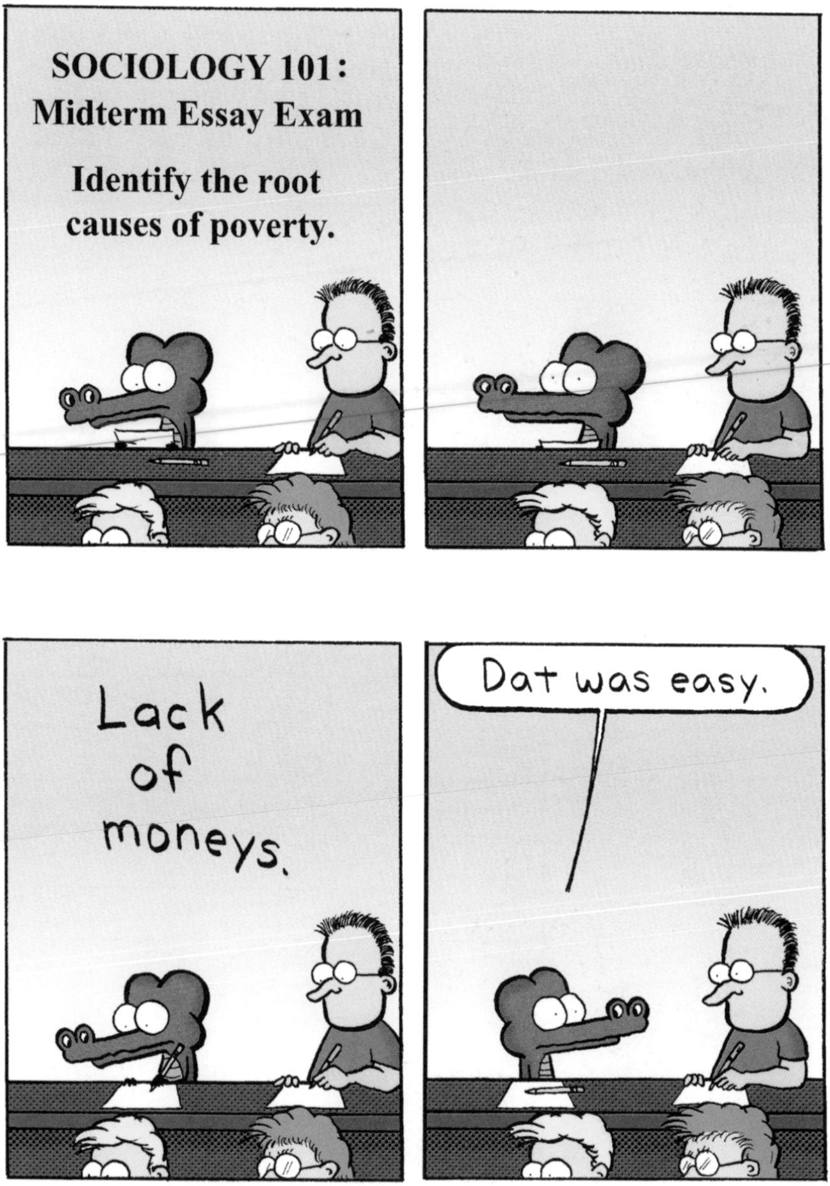
SOCIOLOGY 101:
Midterm Essay Exam
Identify the root causes of poverty.
Lack of moneys.
Dat was easy.

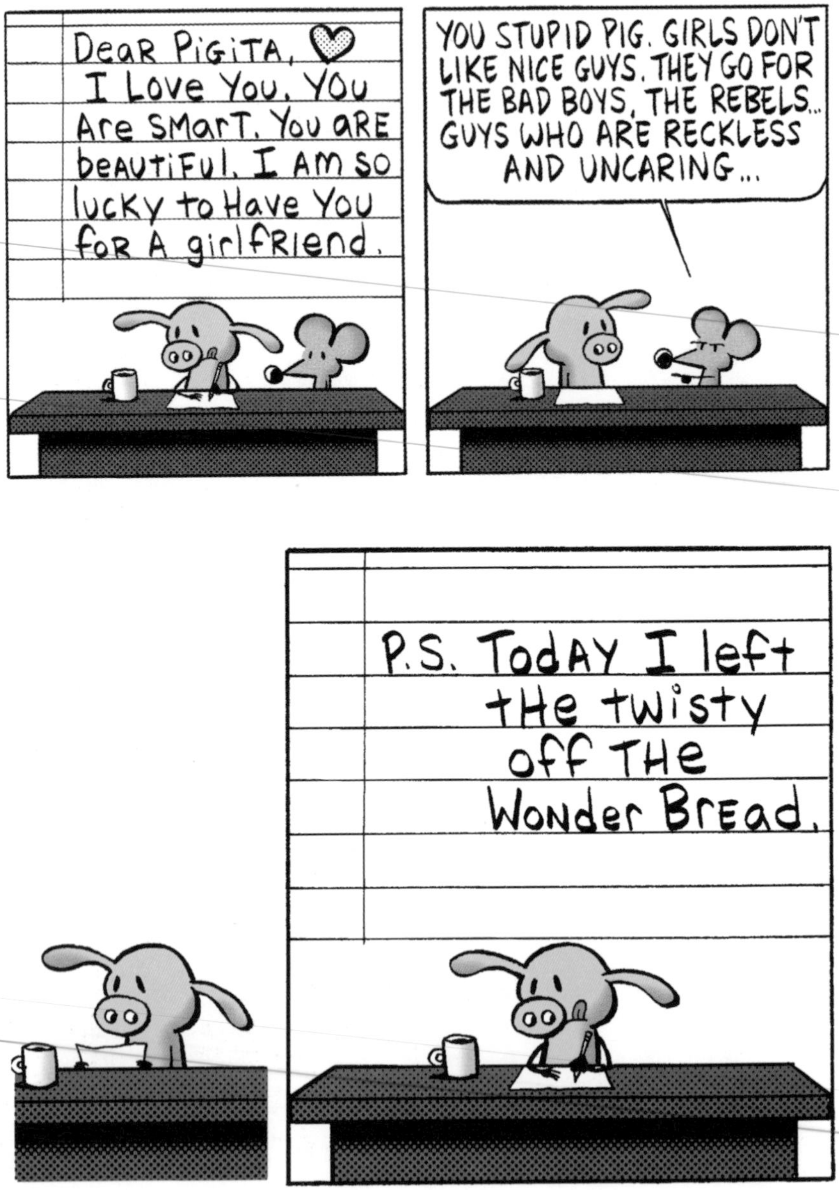
Dear PigiTA,
I Love You. YOu Are SMarT. You aRE beautiful. I Am so lucky to Have You for A girlfriend.
YOU STUPID PIG. GIRLS DON'T LIKE NICE GUYS. THEY GO FOR THE BAD BOYS, THE REBELS... GUYS WHO ARE RECKLESS AND UNCARING...
P.S. TodAY I left tHe twisty off THe Wonder BrEad.

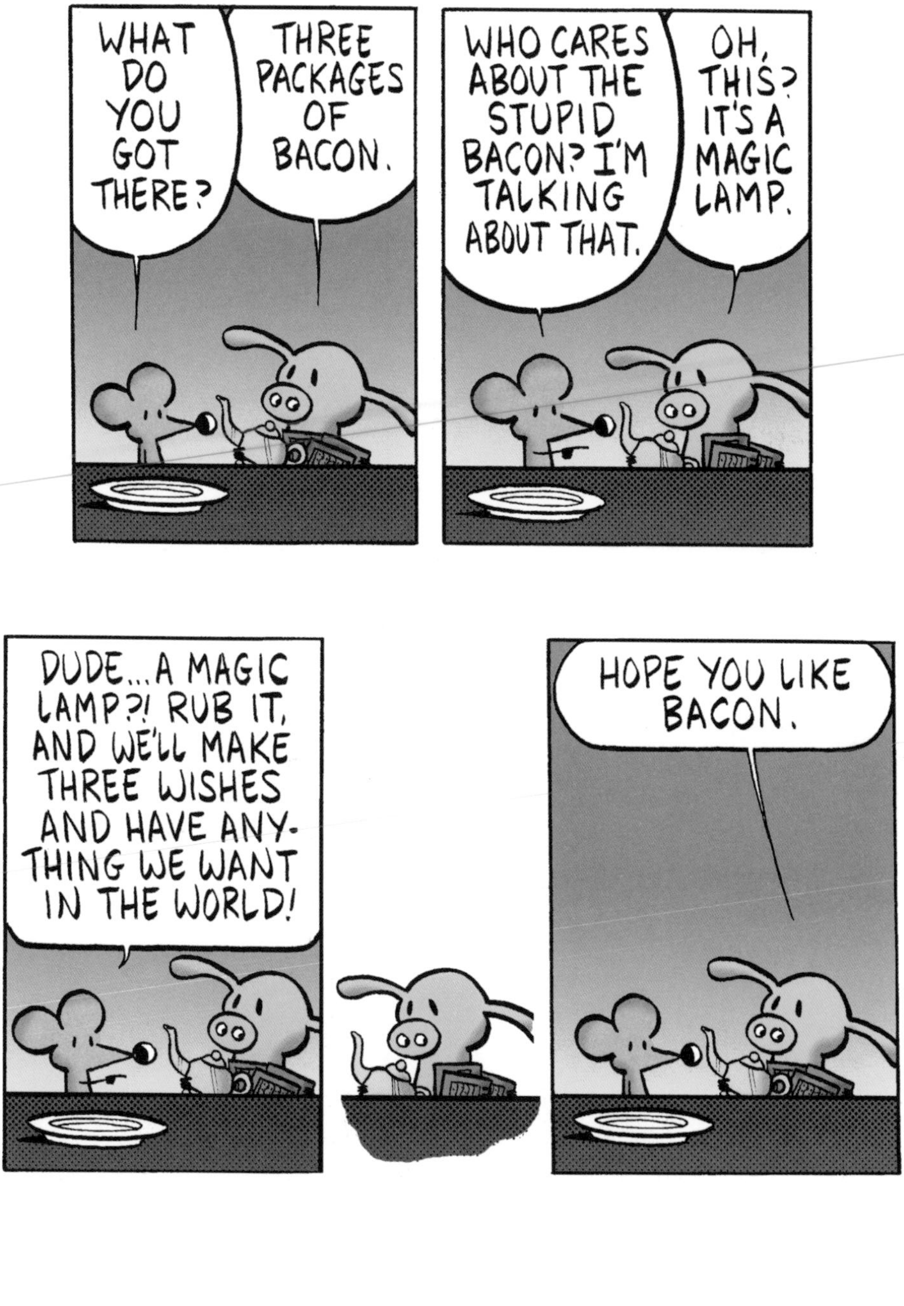
WHAT DO YOU GOT THERE?
THREE PACKAGES OF BACON.
WHO CARES ABOUT THE STUPID BACON? I'M TALKING ABOUT THAT.
OH, THIS? IT'S A MAGIC LAMP.
DUDE...A MAGIC LAMP?! RUB IT, AND WE'LL MAKE THREE WISHES AND HAVE ANYTHING WE WANT IN THE WORLD!
HOPE YOU LIKE BACON.

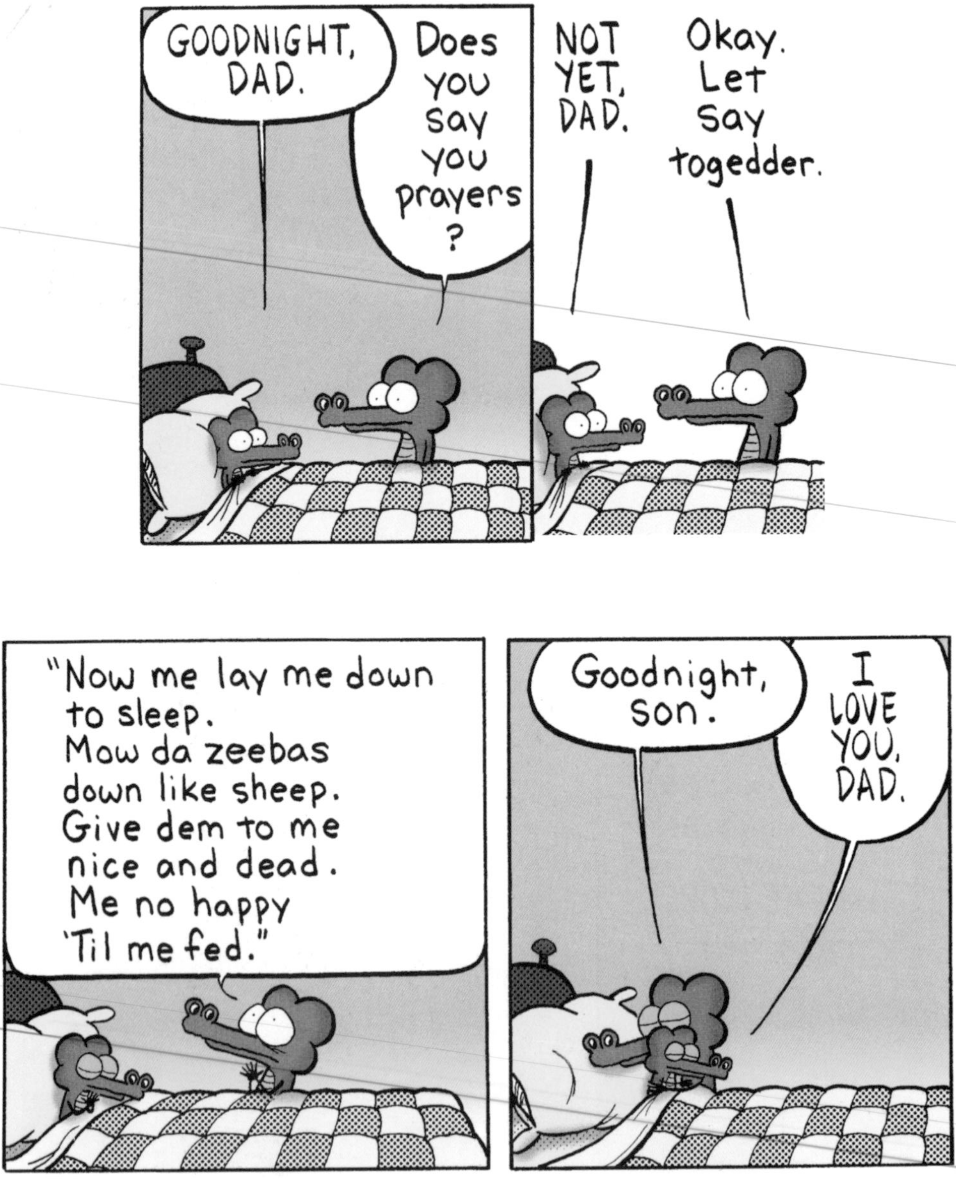
GOODNIGHT, DAD.
Does you say you prayers?
NOT YET, DAD.
Okay. Let say togedder.
"Now me lay me down to sleep. Mow da zeebas down like sheep. Give dem to me nice and dead. Me no happy 'Til me fed."
Goodnight, son.
I LOVE YOU, DAD.

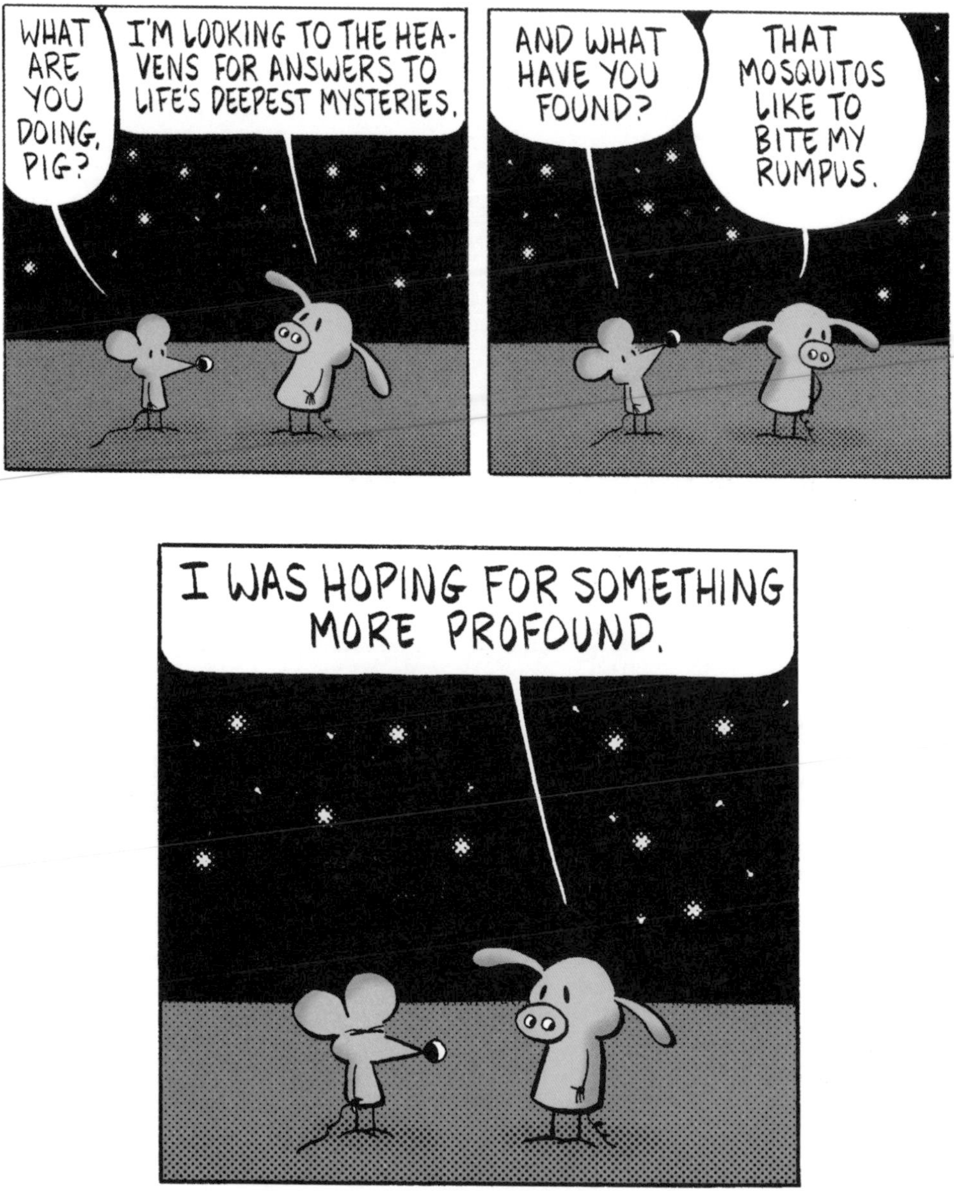
WHAT ARE YOU DOING, PIG?
I'M LOOKING TO THE HEAVENS FOR ANSWERS TO LIFE'S DEEPEST MYSTERIES.
AND WHAT HAVE YOU FOUND?
THAT MOSQUITOS LIKE TO BITE MY RUMPUS.
I WAS HOPING FOR SOMETHING MORE PROFOUND.

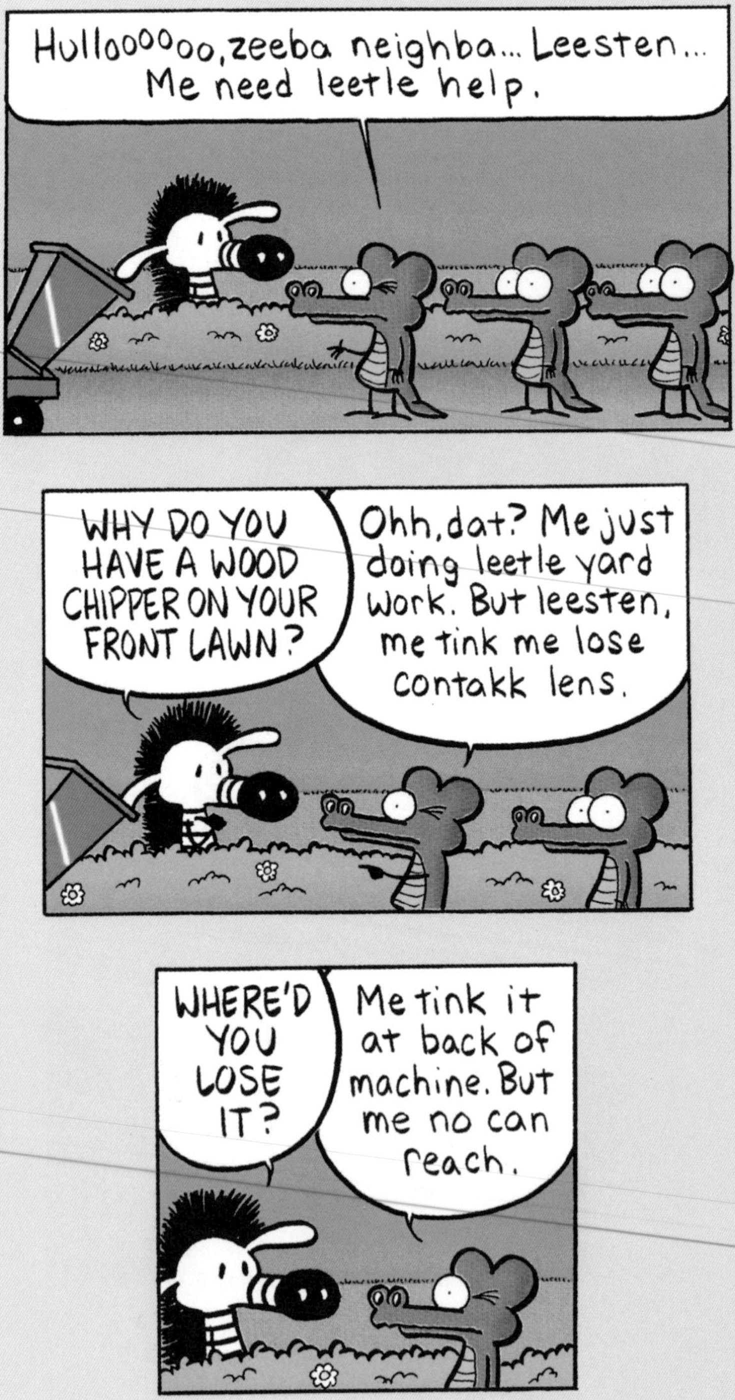
Hulloooooo, zeeba neighba... Leesten... Me need leetle help.
WHY DO YOU HAVE A WOOD CHIPPER ON YOUR FRONT LAWN?
Ohh, dat? Me just doing leetle yard work. But leesten, me tink me lose contakk lens.
WHERE'D YOU LOSE IT?
Me tink it at back of machine. But me no can reach.

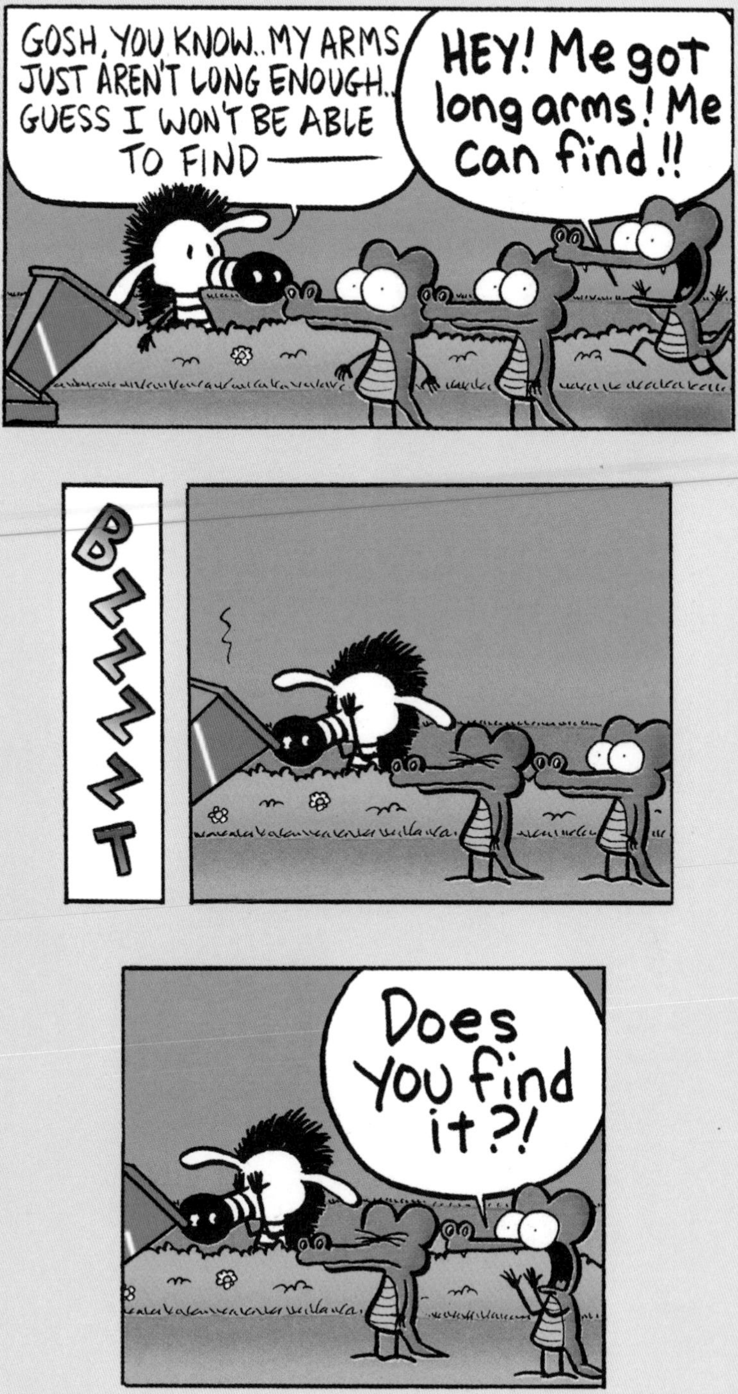
GOSH, YOU KNOW.. MY ARMS JUST AREN'T LONG ENOUGH.. GUESS I WON'T BE ABLE TO FIND——
HEY! Me got long arms! Me can find!!
BZZZZT
Does you find it?!

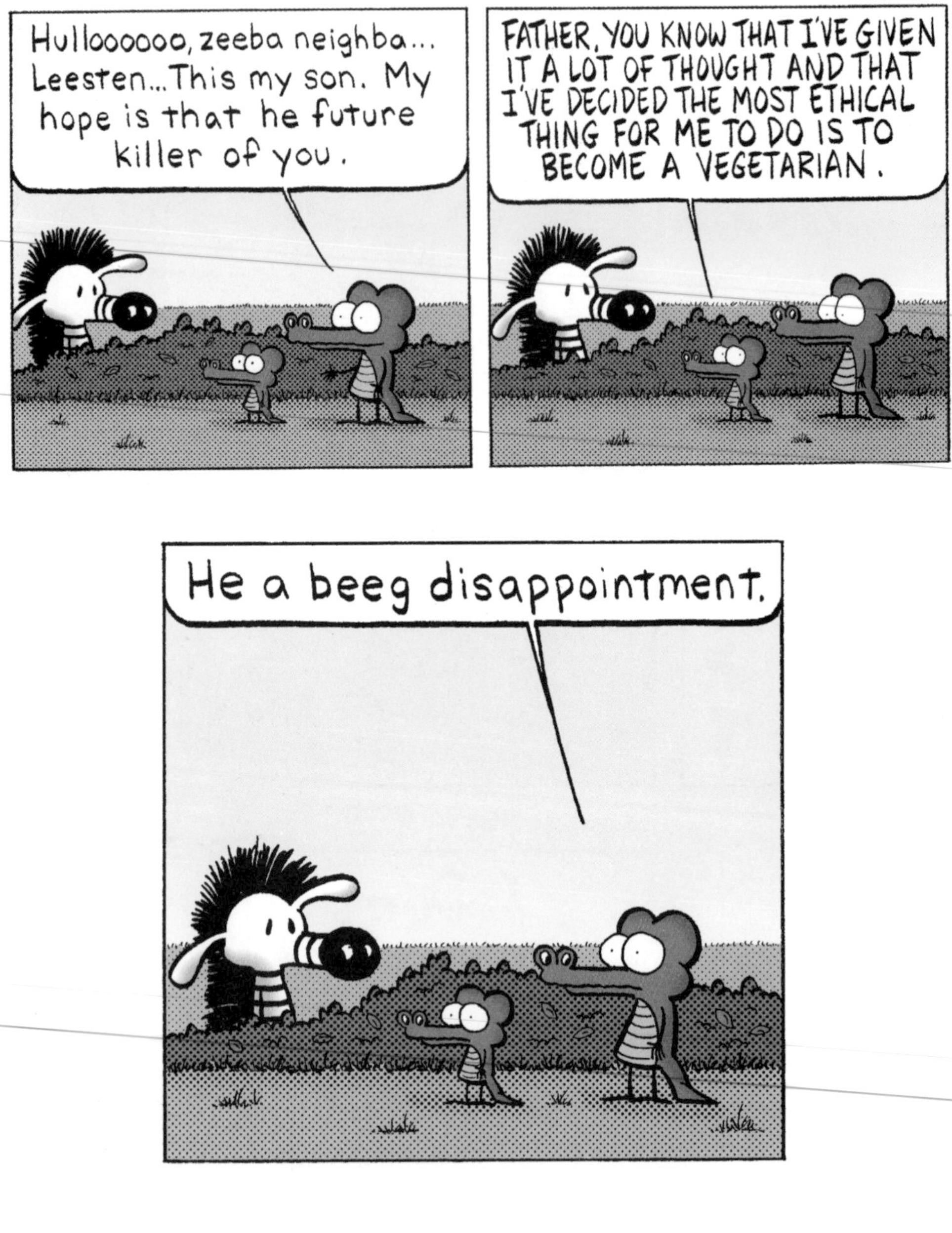
Hulloooooo, zeeba neighba... Leesten...This my son. My hope is that he future killer of you.
FATHER, YOU KNOW THAT I'VE GIVEN IT A LOT OF THOUGHT AND THAT I'VE DECIDED THE MOST ETHICAL THING FOR ME TO DO IS TO BECOME A VEGETARIAN.
He a beeg disappointment.

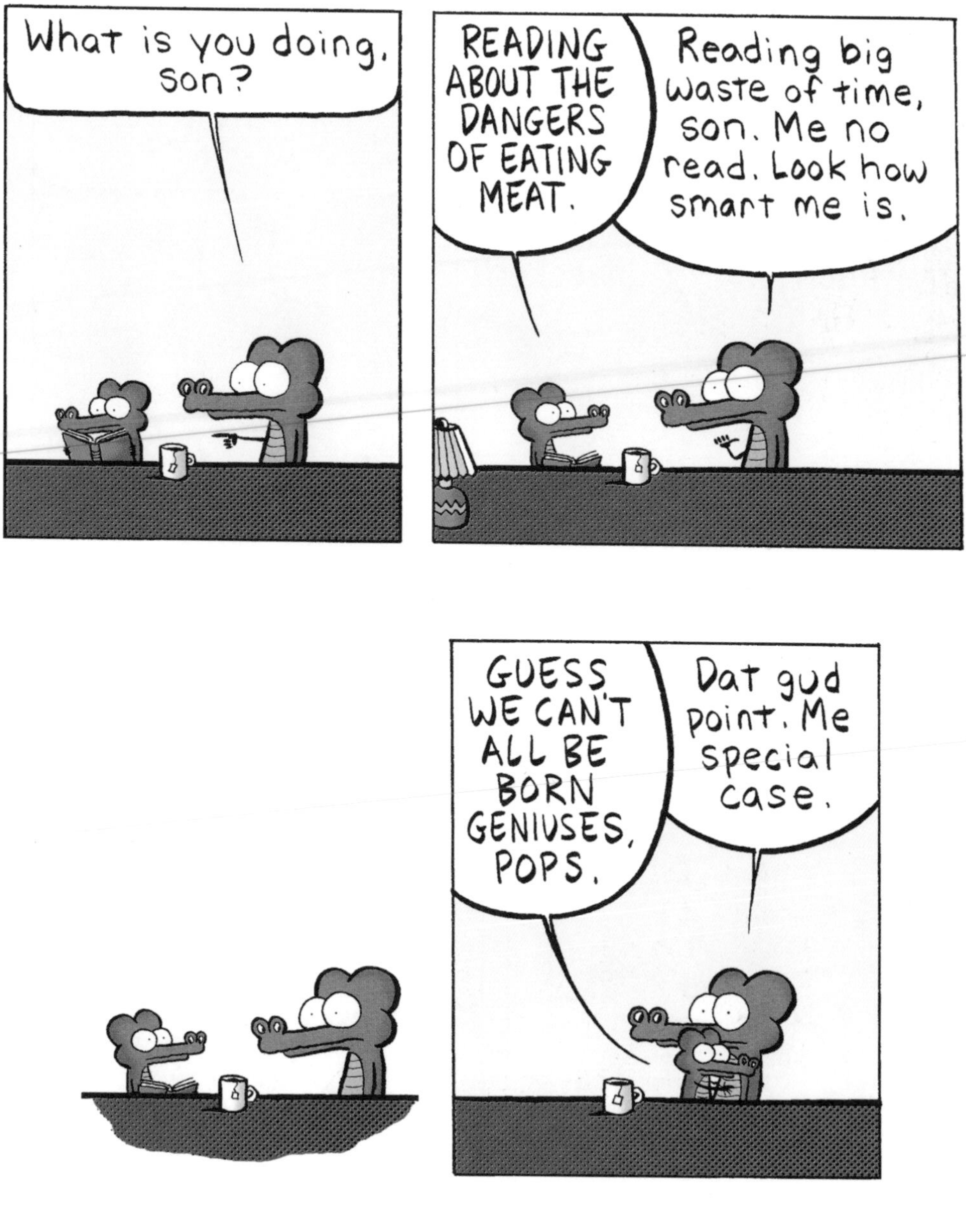
What is you doing, son?
READING ABOUT THE DANGERS OF EATING MEAT.
Reading big waste of time, son. Me no read. Look how smart me is.
GUESS WE CAN'T ALL BE BORN GENIUSES, POPS.
Dat gud point. Me special case.

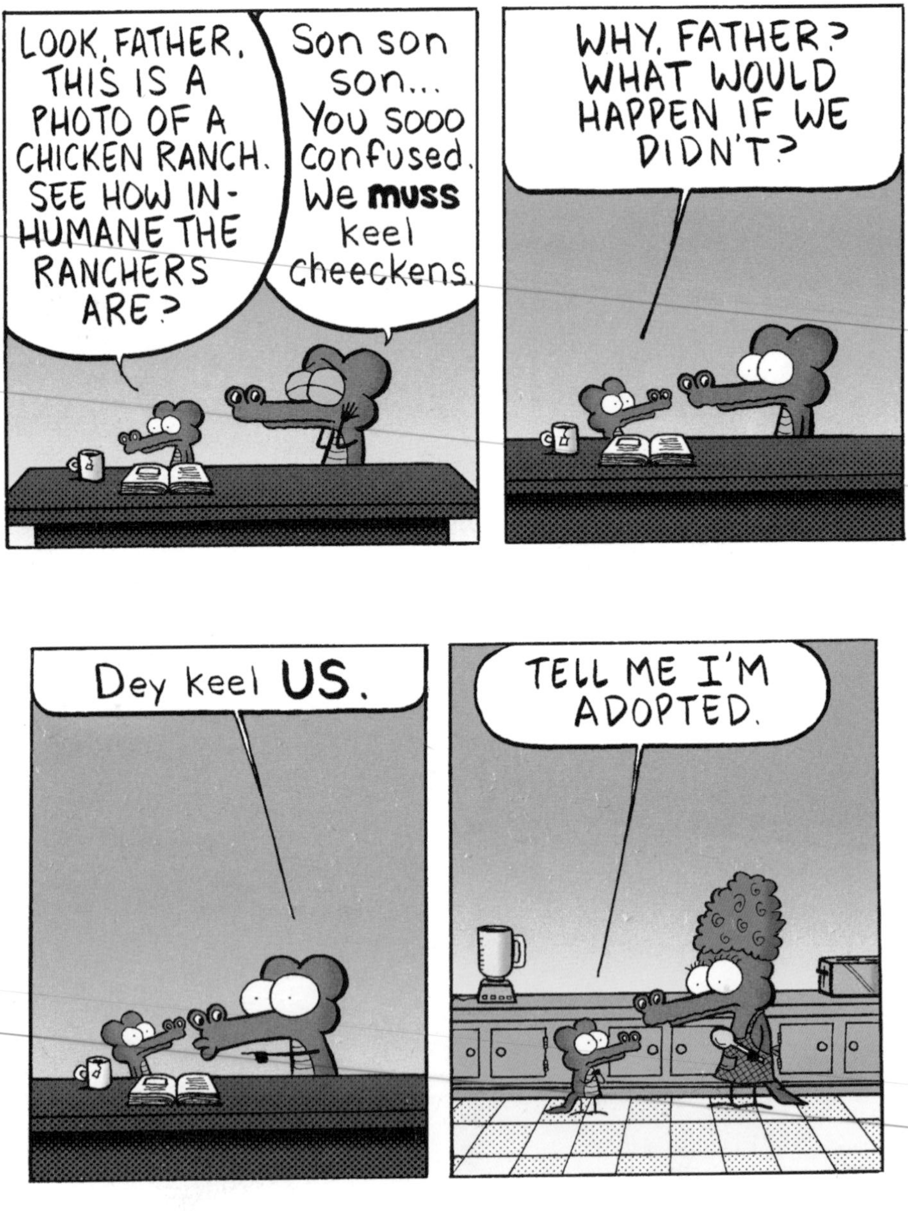

LOOK, FATHER. THIS IS A PHOTO OF A CHICKEN RANCH. SEE HOW INHUMANE THE RANCHERS ARE?
Son son son... You sooo confused. We **muss** keel cheeckens.
WHY, FATHER? WHAT WOULD HAPPEN IF WE DIDN'T?
Dey keel **US**.
TELL ME I'M ADOPTED.

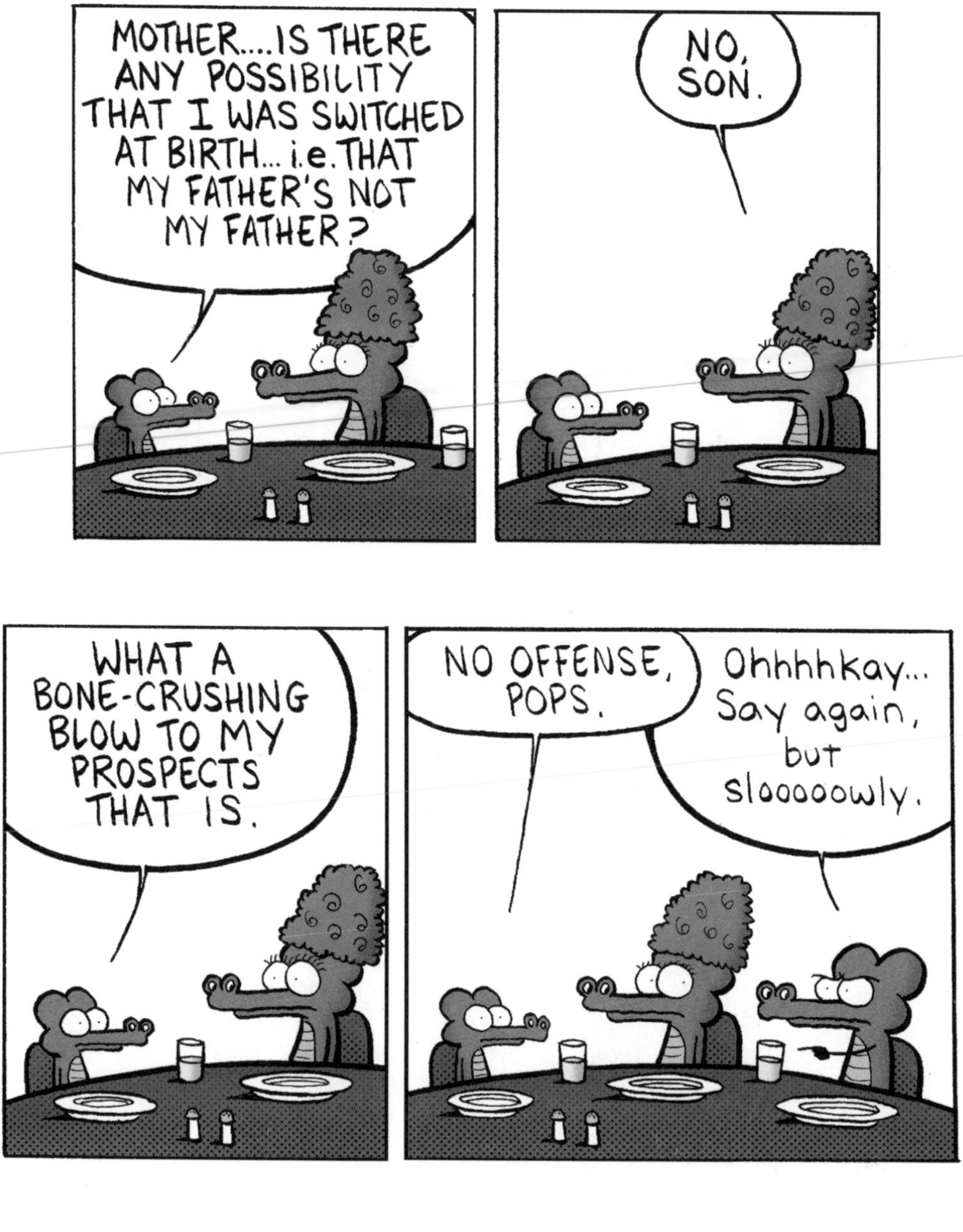
MOTHER....IS THERE ANY POSSIBILITY THAT I WAS SWITCHED AT BIRTH... i.e. THAT MY FATHER'S NOT MY FATHER?
NO, SON.
WHAT A BONE-CRUSHING BLOW TO MY PROSPECTS THAT IS.
NO OFFENSE, POPS.
Ohhhhkay... Say again, but slooooowly.

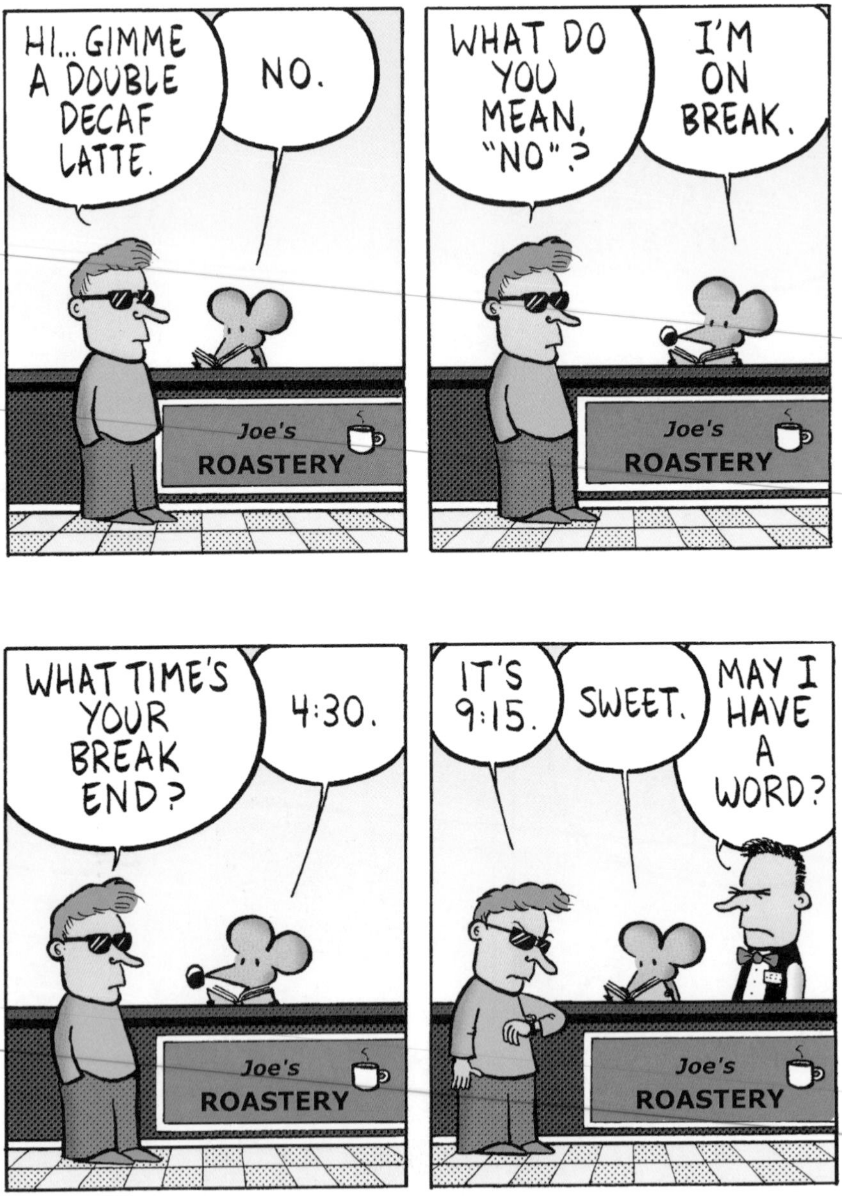
HI... GIMME A DOUBLE DECAF LATTE.
NO.
Joe's ROASTERY
WHAT DO YOU MEAN, "NO"?
I'M ON BREAK.
Joe's ROASTERY
WHAT TIME'S YOUR BREAK END?
4:30.
Joe's ROASTERY
IT'S 9:15.
SWEET.
MAY I HAVE A WORD?
Joe's ROASTERY

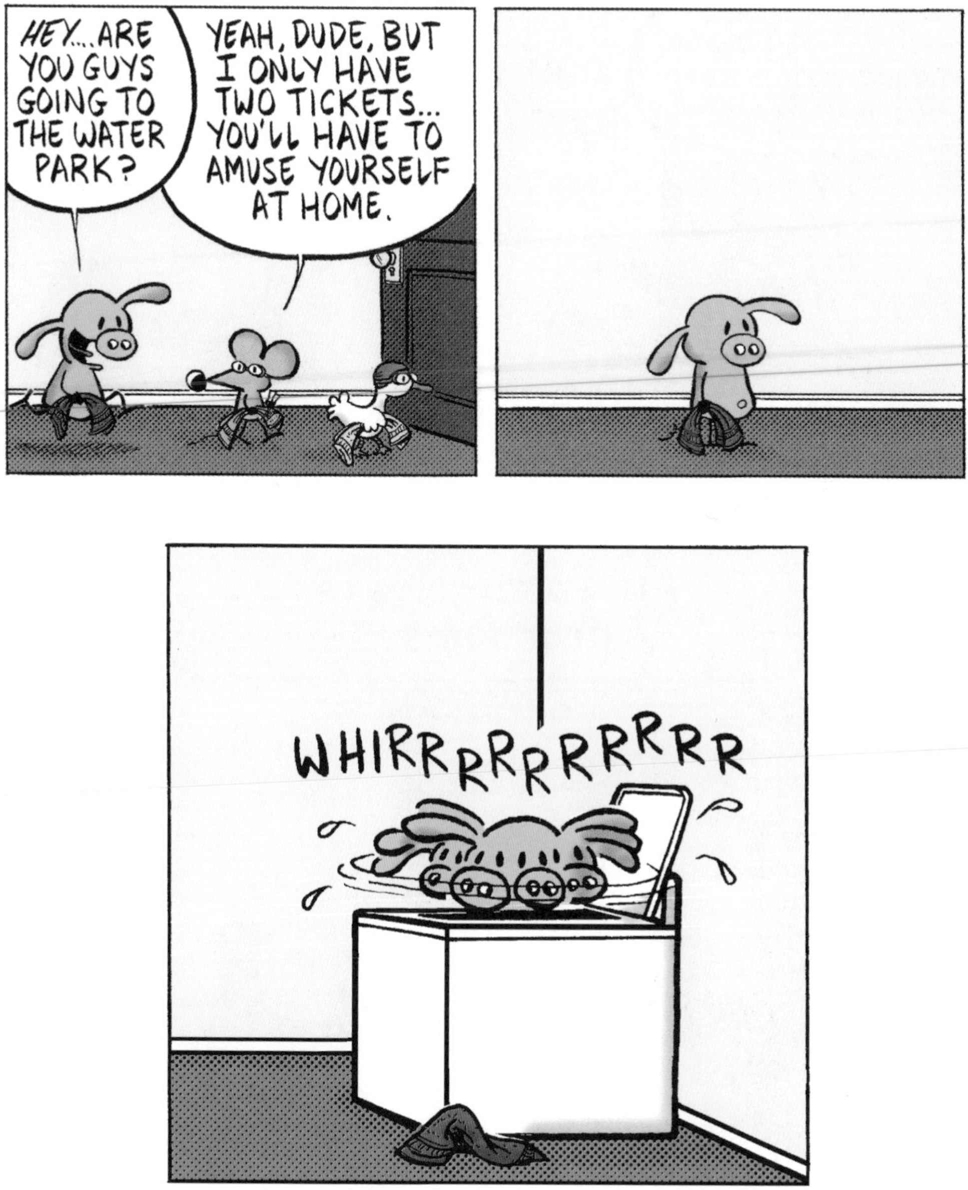
HEY....ARE YOU GUYS GOING TO THE WATER PARK?
YEAH, DUDE, BUT I ONLY HAVE TWO TICKETS... YOU'LL HAVE TO AMUSE YOURSELF AT HOME.
WHIRRRRRRRRRR

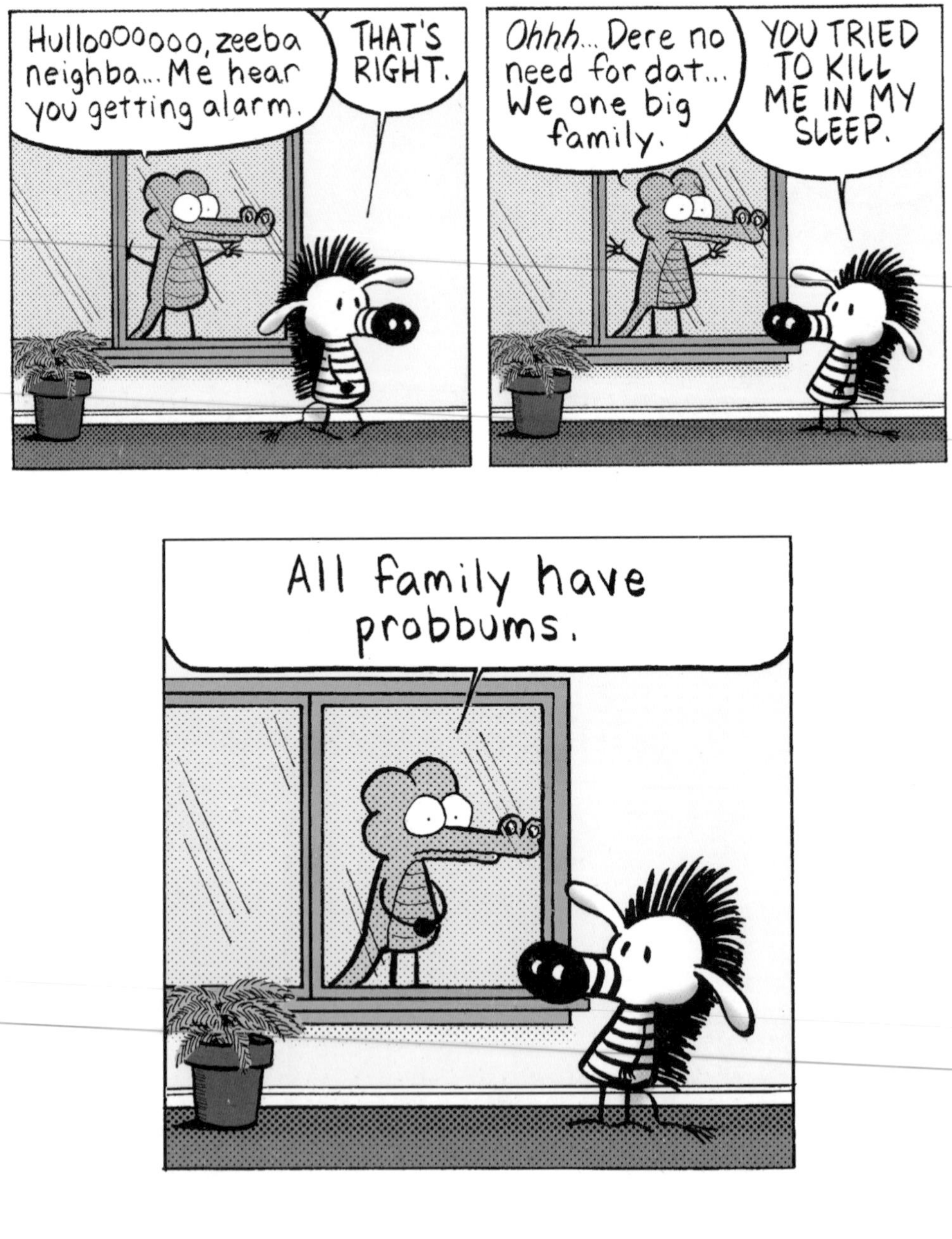
HulloOOOooo, zeeba neighba... Me hear you getting alarm.
THAT'S RIGHT.
Ohhh... Dere no need for dat... We one big family.
YOU TRIED TO KILL ME IN MY SLEEP.
All family have probbums.

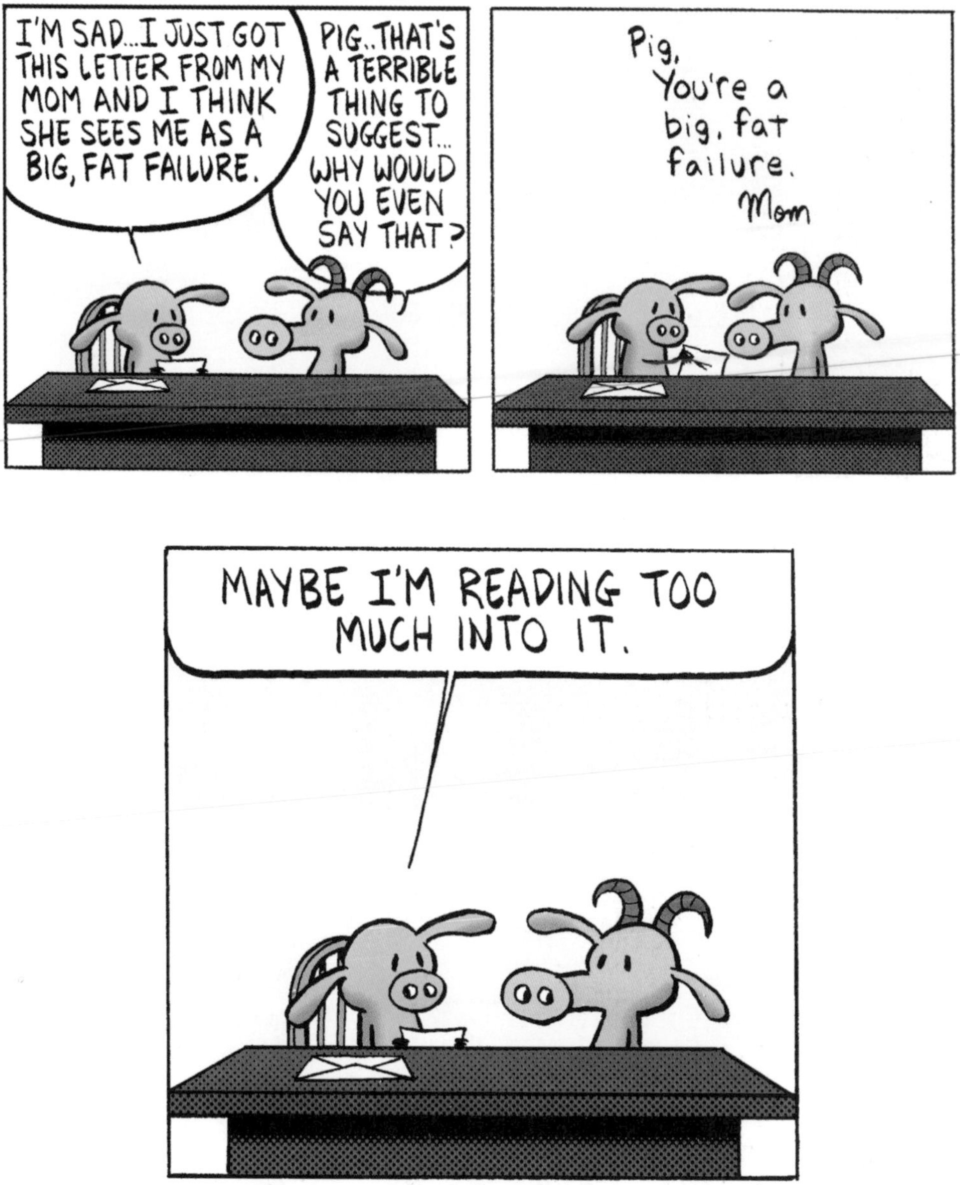
I'M SAD...I JUST GOT THIS LETTER FROM MY MOM AND I THINK SHE SEES ME AS A BIG, FAT FAILURE.
PIG..THAT'S A TERRIBLE THING TO SUGGEST... WHY WOULD YOU EVEN SAY THAT?
Pig,
You're a big, fat failure.
Mom
MAYBE I'M READING TOO MUCH INTO IT.

WHAT ARE YOU DOING?
I JUST GOT A FAX FROM ZEBRA...BUT DON'T TOUCH IT..HE'S GOT A COLD.
WHAT ARE YOU TALKING ABOUT?
HIS GERMS ARE PROBABLY ON IT.
PIG..WHEN SOMEONE SENDS YOU A FAX, THEY'RE NOT SENDING YOU THE ***ACTUAL*** PIECE OF PAPER THEY WERE HOLDING.
YES THEY ARE.

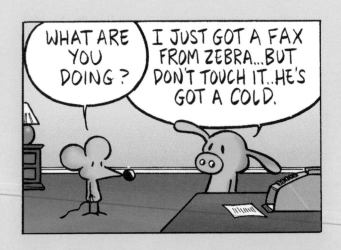

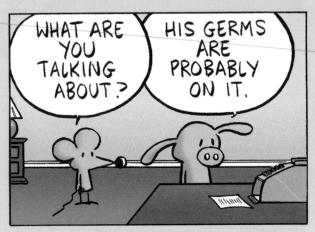

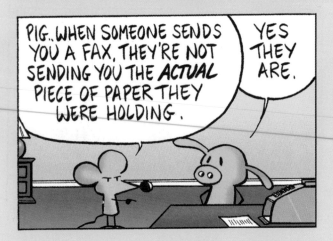

THEN HOW COME WHEN YOU SEND A FAX, THE EXACT PAPER YOU "SENT" COMES OUT AT THE BOTTOM OF YOUR MACHINE?!
THAT'S A COPY... THE ORIGINAL FLIES MAGICALLY TO ZEBRA.
OH, BRILLIANT.. THEN WHY DON'T YOU JUST SHOVE A HAM SANDWICH IN THERE? THAT WAY, ZEBRA'D GET ONE AND YOU'D GET ONE TOO... YOU STUPID PIG!!!!!
HAHAHA HAHAHA.. DON'T BE A SILLY-HEAD!
D'YOU GET IT?

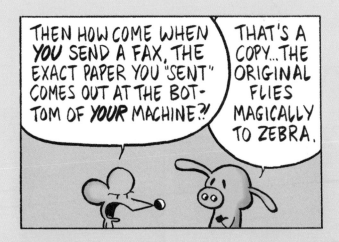

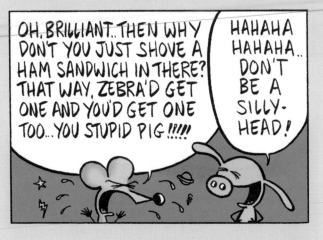

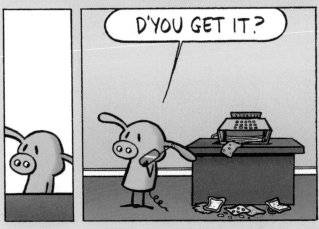

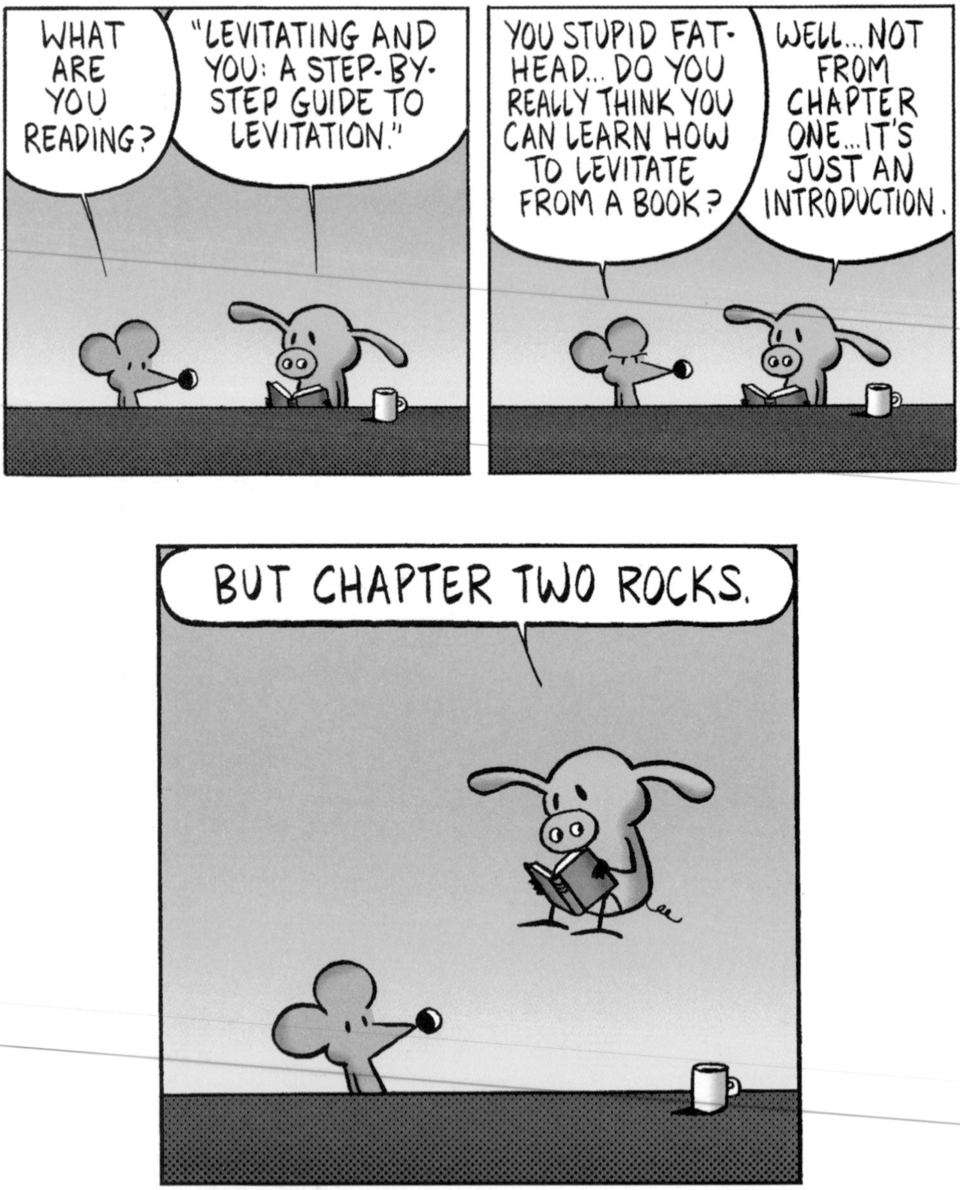
WHAT ARE YOU READING?
"LEVITATING AND YOU: A STEP-BY-STEP GUIDE TO LEVITATION."
YOU STUPID FAT-HEAD... DO YOU REALLY THINK YOU CAN LEARN HOW TO LEVITATE FROM A BOOK?
WELL...NOT FROM CHAPTER ONE...IT'S JUST AN INTRODUCTION.
BUT CHAPTER TWO ROCKS.

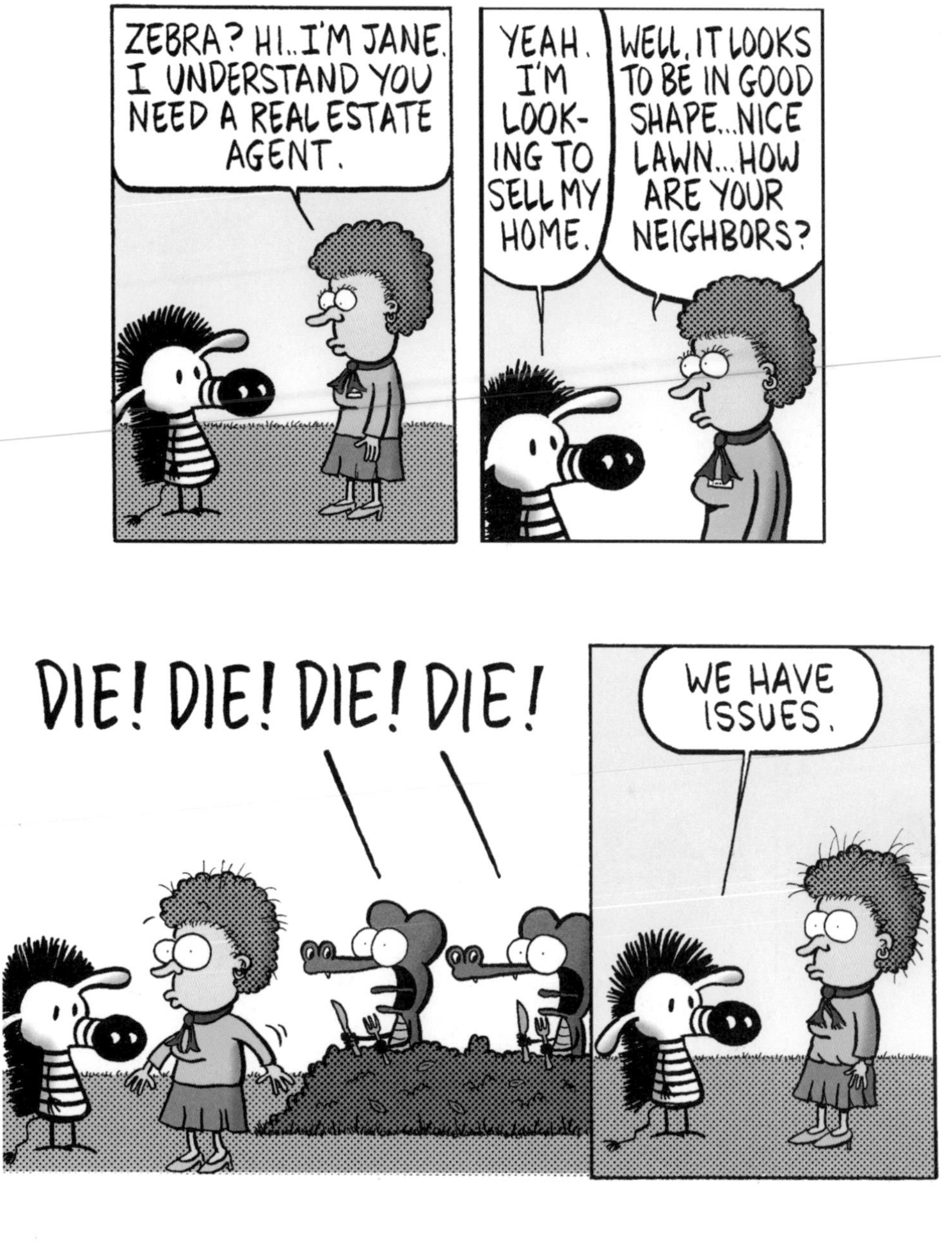
ZEBRA? HI.. I'M JANE. I UNDERSTAND YOU NEED A REAL ESTATE AGENT.
YEAH. I'M LOOKING TO SELL MY HOME.
WELL, IT LOOKS TO BE IN GOOD SHAPE...NICE LAWN...HOW ARE YOUR NEIGHBORS?
DIE! DIE! DIE! DIE!
WE HAVE ISSUES.

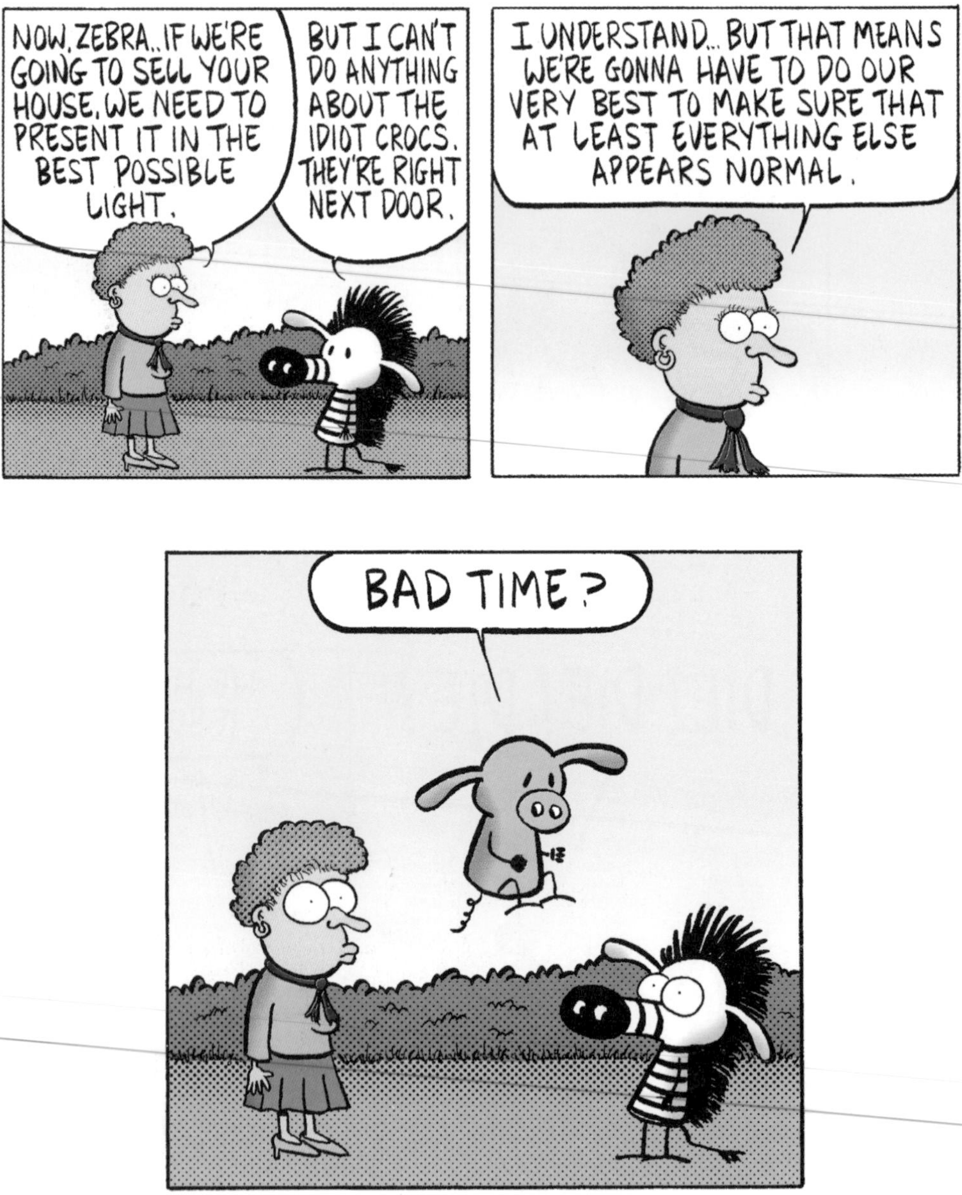
NOW, ZEBRA.. IF WE'RE GOING TO SELL YOUR HOUSE, WE NEED TO PRESENT IT IN THE BEST POSSIBLE LIGHT.
BUT I CAN'T DO ANYTHING ABOUT THE IDIOT CROCS. THEY'RE RIGHT NEXT DOOR.
I UNDERSTAND.. BUT THAT MEANS WE'RE GONNA HAVE TO DO OUR VERY BEST TO MAKE SURE THAT AT LEAST EVERYTHING ELSE APPEARS NORMAL.
BAD TIME?

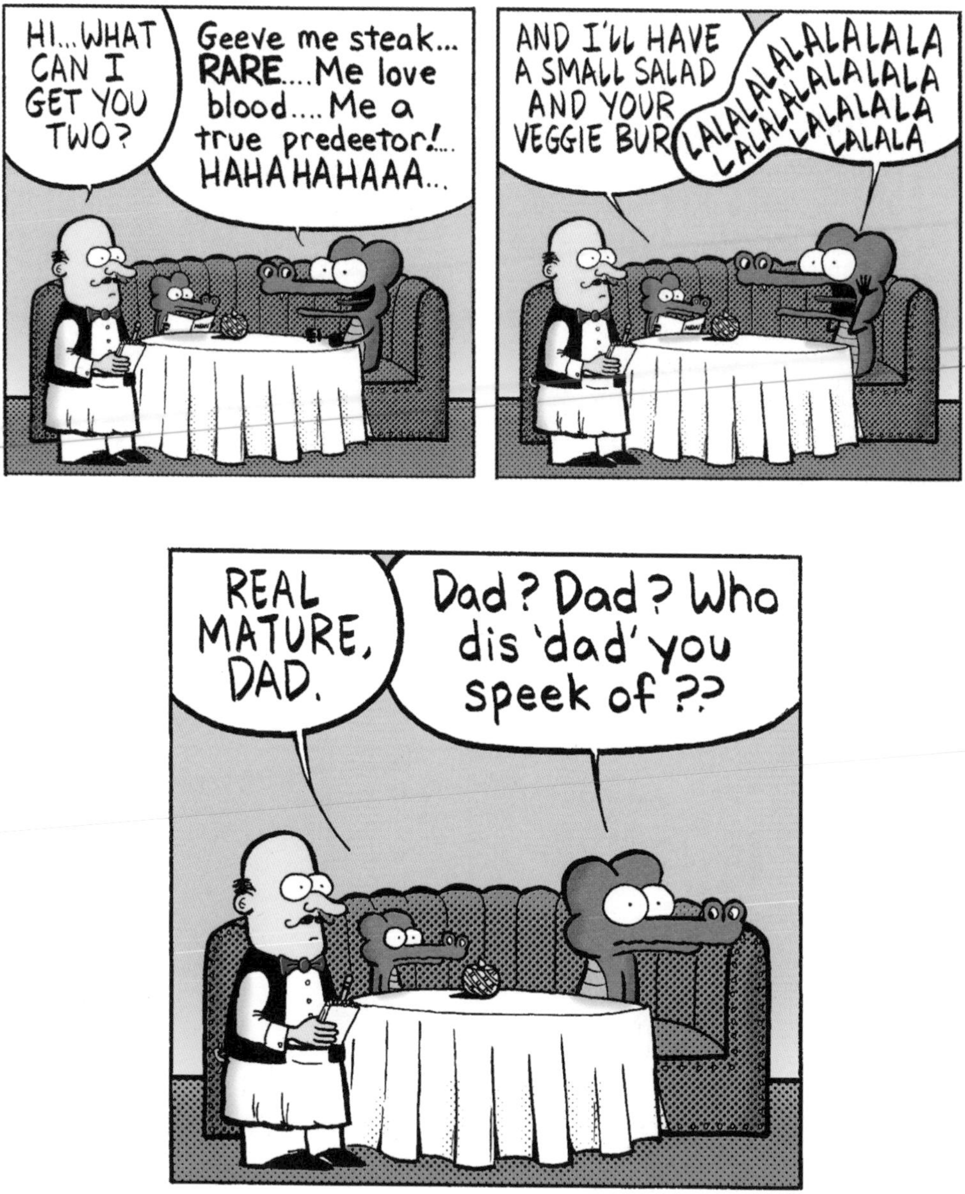
HI...WHAT CAN I GET YOU TWO?
Geeve me steak... RARE....Me love blood.... Me a true predeetor!... HAHAHAHAAA...
AND I'LL HAVE A SMALL SALAD AND YOUR VEGGIE BUR
LALALALALALALALALA LALALALALALALALA LALALALA LALALA
REAL MATURE, DAD.
Dad? Dad? Who dis 'dad' you speek of ??

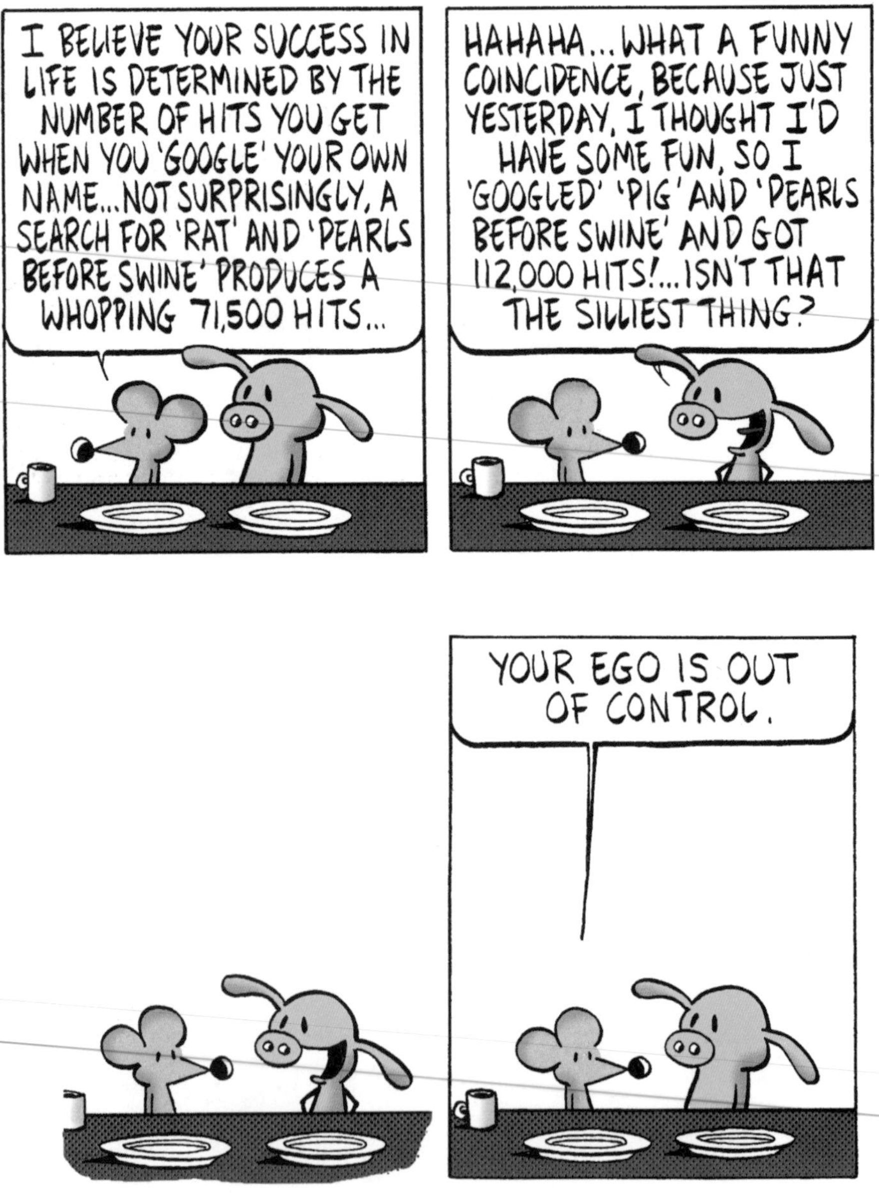
I BELIEVE YOUR SUCCESS IN LIFE IS DETERMINED BY THE NUMBER OF HITS YOU GET WHEN YOU 'GOOGLE' YOUR OWN NAME...NOT SURPRISINGLY, A SEARCH FOR 'RAT' AND 'PEARLS BEFORE SWINE' PRODUCES A WHOPPING 71,500 HITS...
HAHAHA... WHAT A FUNNY COINCIDENCE, BECAUSE JUST YESTERDAY, I THOUGHT I'D HAVE SOME FUN, SO I 'GOOGLED' 'PIG' AND 'PEARLS BEFORE SWINE' AND GOT 112,000 HITS!... ISN'T THAT THE SILLIEST THING?
YOUR EGO IS OUT OF CONTROL.

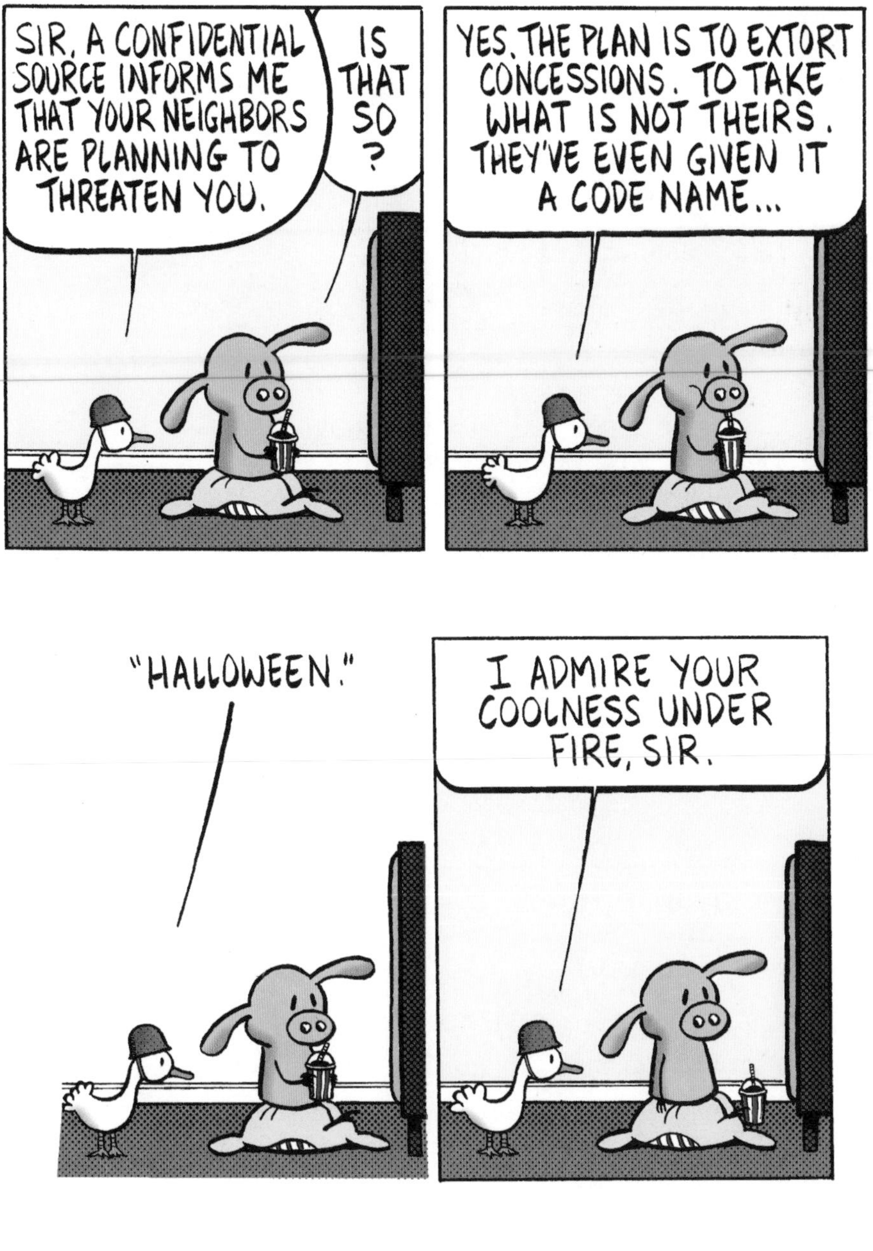
SIR, A CONFIDENTIAL SOURCE INFORMS ME THAT YOUR NEIGHBORS ARE PLANNING TO THREATEN YOU.
IS THAT SO ?
YES. THE PLAN IS TO EXTORT CONCESSIONS. TO TAKE WHAT IS NOT THEIRS. THEY'VE EVEN GIVEN IT A CODE NAME...
"HALLOWEEN."
I ADMIRE YOUR COOLNESS UNDER FIRE, SIR.

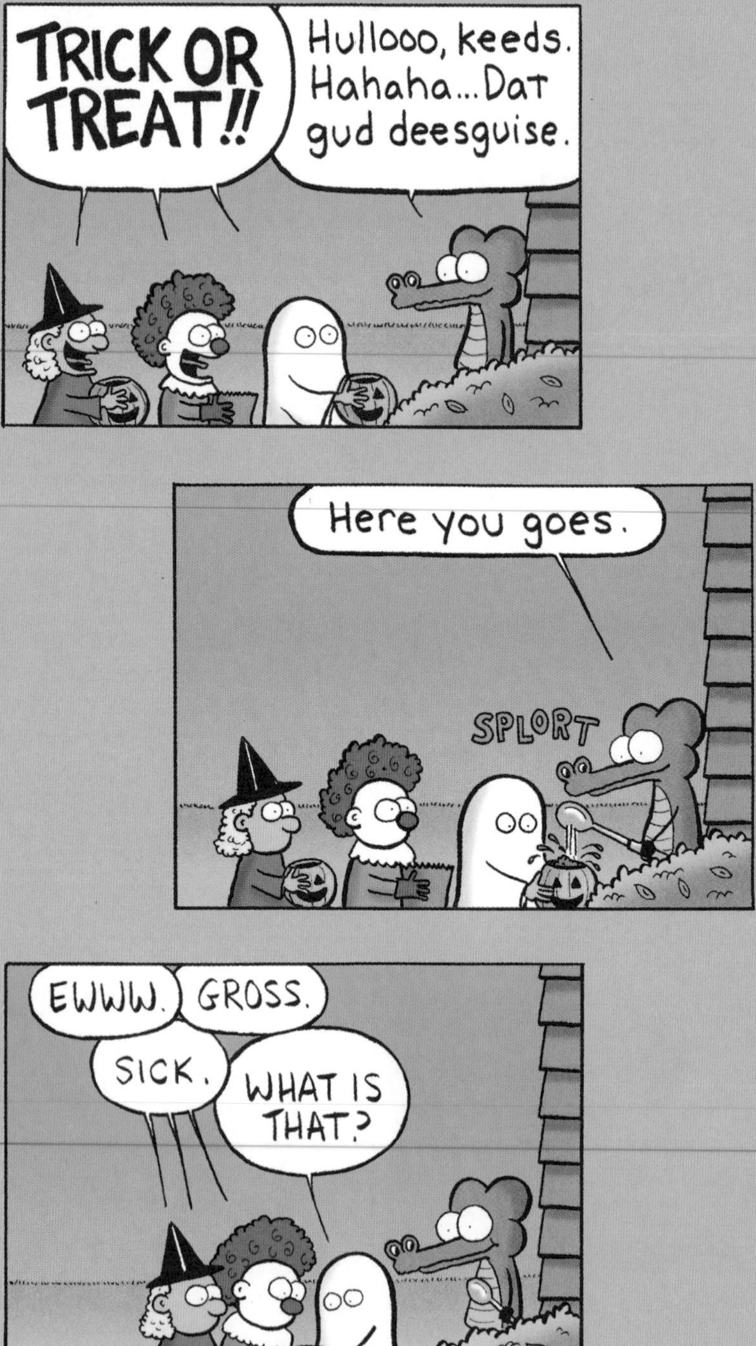
TRICK OR TREAT!!
Hullooo, keeds. Hahaha... Dat gud deesguise.
Here you goes.
SPLORT
EWWW.
GROSS.
SICK.
WHAT IS THAT?

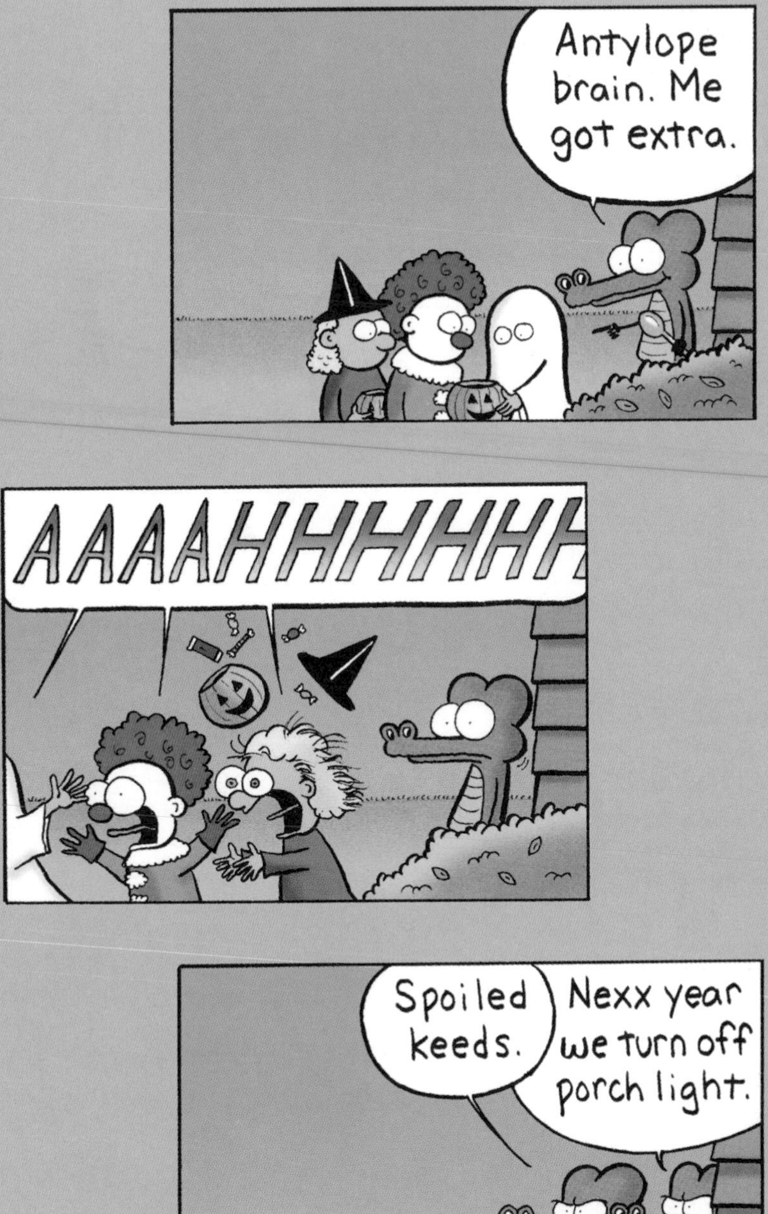
Antylope brain. Me got extra.
AAAAHHHHHH
Spoiled keeds.
Nexx year we turn off porch light.

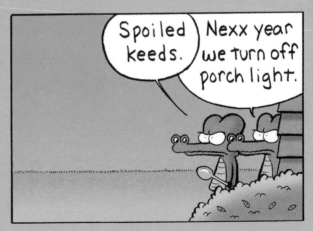

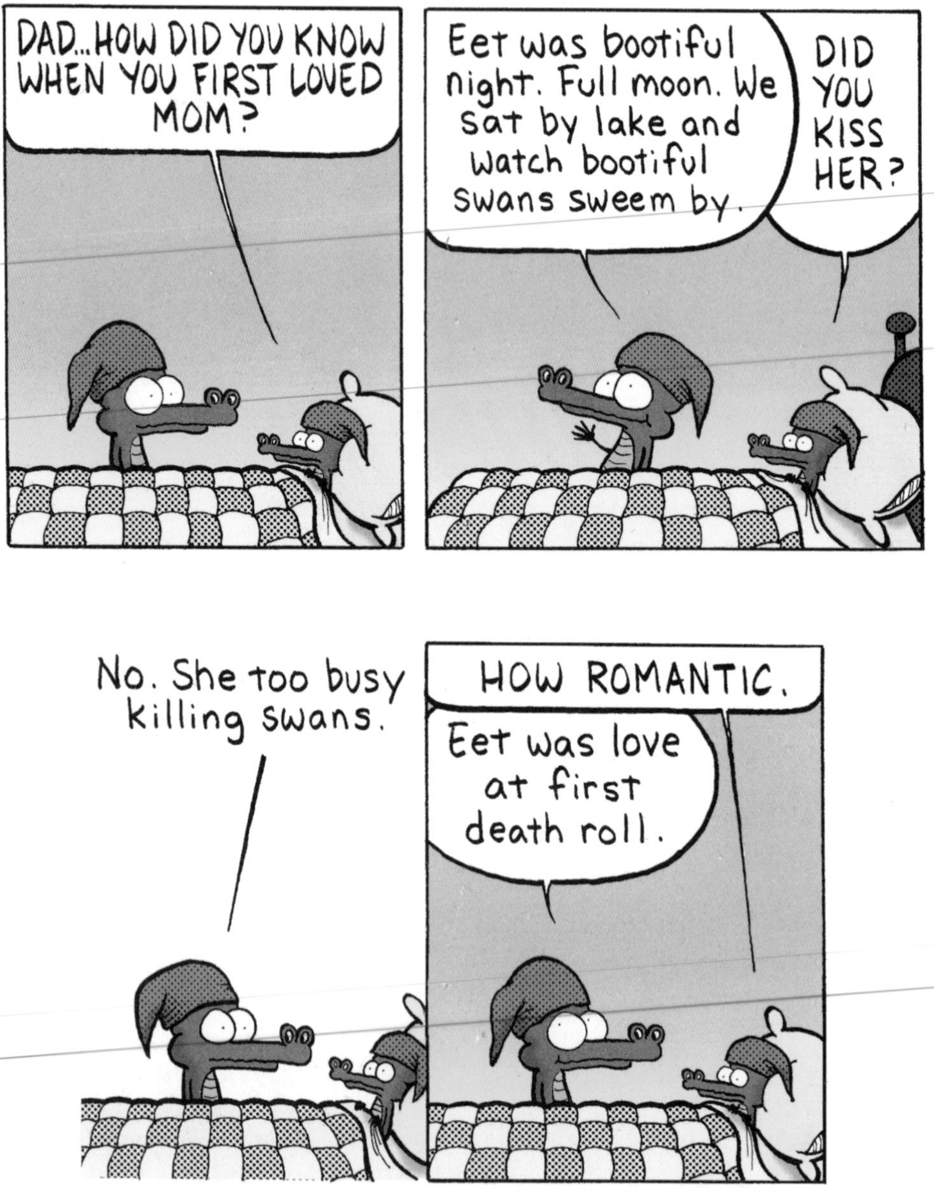
DAD...HOW DID YOU KNOW WHEN YOU FIRST LOVED MOM?
Eet was bootiful night. Full moon. We sat by lake and watch bootiful swans sweem by.
DID YOU KISS HER?
No. She too busy killing swans.
HOW ROMANTIC.
Eet was love at first death roll.

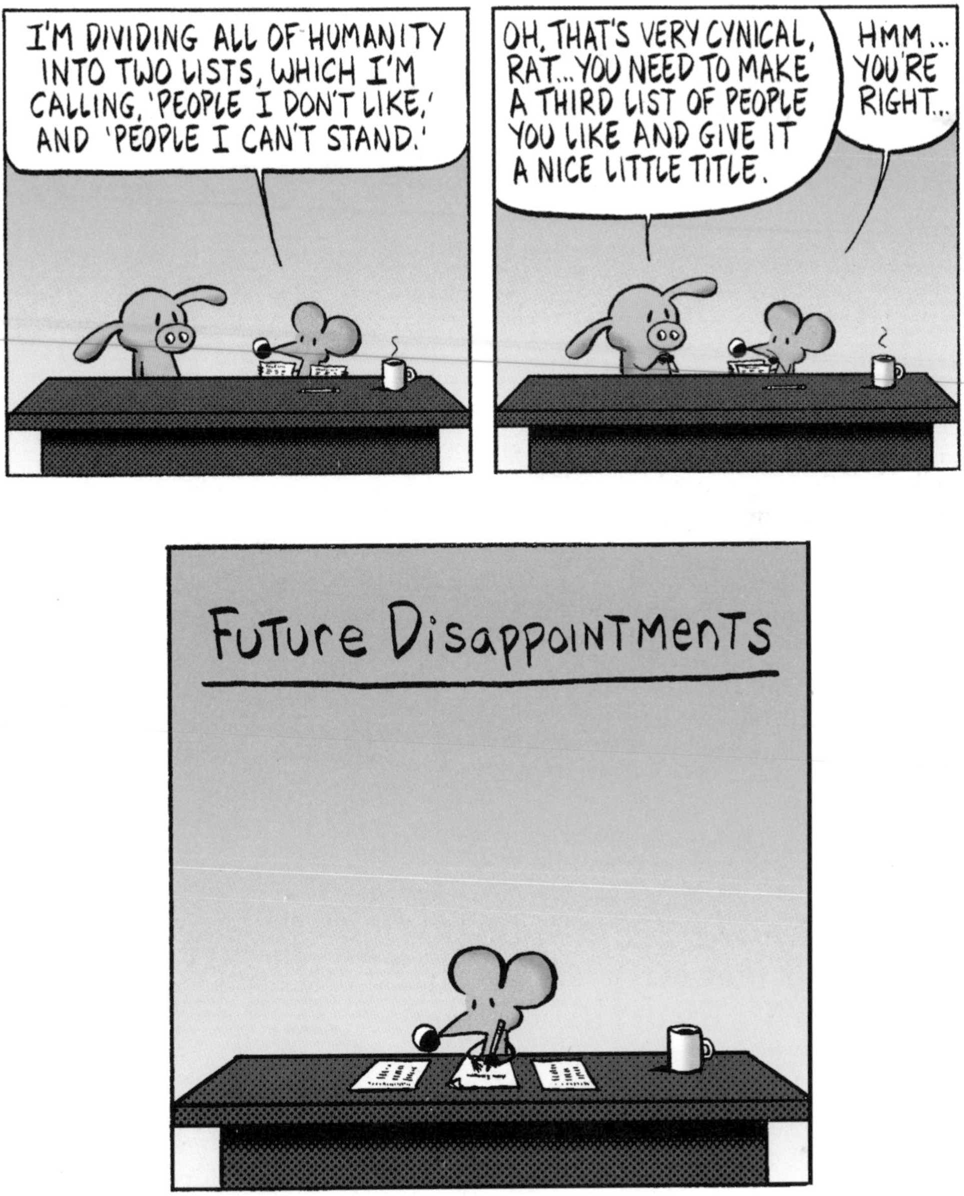
I'M DIVIDING ALL OF HUMANITY INTO TWO LISTS, WHICH I'M CALLING, 'PEOPLE I DON'T LIKE,' AND 'PEOPLE I CAN'T STAND.'
OH, THAT'S VERY CYNICAL, RAT... YOU NEED TO MAKE A THIRD LIST OF PEOPLE YOU LIKE AND GIVE IT A NICE LITTLE TITLE.
HMM... YOU'RE RIGHT...
FUTURE DISAPPOINTMENTS

OKAY, GUYS, EVERYBODY SMILE!
I HATE THESE STUPID CHRISTMAS CARD PHOTOS.
THUD!
OH, BOY! IT'S ONE OF SANTA'S ELVES! I BET HE'S HERE TO PICK UP OUR LISTS FOR SANTA! I GOTTA GET MY LIST FOR SANTA!

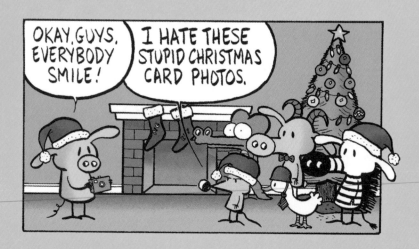

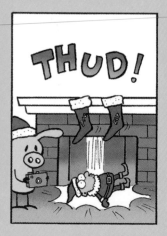

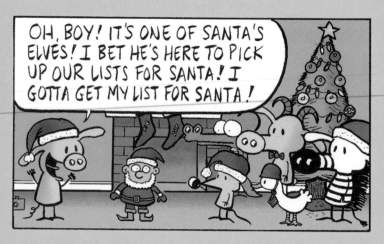

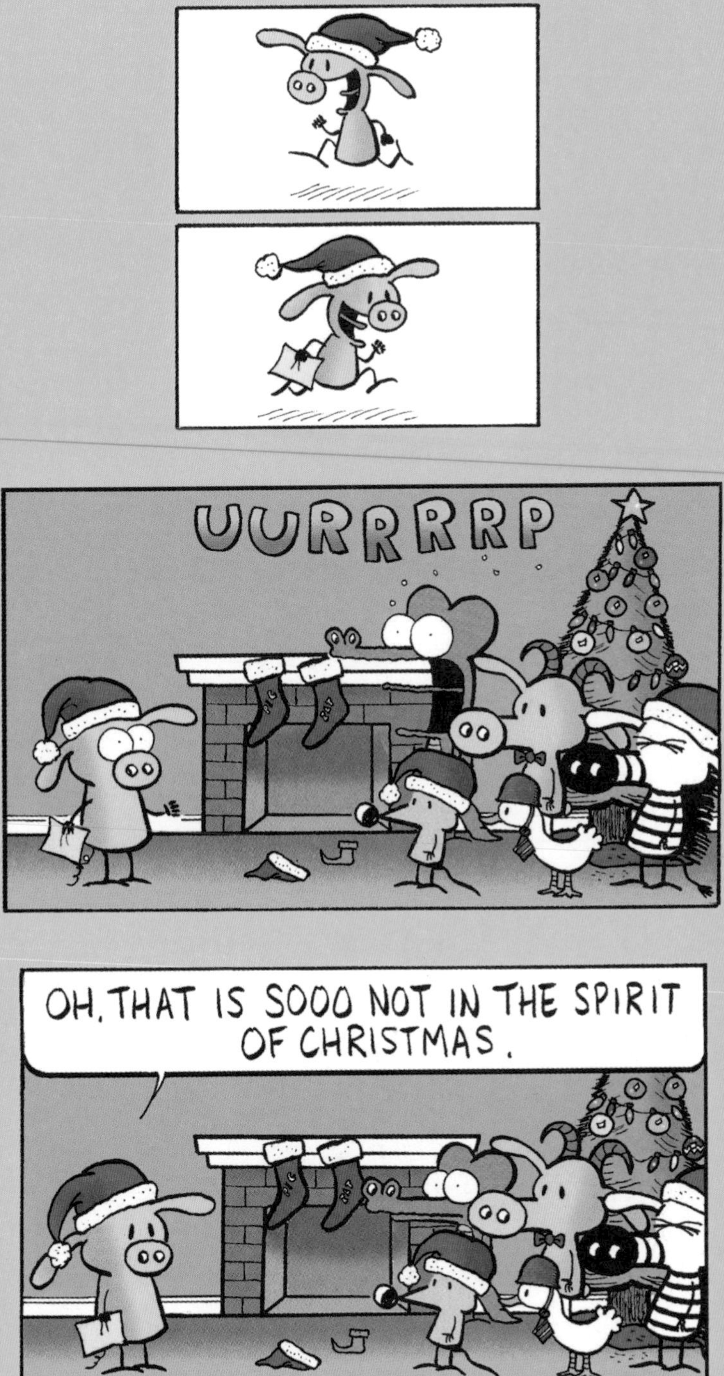
UURRRRP
OH, THAT IS SOOO NOT IN THE SPIRIT OF CHRISTMAS.

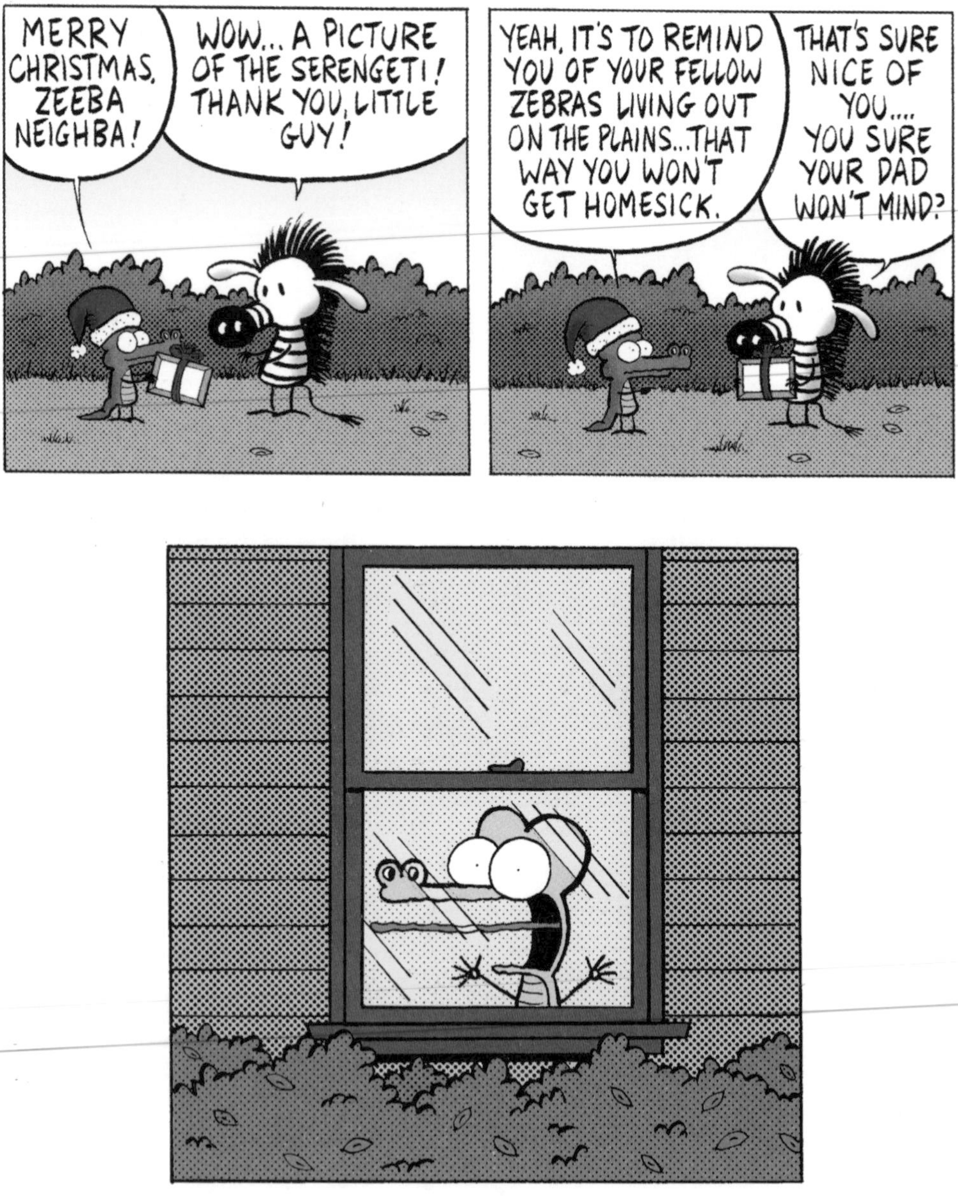
MERRY CHRISTMAS, ZEEBA NEIGHBA!
WOW... A PICTURE OF THE SERENGETI! THANK YOU, LITTLE GUY!
YEAH, IT'S TO REMIND YOU OF YOUR FELLOW ZEBRAS LIVING OUT ON THE PLAINS...THAT WAY YOU WON'T GET HOMESICK.
THAT'S SURE NICE OF YOU.... YOU SURE YOUR DAD WON'T MIND?

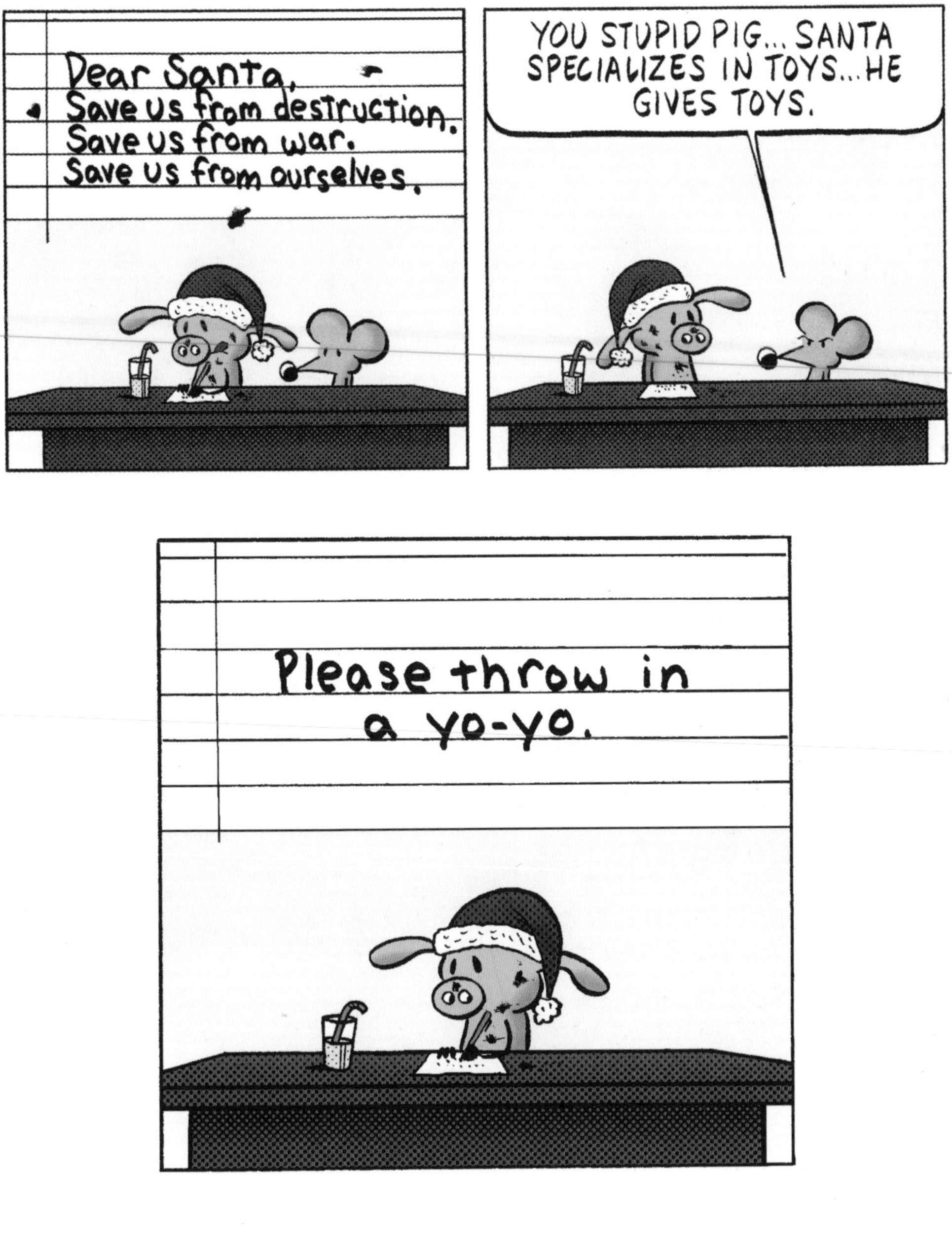
Dear Santa,
Save us from destruction.
Save us from war.
Save us from ourselves.
YOU STUPID PIG... SANTA SPECIALIZES IN TOYS...HE GIVES TOYS.
Please throw in a yo-yo.

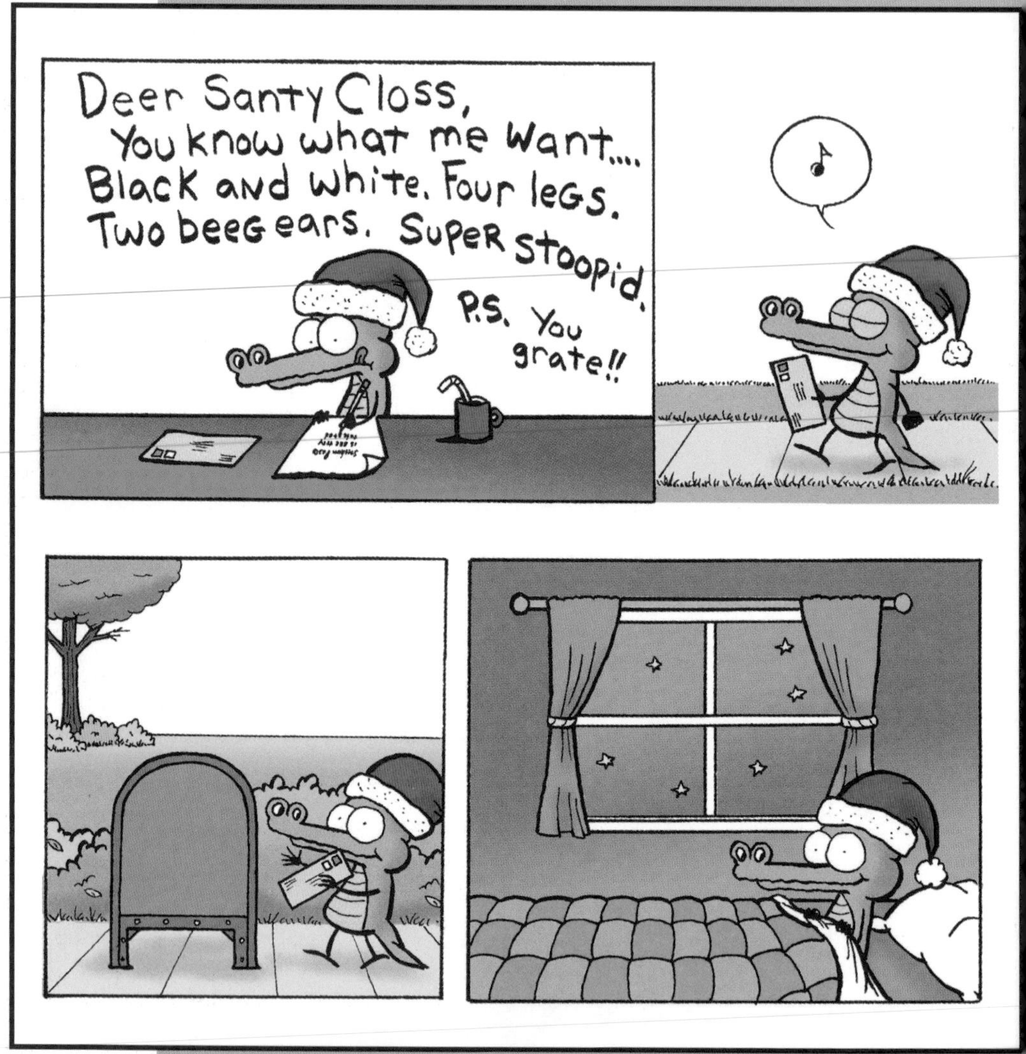
Deer Santy Closs,
You know what me Want....
Black and white. Four legs.
Two beeG ears. Super stoopid.
P.S. You grate!!
♪

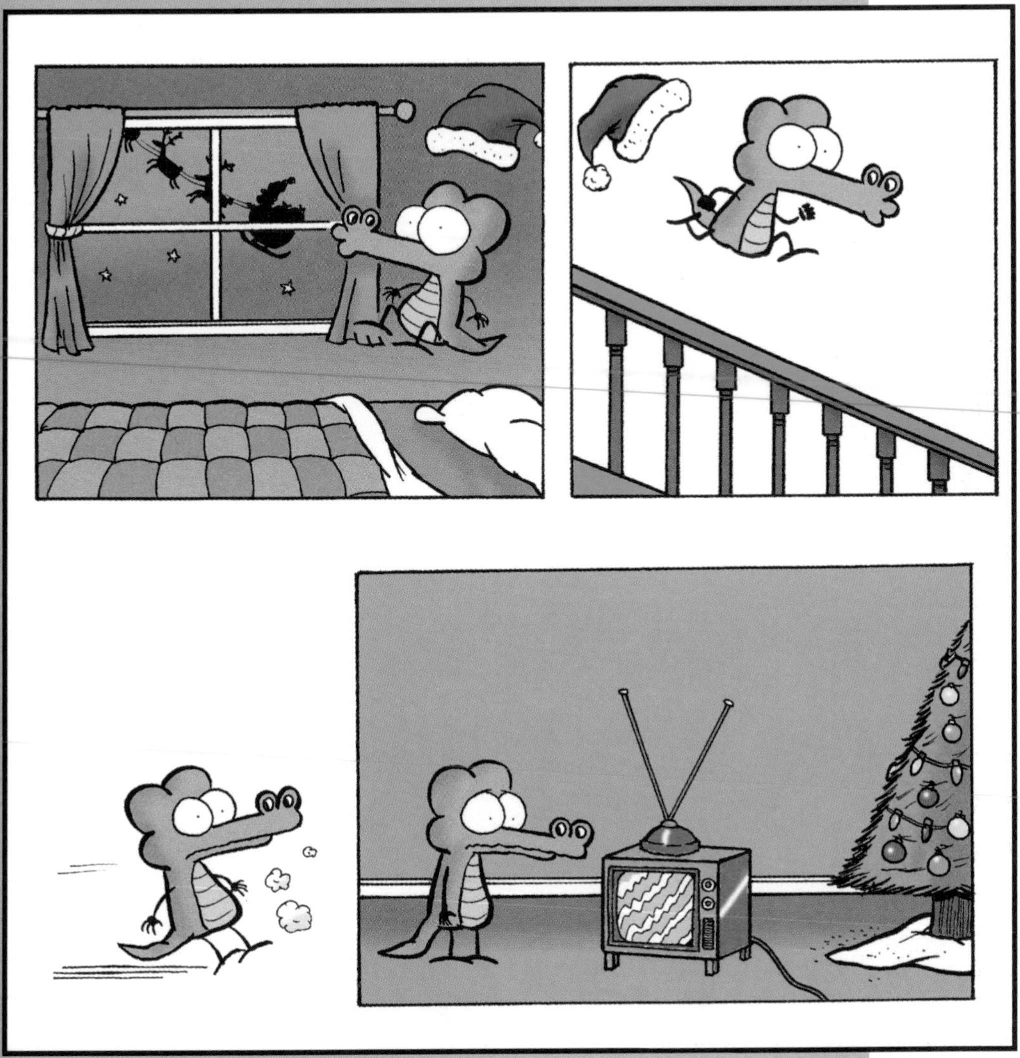

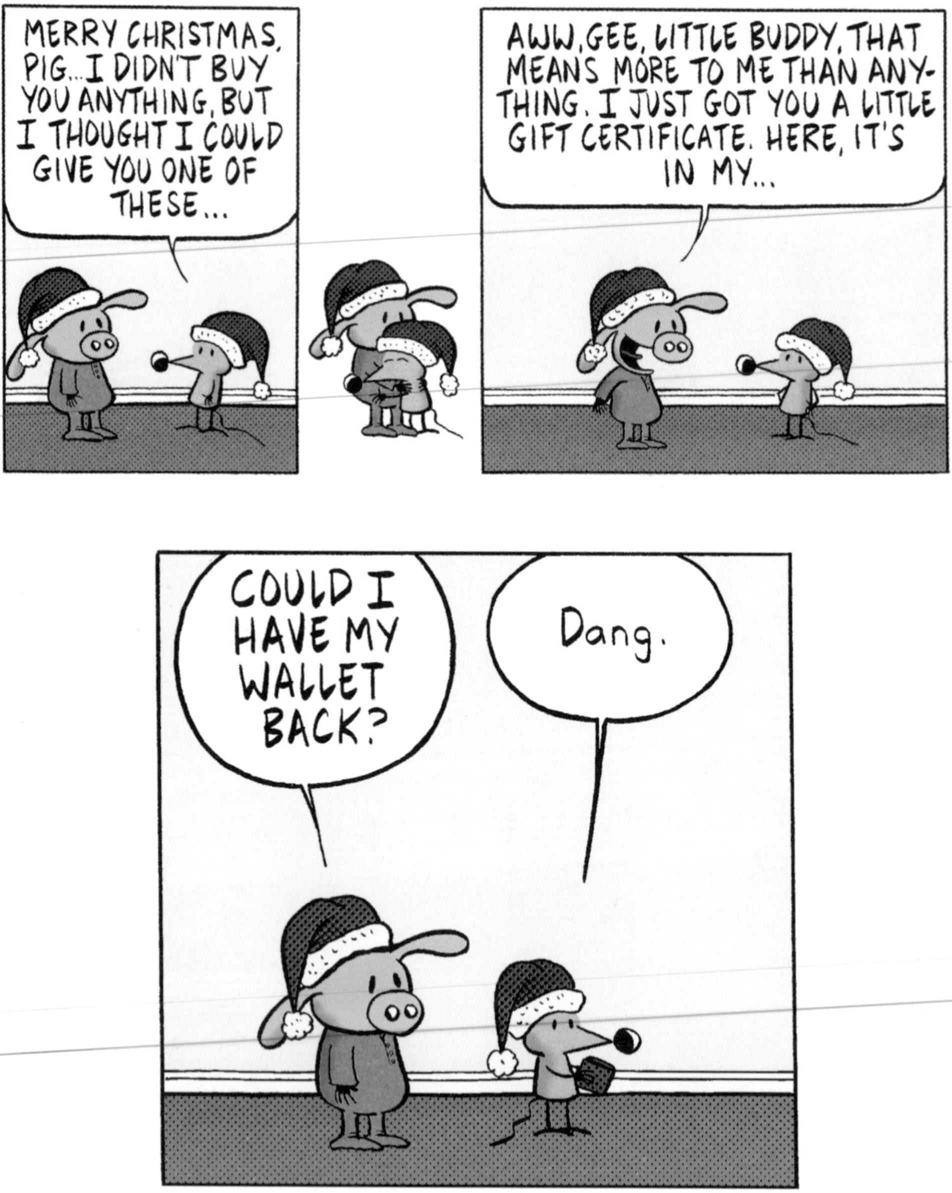
MERRY CHRISTMAS, PIG... I DIDN'T BUY YOU ANYTHING, BUT I THOUGHT I COULD GIVE YOU ONE OF THESE...
AWW, GEE, LITTLE BUDDY, THAT MEANS MORE TO ME THAN ANYTHING. I JUST GOT YOU A LITTLE GIFT CERTIFICATE. HERE, IT'S IN MY...
COULD I HAVE MY WALLET BACK?
Dang.

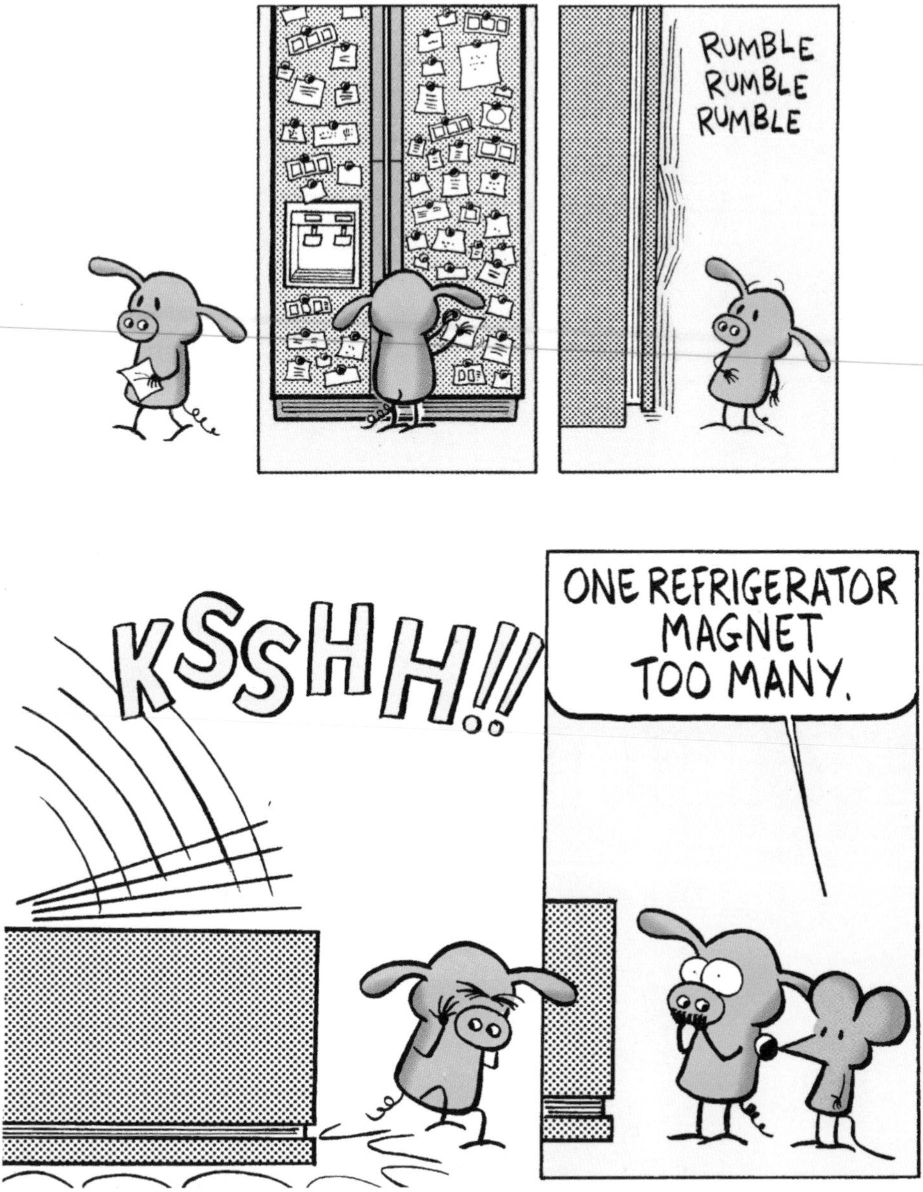
RUMBLE
RUMBLE
RUMBLE
KSSHH!!
ONE REFRIGERATOR MAGNET TOO MANY.

Ohhkay, zeeba neighba.. No more game. We crocs buy F-14 Supersoneecal jet...So geeve up or face conseekences.
SHOW ME THE PLANE.
Uh. Ees in backyard.
I CAN SEE YOUR BACKYARD. IT'S NOT THERE.
Ees behind trash can.
YEAH...THOSE PLANES ARE PROBABLY ABOUT TWENTY FEET HIGH..I DON'T THINK SO.
Ohhkay. FINE. You want truth, Meester Smart Guy?....Plane *inveesible*.
OHH..WELL.. I HADN'T CONSIDERED THAT. SO YOU CAN'T SEE IT EITHER?

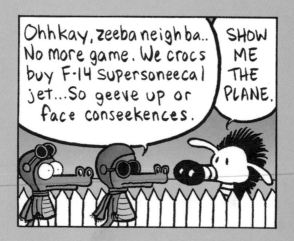

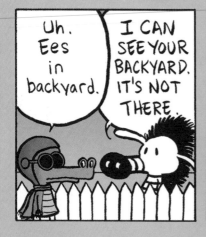

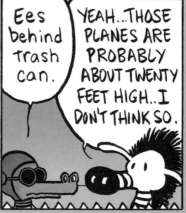

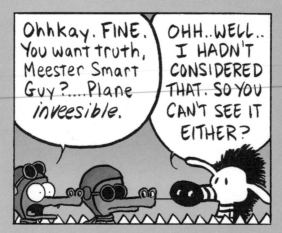

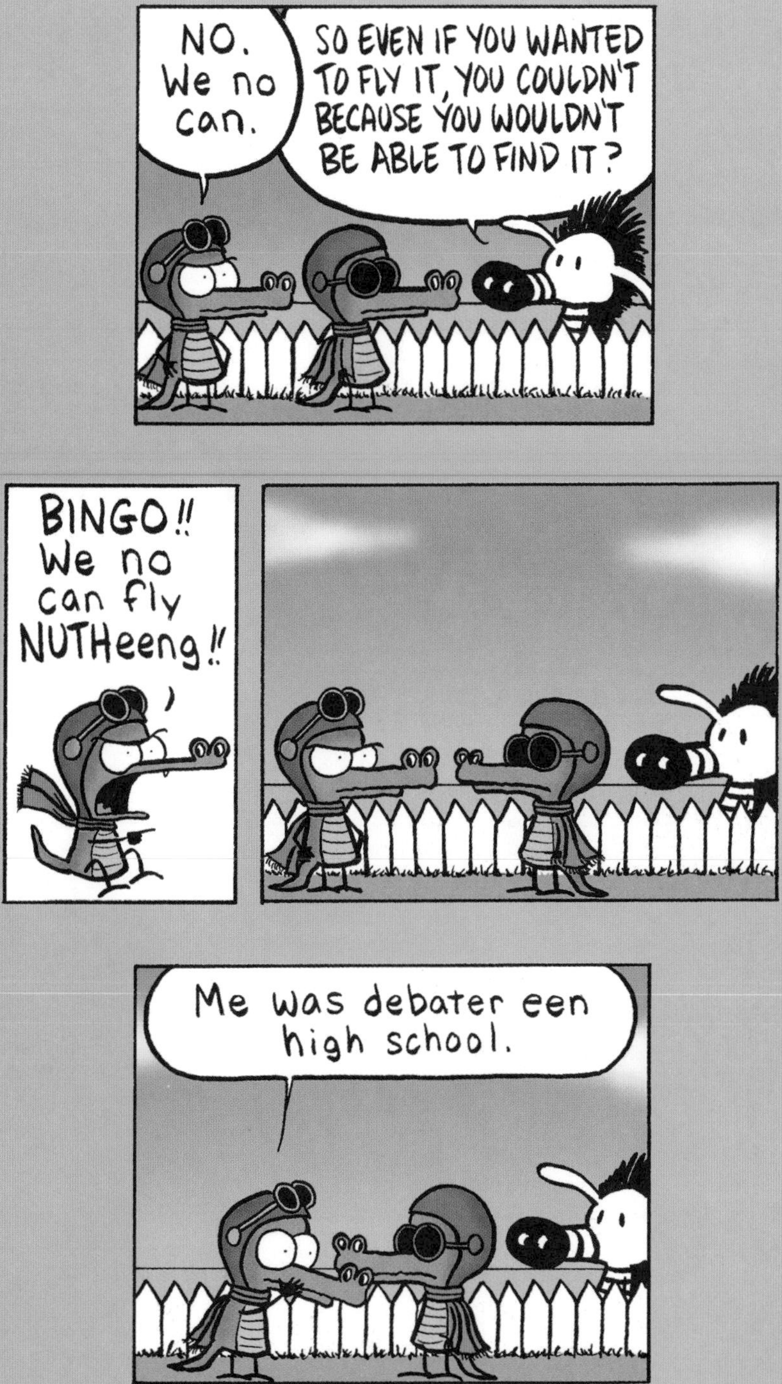
NO. We no can.
SO EVEN IF YOU WANTED TO FLY IT, YOU COULDN'T BECAUSE YOU WOULDN'T BE ABLE TO FIND IT?
BINGO!! We no can fly NUTHeeng!!
Me was debater een high school.

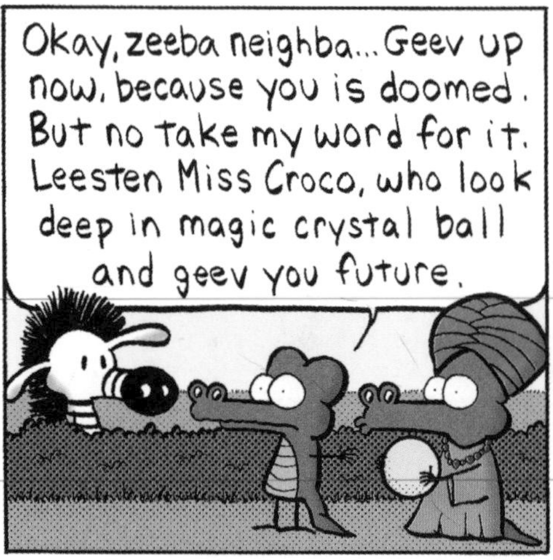
Okay, zeeba neighba... Geev up now, because you is doomed. But no take my word for it. Leesten Miss Croco, who look deep in magic crystal ball and geev you future.

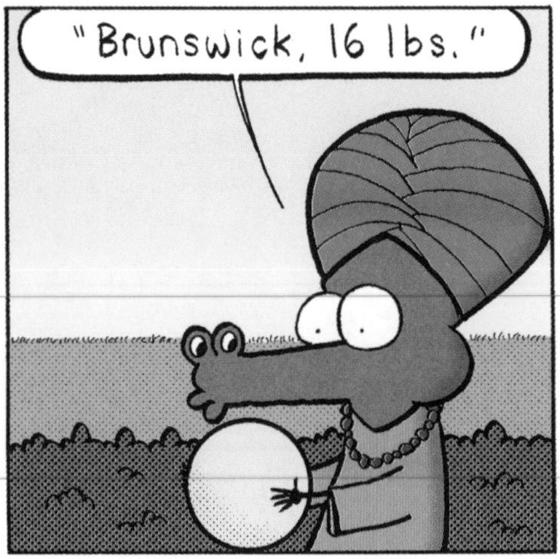
"Brunswick, 16 lbs."

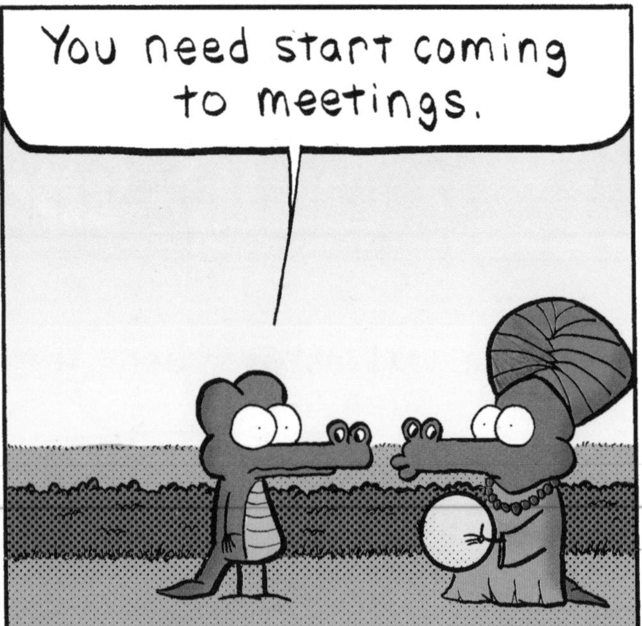
You need start coming to meetings.

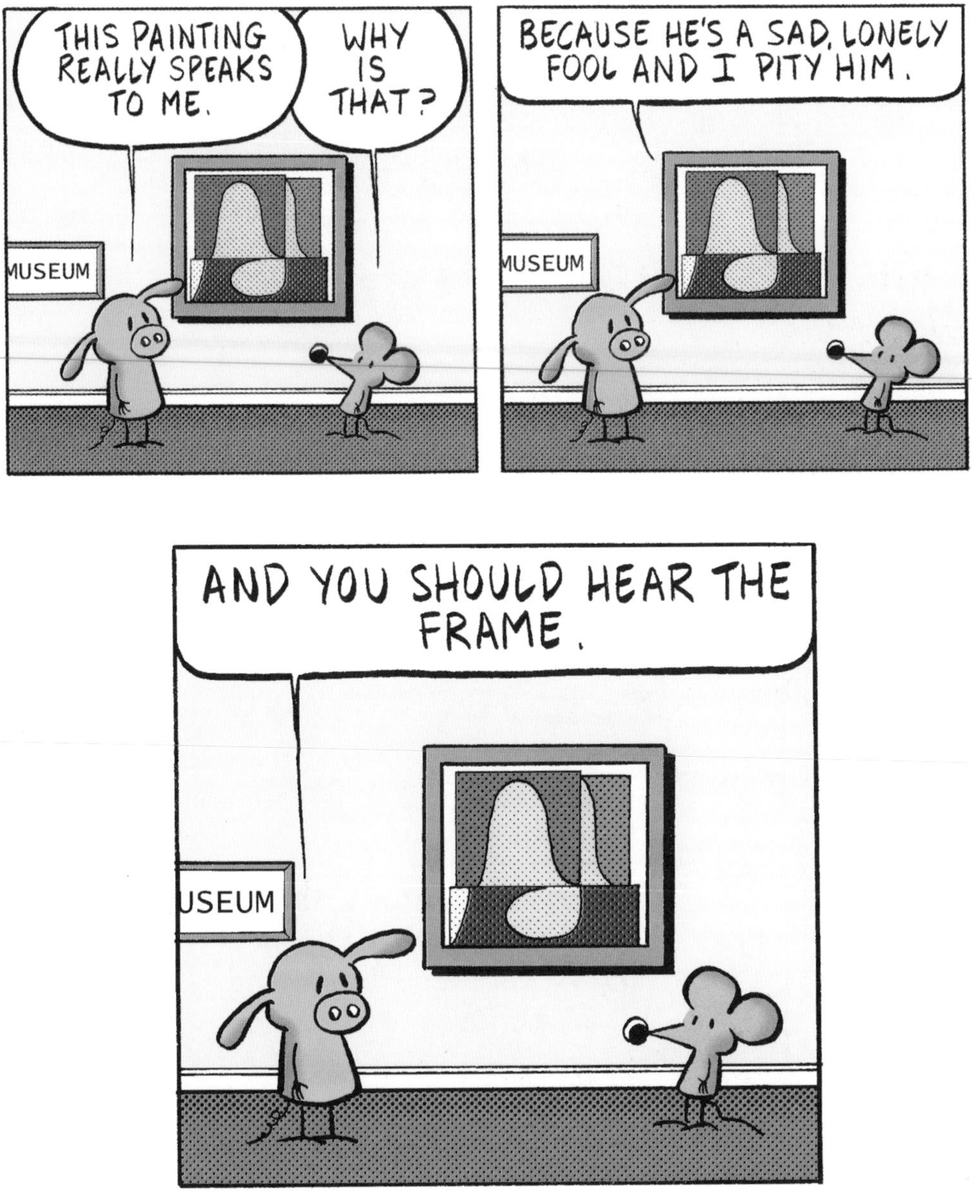
THIS PAINTING REALLY SPEAKS TO ME.
WHY IS THAT?
MUSEUM
BECAUSE HE'S A SAD, LONELY FOOL AND I PITY HIM.
MUSEUM
AND YOU SHOULD HEAR THE FRAME.
USEUM

Larry... What you doing?
Me is tree-climbing assassin monkey.
Larry... You juss crockydile.
Haha.. You know me crockydile. Me know me crockydile. But zeeba not know nutheeng.
You tink ?
Me know...Zeeba juss over fence... He at birthday party for neighba's keed. When he leave, me pounce.

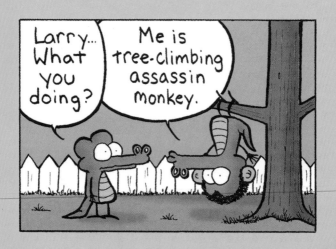

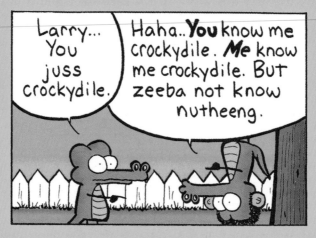

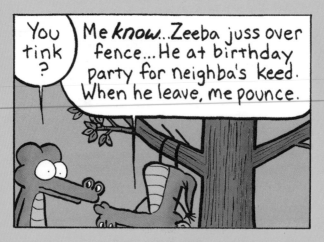

And dat work?
Of course dat work...Once zeeba see he in jaws of tree-climbing assassin monkey, he geeve up so fast dat —
WHAM
Ohhh... SORRY, KIDS.. LOOKS LIKE THE PIÑATA'S OVER *HERE*.
GOOD...THIS ONE'S A RIP-OFF.
GIMME CANDY! CANDY! CANDY!

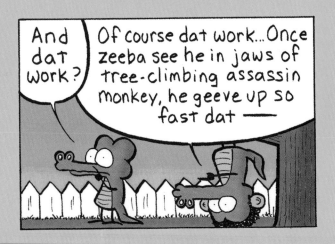

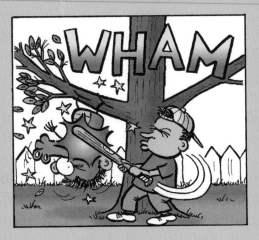

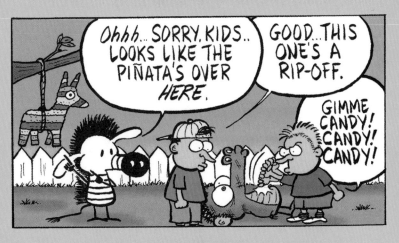

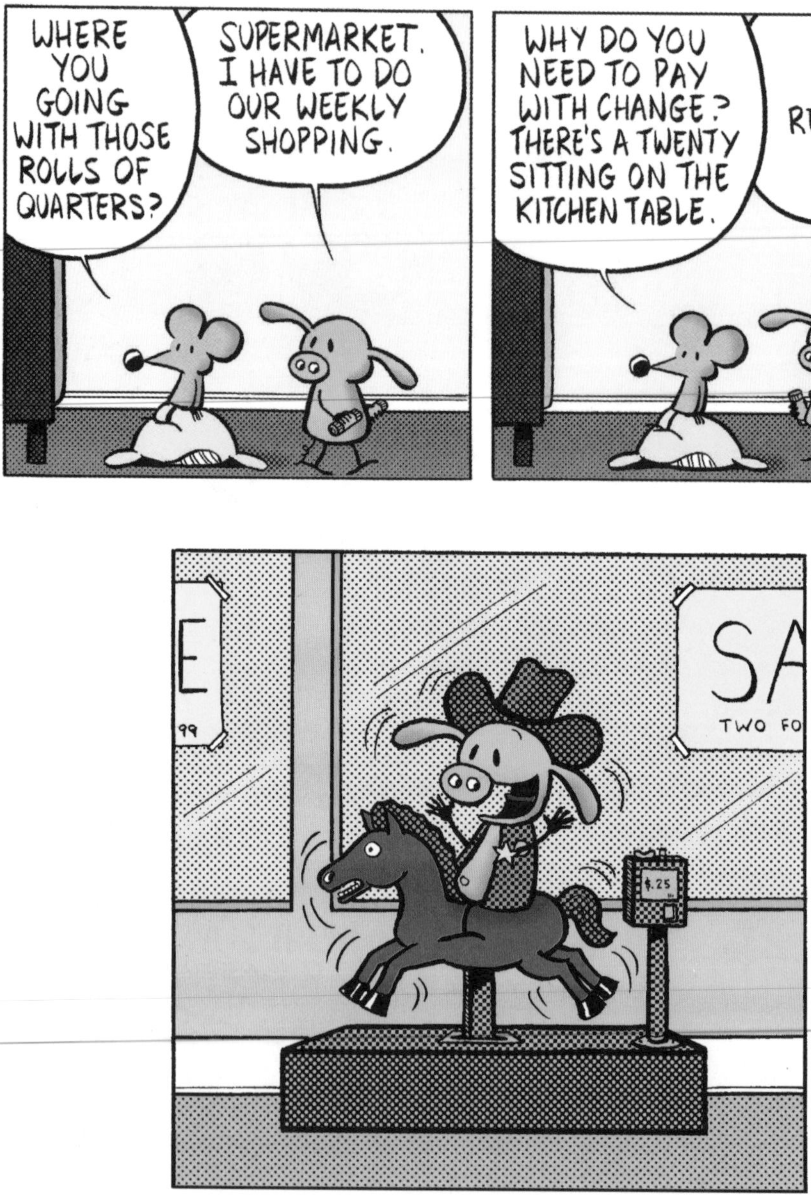
WHERE YOU GOING WITH THOSE ROLLS OF QUARTERS?
SUPERMARKET. I HAVE TO DO OUR WEEKLY SHOPPING.
WHY DO YOU NEED TO PAY WITH CHANGE? THERE'S A TWENTY SITTING ON THE KITCHEN TABLE.
NO REASON.
E
99
SA
TWO FO
$.25

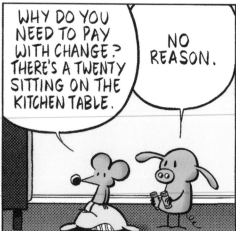

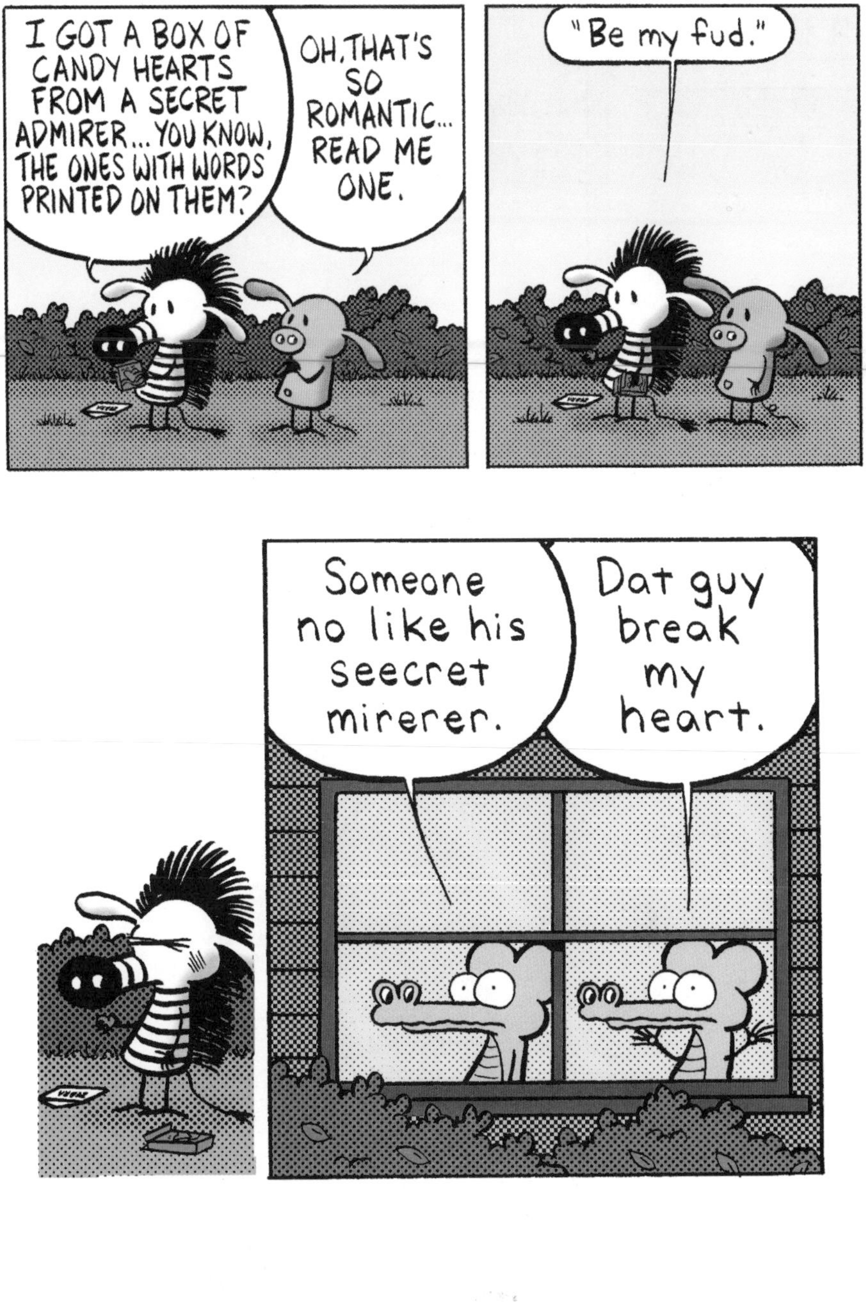
I GOT A BOX OF CANDY HEARTS FROM A SECRET ADMIRER... YOU KNOW, THE ONES WITH WORDS PRINTED ON THEM?
OH, THAT'S SO ROMANTIC... READ ME ONE.
"Be my fud."
Someone no like his seecret mirerer.
Dat guy break my heart.

I'M LEAVING YOU, PIG.
WHY?
YOU'RE A WIMP. I WANT A BOY-FRIEND WHO'S THE TOUGH, OUTDOORSY TYPE. I WANT A MANLY MAN.
BUT THAT'S ME.
PROVE IT.

E
99
S
TW
$.25

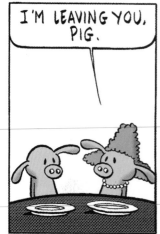

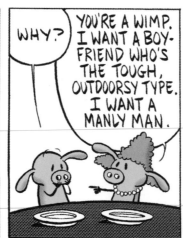

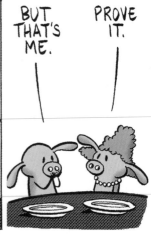

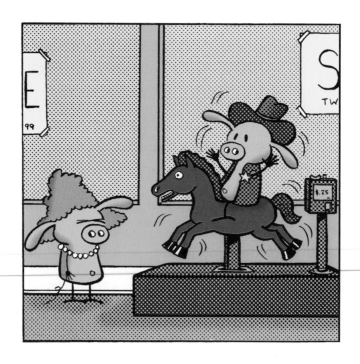

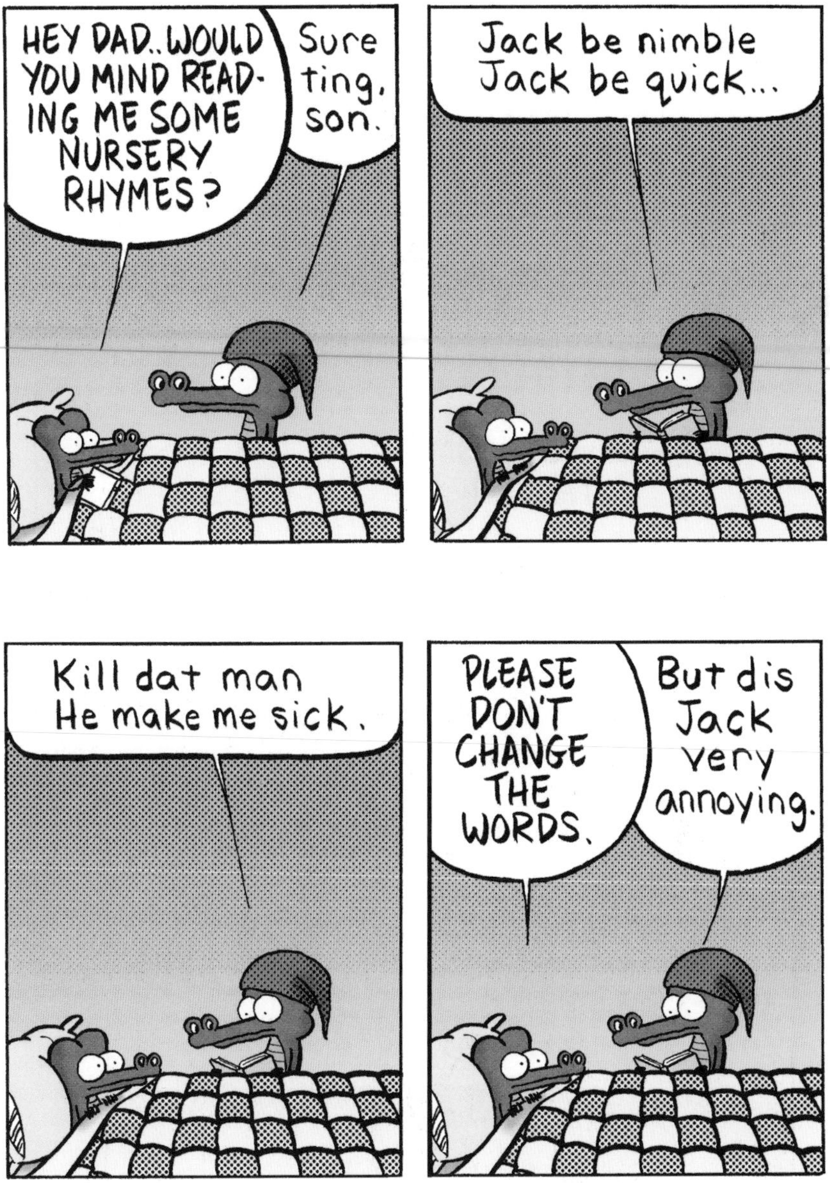
HEY DAD.. WOULD YOU MIND READ-ING ME SOME NURSERY RHYMES?
Sure ting, son.
Jack be nimble Jack be quick...
Kill dat man He make me sick.
PLEASE DON'T CHANGE THE WORDS.
But dis Jack very annoying.

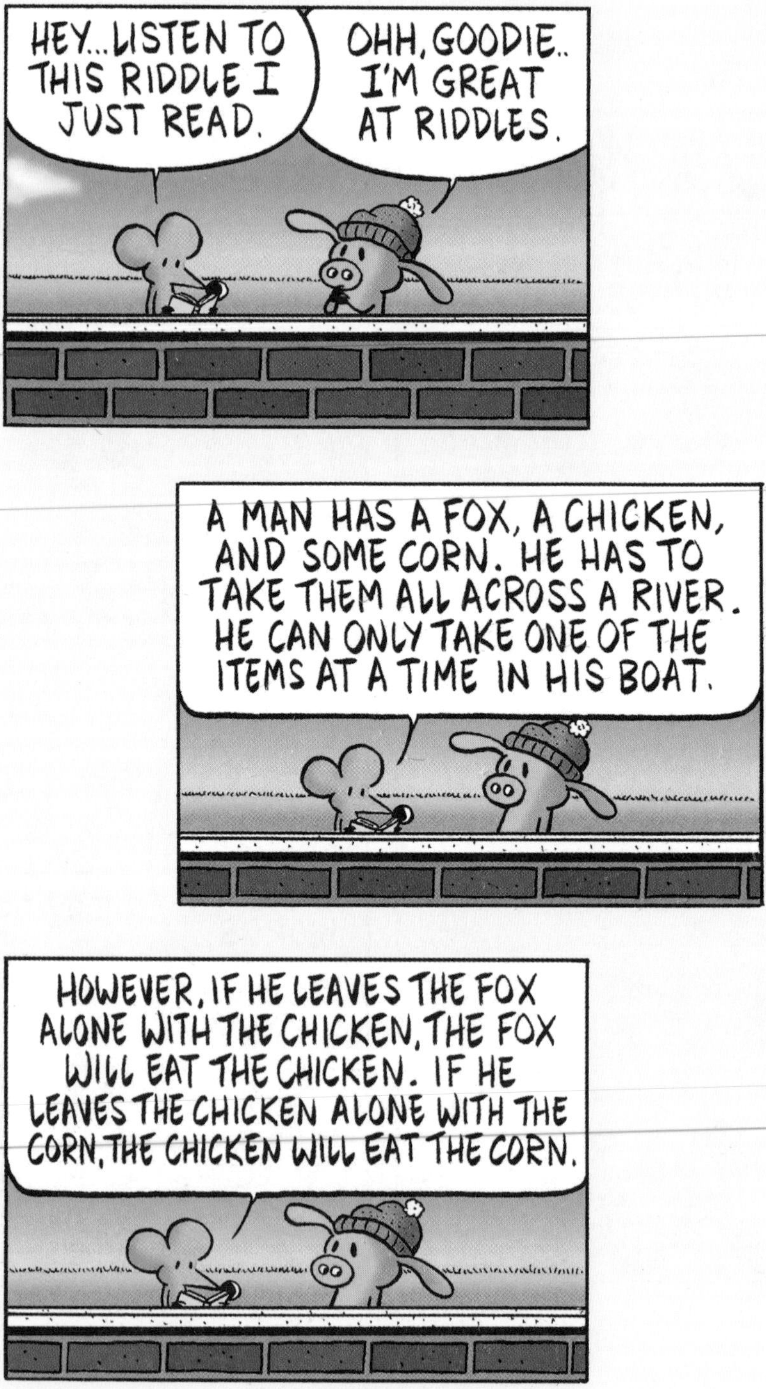
HEY...LISTEN TO THIS RIDDLE I JUST READ.
OHH, GOODIE.. I'M GREAT AT RIDDLES.
A MAN HAS A FOX, A CHICKEN, AND SOME CORN. HE HAS TO TAKE THEM ALL ACROSS A RIVER. HE CAN ONLY TAKE ONE OF THE ITEMS AT A TIME IN HIS BOAT.
HOWEVER, IF HE LEAVES THE FOX ALONE WITH THE CHICKEN, THE FOX WILL EAT THE CHICKEN. IF HE LEAVES THE CHICKEN ALONE WITH THE CORN, THE CHICKEN WILL EAT THE CORN.

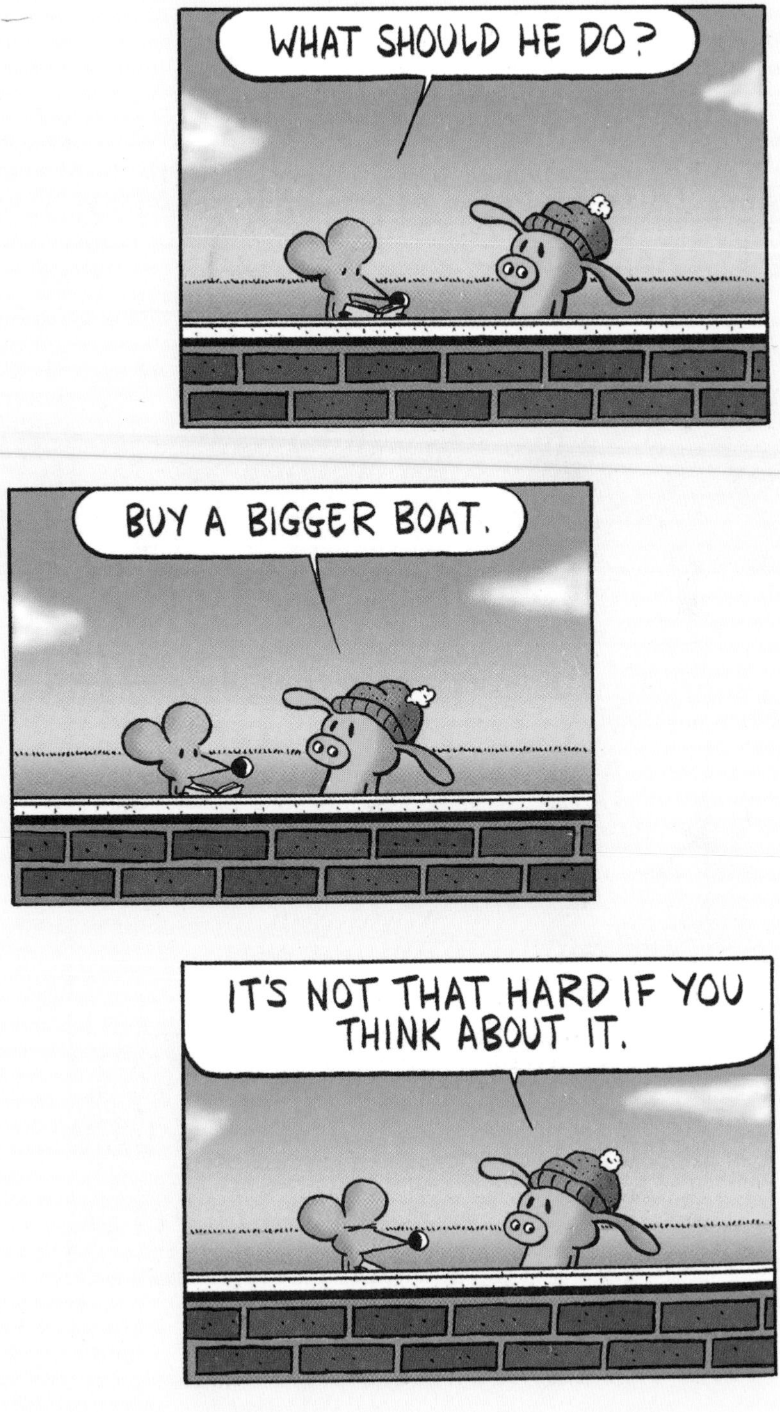
WHAT SHOULD HE DO?
BUY A BIGGER BOAT.
IT'S NOT THAT HARD IF YOU THINK ABOUT IT.

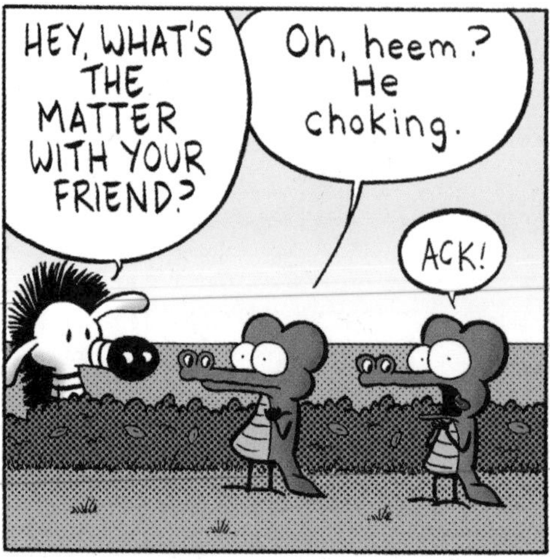
HEY, WHAT'S THE MATTER WITH YOUR FRIEND?
Oh, heem? He choking.
ACK!

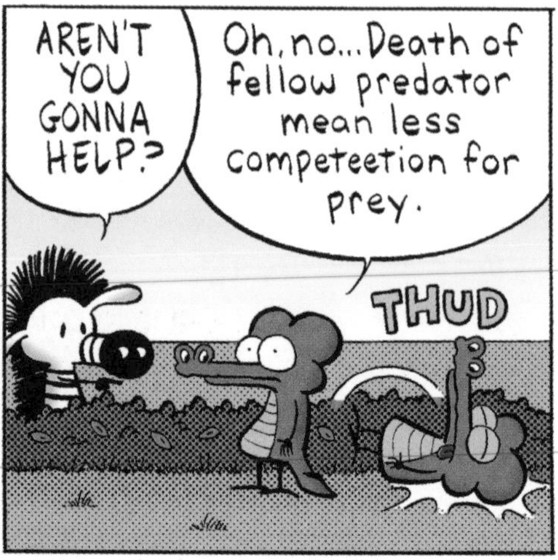
AREN'T YOU GONNA HELP?
Oh, no... Death of fellow predator mean less competeetion for prey.
THUD

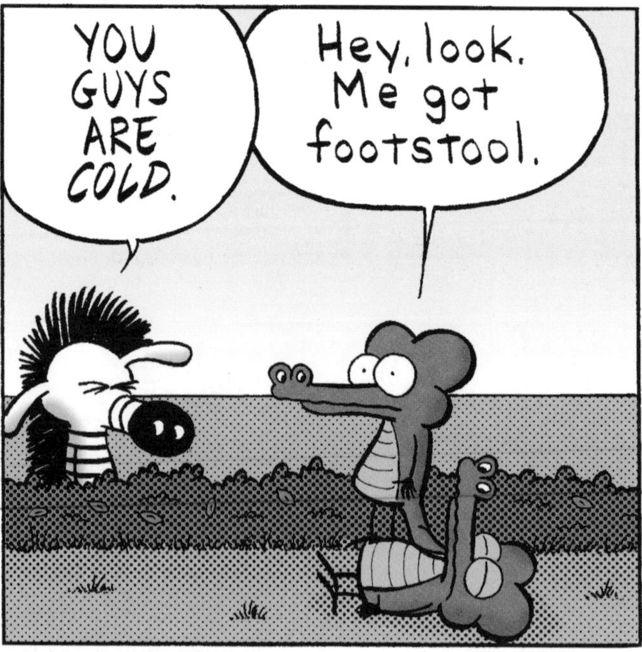
YOU GUYS ARE COLD.
Hey, look. Me got footstool.

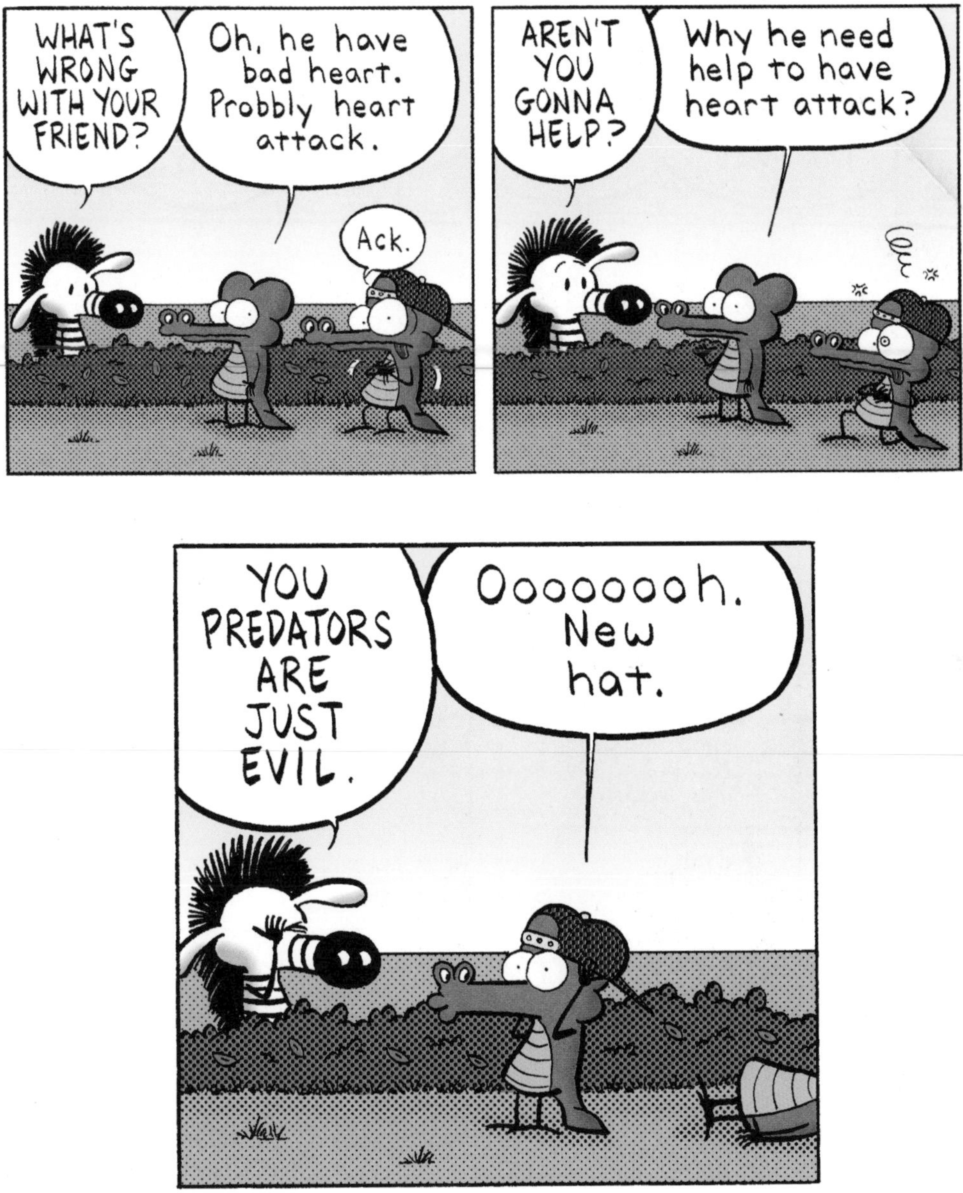
WHAT'S WRONG WITH YOUR FRIEND?
Oh, he have bad heart. Probbly heart attack.
Ack.
AREN'T YOU GONNA HELP?
Why he need help to have heart attack?
YOU PREDATORS ARE JUST EVIL.
Oooooooh. New hat.

WHOA. THAT BOAT'S ABOUT TO GO OVER THE EDGE.
THE EDGE OF WHAT?
THE WORLD THERE.
THE WORLD'S ROUND, PIG.
SO IS MY KITCHEN TABLE, BUT YOU CAN STILL KNOCK OFF THE CEREAL BOWL.
I GUESS 'SORRY' ISN'T IN YOUR VOCABULARY.

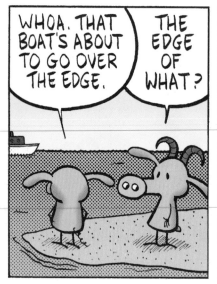

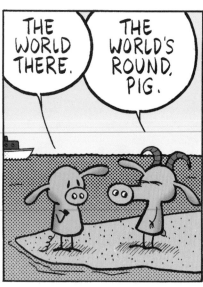

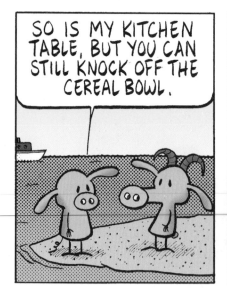

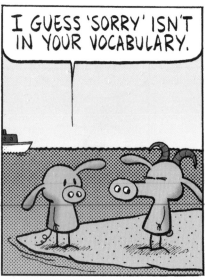

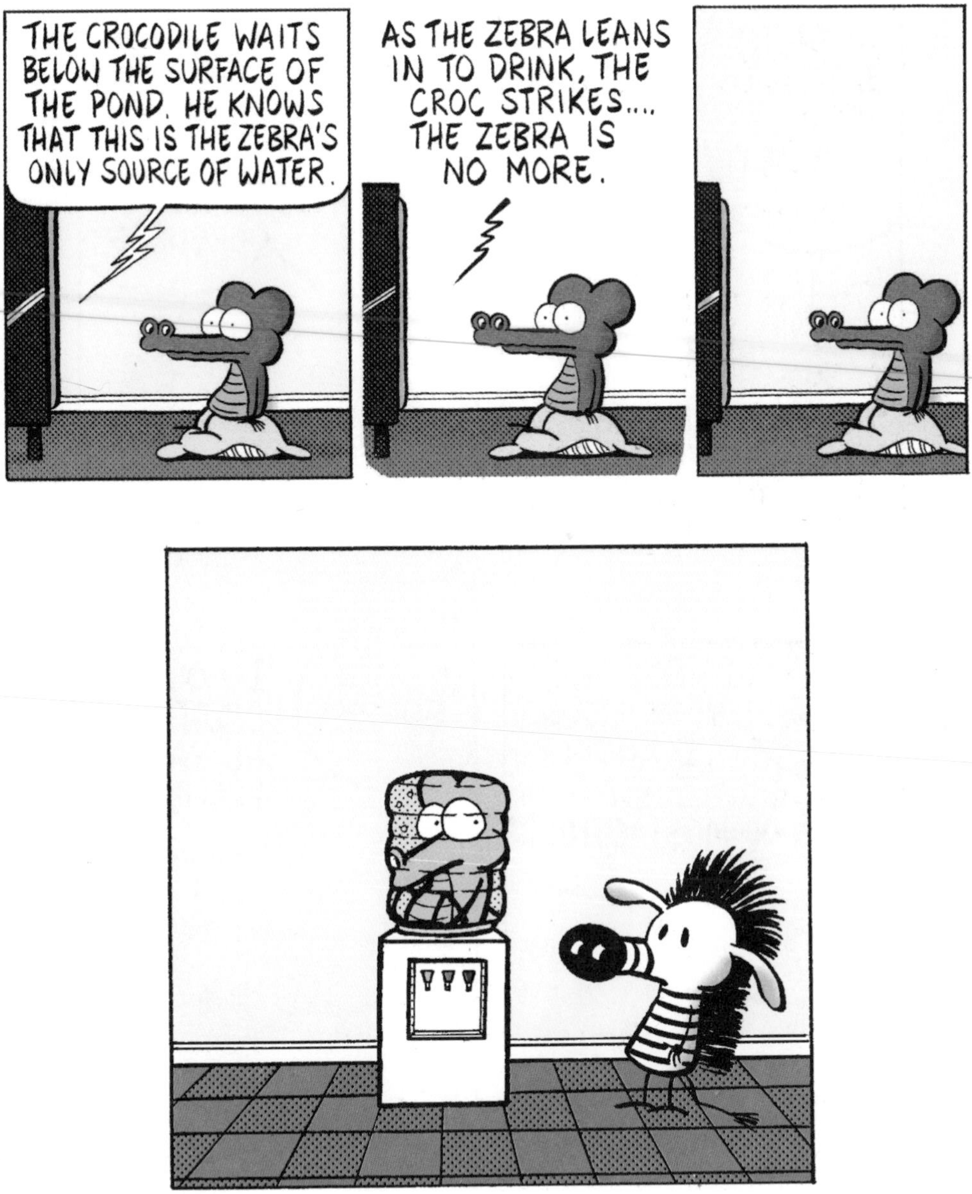
THE CROCODILE WAITS BELOW THE SURFACE OF THE POND. HE KNOWS THAT THIS IS THE ZEBRA'S ONLY SOURCE OF WATER.
AS THE ZEBRA LEANS IN TO DRINK, THE CROC STRIKES.... THE ZEBRA IS NO MORE.

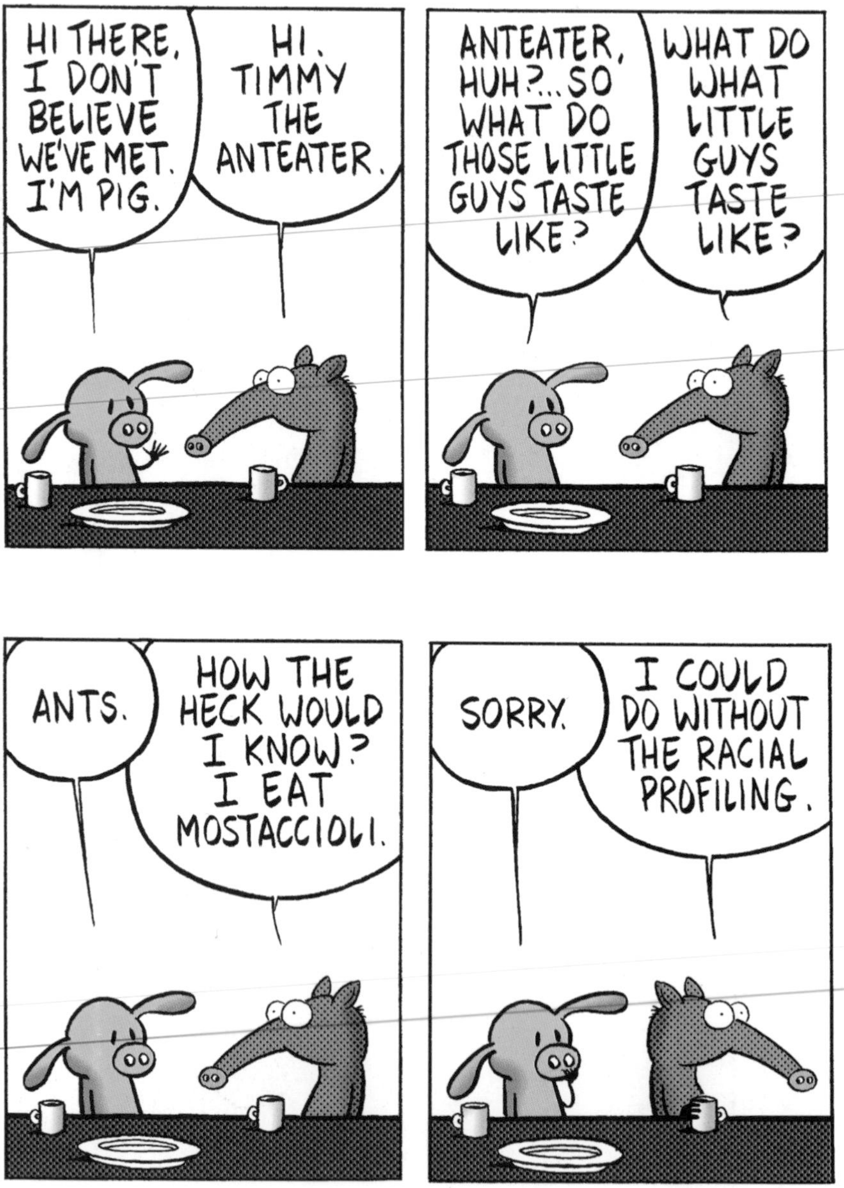
HI THERE, I DON'T BELIEVE WE'VE MET. I'M PIG.
HI. TIMMY THE ANTEATER.
ANTEATER, HUH?...SO WHAT DO THOSE LITTLE GUYS TASTE LIKE?
WHAT DO WHAT LITTLE GUYS TASTE LIKE?
ANTS.
HOW THE HECK WOULD I KNOW? I EAT MOSTACCIOLI.
SORRY.
I COULD DO WITHOUT THE RACIAL PROFILING.

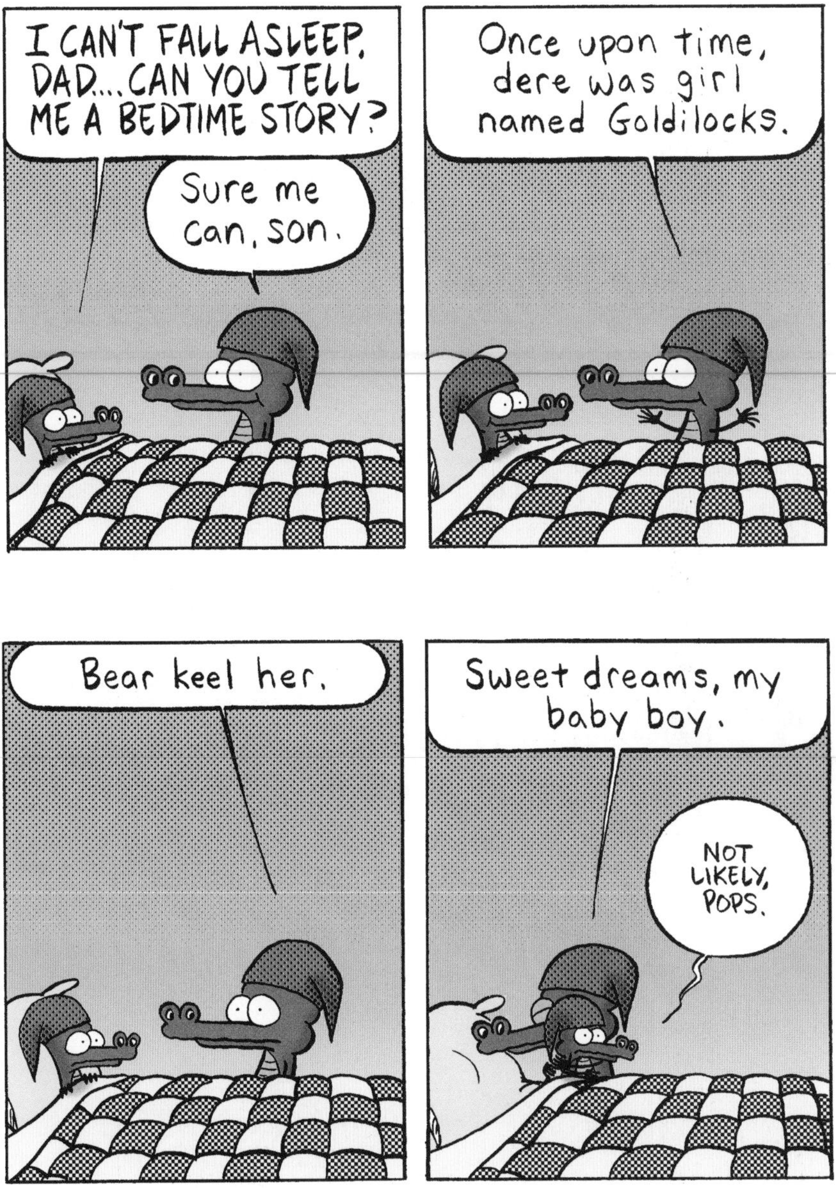
I CAN'T FALL ASLEEP, DAD....CAN YOU TELL ME A BEDTIME STORY?
Sure me can, son.
Once upon time, dere was girl named Goldilocks.
Bear keel her.
Sweet dreams, my baby boy.
NOT LIKELY, POPS.

THE UNSUSPECTING ZEBRA APPROACHES THE WATERING HOLE....
HE TAKES A DRINK...HE DOES NOT SEE THE CROCODILE LURKING JUST BENEATH THE SURFACE...
THE CROC STRIKES.

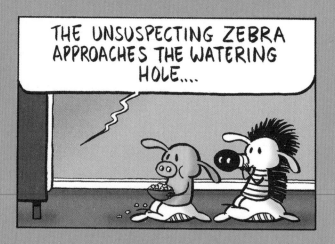

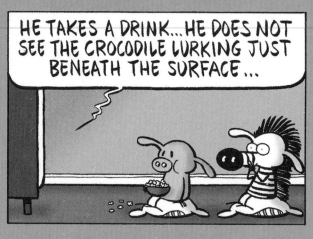

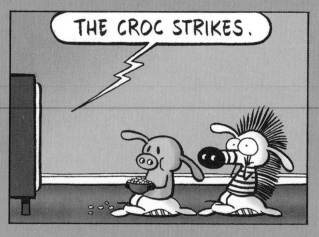

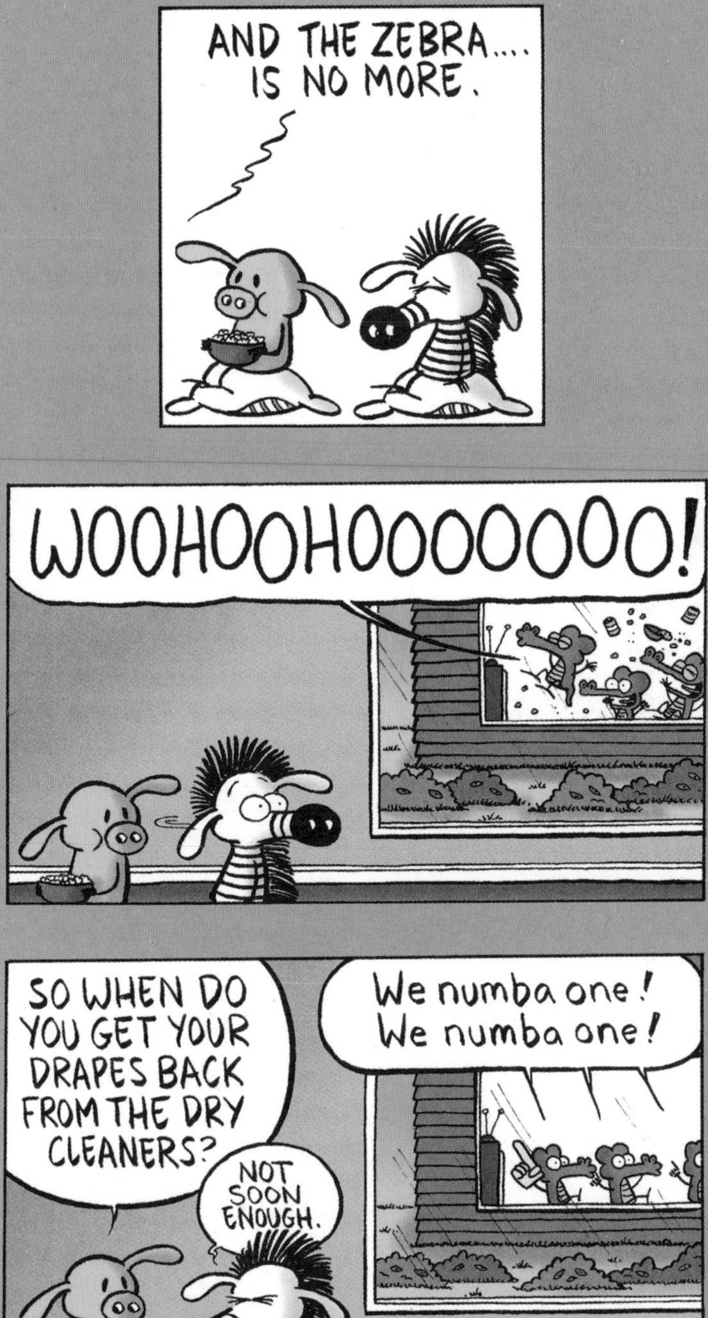
AND THE ZEBRA.... IS NO MORE.
WOOHOOHOOOOOOO!
SO WHEN DO YOU GET YOUR DRAPES BACK FROM THE DRY CLEANERS?
We numba one! We numba one!
NOT SOON ENOUGH.

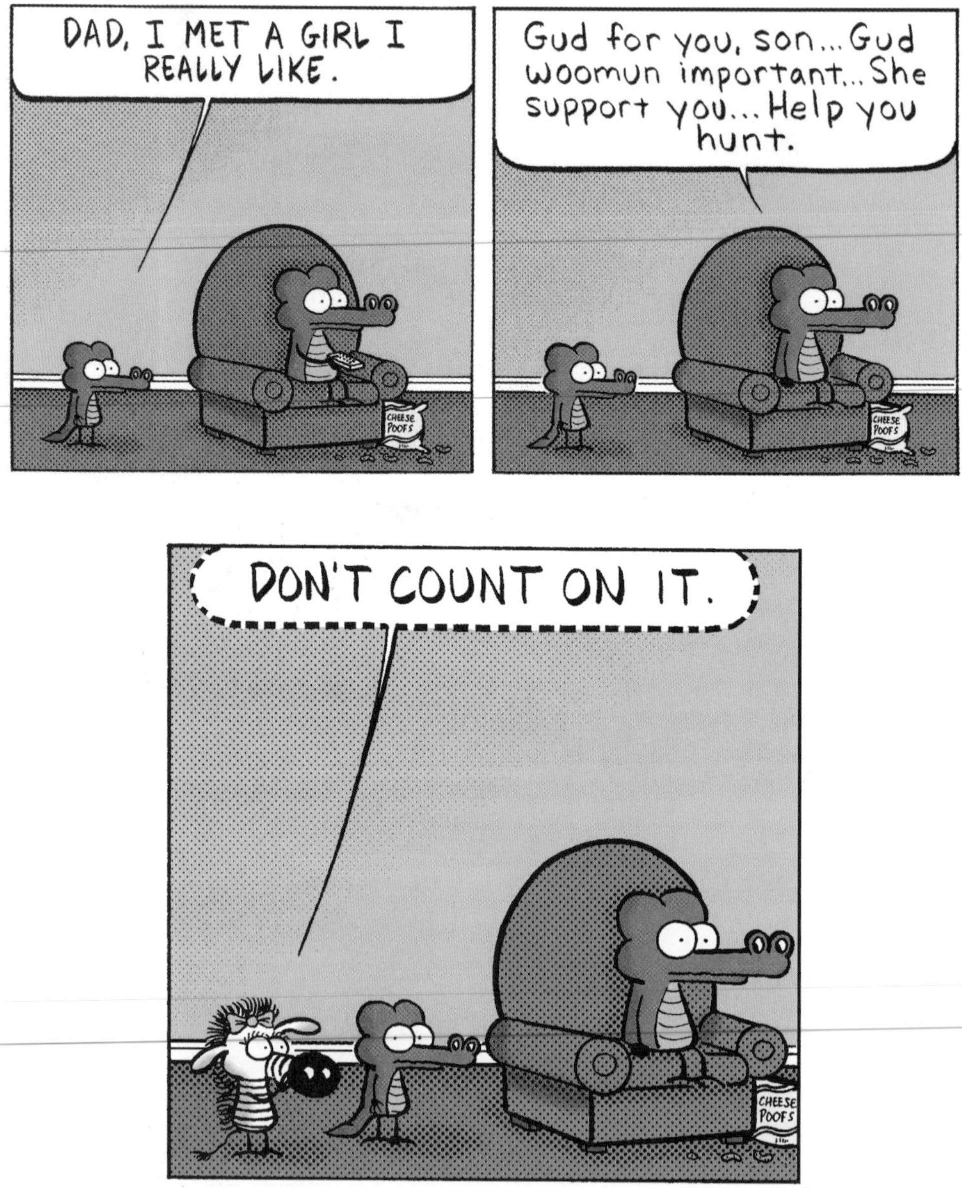
DAD, I MET A GIRL I REALLY LIKE.
CHEESE POOFS
Gud for you, son... Gud woomun important... She support you... Help you hunt.
CHEESE POOFS
DON'T COUNT ON IT.
CHEESE POOFS

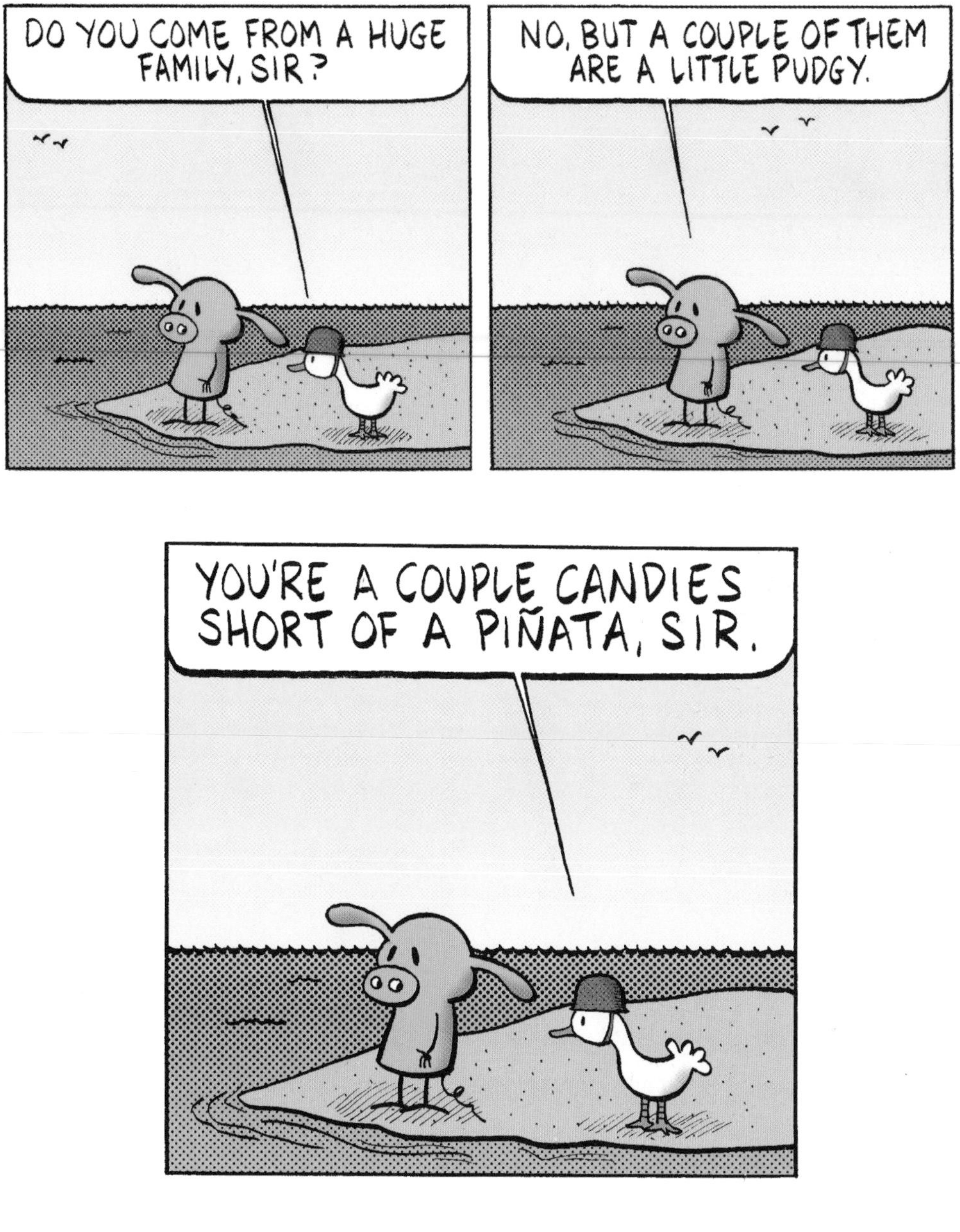
DO YOU COME FROM A HUGE FAMILY, SIR?
NO, BUT A COUPLE OF THEM ARE A LITTLE PUDGY.
YOU'RE A COUPLE CANDIES SHORT OF A PIÑATA, SIR.

DAD, I'M GOING ON A DINNER DATE.

Me see you dinner. Where you date?

WE SHOULD TALK, DAD.

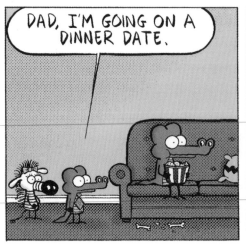

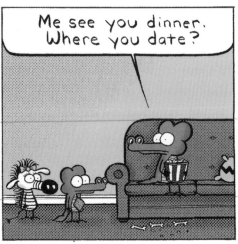

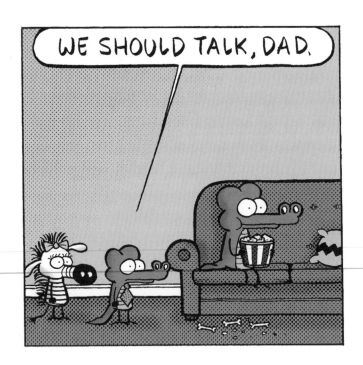

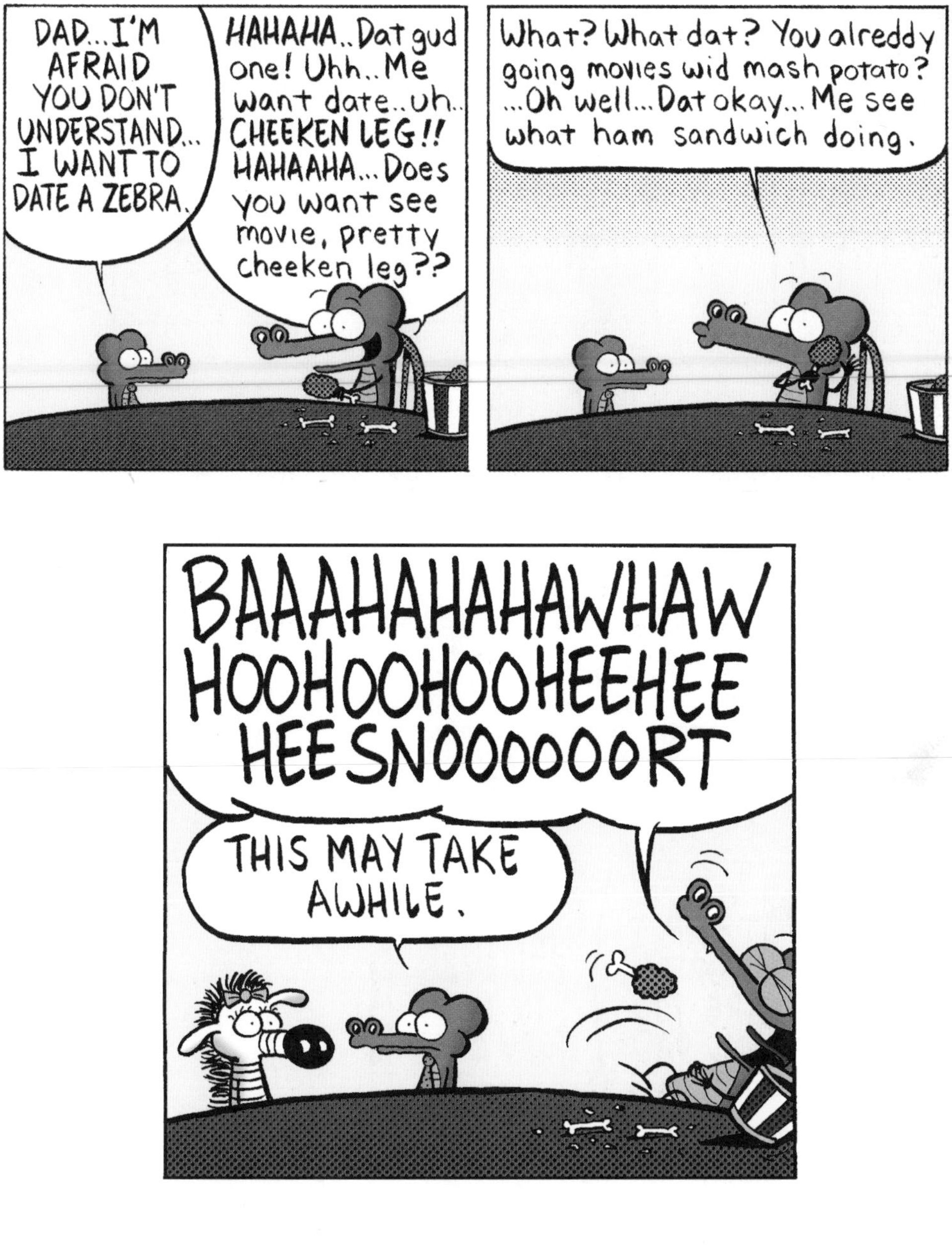
DAD... I'M AFRAID YOU DON'T UNDERSTAND... I WANT TO DATE A ZEBRA.
HAHAHA.. Dat gud one! Uhh.. Me want date.. uh.. CHEEKEN LEG!! HAHAAHA... Does you want see movie, pretty cheeken leg??
What? What dat? You alreddy going movies wid mash potato? ...Oh well... Dat okay... Me see what ham sandwich doing.
BAAAHAHAHAWHAW HOOHOOHOOHEEHEE HEESNOOOOOORT
THIS MAY TAKE AWHILE.

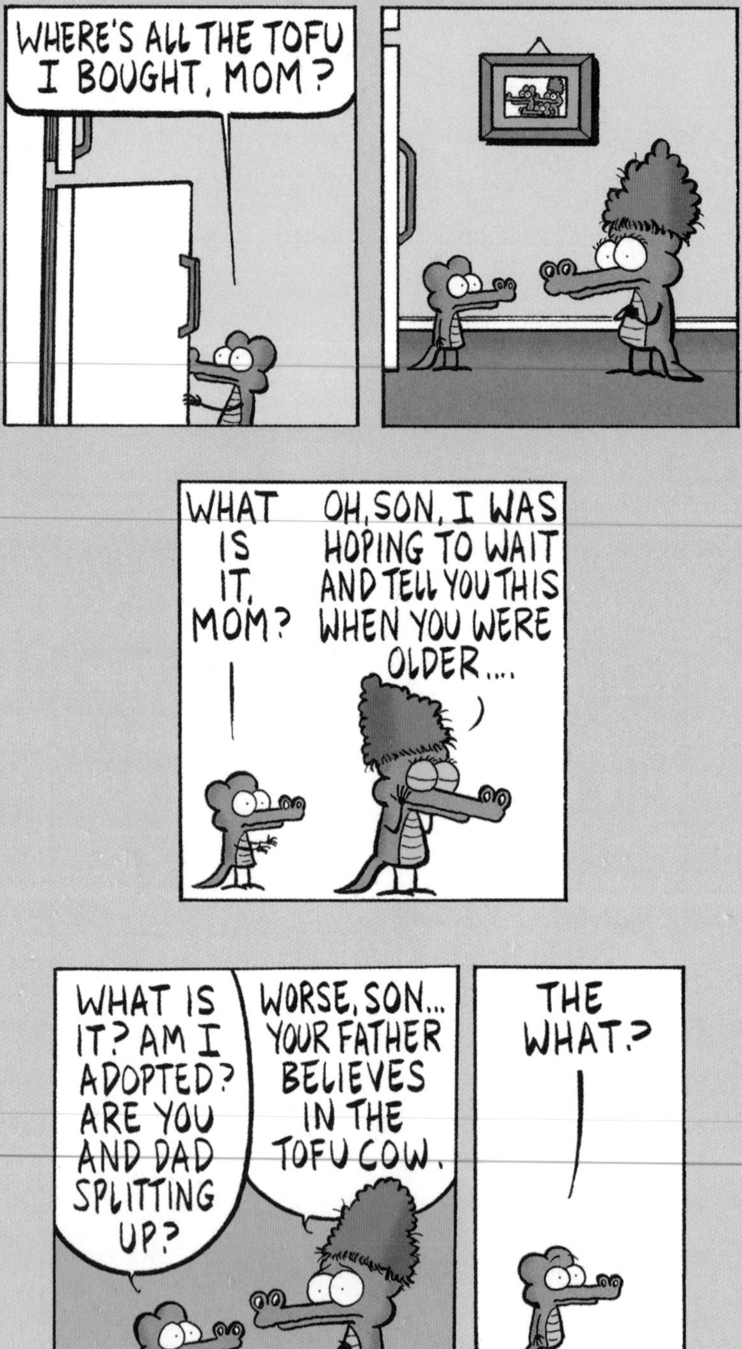
WHERE'S ALL THE TOFU I BOUGHT, MOM?
WHAT IS IT, MOM?
OH, SON, I WAS HOPING TO WAIT AND TELL YOU THIS WHEN YOU WERE OLDER....
WHAT IS IT? AM I ADOPTED? ARE YOU AND DAD SPLITTING UP?
WORSE, SON... YOUR FATHER BELIEVES IN THE TOFU COW.
THE WHAT?

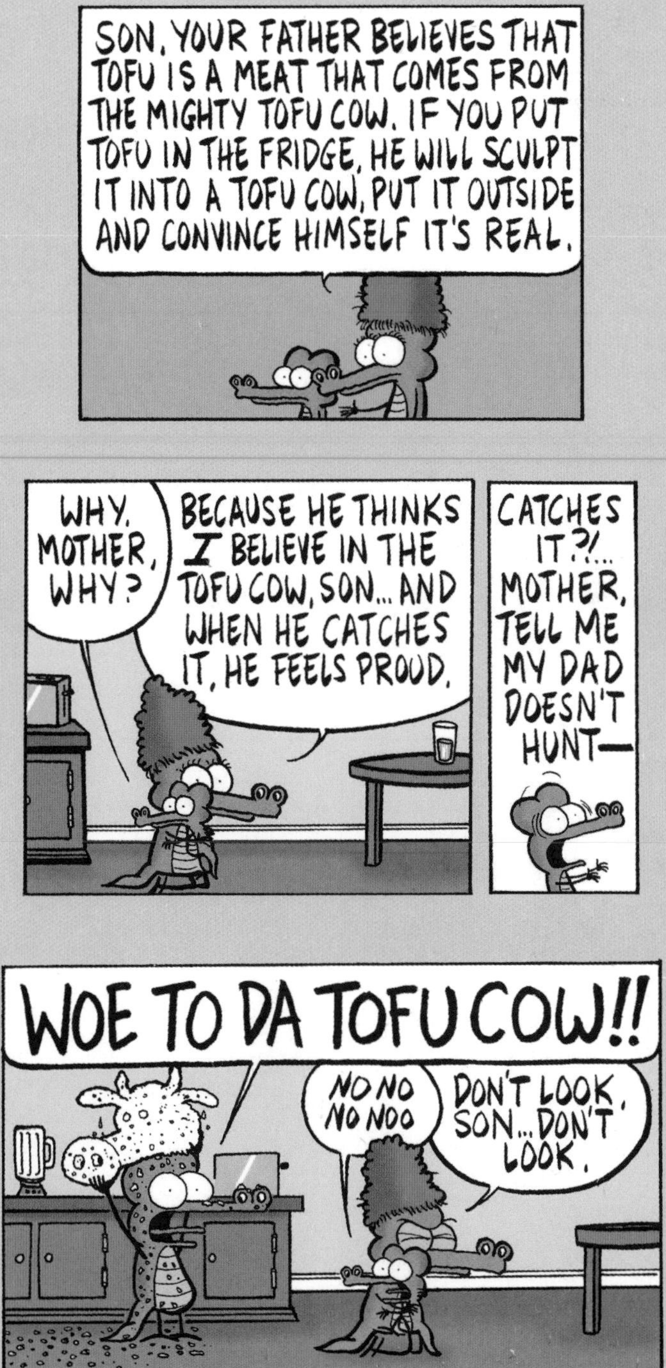
SON, YOUR FATHER BELIEVES THAT TOFU IS A MEAT THAT COMES FROM THE MIGHTY TOFU COW. IF YOU PUT TOFU IN THE FRIDGE, HE WILL SCULPT IT INTO A TOFU COW, PUT IT OUTSIDE AND CONVINCE HIMSELF IT'S REAL.
WHY, MOTHER, WHY?
BECAUSE HE THINKS I BELIEVE IN THE TOFU COW, SON... AND WHEN HE CATCHES IT, HE FEELS PROUD.
CATCHES IT?!... MOTHER, TELL ME MY DAD DOESN'T HUNT—
WOE TO DA TOFU COW!!
NO NO NO NOO
DON'T LOOK, SON... DON'T LOOK.

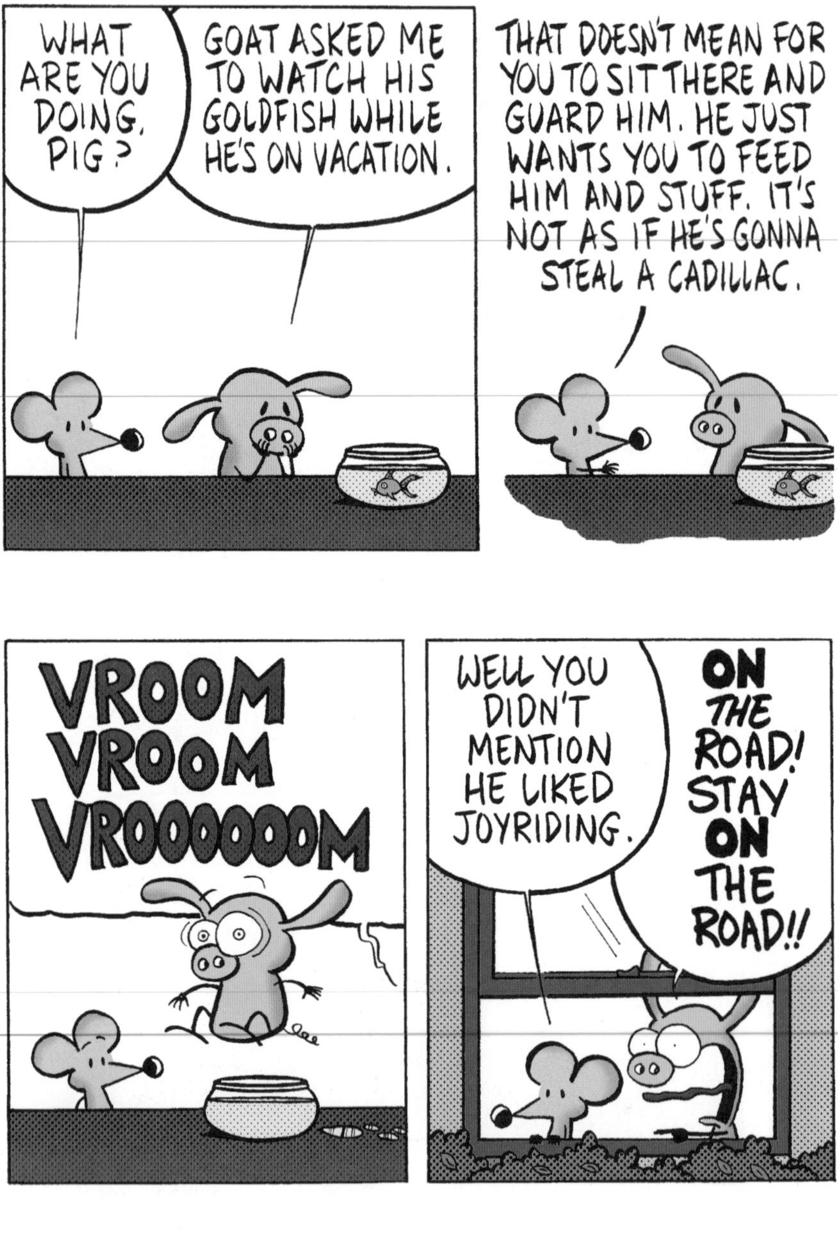
WHAT ARE YOU DOING, PIG?
GOAT ASKED ME TO WATCH HIS GOLDFISH WHILE HE'S ON VACATION.
THAT DOESN'T MEAN FOR YOU TO SIT THERE AND GUARD HIM. HE JUST WANTS YOU TO FEED HIM AND STUFF. IT'S NOT AS IF HE'S GONNA STEAL A CADILLAC.
VROOM VROOM VROOOOOOM
WELL YOU DIDN'T MENTION HE LIKED JOYRIDING.
ON THE ROAD! STAY ON THE ROAD!!

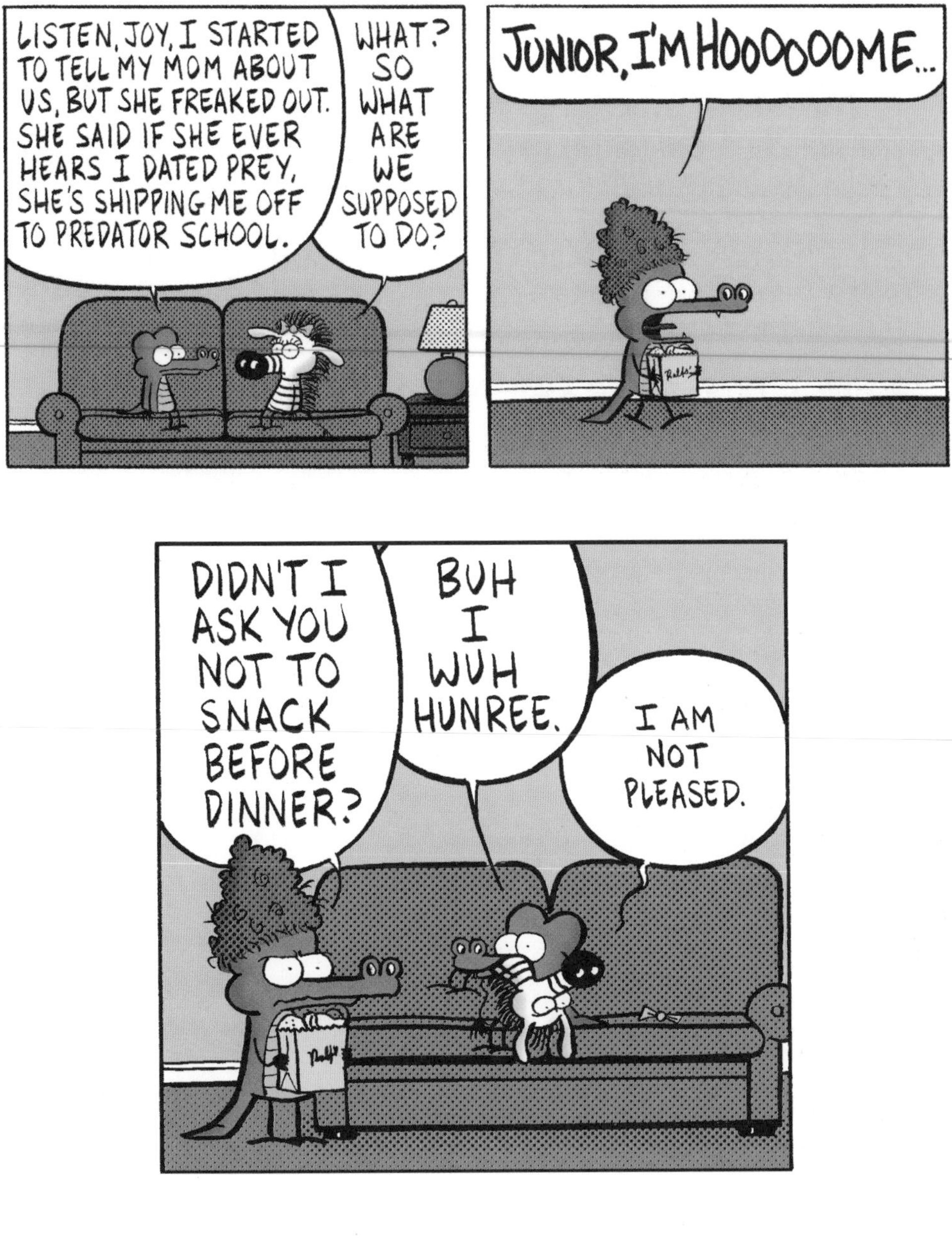
LISTEN, JOY, I STARTED TO TELL MY MOM ABOUT US, BUT SHE FREAKED OUT. SHE SAID IF SHE EVER HEARS I DATED PREY, SHE'S SHIPPING ME OFF TO PREDATOR SCHOOL.
WHAT? SO WHAT ARE WE SUPPOSED TO DO?
JUNIOR, I'M HOOOOOOME...
Ralph's
DIDN'T I ASK YOU NOT TO SNACK BEFORE DINNER?
BUH I WUH HUNREE.
I AM NOT PLEASED.

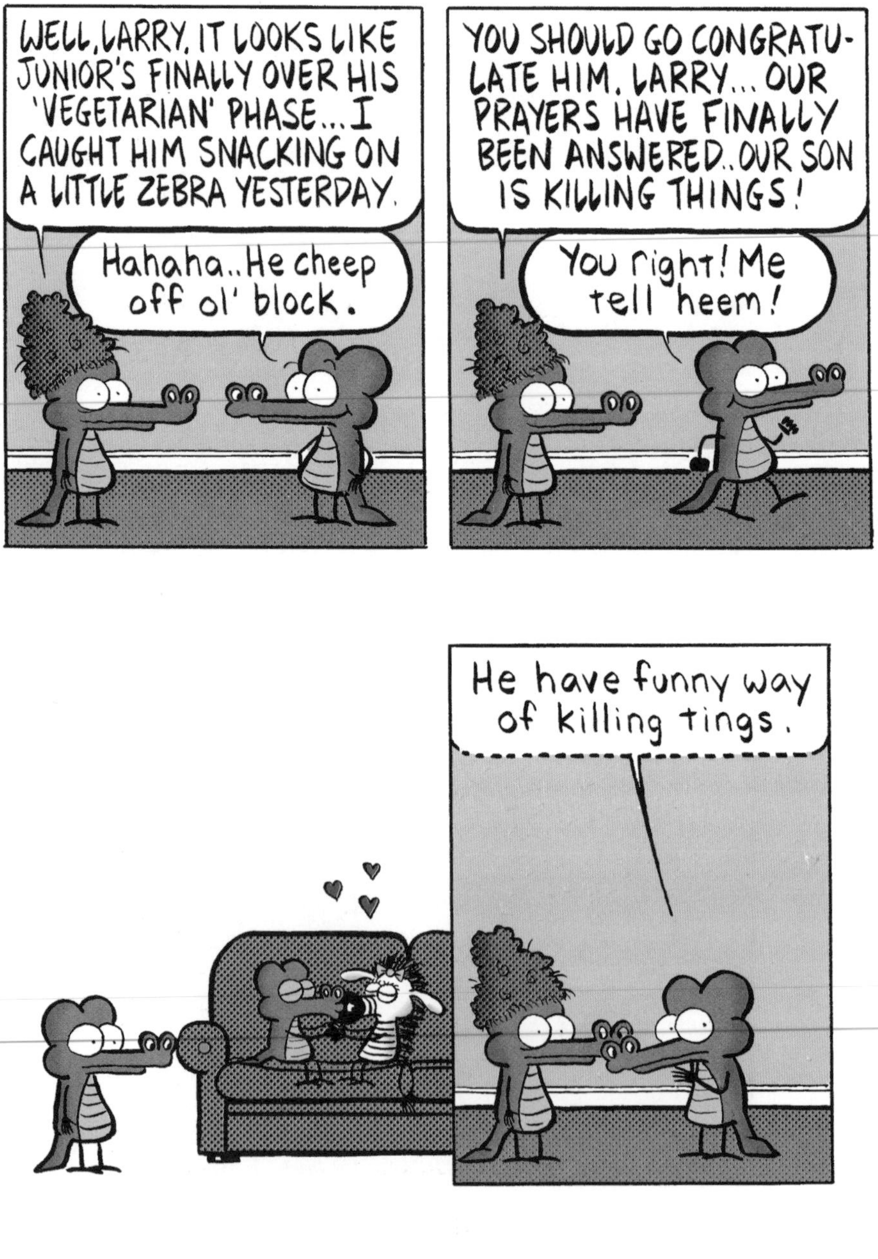
WELL, LARRY, IT LOOKS LIKE JUNIOR'S FINALLY OVER HIS 'VEGETARIAN' PHASE... I CAUGHT HIM SNACKING ON A LITTLE ZEBRA YESTERDAY.
Hahaha.. He cheep off ol' block.
YOU SHOULD GO CONGRATU-LATE HIM, LARRY... OUR PRAYERS HAVE FINALLY BEEN ANSWERED.. OUR SON IS KILLING THINGS!
You right! Me tell heem!
He have funny way of killing tings.

WHAT'S THE MATTER WITH YOU, PATTY?
OH, MYRNA, YOU CAN'T TELL ANYONE. IT'S SO HUMILIATING.
I WON'T. I SWEAR. WHAT IS IT?
I CAUGHT JUNIOR DATING A ZEBRA.
YOU WHAT ?!?
SHE'S THE NIECE OF THAT ZEBRA NEXT DOOR... BUT I'VE LOCKED HIM IN HIS ROOM AND TAKEN AWAY HIS CELL PHONE AND COMPUTER, SO AT LEAST THEY'LL HAVE NO WAY TO COMMUNICATE.

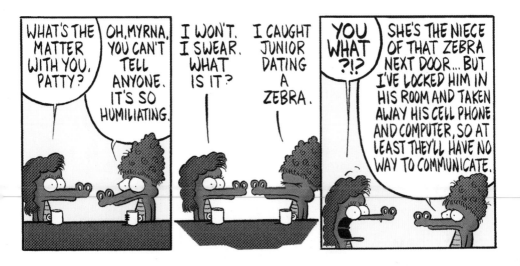

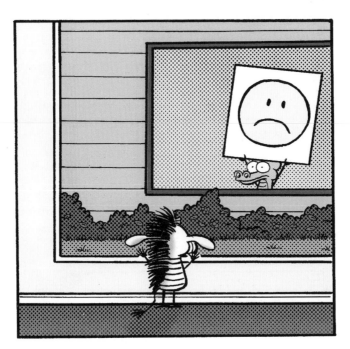

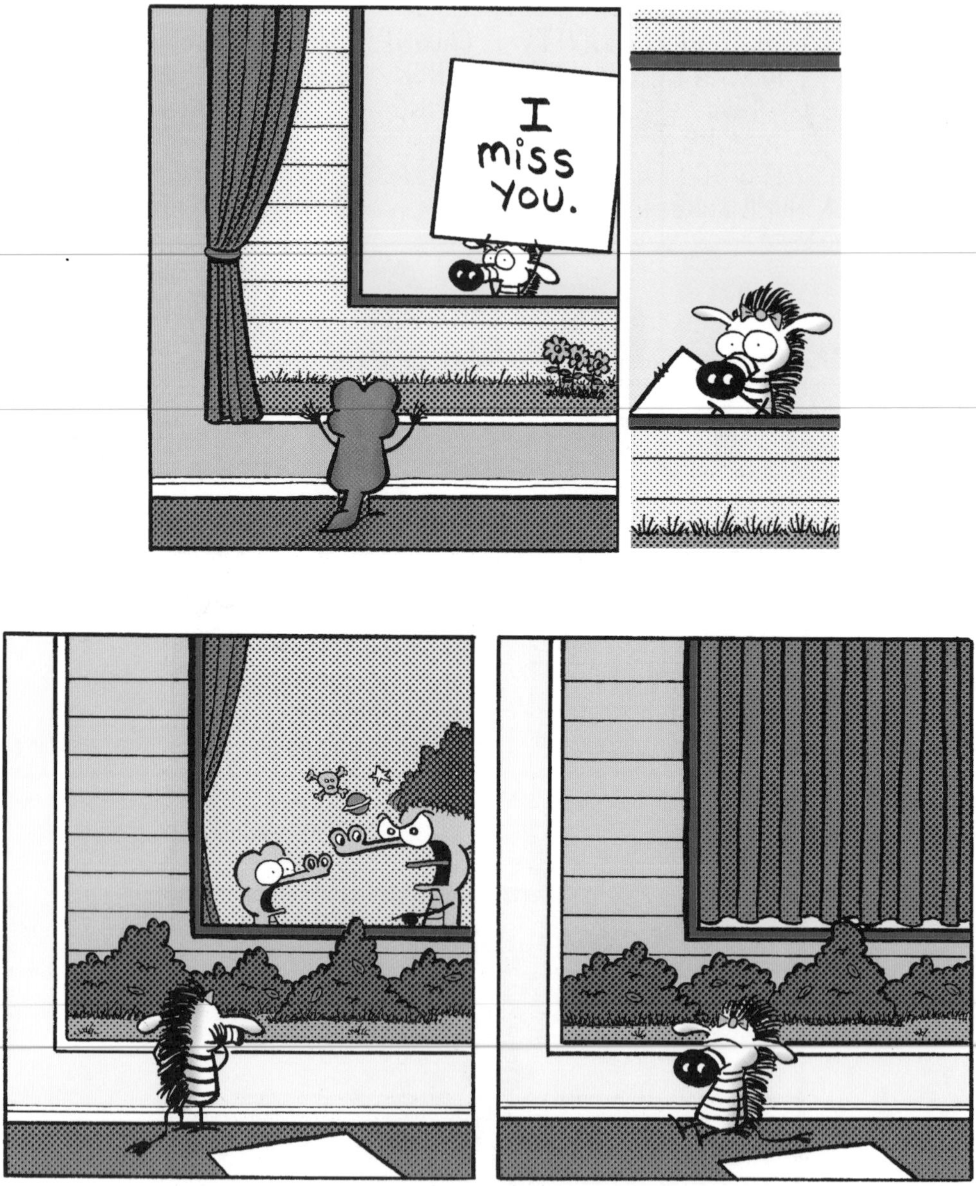
I miss you.

HOW'S YOUR SON DOING?
GOOD. THAT LITTLE ZEBRA HE WAS DATING IS LEAVING TO GO BACK TO SCHOOL...I GUESS HER SPRING BREAK IS OVER, THANK GOD.
WONDERFUL. AND HOW'S YOUR SON TAKING IT?
OH, HAHAHA...HE'S FINE. HE KNOWS IT WAS JUST A SILLY CHILDHOOD CRUSH...

World ending.

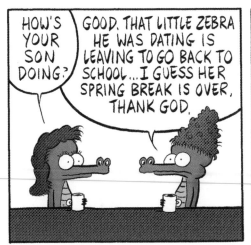

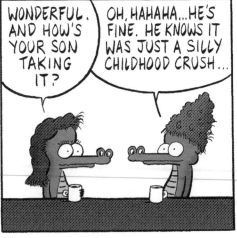

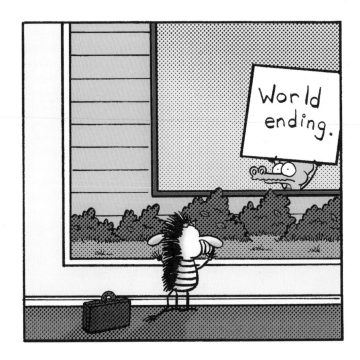

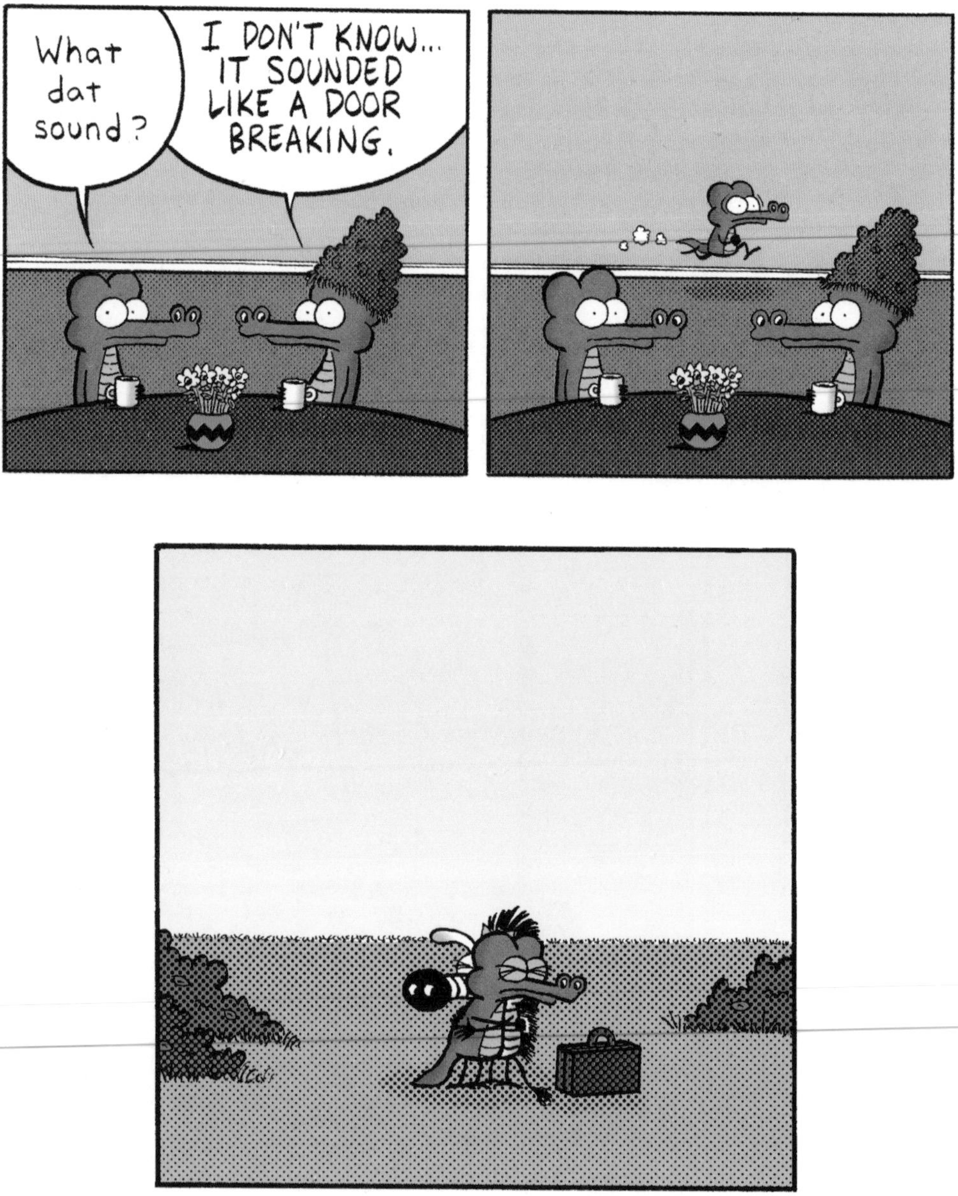
What dat sound?
I DON'T KNOW... IT SOUNDED LIKE A DOOR BREAKING.

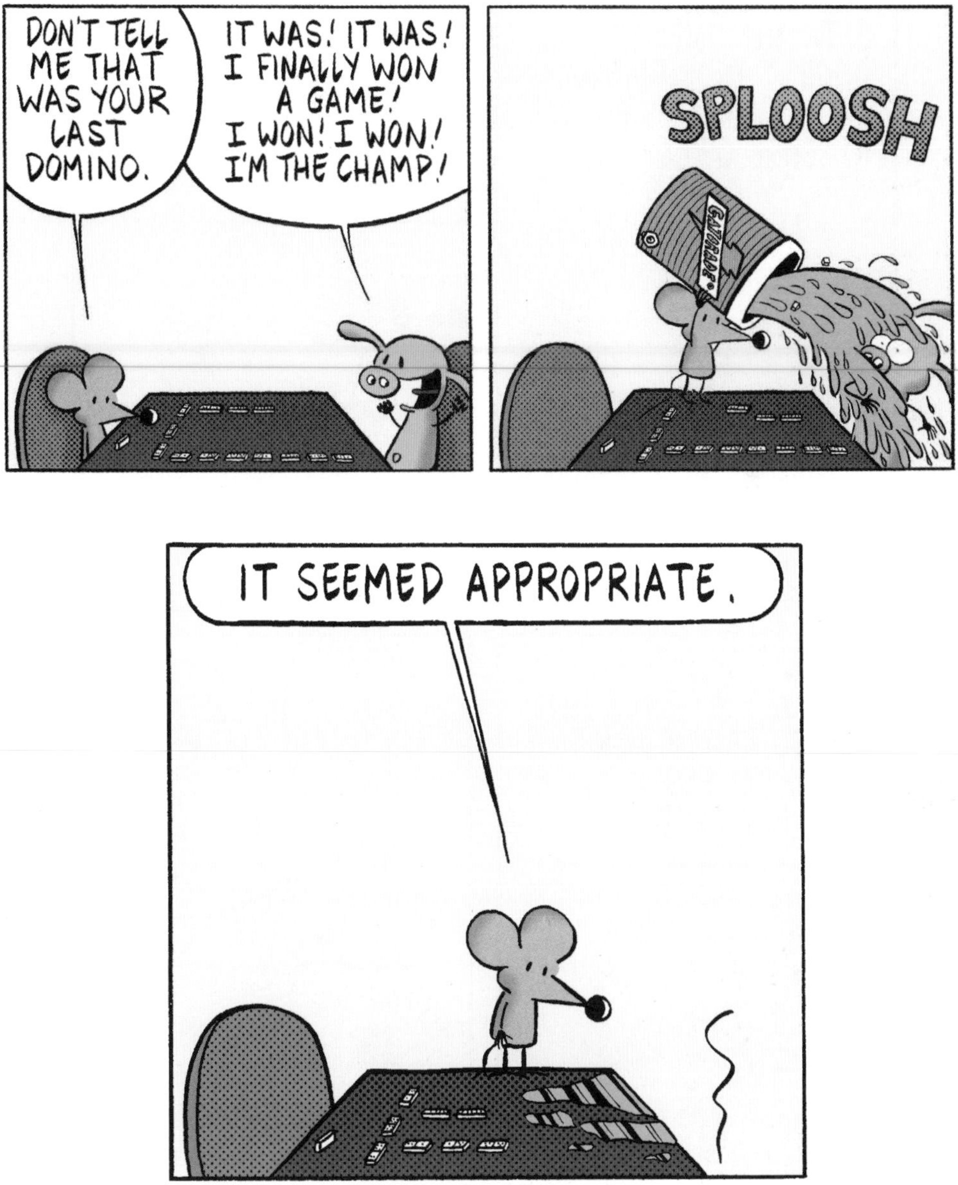
DON'T TELL ME THAT WAS YOUR LAST DOMINO.
IT WAS! IT WAS! I FINALLY WON A GAME! I WON! I WON! I'M THE CHAMP!
SPLOOSH
GATORADE®
IT SEEMED APPROPRIATE.

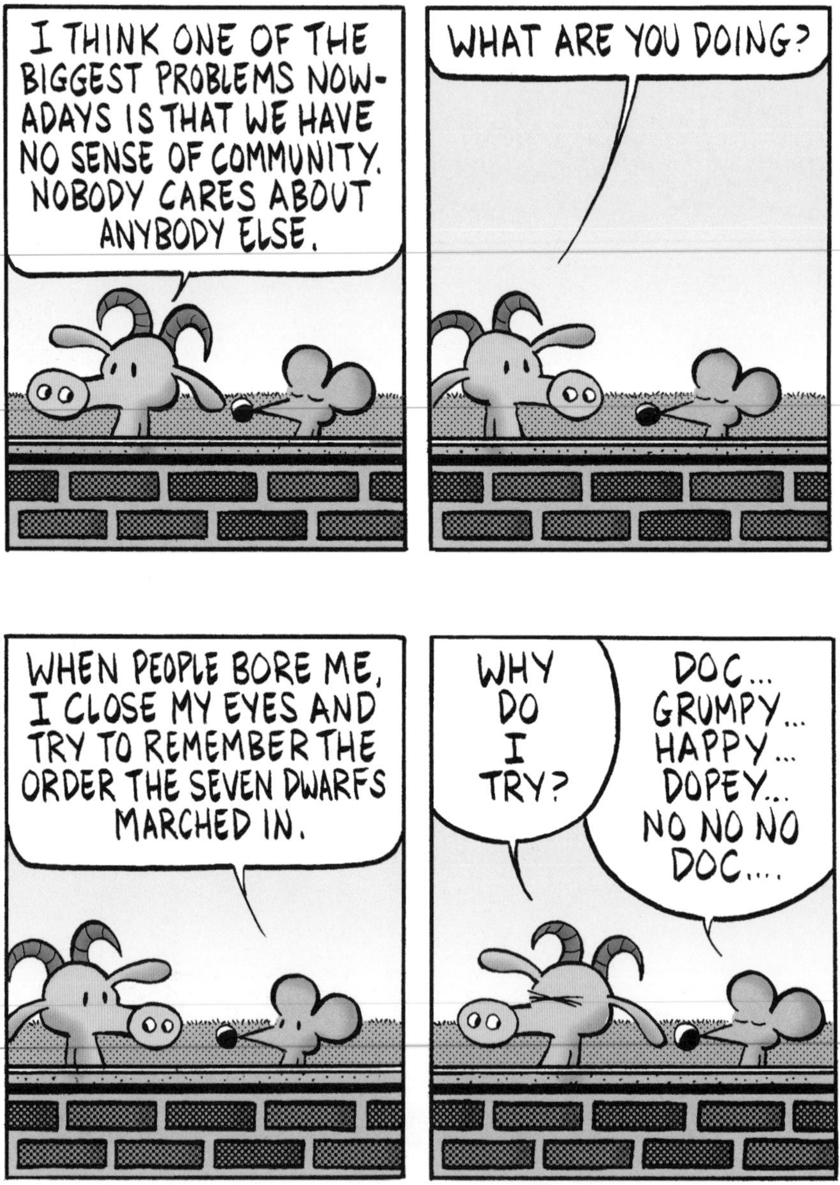
I THINK ONE OF THE BIGGEST PROBLEMS NOWADAYS IS THAT WE HAVE NO SENSE OF COMMUNITY. NOBODY CARES ABOUT ANYBODY ELSE.
WHAT ARE YOU DOING?
WHEN PEOPLE BORE ME, I CLOSE MY EYES AND TRY TO REMEMBER THE ORDER THE SEVEN DWARFS MARCHED IN.
WHY DO I TRY?
DOC... GRUMPY... HAPPY... DOPEY... NO NO NO DOC....

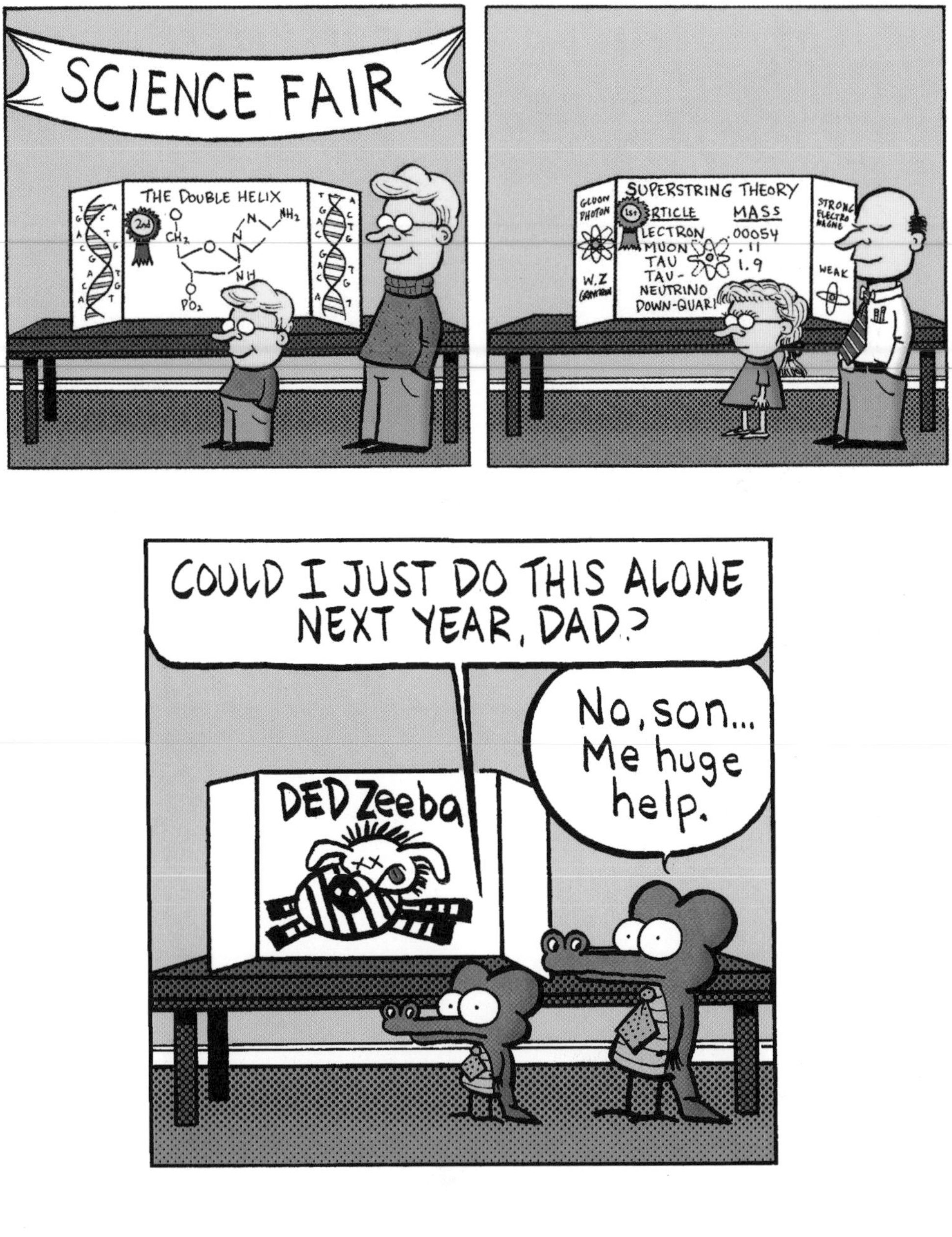
SCIENCE FAIR
THE DOUBLE HELIX
2nd
SUPERSTRING THEORY
1st
MASS
GLUON
PHOTON
WEAK
COULD I JUST DO THIS ALONE NEXT YEAR, DAD?
No, son... Me huge help.
DED Zeeba

Oh wooOomuuunn.. Me get you biiiiiiiirtday present!
WHAT IS IT, LARRY?
Ees a Zeeb-O'-Matic...It chop, slice and dice ded zeeba..HAHA.. Now we have zeeba milkshake, zeeba smoodie... Even zeeba mahgareeta!
Just tink, woomun! Now we have zeeba coming out ears!!

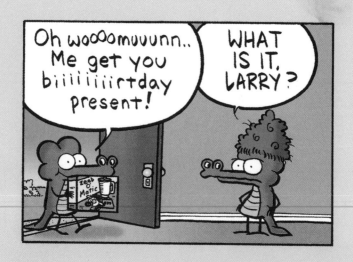

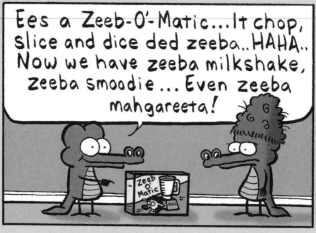

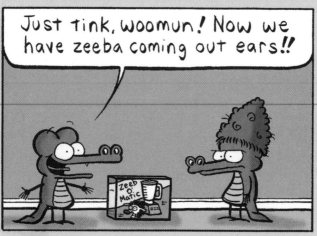

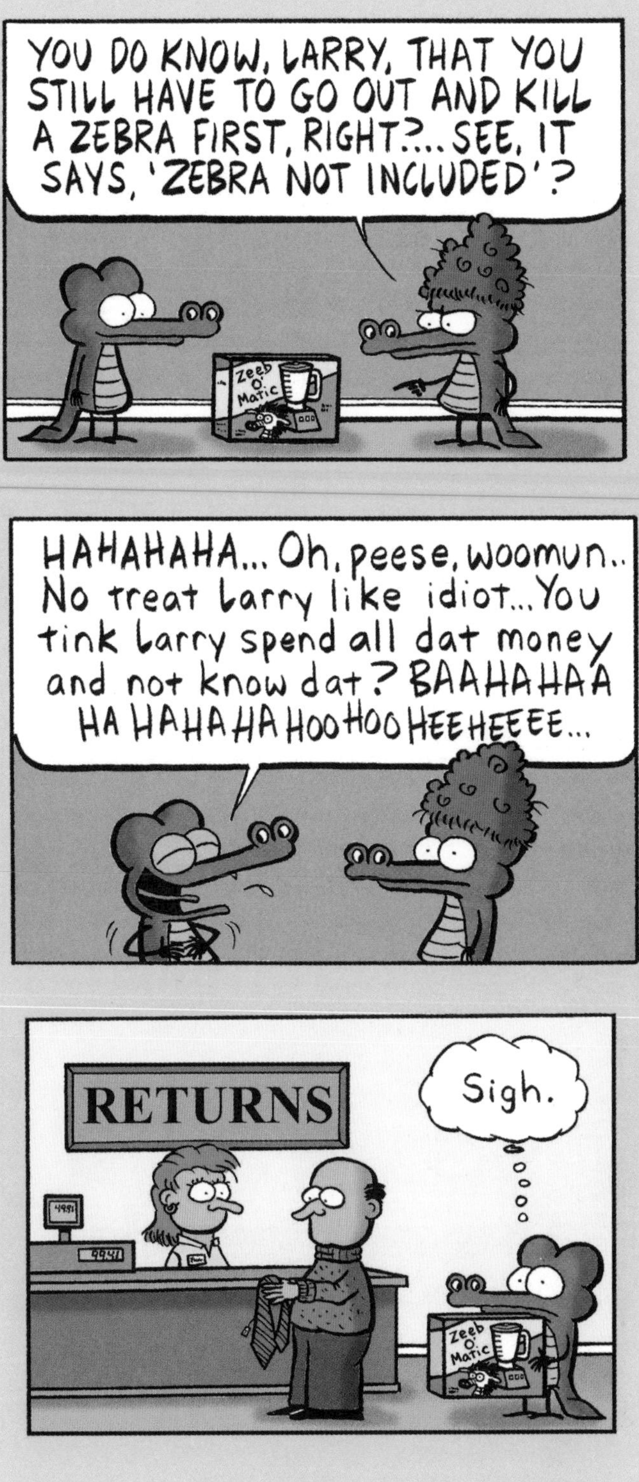
YOU DO KNOW, LARRY, THAT YOU STILL HAVE TO GO OUT AND KILL A ZEBRA FIRST, RIGHT?... SEE, IT SAYS, 'ZEBRA NOT INCLUDED'?
HAHAHAHA... Oh, peese, woomun.. No treat Larry like idiot... You tink Larry spend all dat money and not know dat? BAAHAHAA HA HAHAHA HOOHOO HEEHEEEE...
RETURNS
Sigh.

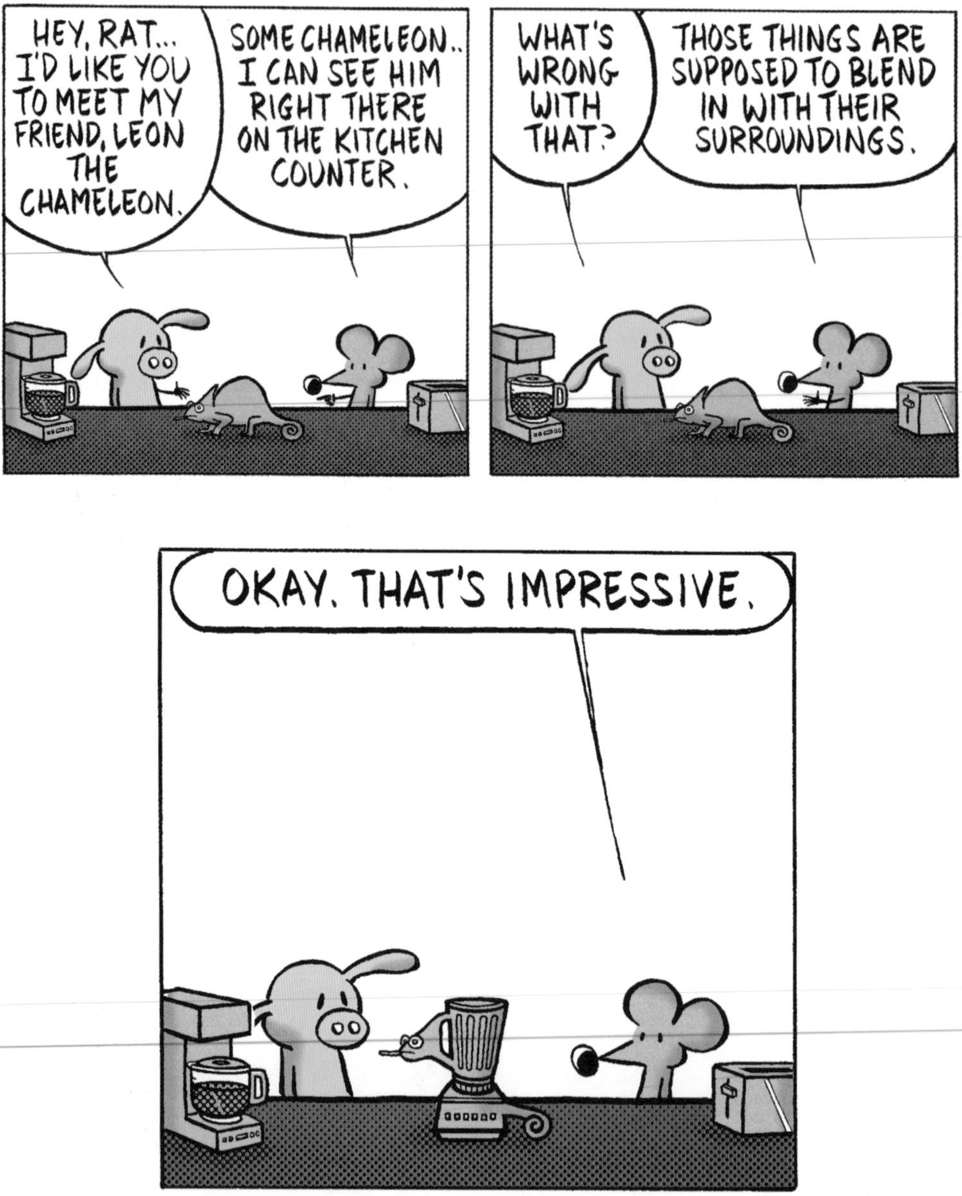
HEY, RAT... I'D LIKE YOU TO MEET MY FRIEND, LEON THE CHAMELEON.
SOME CHAMELEON.. I CAN SEE HIM RIGHT THERE ON THE KITCHEN COUNTER.
WHAT'S WRONG WITH THAT?
THOSE THINGS ARE SUPPOSED TO BLEND IN WITH THEIR SURROUNDINGS.
OKAY. THAT'S IMPRESSIVE.

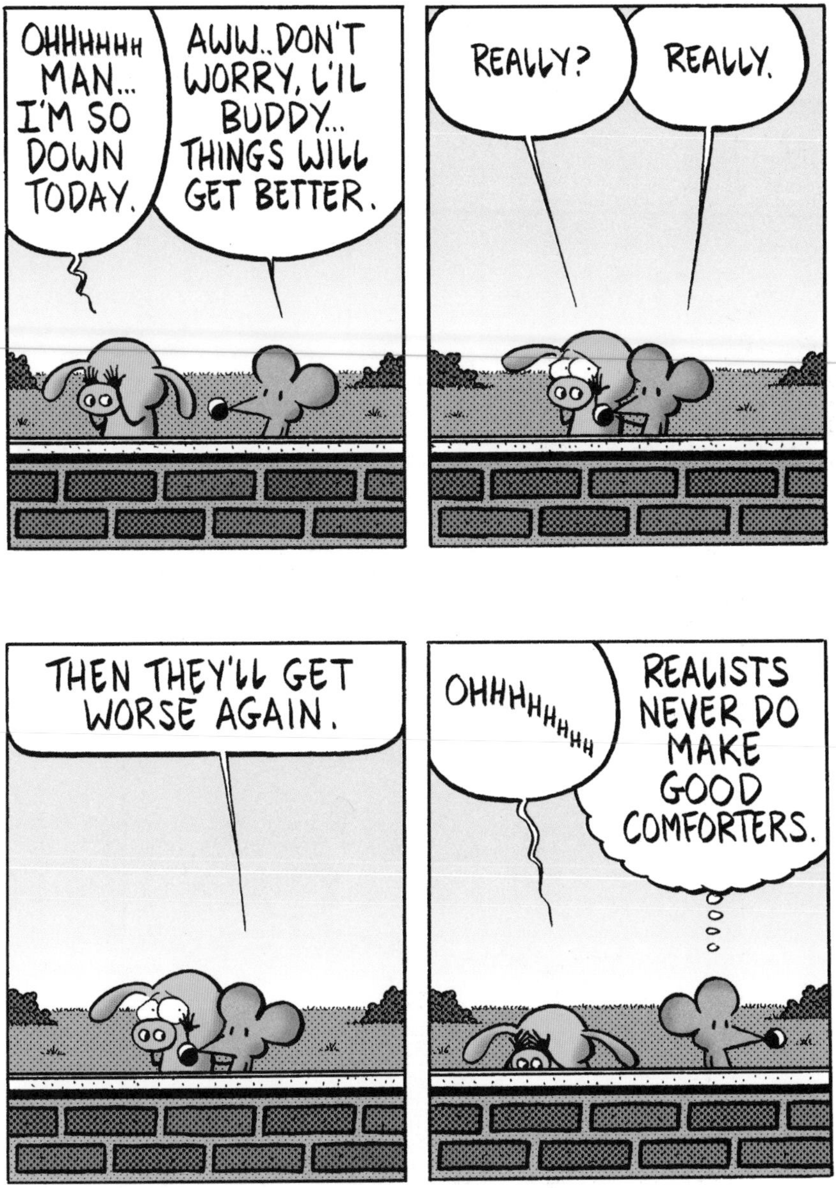
OHHHHHH MAN... I'M SO DOWN TODAY.
AWW..DON'T WORRY, L'IL BUDDY... THINGS WILL GET BETTER.
REALLY?
REALLY.
THEN THEY'LL GET WORSE AGAIN.
OHHHHHHHHH
REALISTS NEVER DO MAKE GOOD COMFORTERS.

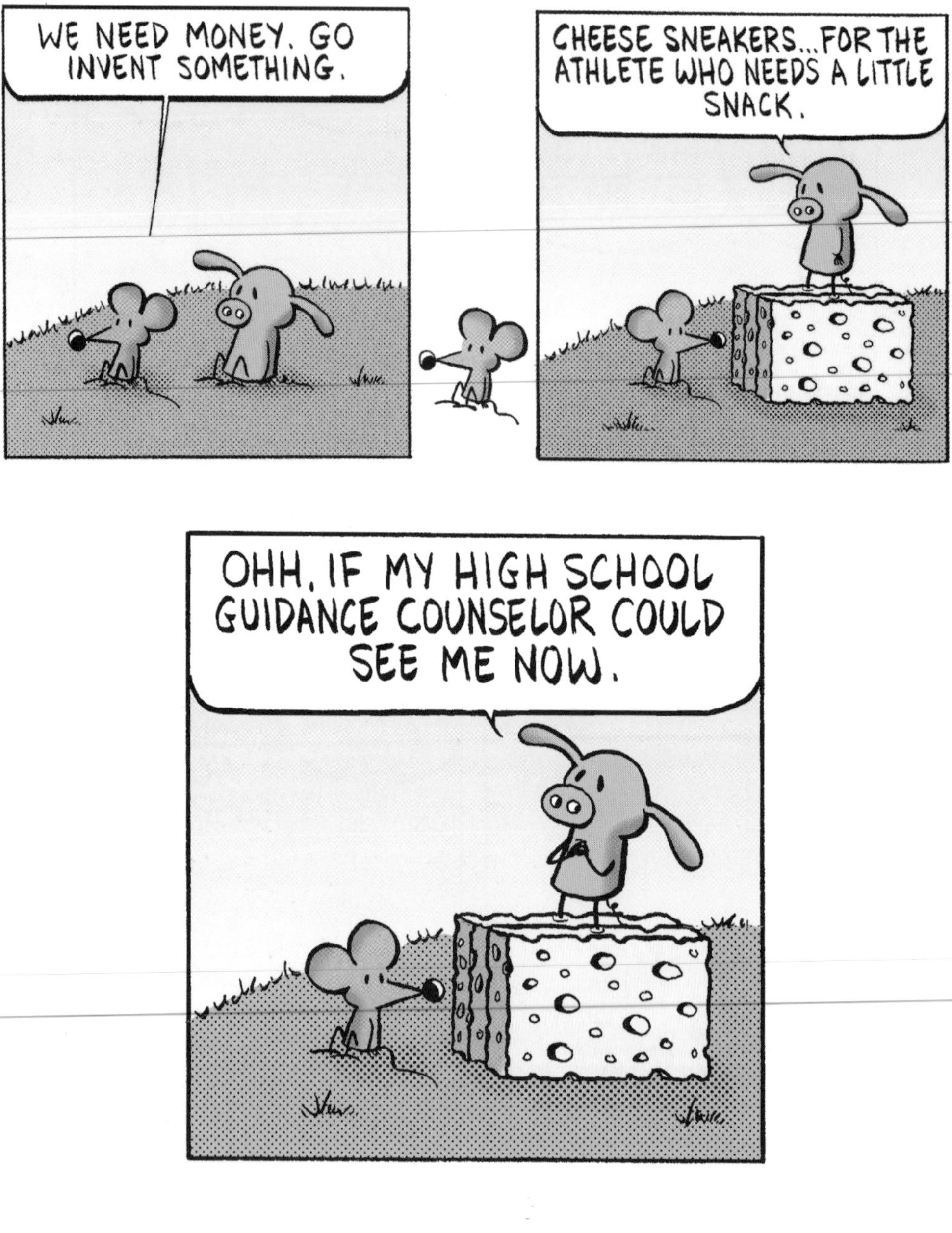
WE NEED MONEY. GO INVENT SOMETHING.
CHEESE SNEAKERS...FOR THE ATHLETE WHO NEEDS A LITTLE SNACK.
OHH, IF MY HIGH SCHOOL GUIDANCE COUNSELOR COULD SEE ME NOW.

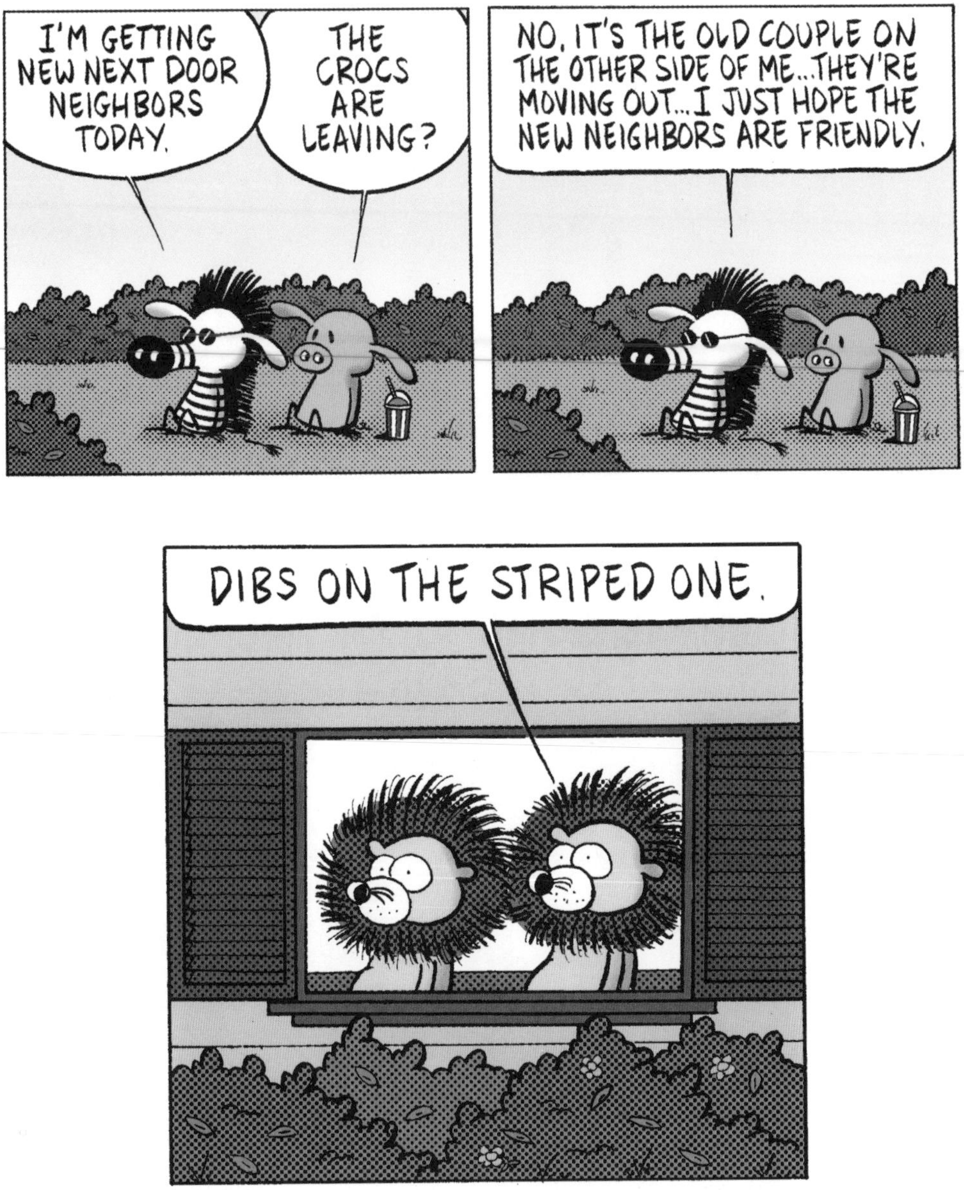
I'M GETTING NEW NEXT DOOR NEIGHBORS TODAY.
THE CROCS ARE LEAVING?
NO, IT'S THE OLD COUPLE ON THE OTHER SIDE OF ME...THEY'RE MOVING OUT...I JUST HOPE THE NEW NEIGHBORS ARE FRIENDLY.
DIBS ON THE STRIPED ONE.

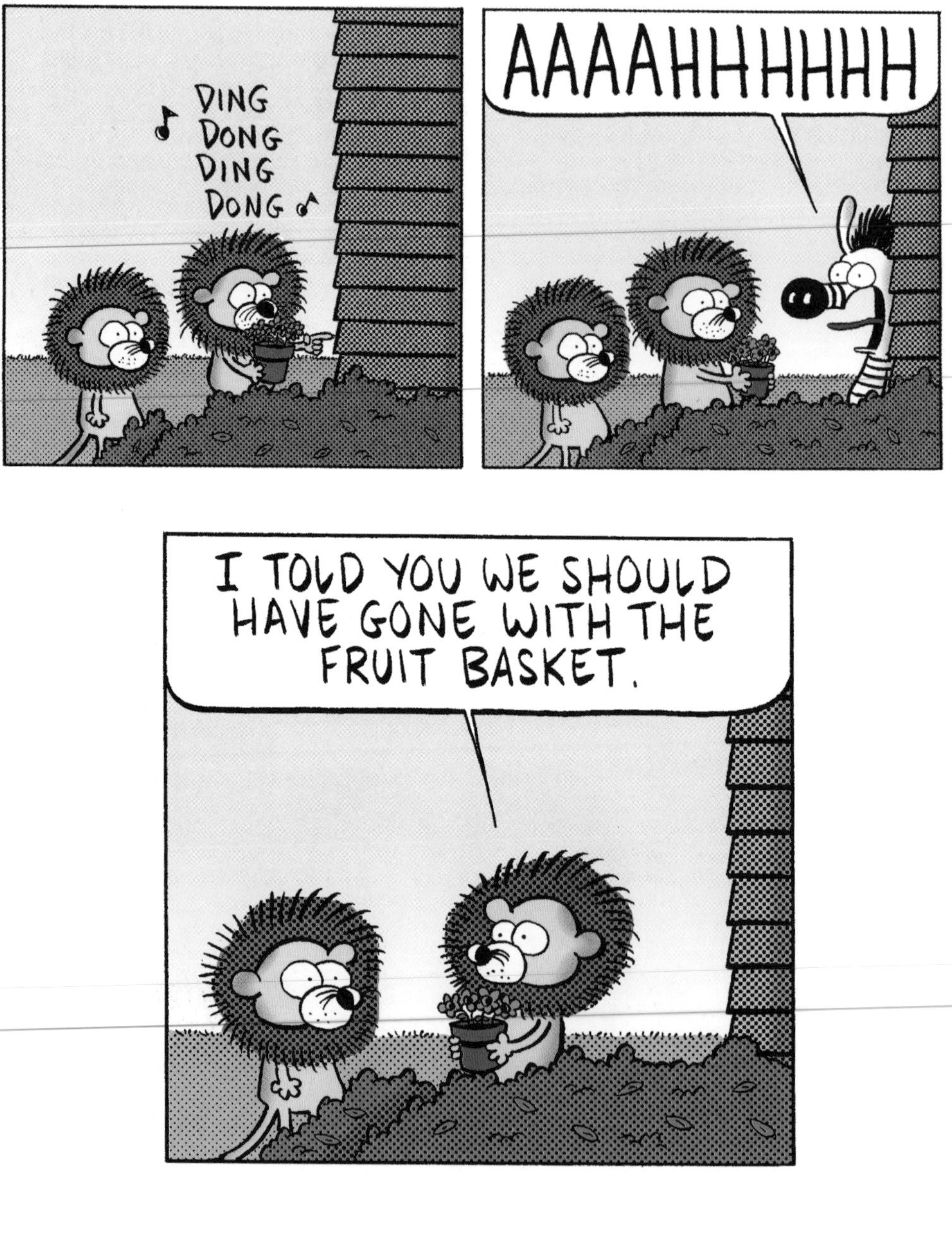
DING
DONG
DING
DONG
AAAAHHHHHH
I TOLD YOU WE SHOULD HAVE GONE WITH THE FRUIT BASKET.

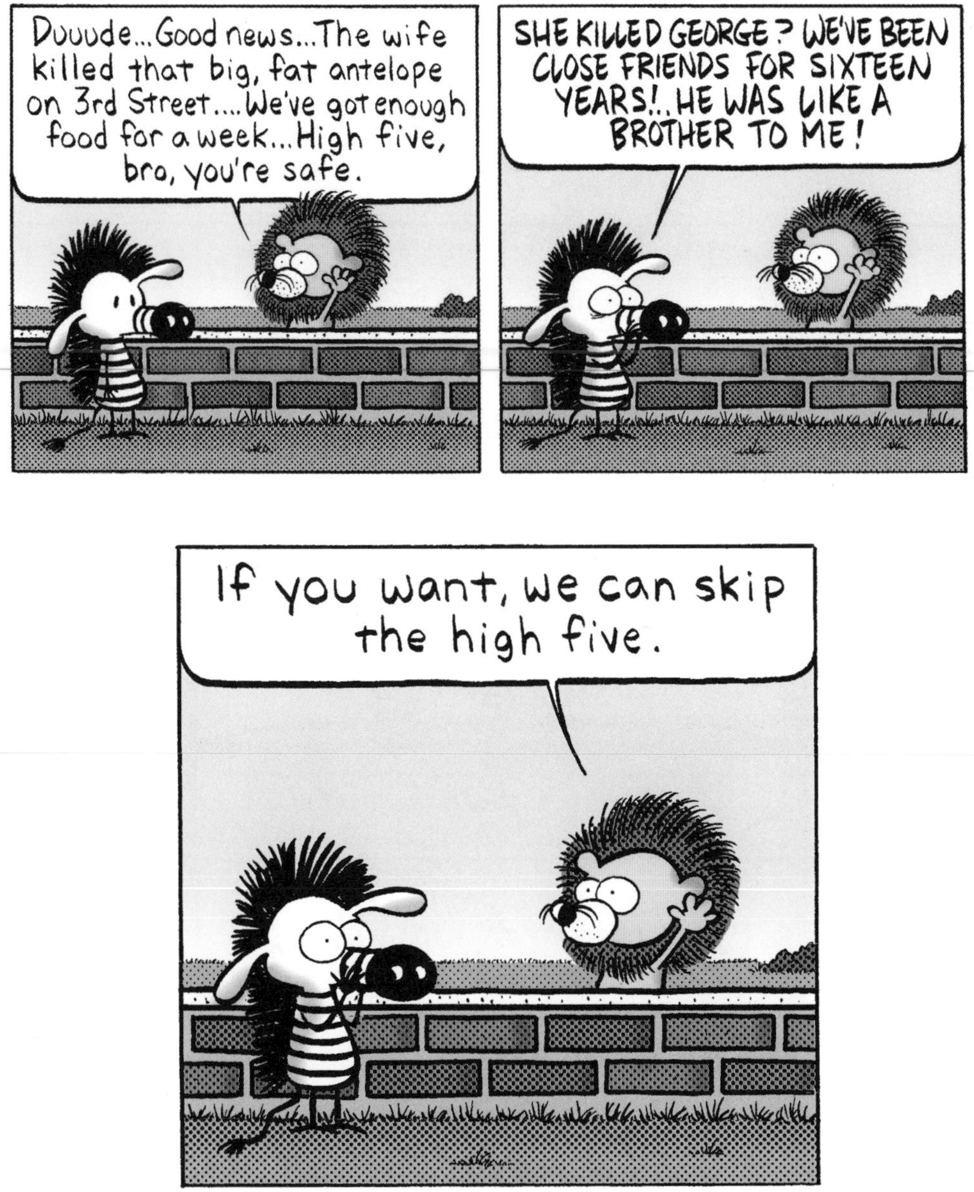
Duuude...Good news...The wife killed that big, fat antelope on 3rd Street....We've got enough food for a week...High five, bro, you're safe.
SHE KILLED GEORGE? WE'VE BEEN CLOSE FRIENDS FOR SIXTEEN YEARS!..HE WAS LIKE A BROTHER TO ME!
If you want, we can skip the high five.

Dear Zebra,
We are your new neighbors,
Max and Zach.
Do not fear us.
We will not hunt you.
We will not kill you.
Why is that, you ask?

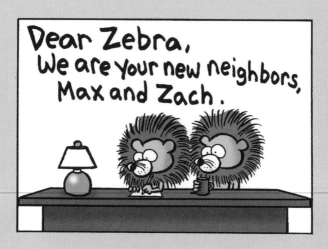

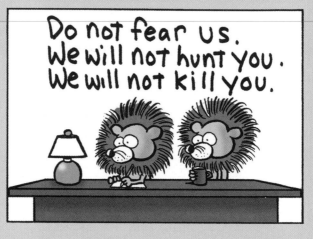

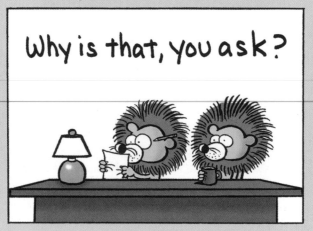

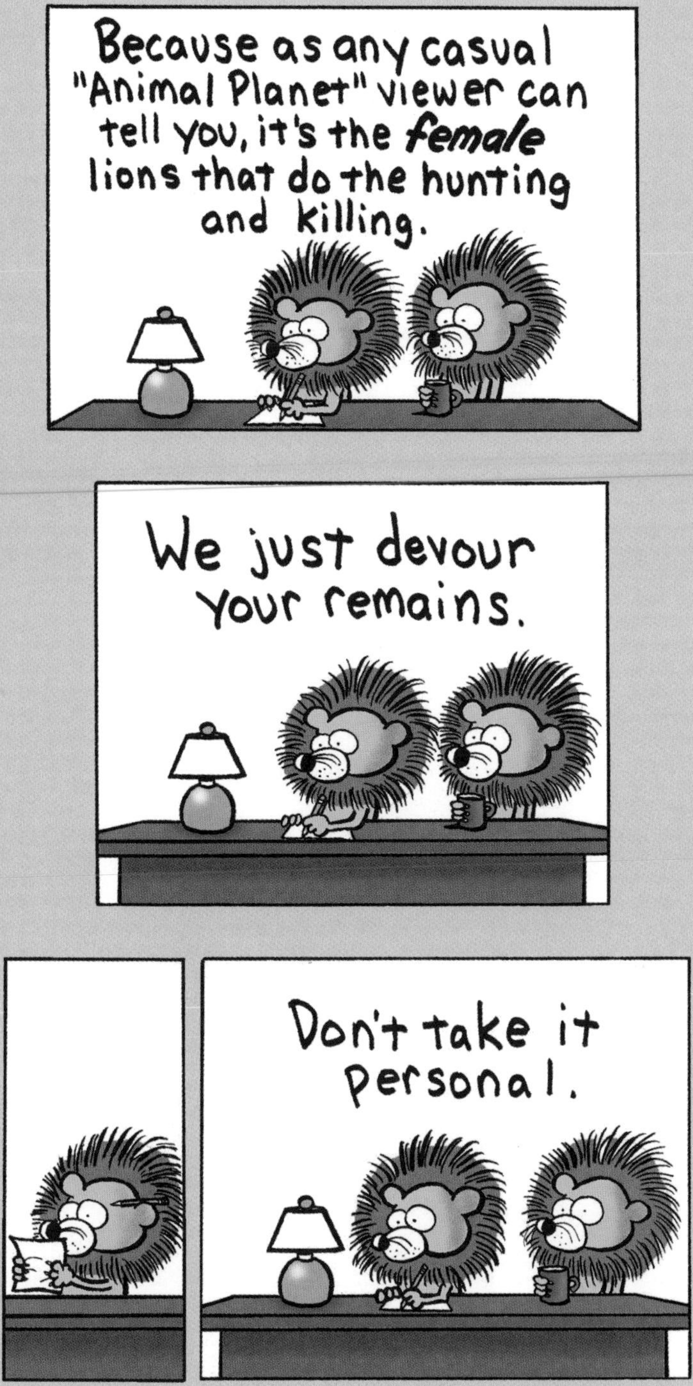
Because as any casual "Animal Planet" viewer can tell you, it's the *female* lions that do the hunting and killing.
We just devour your remains.
Don't take it personal.

WHERE WERE YOU THIS MORNING?

I WAS TALKING TO ANDY, THAT LITTLE DOG ACROSS THE STREET... BOY, DOES HE HAVE BIG PLANS... HE'S GONNA BACKPACK THROUGH ITALY, SAFARI IN KENYA AND SIP TEA IN SHANGHAI.

DUDE...IT'S ONE THING TO HAVE DREAMS... IT'S ANOTHER TO BE DELUSIONAL.

WHAT'S SO DELUSIONAL ABOUT WANTING TO SEE THE WORLD?

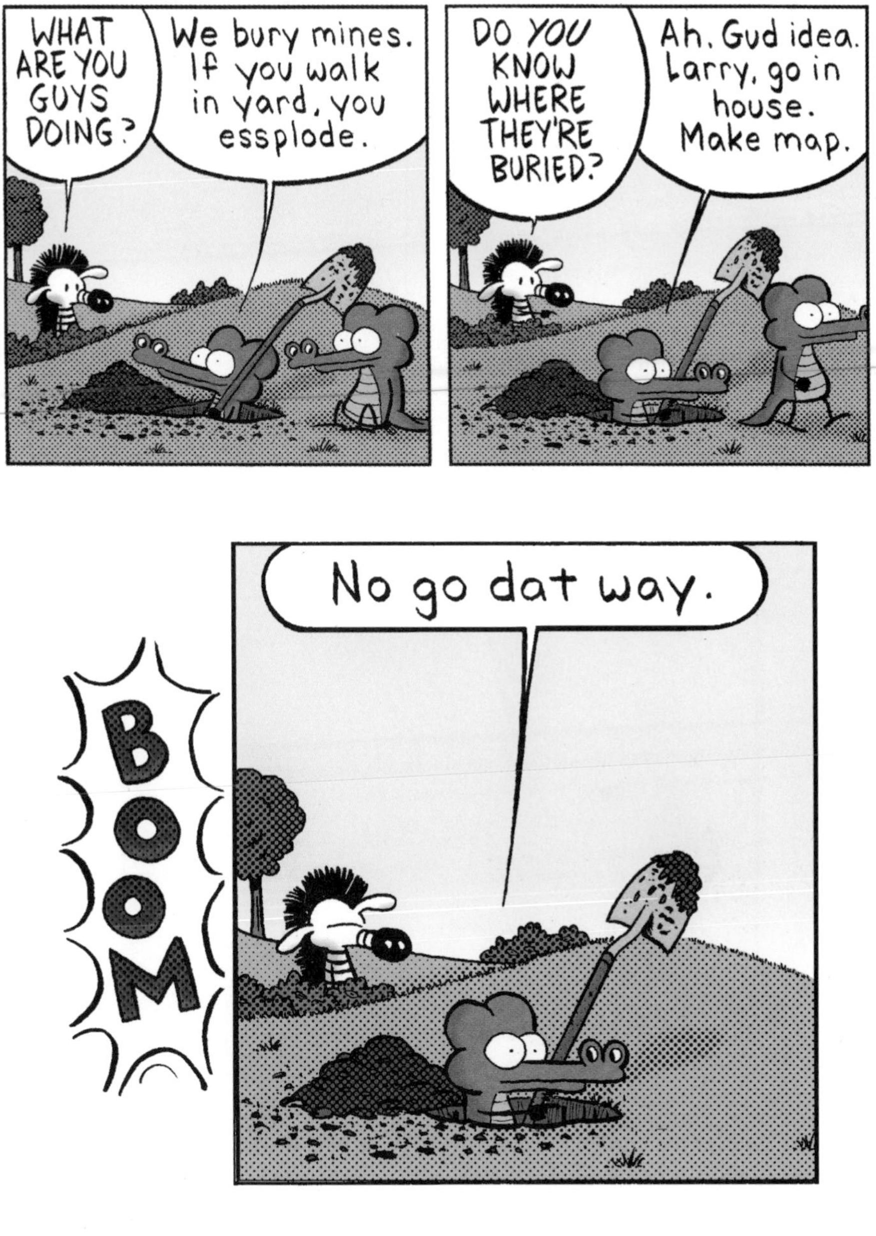
WHAT ARE YOU GUYS DOING?
We bury mines. If you walk in yard, you essplode.
DO *YOU* KNOW WHERE THEY'RE BURIED?
Ah. Gud idea. Larry, go in house. Make map.
BOOM
No go dat way.

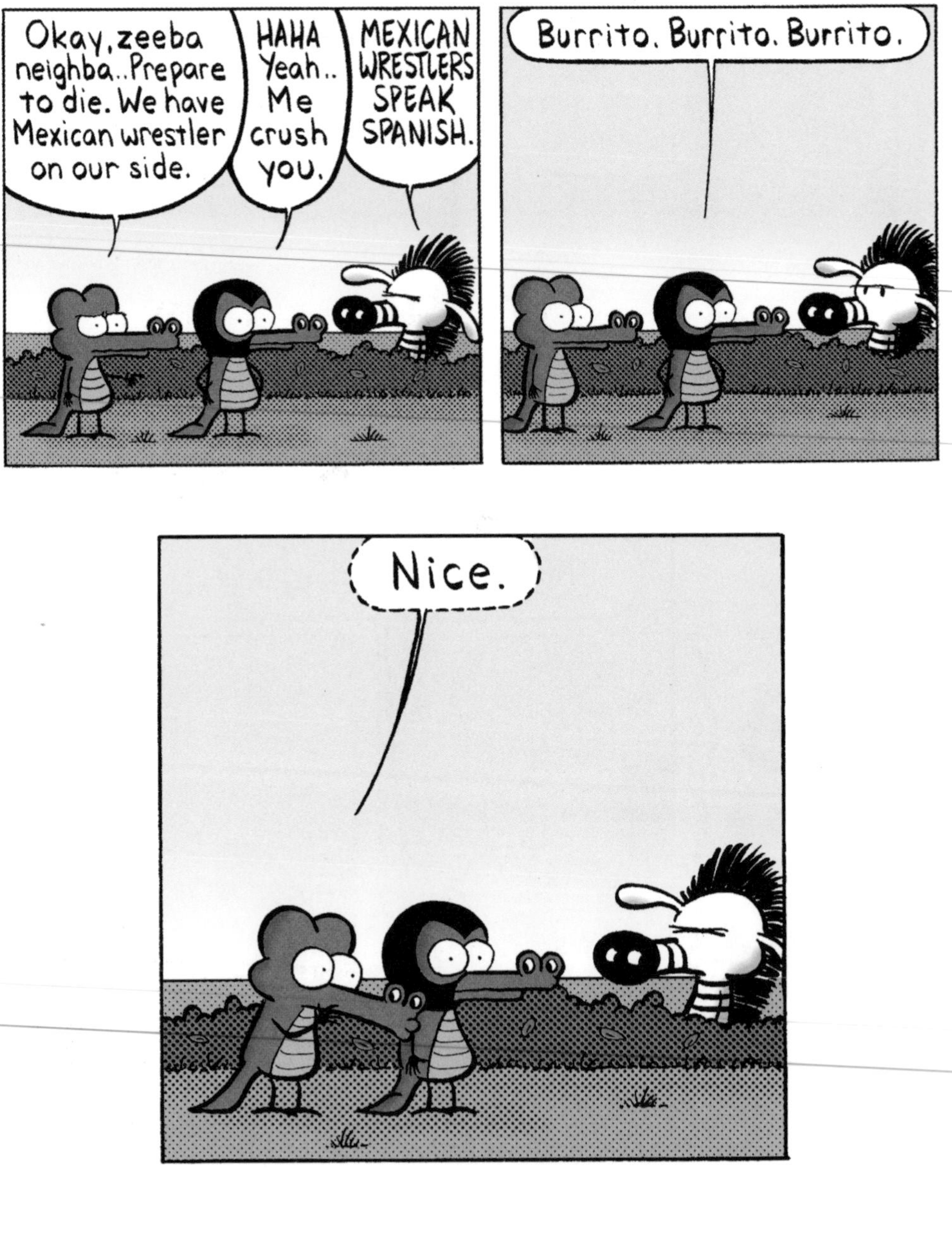
Okay, zeeba neighba.. Prepare to die. We have Mexican wrestler on our side.
HAHA Yeah.. Me crush you.
MEXICAN WRESTLERS SPEAK SPANISH.
Burrito. Burrito. Burrito.
Nice.

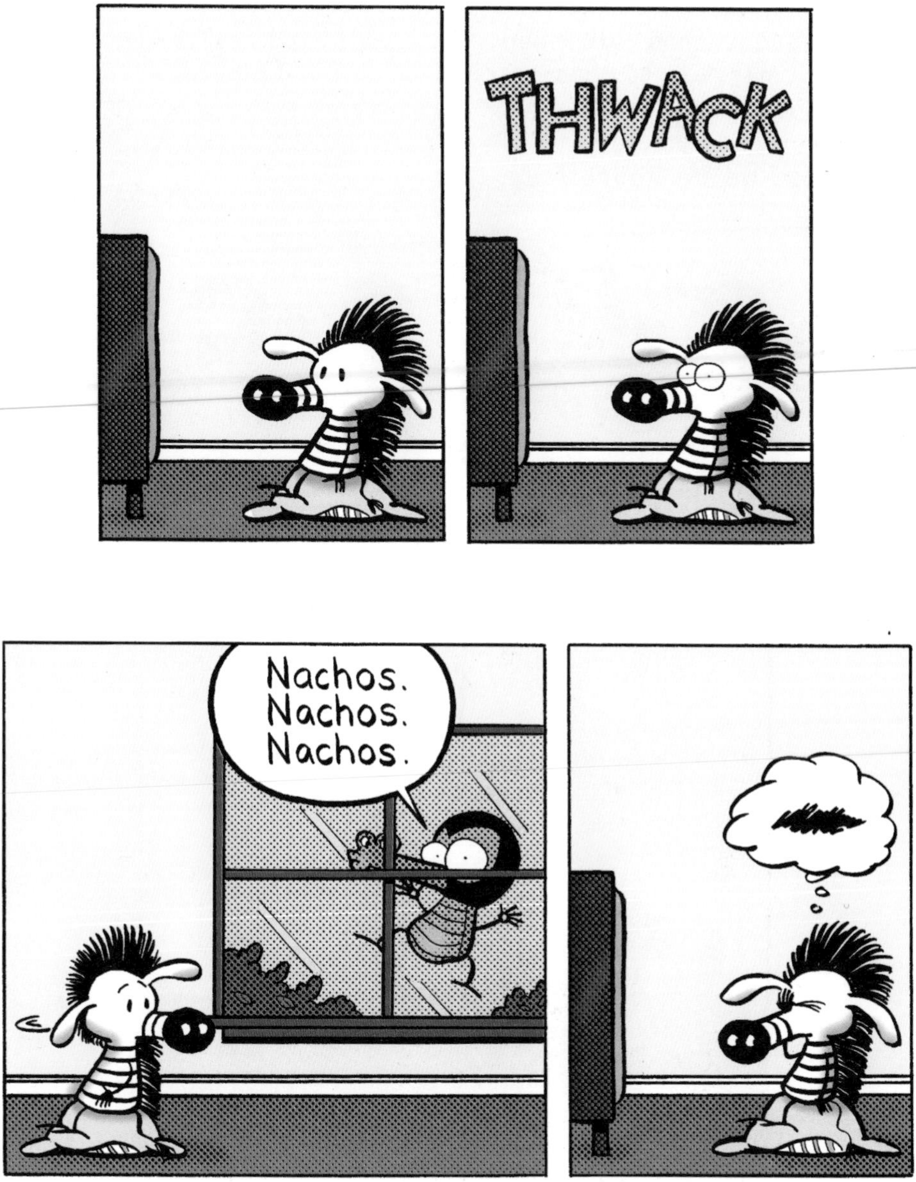
THWACK
Nachos.
Nachos.
Nachos.

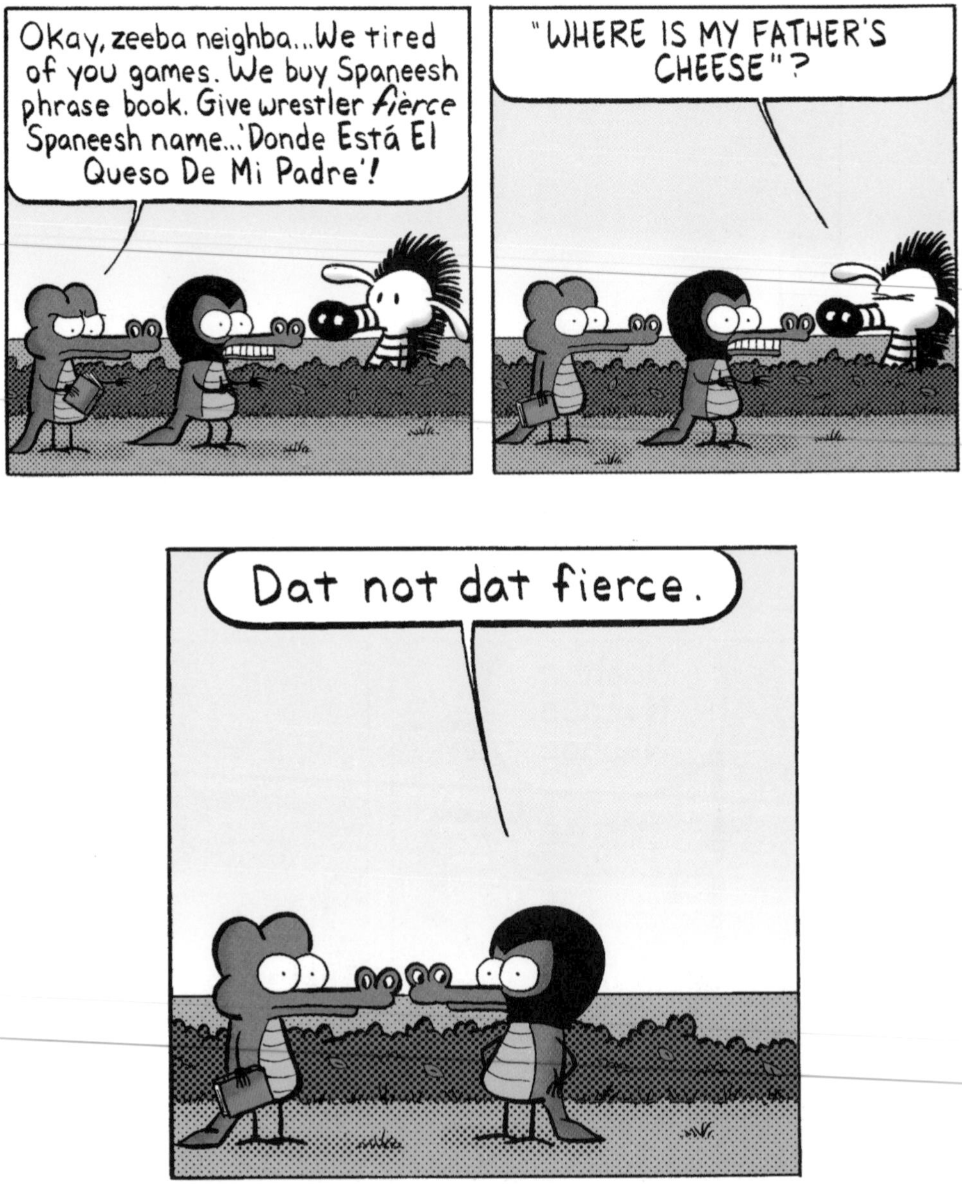
Okay, zeeba neighba...We tired of you games. We buy Spaneesh phrase book. Give wrestler fièrce Spaneesh name...'Donde Está El Queso De Mi Padre'!
"WHERE IS MY FATHER'S CHEESE"?
Dat not dat fierce.

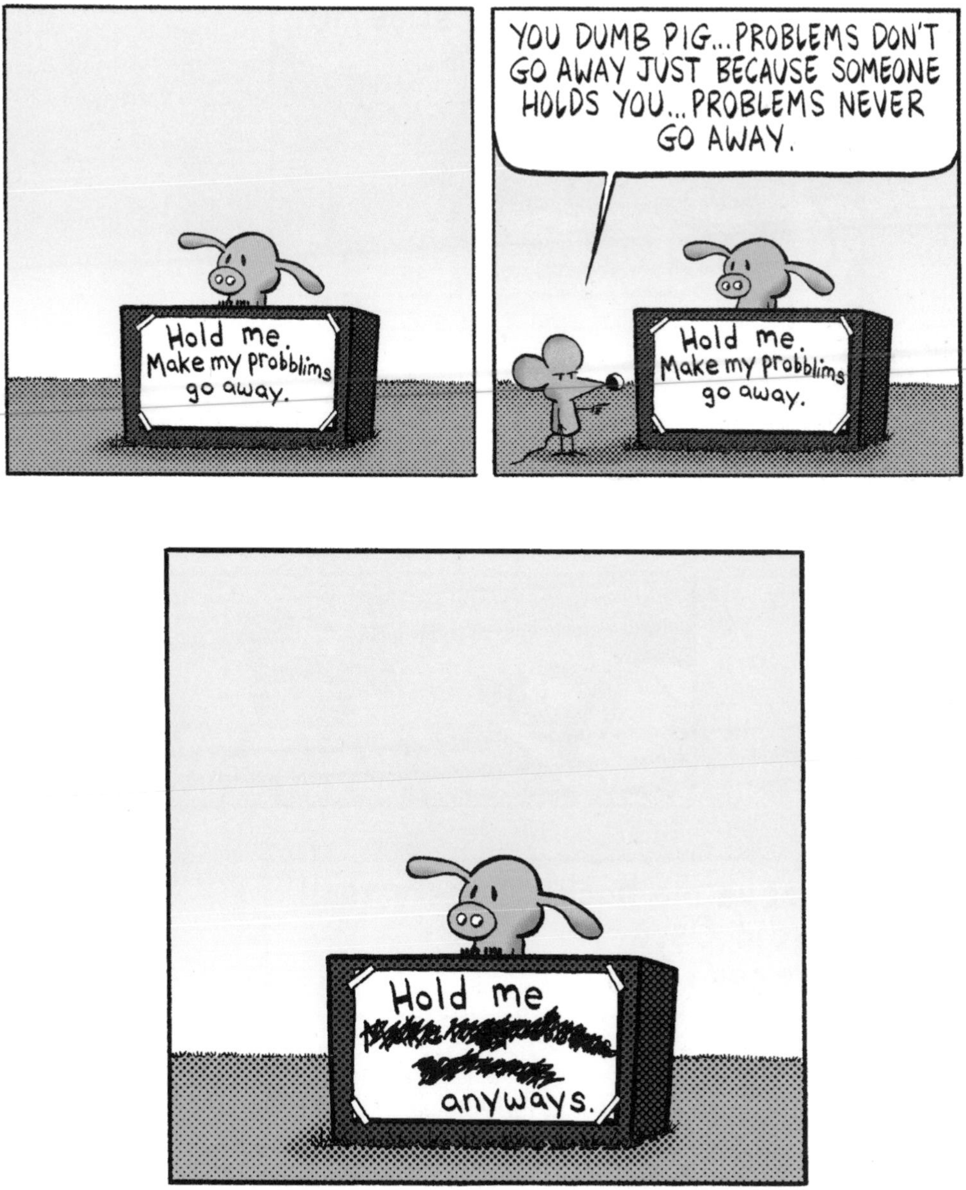
Hold me.
Make my probblims go away.
YOU DUMB PIG...PROBLEMS DON'T GO AWAY JUST BECAUSE SOMEONE HOLDS YOU...PROBLEMS NEVER GO AWAY.
Hold me.
Make my probblims go away.
Hold me
anyways.

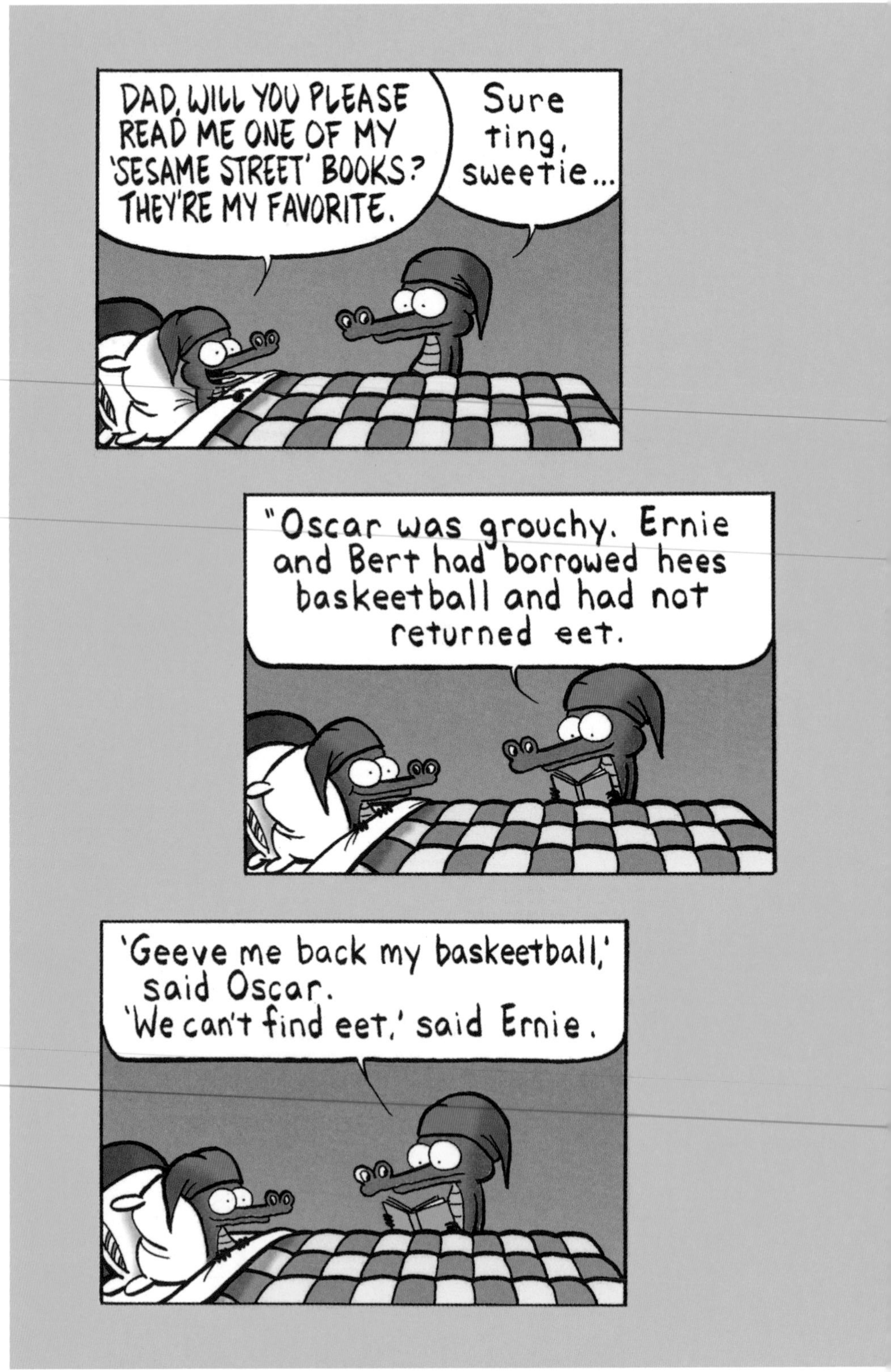
DAD, WILL YOU PLEASE READ ME ONE OF MY 'SESAME STREET' BOOKS? THEY'RE MY FAVORITE.
Sure ting, sweetie...
"Oscar was grouchy. Ernie and Bert had borrowed hees baskeetball and had not returned eet.
'Geeve me back my baskeetball,' said Oscar.
'We can't find eet,' said Ernie.

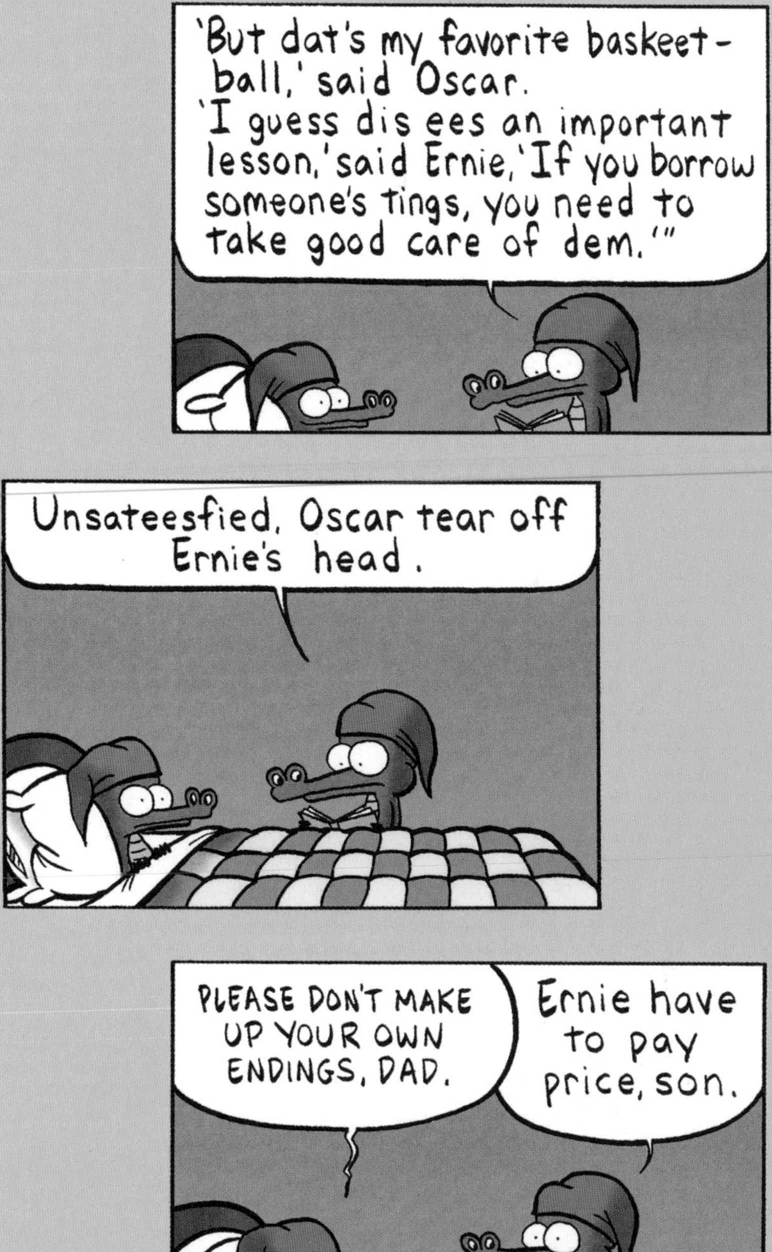
'But dat's my favorite baskeet-ball,' said Oscar. 'I guess dis ees an important lesson,' said Ernie, 'If you borrow someone's tings, you need to take good care of dem.'"
Unsateesfied, Oscar tear off Ernie's head.
PLEASE DON'T MAKE UP YOUR OWN ENDINGS, DAD.
Ernie have to pay price, son.

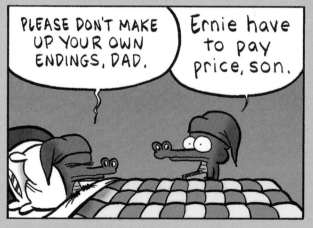

WHOA!...WHERE ARE YOU GOING, RAT?

I'M RUNNING AWAY FROM LIFE AND ALL MY PROBLEMS.

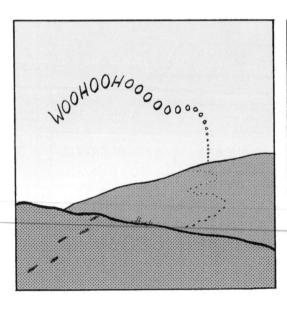

WOOHOOHOOOOOOOoooo

I DIDN'T KNOW IT WAS THAT EASY.

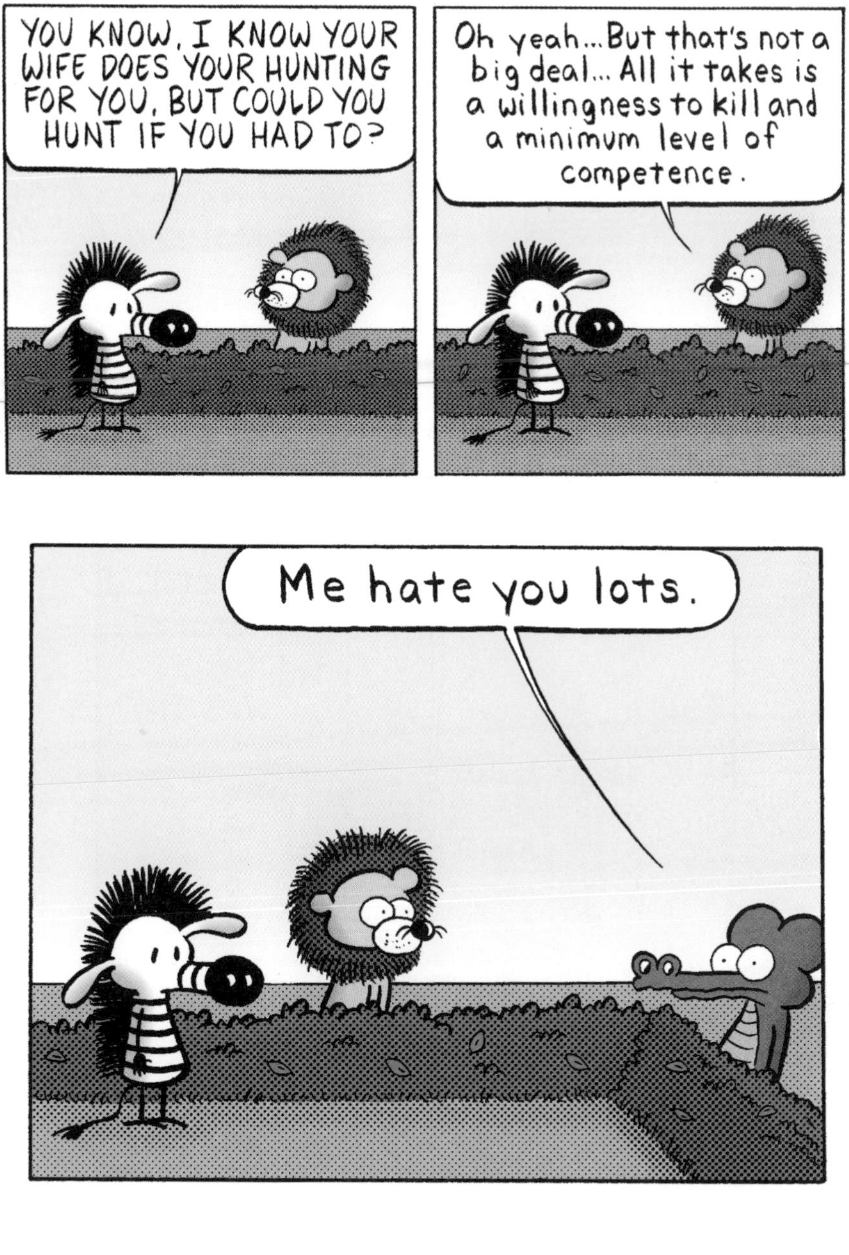
YOU KNOW, I KNOW YOUR WIFE DOES YOUR HUNTING FOR YOU, BUT COULD YOU HUNT IF YOU HAD TO?
Oh yeah... But that's not a big deal... All it takes is a willingness to kill and a minimum level of competence.
Me hate you lots.

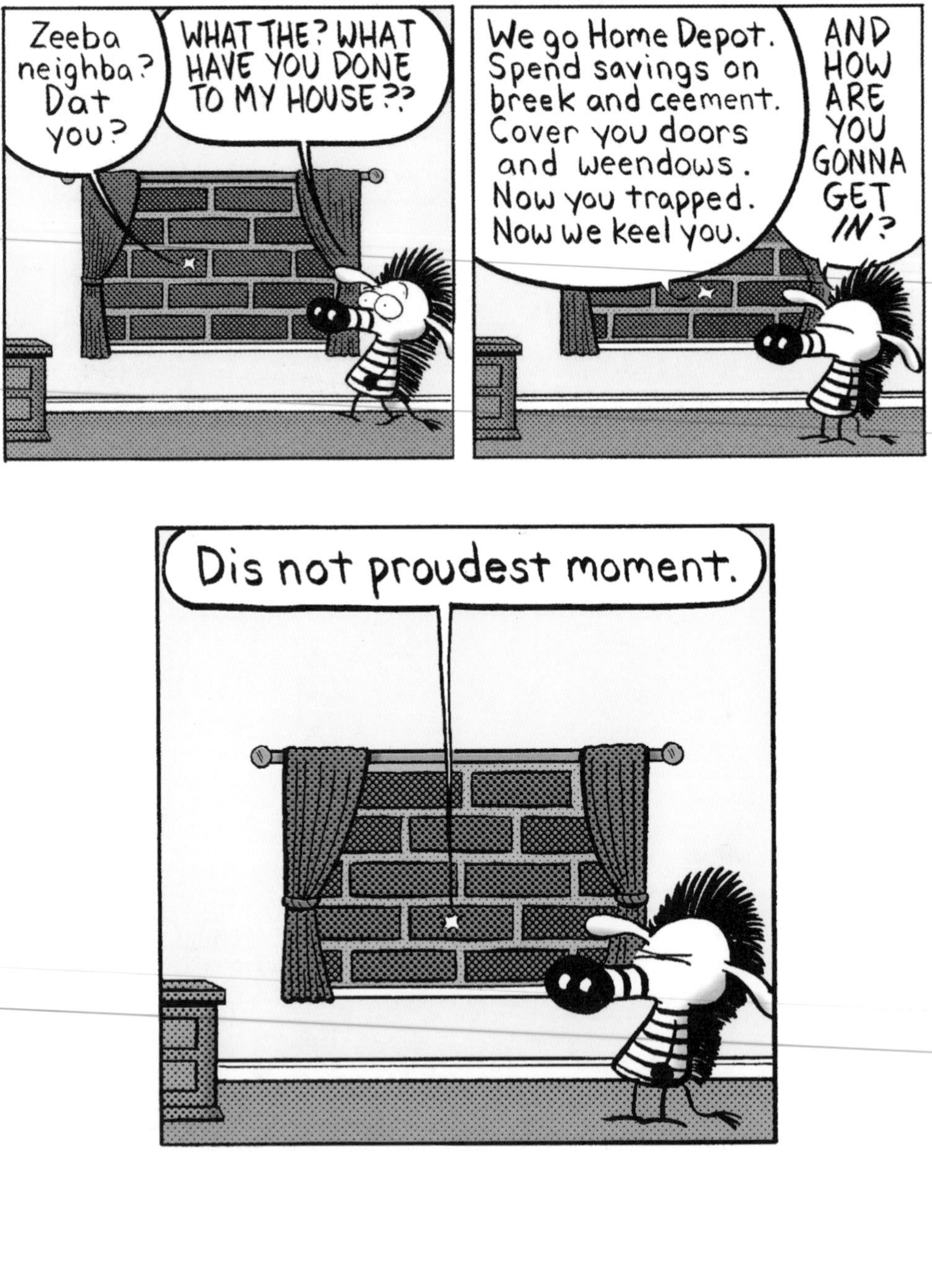
Zeeba neighba? Dat you?
WHAT THE? WHAT HAVE YOU DONE TO MY HOUSE??
We go Home Depot. Spend savings on breek and ceement. Cover you doors and weendows. Now you trapped. Now we keel you.
AND HOW ARE YOU GONNA GET IN?
Dis not proudest moment.

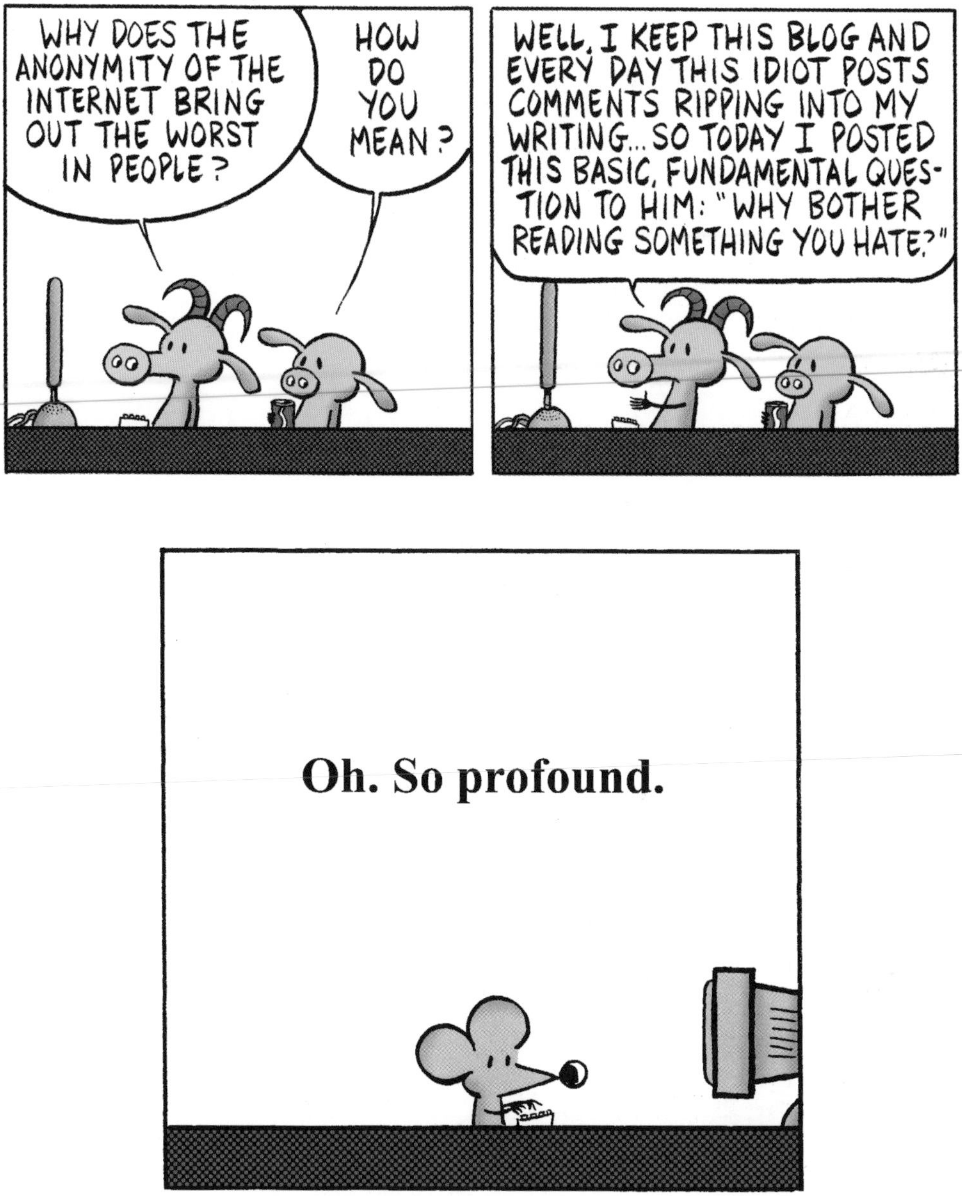
WHY DOES THE ANONYMITY OF THE INTERNET BRING OUT THE WORST IN PEOPLE?
HOW DO YOU MEAN?
WELL, I KEEP THIS BLOG AND EVERY DAY THIS IDIOT POSTS COMMENTS RIPPING INTO MY WRITING... SO TODAY I POSTED THIS BASIC, FUNDAMENTAL QUESTION TO HIM: "WHY BOTHER READING SOMETHING YOU HATE?"
Oh. So profound.

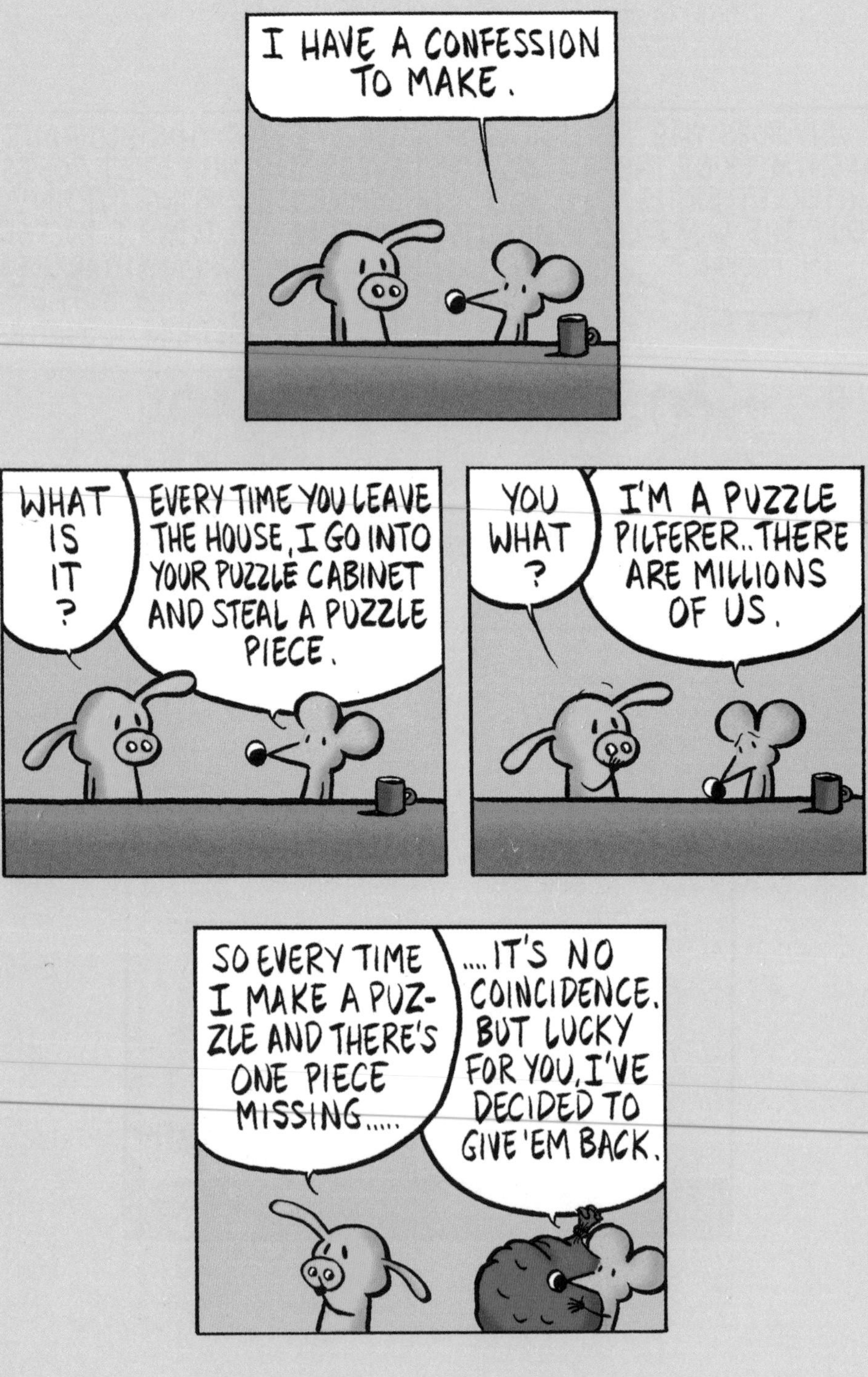
I HAVE A CONFESSION TO MAKE.
WHAT IS IT ?
EVERY TIME YOU LEAVE THE HOUSE, I GO INTO YOUR PUZZLE CABINET AND STEAL A PUZZLE PIECE.
YOU WHAT ?
I'M A PUZZLE PILFERER.. THERE ARE MILLIONS OF US.
SO EVERY TIME I MAKE A PUZZLE AND THERE'S ONE PIECE MISSING.....
....IT'S NO COINCIDENCE. BUT LUCKY FOR YOU, I'VE DECIDED TO GIVE 'EM BACK.

FOOOOSH....
.... STILL FRIENDS?
YOU BET... I'M JUST HAPPY YOU DECIDED TO GIVE 'EM BACK.
SNATCH
PEOPLE CAN CHANGE.

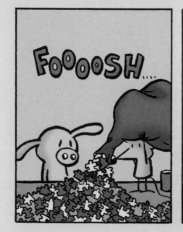

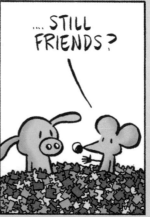

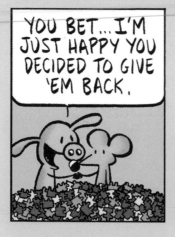

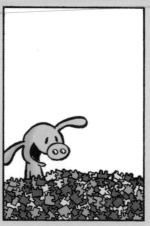

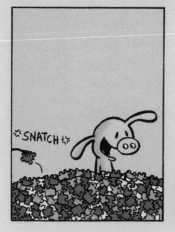

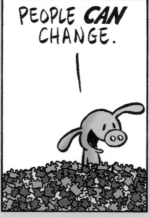

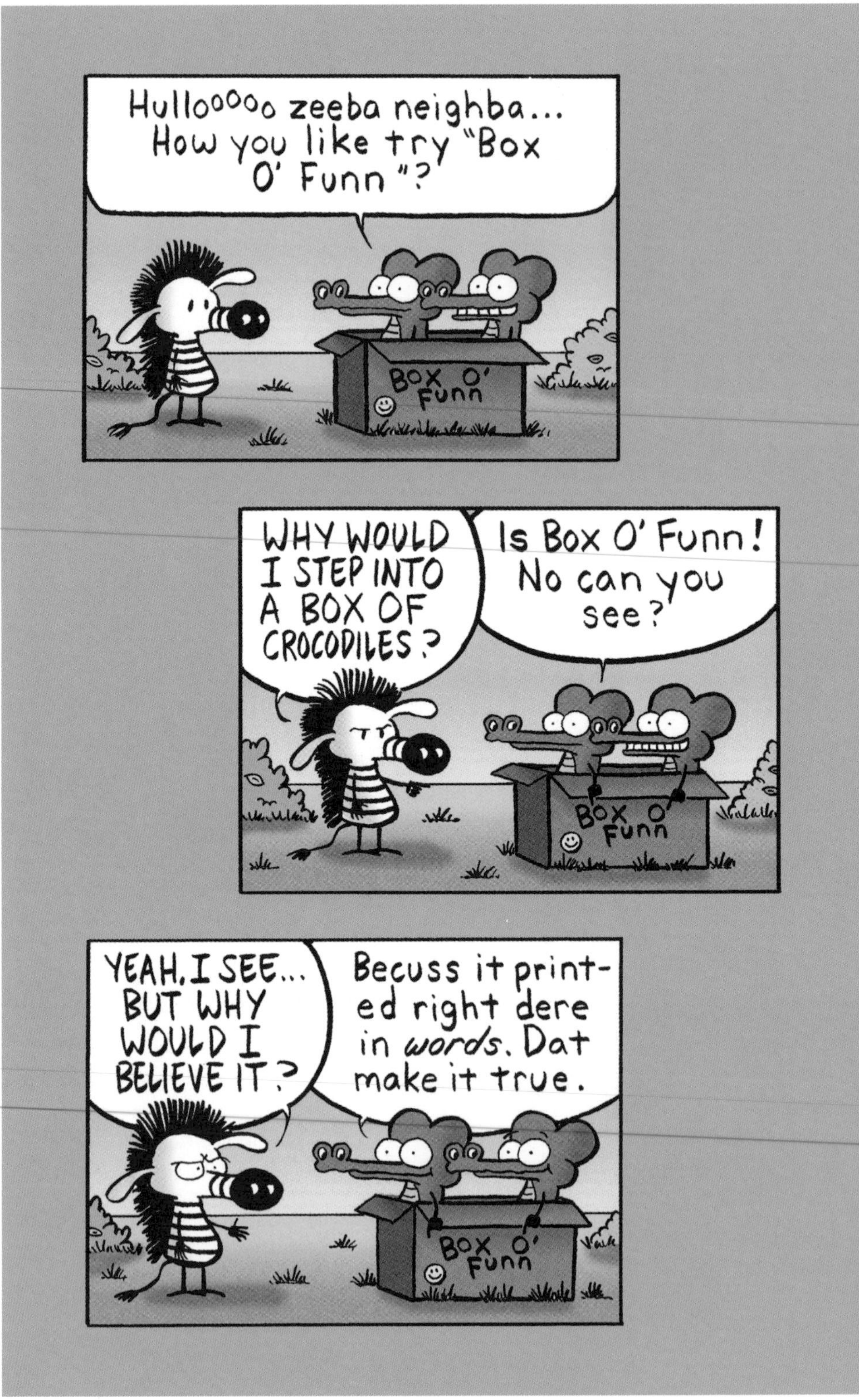
Hulloooooo zeeba neighba... How you like try "Box O' Funn"?
BOX O' FUNN
WHY WOULD I STEP INTO A BOX OF CROCODILES?
Is Box O' Funn! No can you see?
BOX O' FUNN
YEAH, I SEE... BUT WHY WOULD I BELIEVE IT?
Becuss it printed right dere in *words*. Dat make it true.
BOX O' FUNN

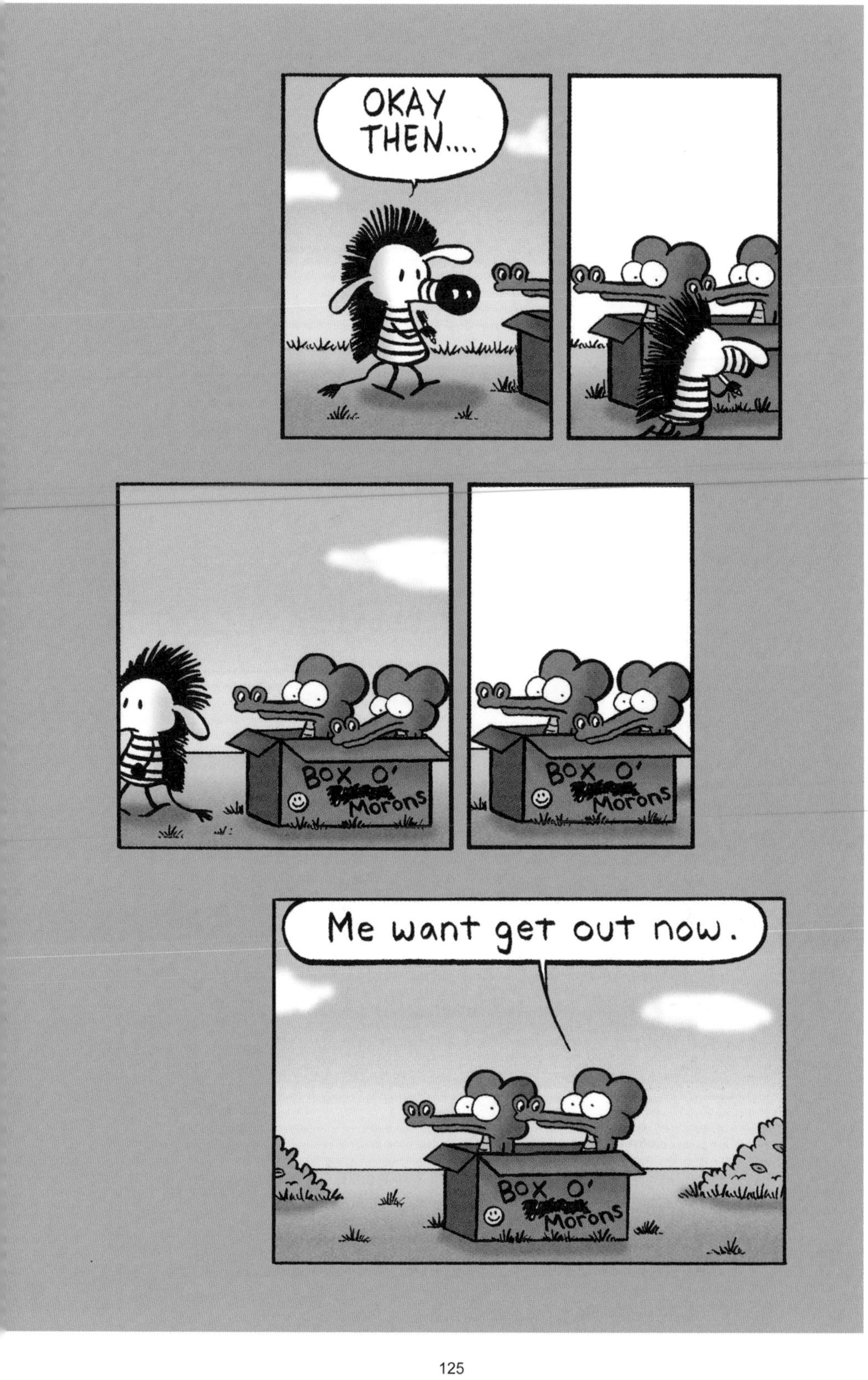
OKAY THEN....
BOX O' Morons
BOX O' Morons
Me want get out now.
BOX O' Morons

WHAT HAPPENED TO YOUR HOUSE?
We tear down. Swamp natural advannage. Ees all part of BEEG plan.
THAT'S MORONIC.
Ohhhhhh... Moroneec, huh? You not say dat when you ees keeled.
OH? AND HOW DO YOU PLAN TO DO THAT?
Unnerwater spear-gun. You fall een. We shoot. FOOM! You not know what happen.

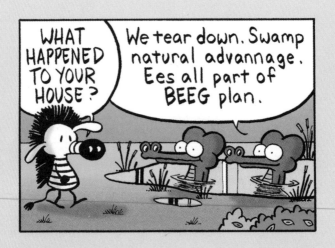

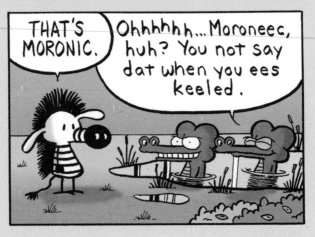

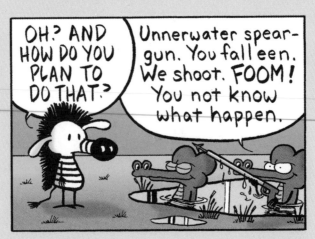

WHERE'D YOU LEARN TO WORK ONE OF THOSE?
Learn? What dere learn? You juss pull—
FOOM!
Good ting he not know what happen.

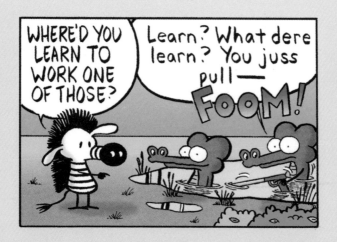

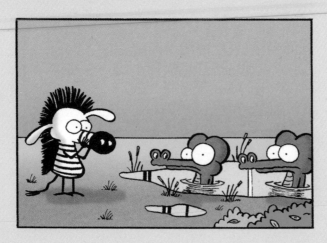

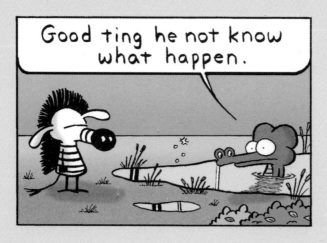

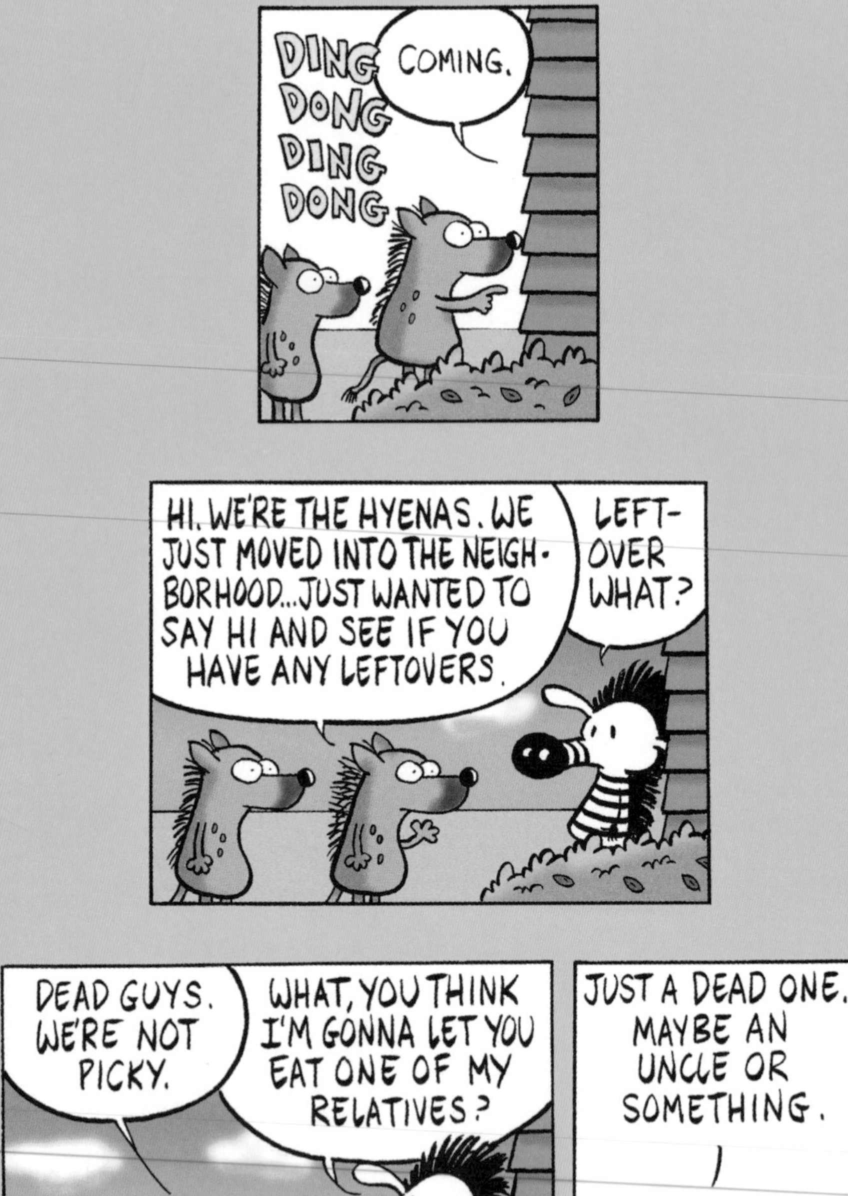
DING DONG DING DONG
COMING.
HI. WE'RE THE HYENAS. WE JUST MOVED INTO THE NEIGHBORHOOD...JUST WANTED TO SAY HI AND SEE IF YOU HAVE ANY LEFTOVERS.
LEFT-OVER WHAT?
DEAD GUYS. WE'RE NOT PICKY.
WHAT, YOU THINK I'M GONNA LET YOU EAT ONE OF MY RELATIVES?
JUST A DEAD ONE. MAYBE AN UNCLE OR SOMETHING.

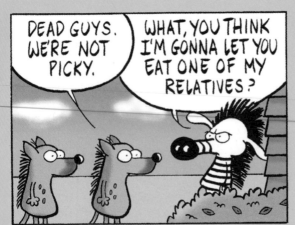

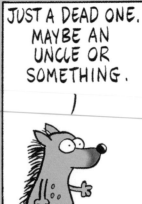

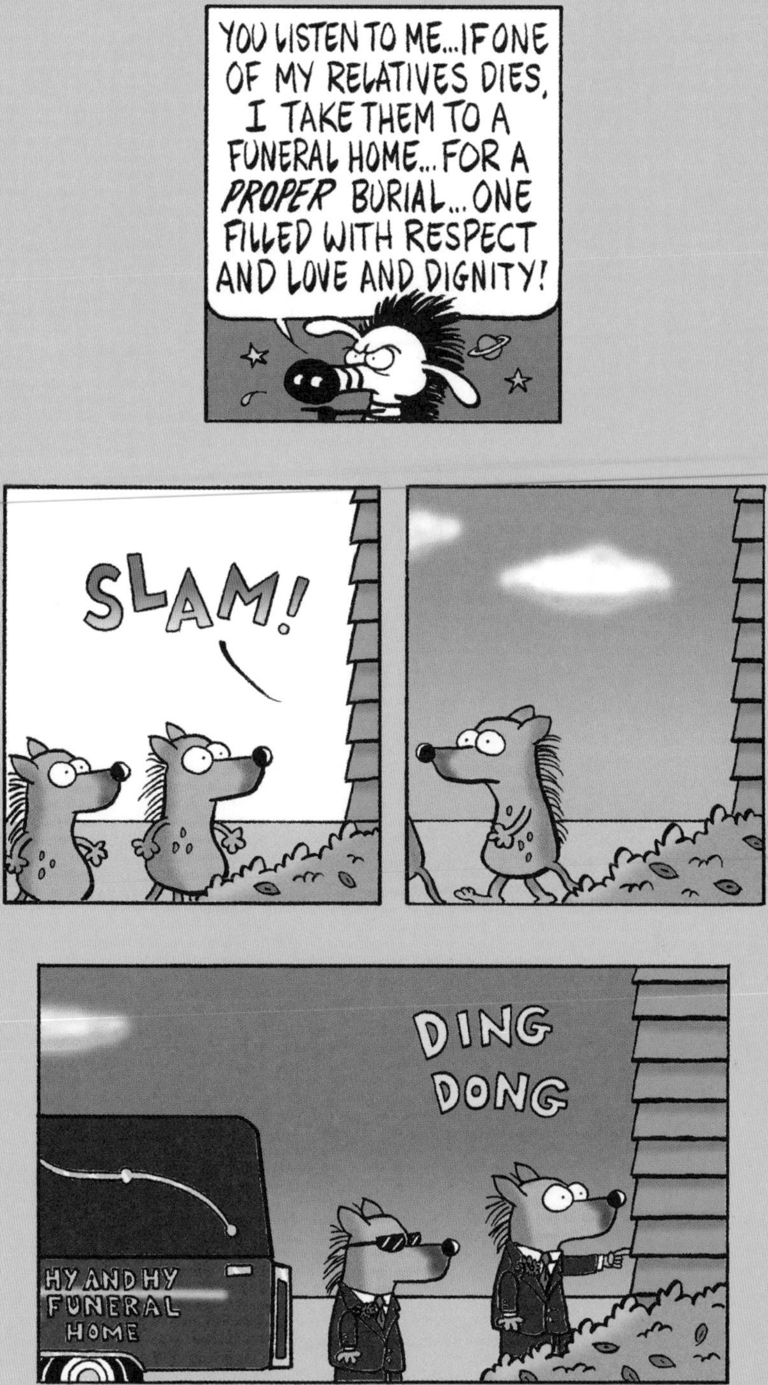
YOU LISTEN TO ME...IF ONE OF MY RELATIVES DIES, I TAKE THEM TO A FUNERAL HOME... FOR A *PROPER* BURIAL... ONE FILLED WITH RESPECT AND LOVE AND DIGNITY!
SLAM!
DING DONG
HY AND HY FUNERAL HOME

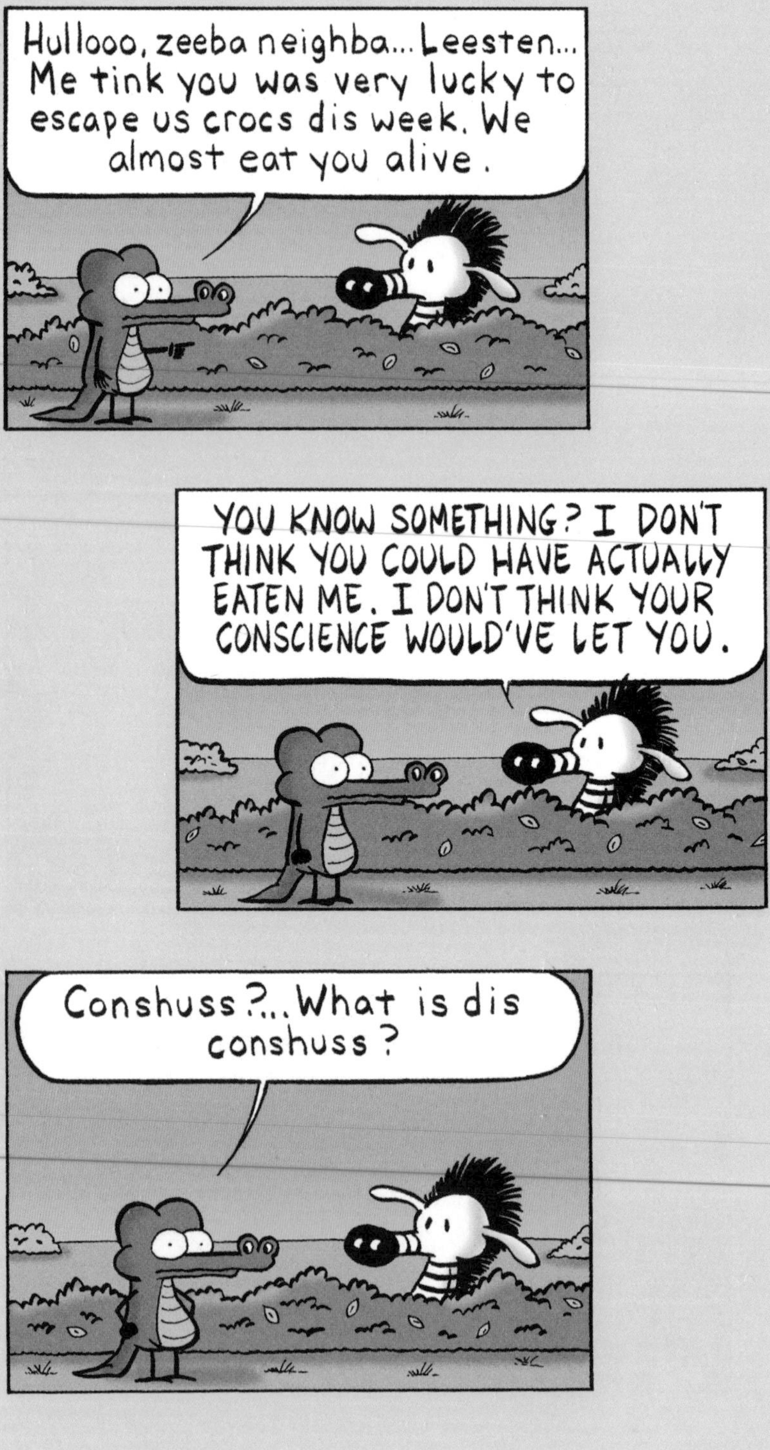
Hullooo, zeeba neighba... Leesten... Me tink you was very lucky to escape us crocs dis week. We almost eat you alive.
YOU KNOW SOMETHING? I DON'T THINK YOU COULD HAVE ACTUALLY EATEN ME. I DON'T THINK YOUR CONSCIENCE WOULD'VE LET YOU.
Conshuss?... What is dis conshuss?

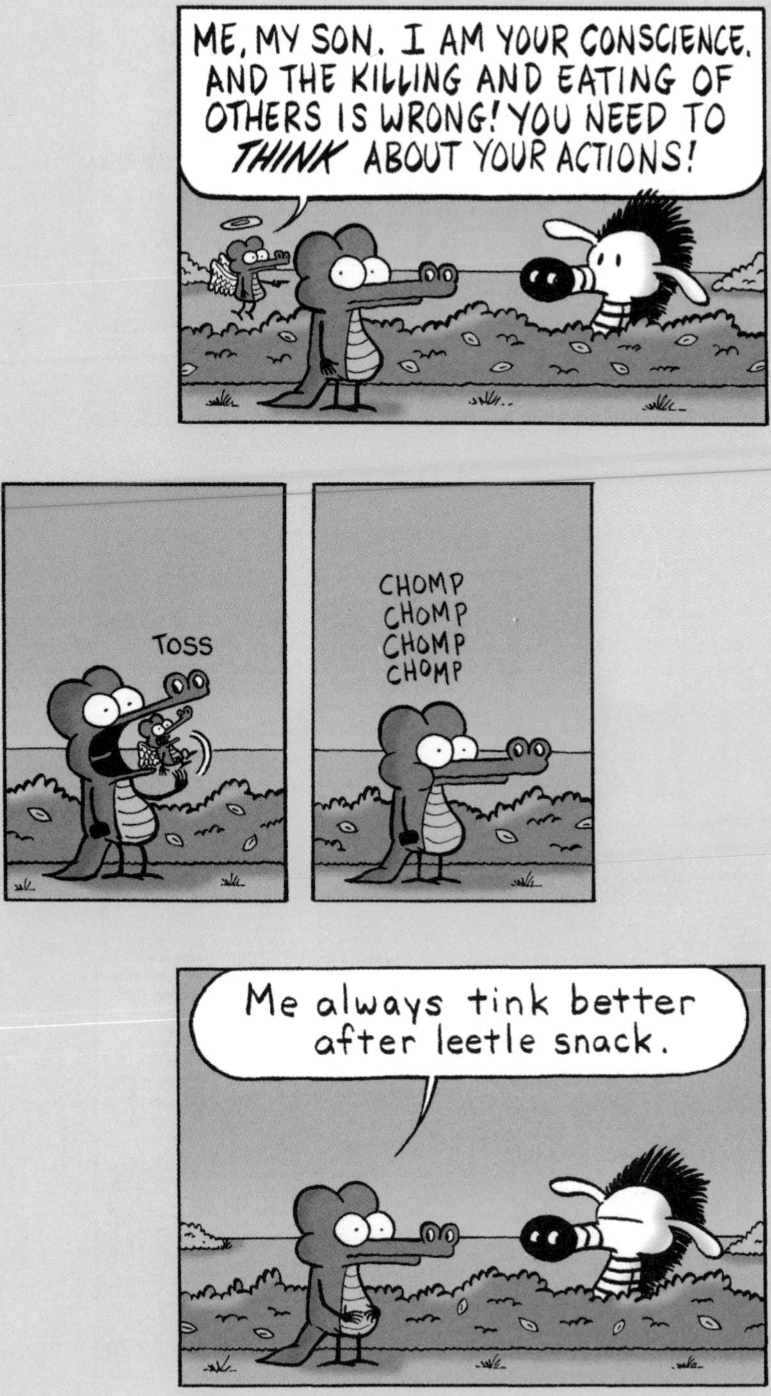
ME, MY SON. I AM YOUR CONSCIENCE. AND THE KILLING AND EATING OF OTHERS IS WRONG! YOU NEED TO *THINK* ABOUT YOUR ACTIONS!
TOSS
CHOMP
CHOMP
CHOMP
CHOMP
Me always tink better after leetle snack.

...THANKS AGAIN FOR ADOPTING THIS CAT... NOT EVERY PERSON THAT COMES IN HERE ASKS FOR THE CAT THAT SCRATCHES AND BITES THE MOST.
Oh... Ees no probbum. We nice guy.
ANIMAL SHELTER
HEY... WHAT ARE YOU GUYS DOING WITH A—
KEEL ZEEBA
REEP TO SHRED

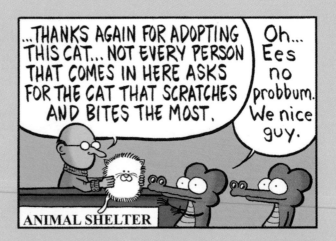

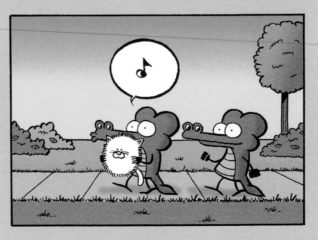

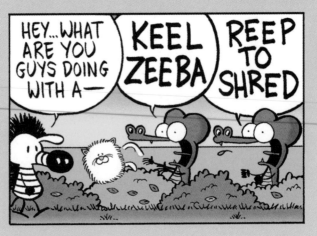

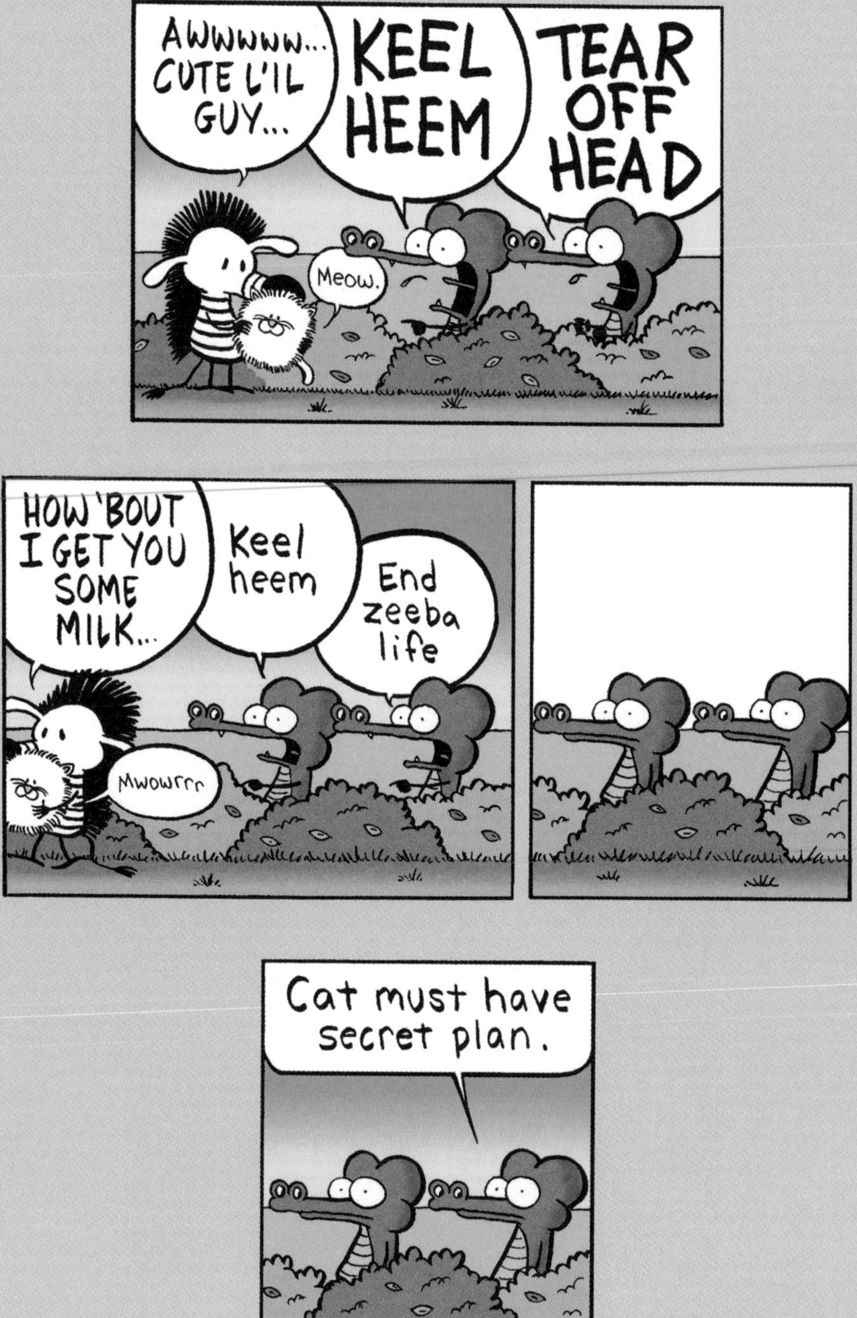
AWWWWW... CUTE L'IL GUY...
KEEL HEEM
TEAR OFF HEAD
Meow.
HOW 'BOUT I GET YOU SOME MILK...
Keel heem
End zeeba life
Mwowrrr
Cat must have secret plan.

LEMME MAKE SURE I UNDERSTAND...YOU MORONS ADOPTED A MEAN CAT TO KILL THE ZEBRA, BUT THE CAT TURNED OUT TO *LIKE* THE ZEBRA.
Peese shut mouf, woomun. You no unnerstan nutting.
OH. TELL ME. LARRY.... WHAT AM I MISSING?
Cat **VEESHUS**... Once eenside zeeba house, cat will **KEEL** heem! **KEEL** heem! ***KEEL*** heem!

ZZZZZZZ
PURRRRRRRRRRRRRR

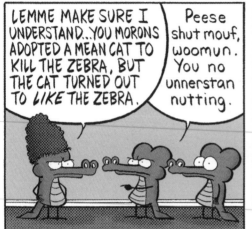

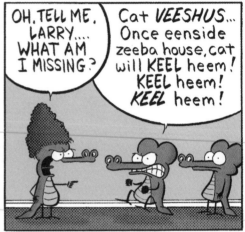

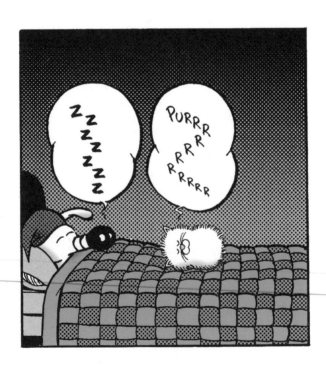

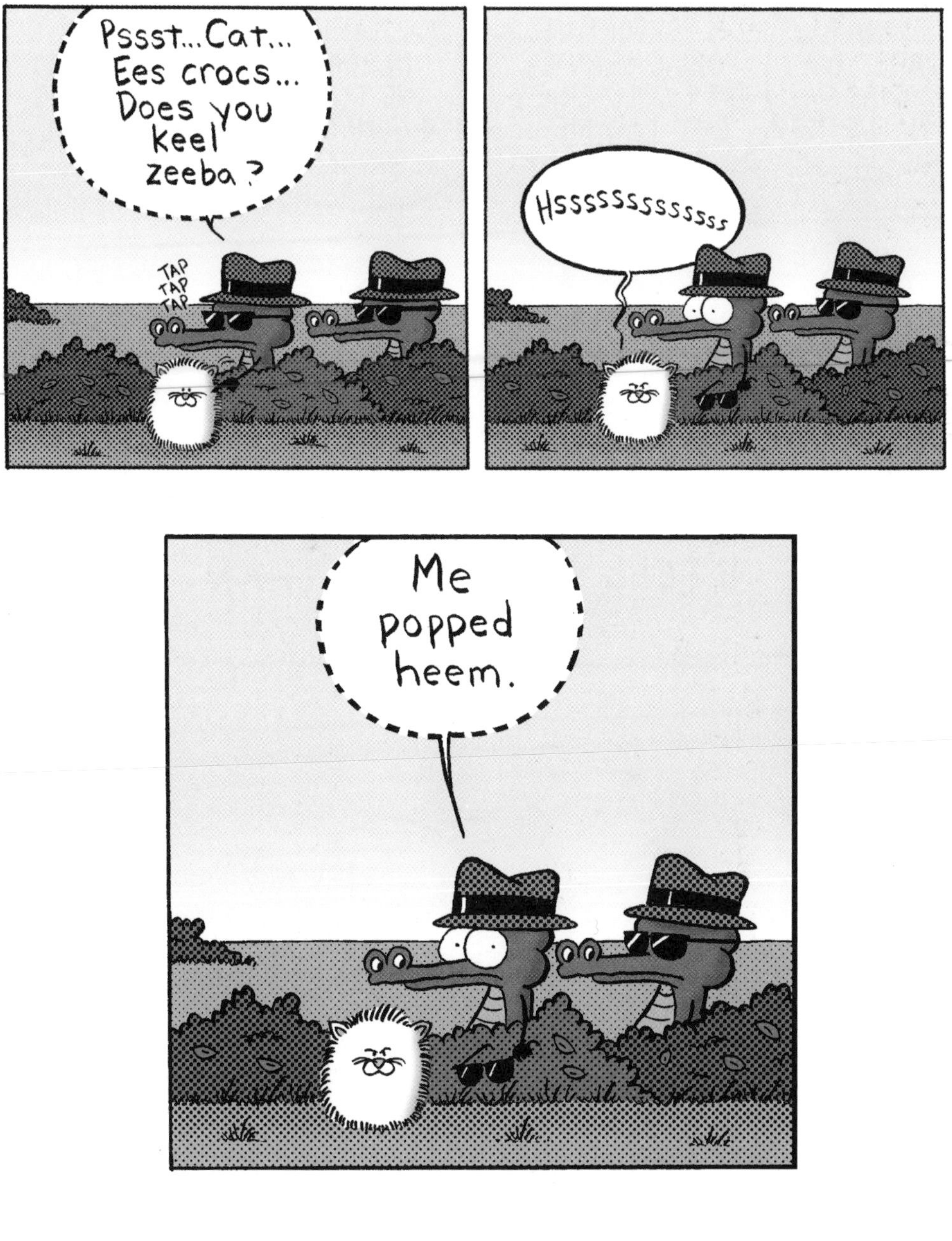
Pssst...Cat...
Ees crocs...
Does you
keel
zeeba?
TAP
TAP
TAP
Hssssssssssss
Me
popped
heem.

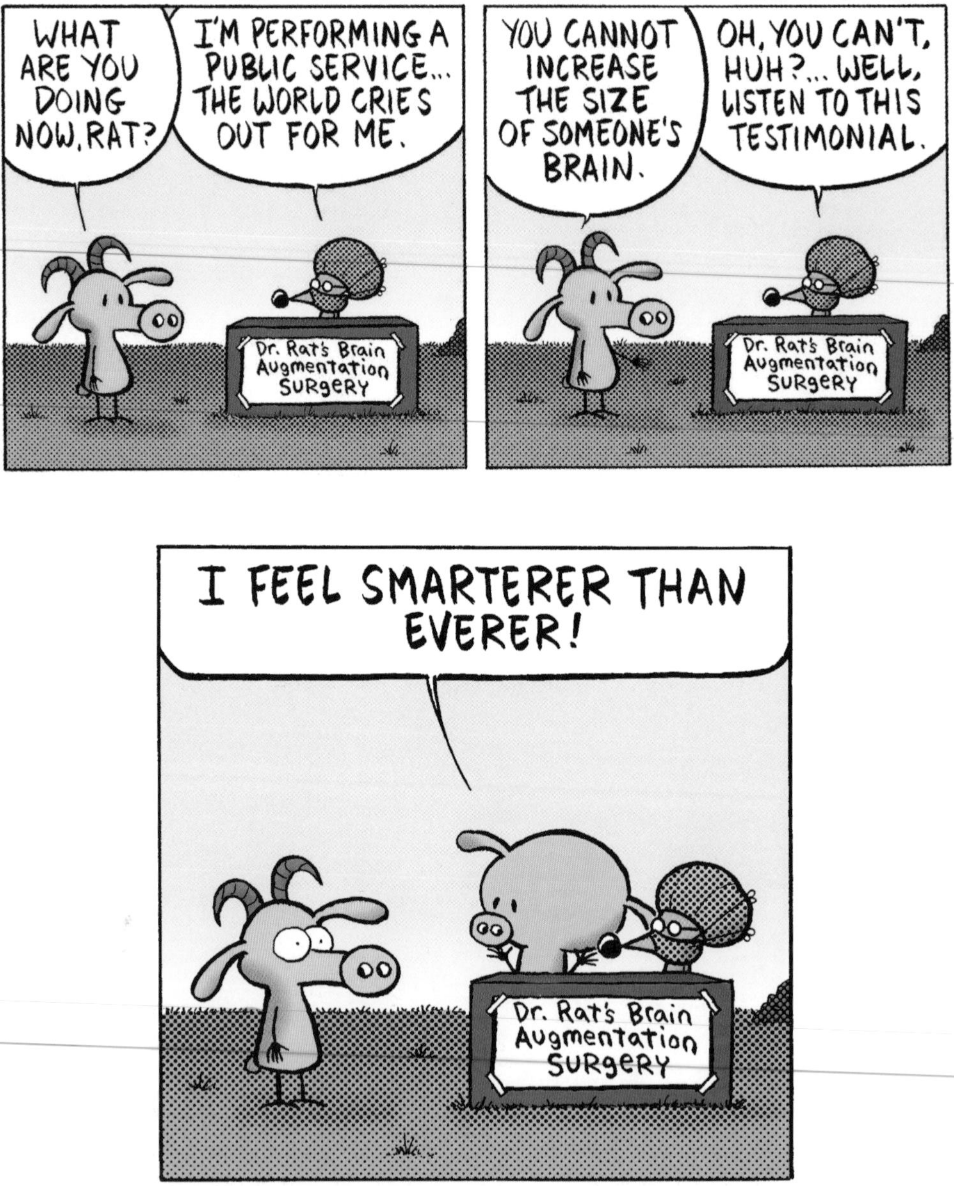
WHAT ARE YOU DOING NOW, RAT?
I'M PERFORMING A PUBLIC SERVICE... THE WORLD CRIES OUT FOR ME.
Dr. Rat's Brain Augmentation SURGERY
YOU CANNOT INCREASE THE SIZE OF SOMEONE'S BRAIN.
OH, YOU CAN'T, HUH?... WELL, LISTEN TO THIS TESTIMONIAL.
Dr. Rat's Brain Augmentation SURGERY
I FEEL SMARTERER THAN EVERER!
Dr. Rat's Brain Augmentation SURGERY

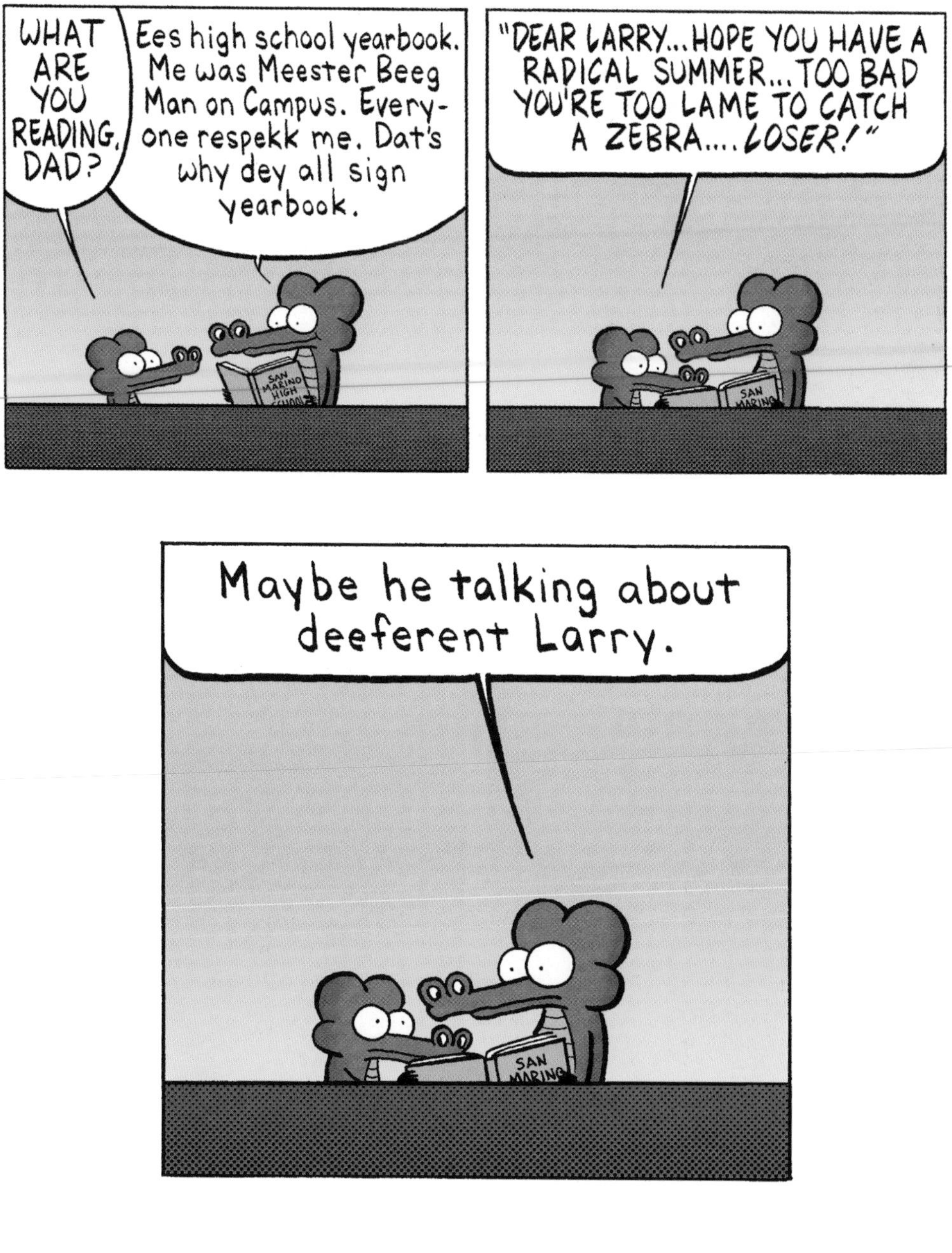
WHAT ARE YOU READING, DAD?
Ees high school yearbook. Me was Meester Beeg Man on Campus. Every-one respekk me. Dat's why dey all sign yearbook.
"DEAR LARRY... HOPE YOU HAVE A RADICAL SUMMER... TOO BAD YOU'RE TOO LAME TO CATCH A ZEBRA.... *LOSER!*"
Maybe he talking about deeferent Larry.

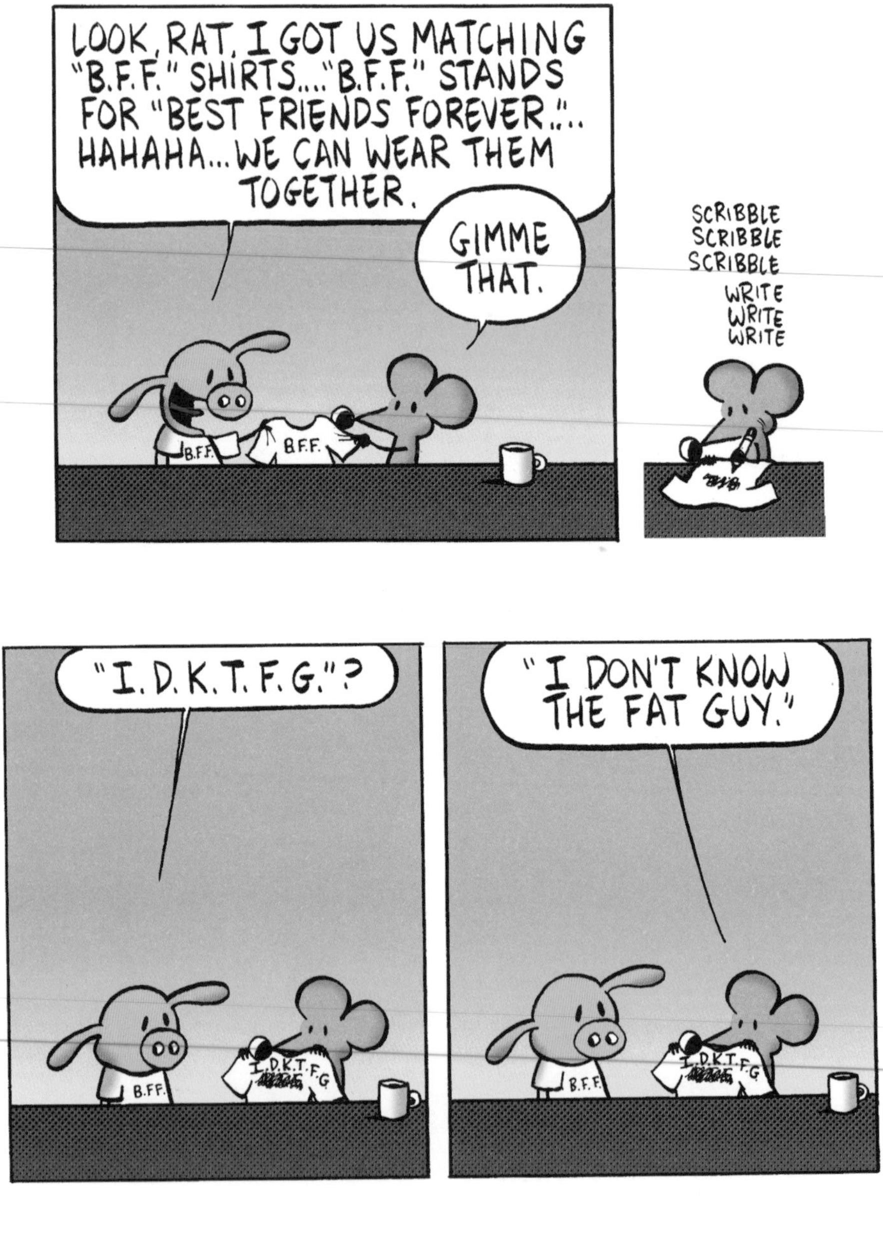
LOOK, RAT, I GOT US MATCHING "B.F.F." SHIRTS...."B.F.F." STANDS FOR "BEST FRIENDS FOREVER."... HAHAHA... WE CAN WEAR THEM TOGETHER.
GIMME THAT.
B.F.F.
B.F.F.
SCRIBBLE
SCRIBBLE
SCRIBBLE
WRITE
WRITE
WRITE
"I.D.K.T.F.G."?
B.F.F.
I.D.K.T.F.G.
"I DON'T KNOW THE FAT GUY."
B.F.F.
I.D.K.T.F.G.

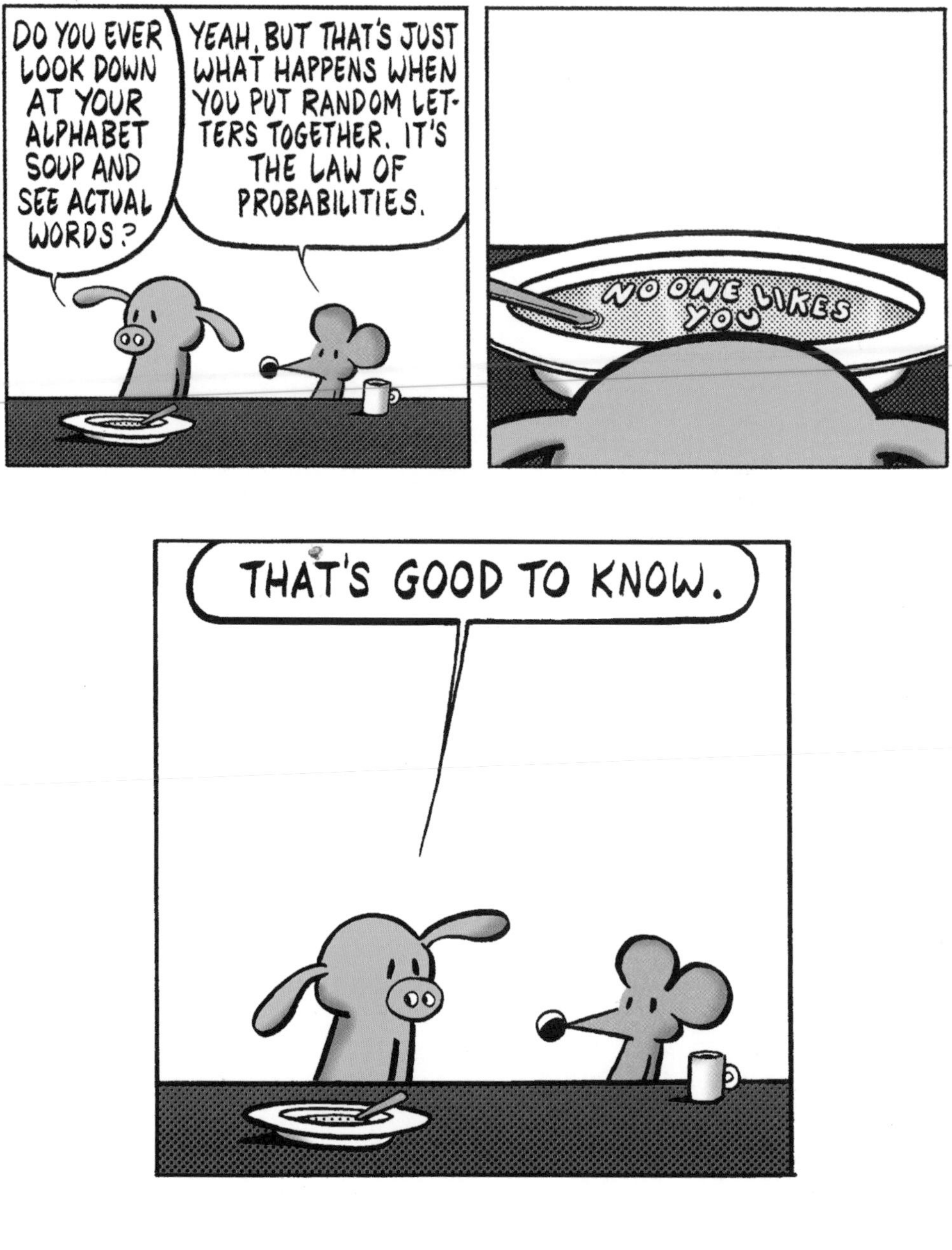
DO YOU EVER LOOK DOWN AT YOUR ALPHABET SOUP AND SEE ACTUAL WORDS?
YEAH, BUT THAT'S JUST WHAT HAPPENS WHEN YOU PUT RANDOM LETTERS TOGETHER. IT'S THE LAW OF PROBABILITIES.
NO ONE LIKES YOU
THAT'S GOOD TO KNOW.

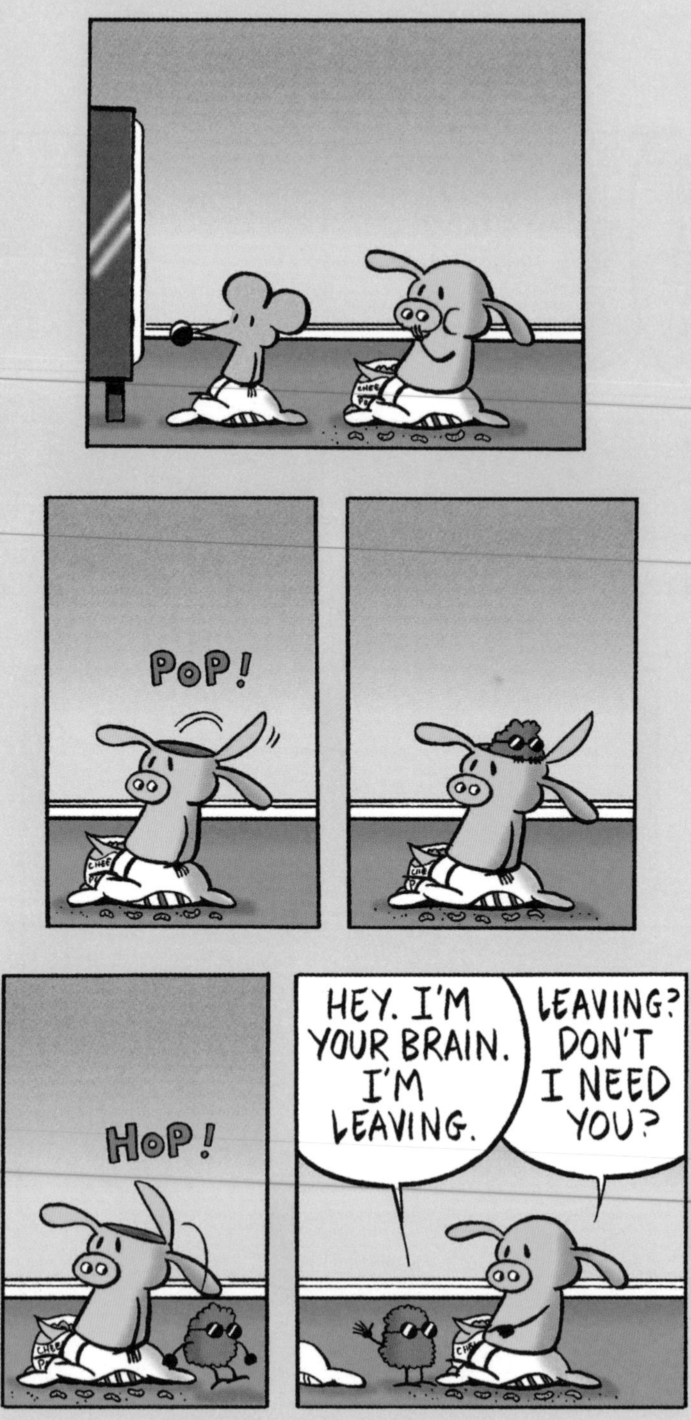
POP!
HOP!
HEY. I'M YOUR BRAIN. I'M LEAVING.
LEAVING? DON'T I NEED YOU?

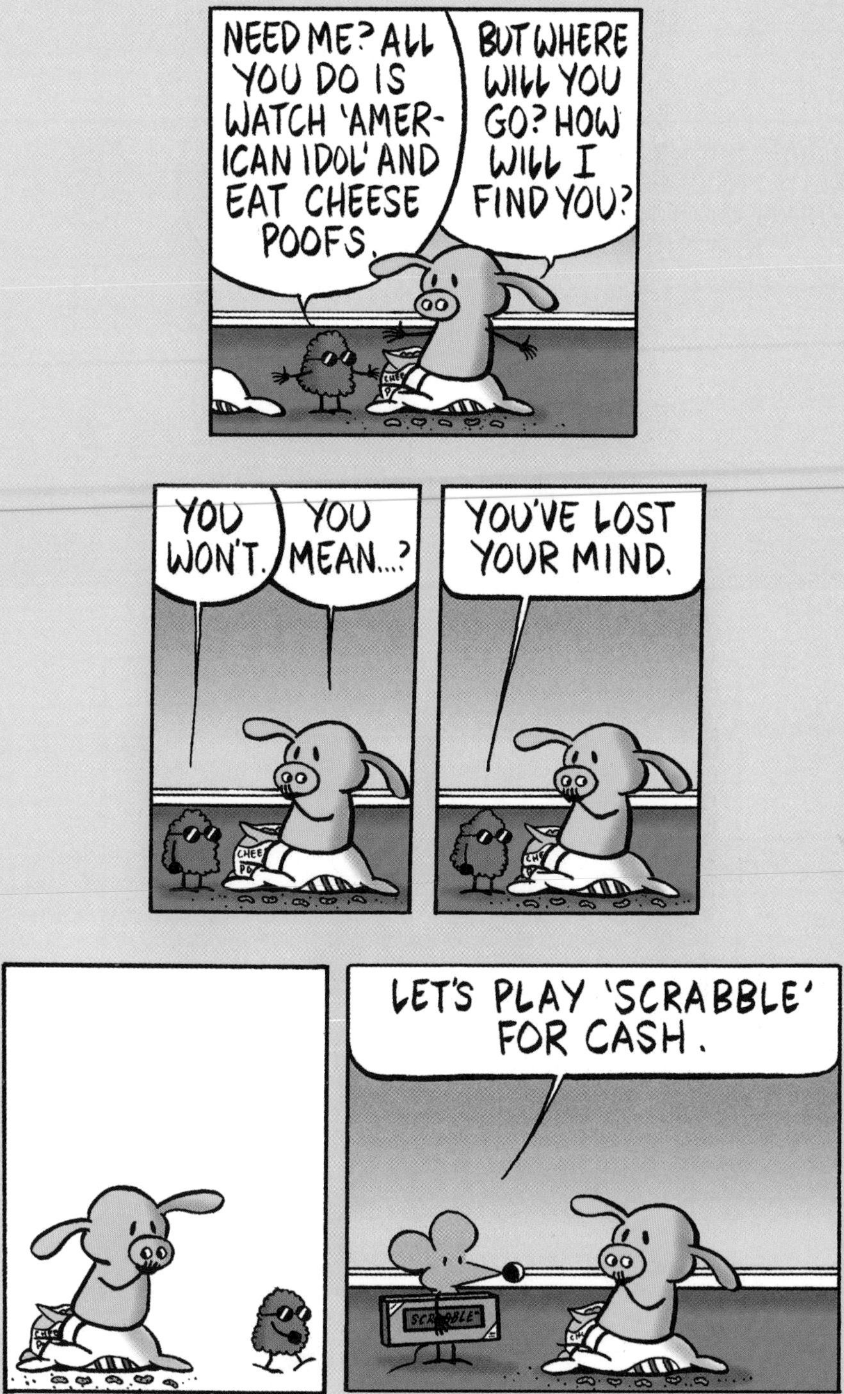
NEED ME? ALL YOU DO IS WATCH 'AMERICAN IDOL' AND EAT CHEESE POOFS.
BUT WHERE WILL YOU GO? HOW WILL I FIND YOU?
YOU WON'T.
YOU MEAN...?
YOU'VE LOST YOUR MIND.
LET'S PLAY 'SCRABBLE' FOR CASH.
SCRABBLE

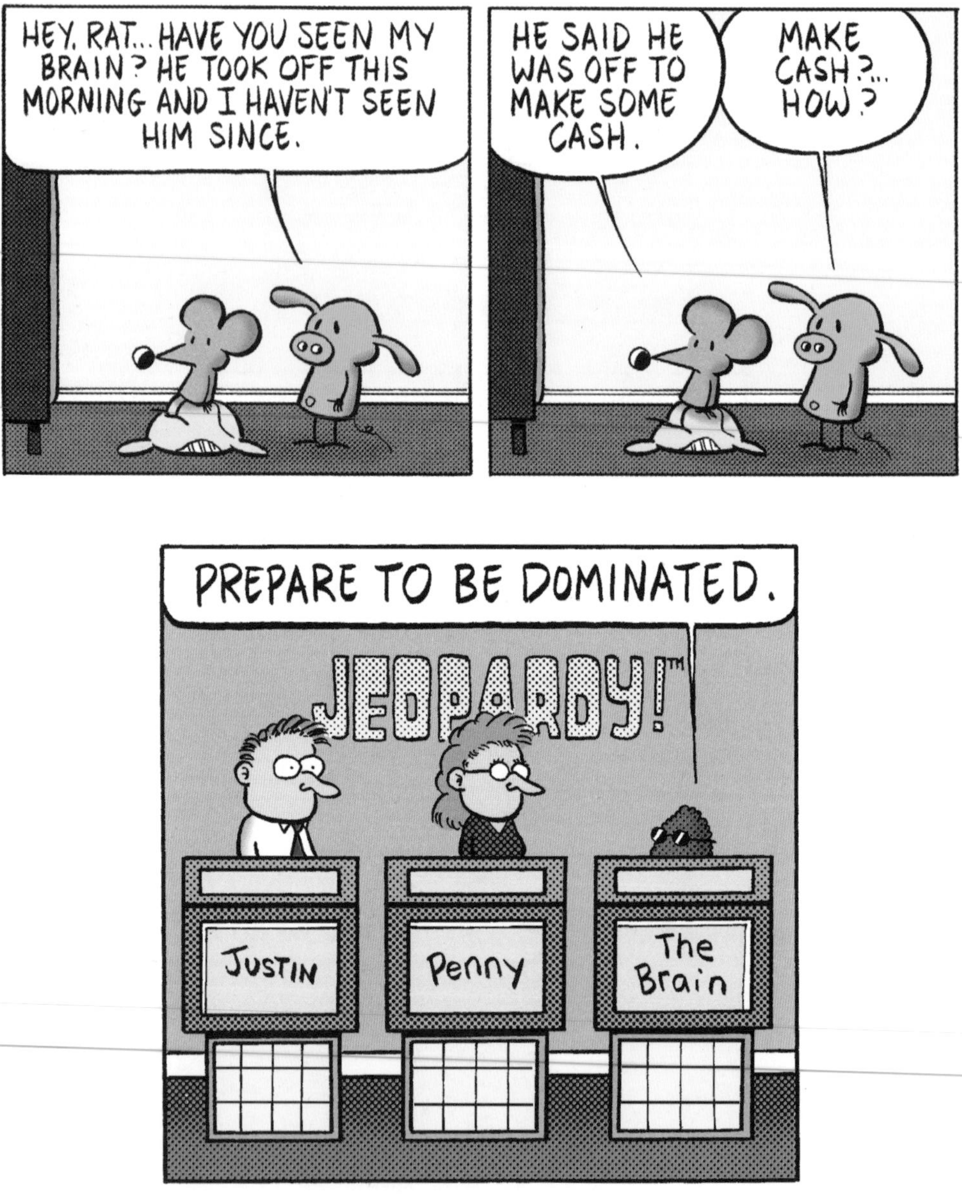

HEY, RAT... HAVE YOU SEEN MY BRAIN? HE TOOK OFF THIS MORNING AND I HAVEN'T SEEN HIM SINCE.
HE SAID HE WAS OFF TO MAKE SOME CASH.
MAKE CASH?... HOW?
PREPARE TO BE DOMINATED.
JEOPARDY!™
JUSTIN
Penny
The Brain

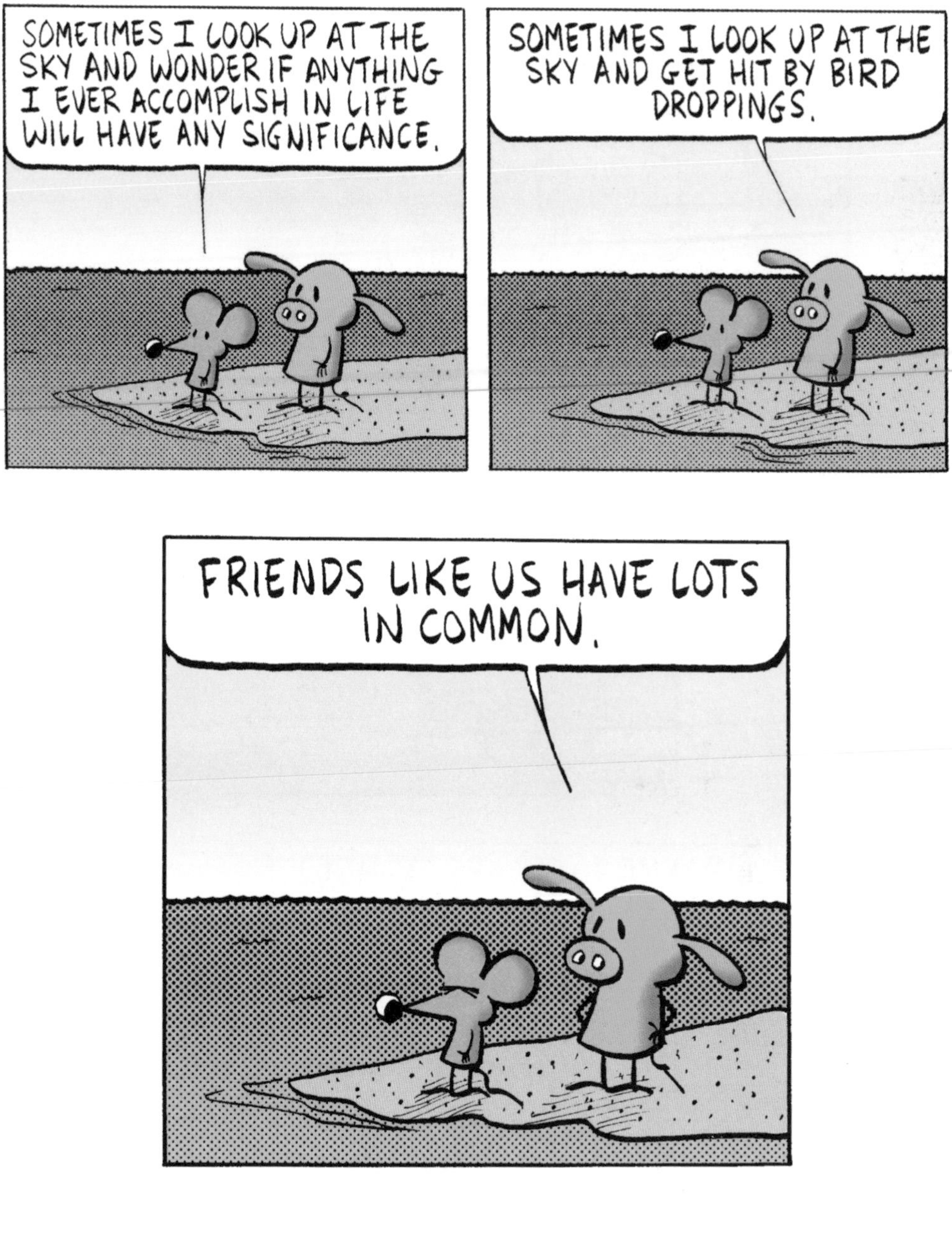
SOMETIMES I LOOK UP AT THE SKY AND WONDER IF ANYTHING I EVER ACCOMPLISH IN LIFE WILL HAVE ANY SIGNIFICANCE.
SOMETIMES I LOOK UP AT THE SKY AND GET HIT BY BIRD DROPPINGS.
FRIENDS LIKE US HAVE LOTS IN COMMON.

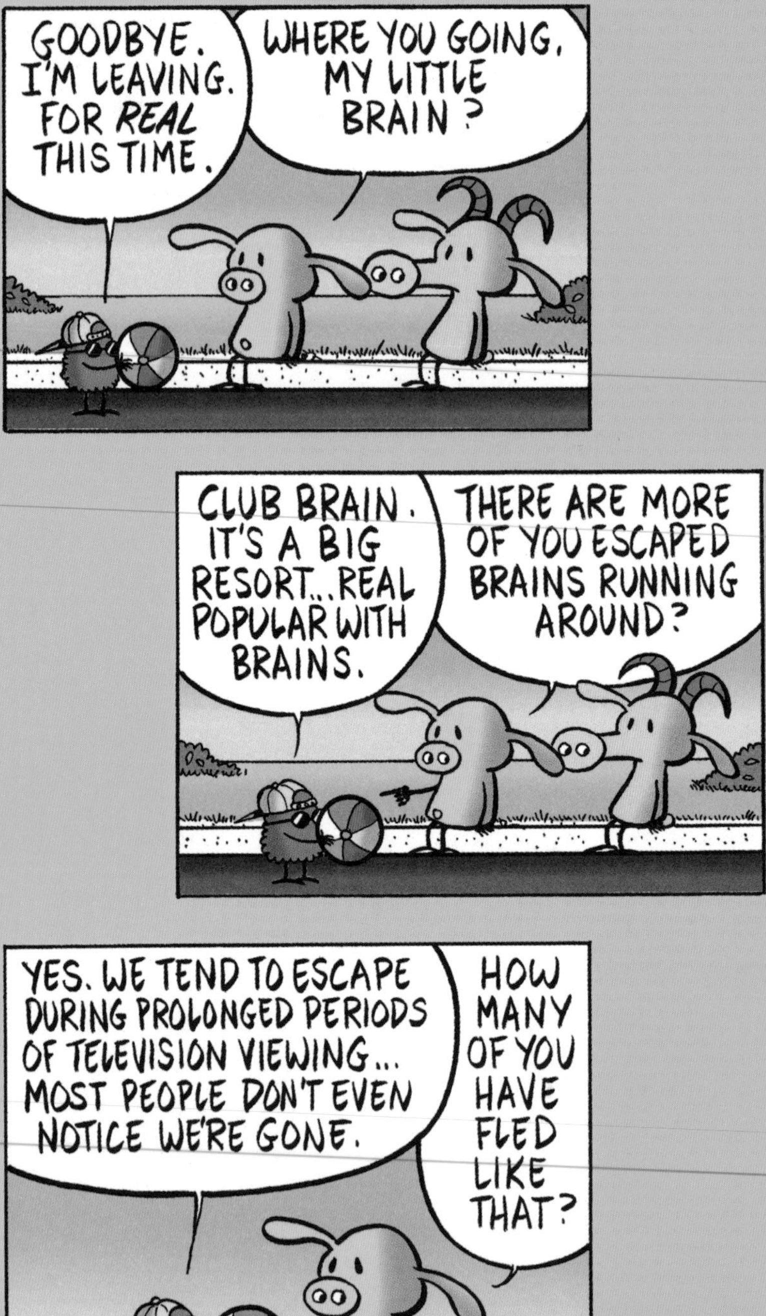
GOODBYE. I'M LEAVING. FOR REAL THIS TIME.
WHERE YOU GOING, MY LITTLE BRAIN?
CLUB BRAIN. IT'S A BIG RESORT...REAL POPULAR WITH BRAINS.
THERE ARE MORE OF YOU ESCAPED BRAINS RUNNING AROUND?
YES. WE TEND TO ESCAPE DURING PROLONGED PERIODS OF TELEVISION VIEWING... MOST PEOPLE DON'T EVEN NOTICE WE'RE GONE.
HOW MANY OF YOU HAVE FLED LIKE THAT?

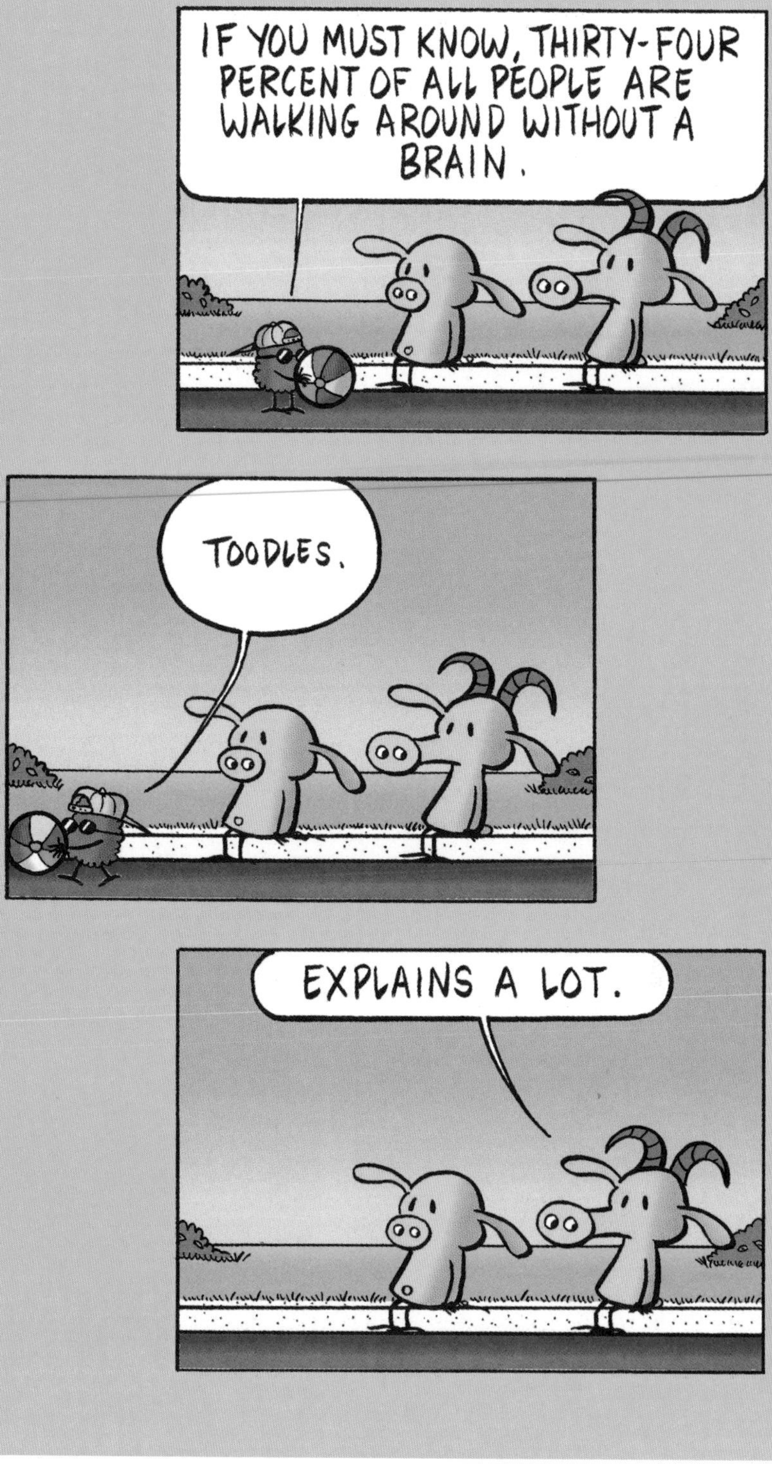
IF YOU MUST KNOW, THIRTY-FOUR PERCENT OF ALL PEOPLE ARE WALKING AROUND WITHOUT A BRAIN.
TOODLES.
EXPLAINS A LOT.

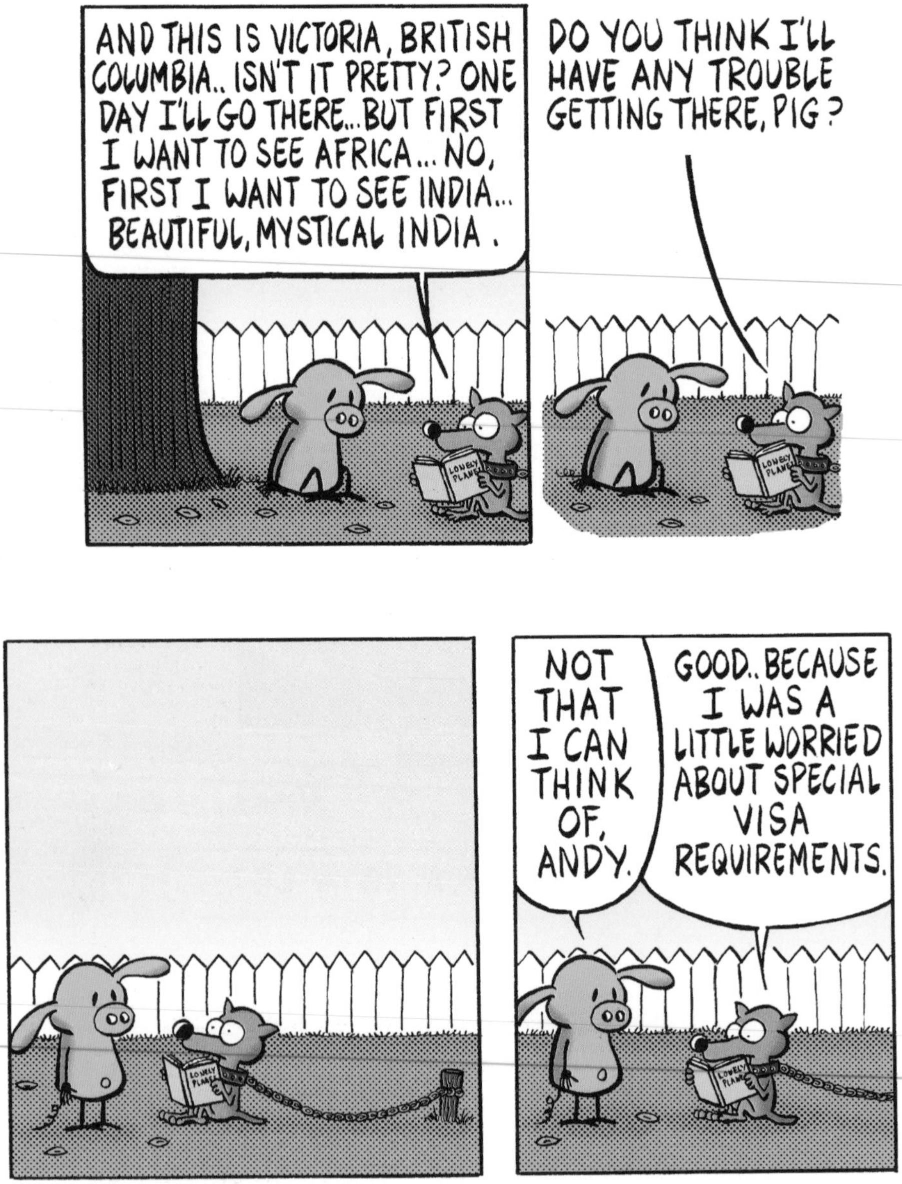
AND THIS IS VICTORIA, BRITISH COLUMBIA.. ISN'T IT PRETTY? ONE DAY I'LL GO THERE...BUT FIRST I WANT TO SEE AFRICA... NO, FIRST I WANT TO SEE INDIA... BEAUTIFUL, MYSTICAL INDIA.
DO YOU THINK I'LL HAVE ANY TROUBLE GETTING THERE, PIG?
NOT THAT I CAN THINK OF, ANDY.
GOOD.. BECAUSE I WAS A LITTLE WORRIED ABOUT SPECIAL VISA REQUIREMENTS.

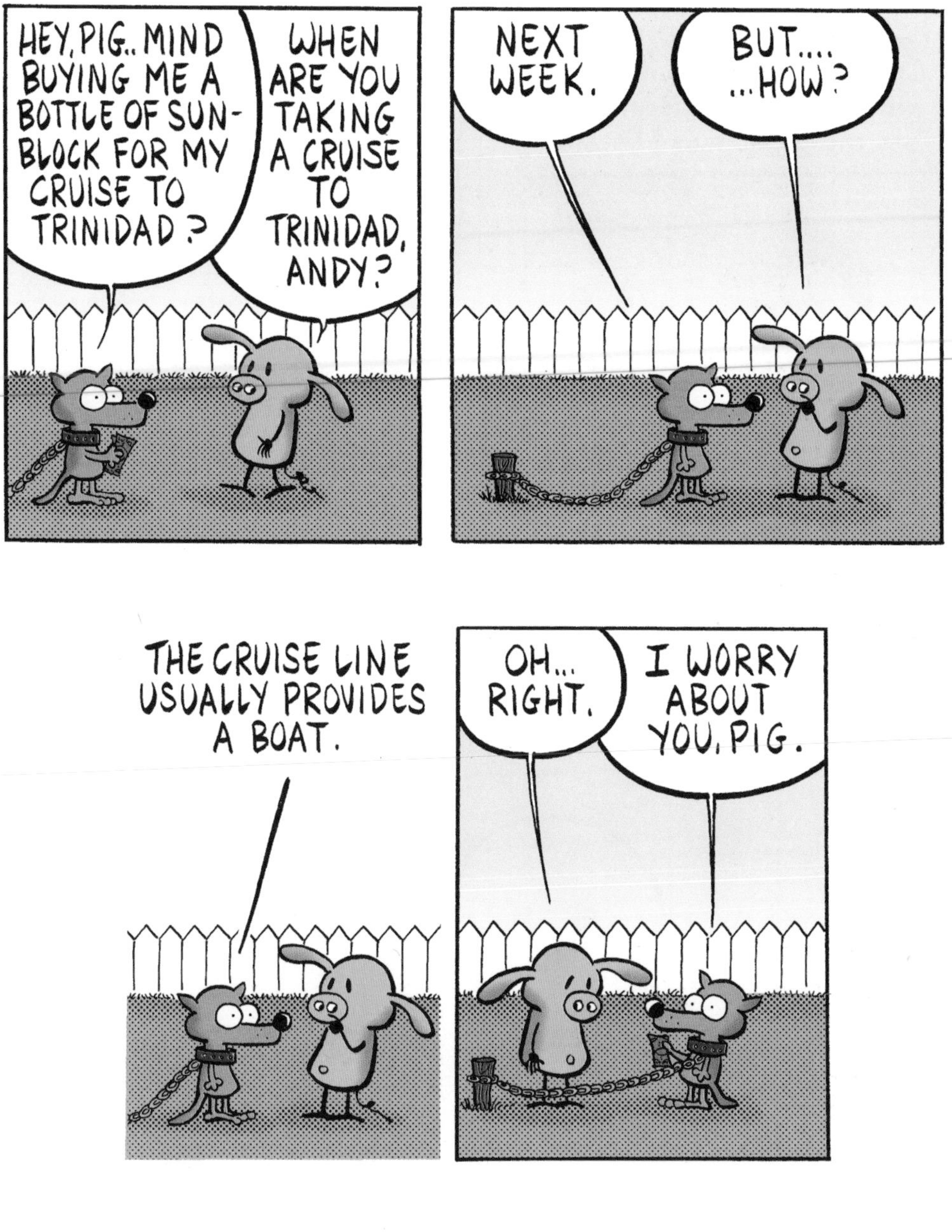
HEY, PIG.. MIND BUYING ME A BOTTLE OF SUN-BLOCK FOR MY CRUISE TO TRINIDAD?
WHEN ARE YOU TAKING A CRUISE TO TRINIDAD, ANDY?
NEXT WEEK.
BUT.... ...HOW?
THE CRUISE LINE USUALLY PROVIDES A BOAT.
OH... RIGHT.
I WORRY ABOUT YOU, PIG.

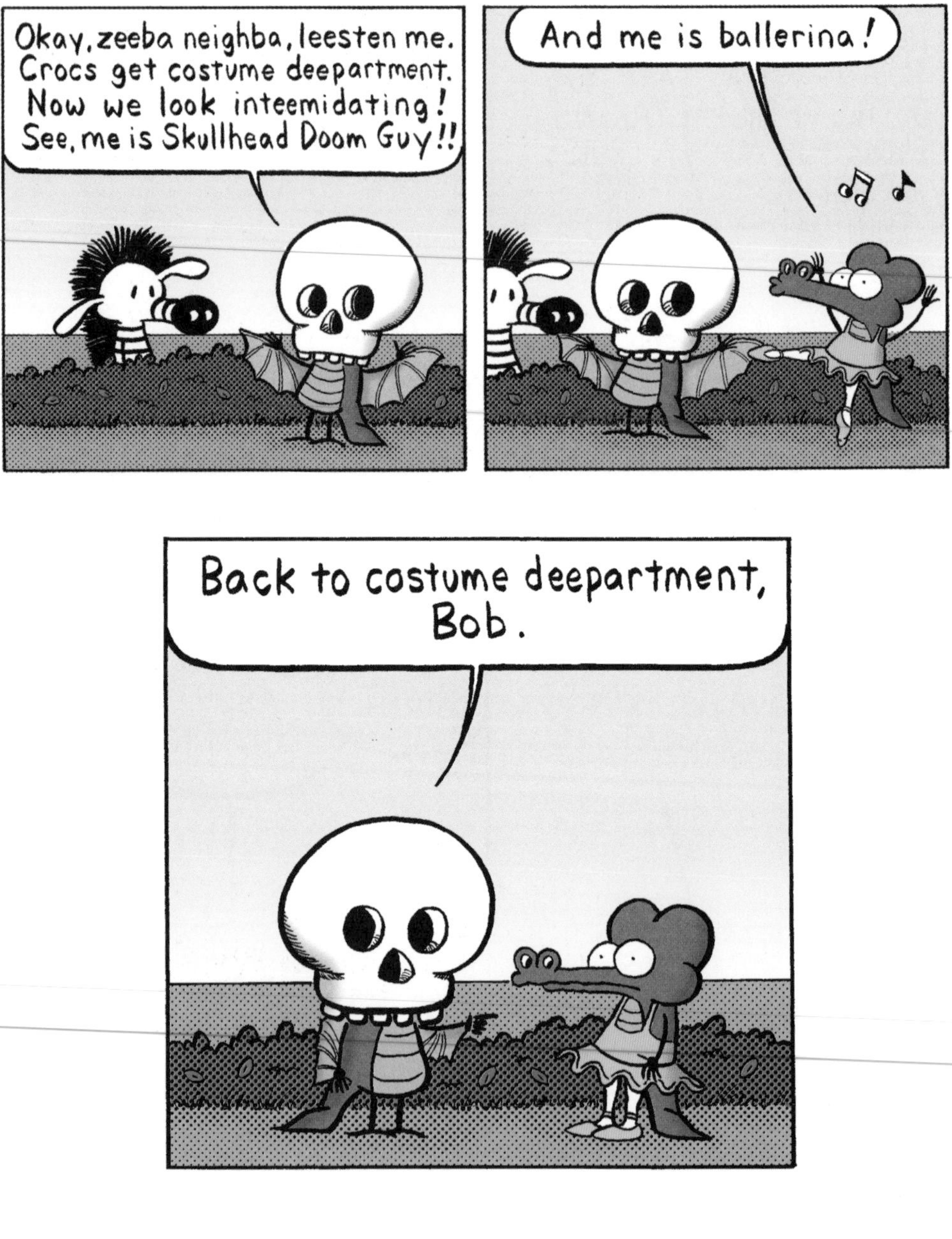
Okay, zeeba neighba, leesten me. Crocs get costume deepartment. Now we look inteemidating! See, me is Skullhead Doom Guy!!
And me is ballerina!
Back to costume deepartment, Bob.

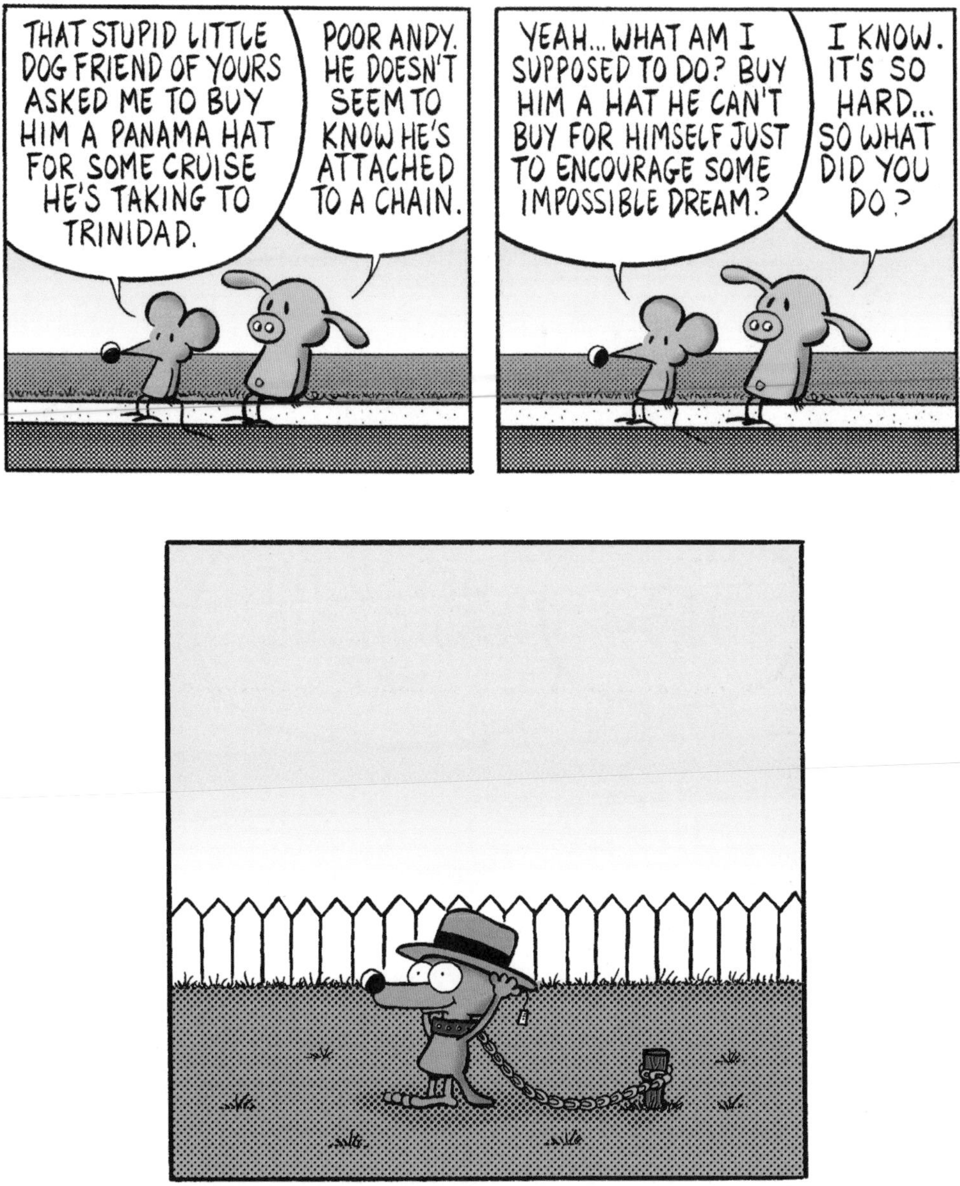
THAT STUPID LITTLE DOG FRIEND OF YOURS ASKED ME TO BUY HIM A PANAMA HAT FOR SOME CRUISE HE'S TAKING TO TRINIDAD.
POOR ANDY. HE DOESN'T SEEM TO KNOW HE'S ATTACHED TO A CHAIN.
YEAH... WHAT AM I SUPPOSED TO DO? BUY HIM A HAT HE CAN'T BUY FOR HIMSELF JUST TO ENCOURAGE SOME IMPOSSIBLE DREAM?
I KNOW. IT'S SO HARD... SO WHAT DID YOU DO?

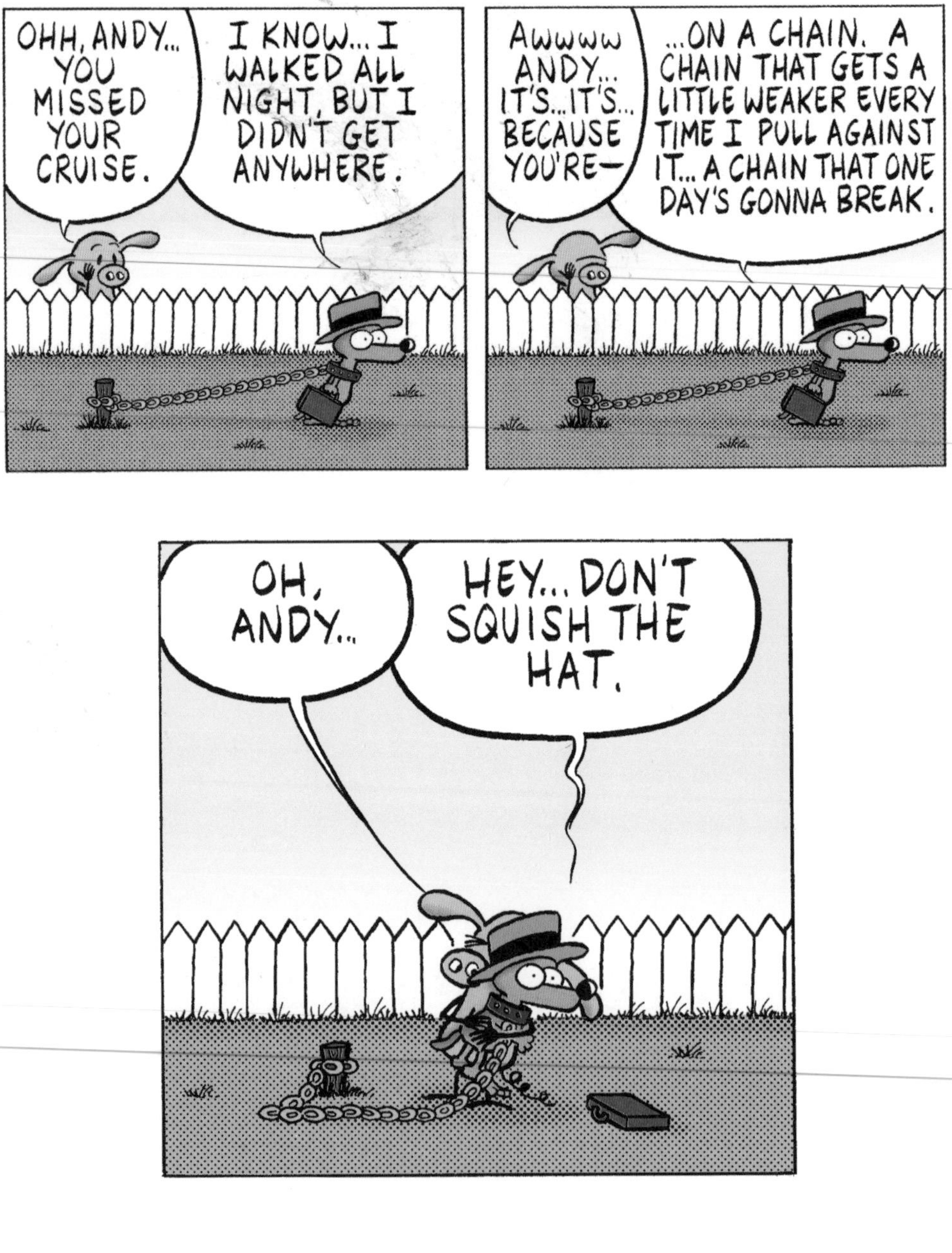
OHH, ANDY... YOU MISSED YOUR CRUISE.
I KNOW... I WALKED ALL NIGHT, BUT I DIDN'T GET ANYWHERE.
Awwww ANDY... IT'S... IT'S... BECAUSE YOU'RE—
...ON A CHAIN. A CHAIN THAT GETS A LITTLE WEAKER EVERY TIME I PULL AGAINST IT... A CHAIN THAT ONE DAY'S GONNA BREAK.
OH, ANDY...
HEY... DON'T SQUISH THE HAT.

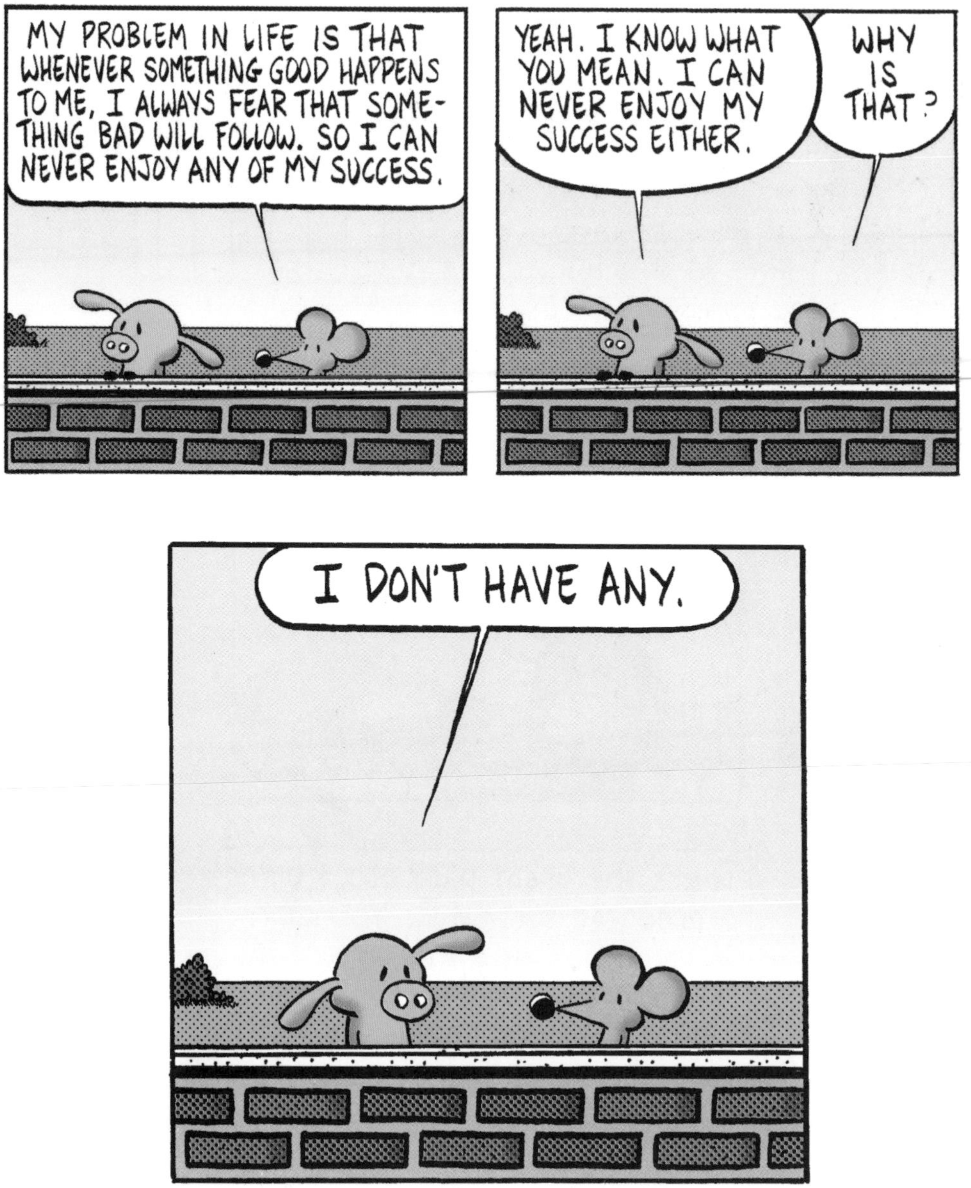
MY PROBLEM IN LIFE IS THAT WHENEVER SOMETHING GOOD HAPPENS TO ME, I ALWAYS FEAR THAT SOMETHING BAD WILL FOLLOW. SO I CAN NEVER ENJOY ANY OF MY SUCCESS.
YEAH. I KNOW WHAT YOU MEAN. I CAN NEVER ENJOY MY SUCCESS EITHER.
WHY IS THAT?
I DON'T HAVE ANY.

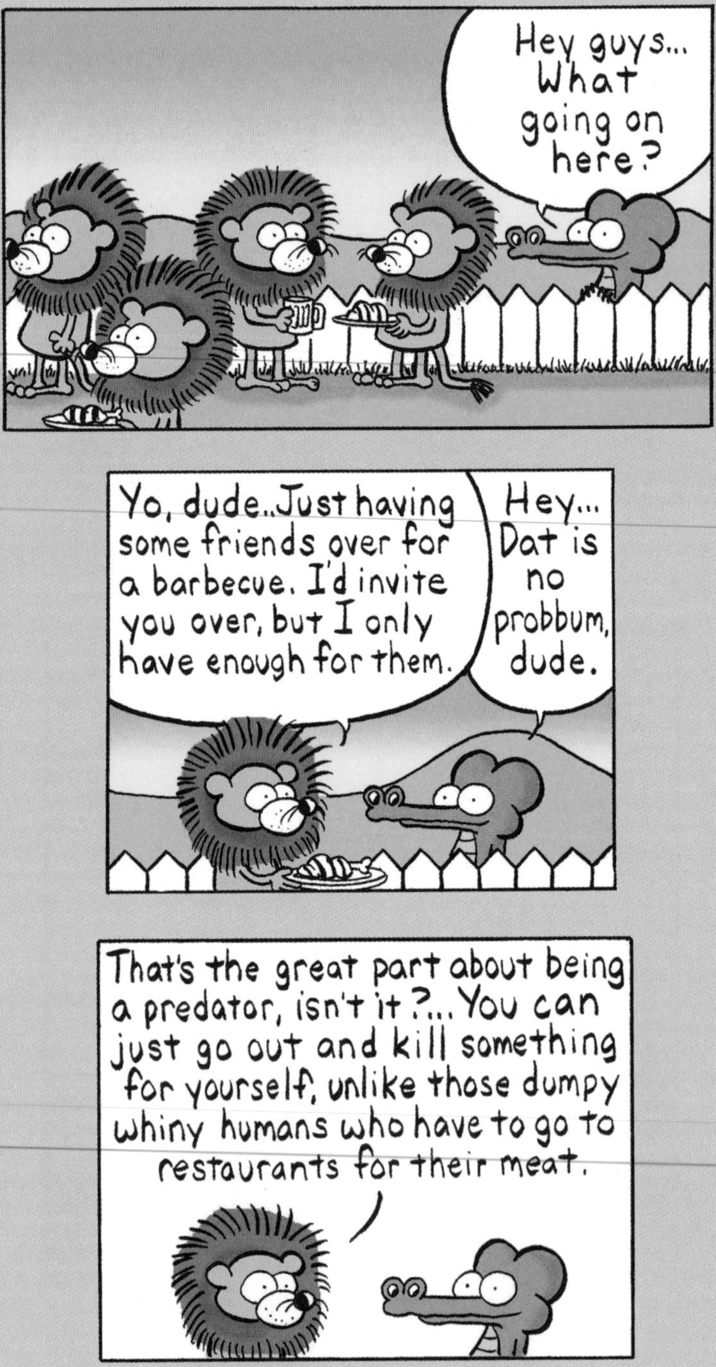

Hey guys... What going on here?
Yo, dude..Just having some friends over for a barbecue. I'd invite you over, but I only have enough for them.
Hey... Dat is no probbum, dude.
That's the great part about being a predator, isn't it?... You can just go out and kill something for yourself, unlike those dumpy whiny humans who have to go to restaurants for their meat.

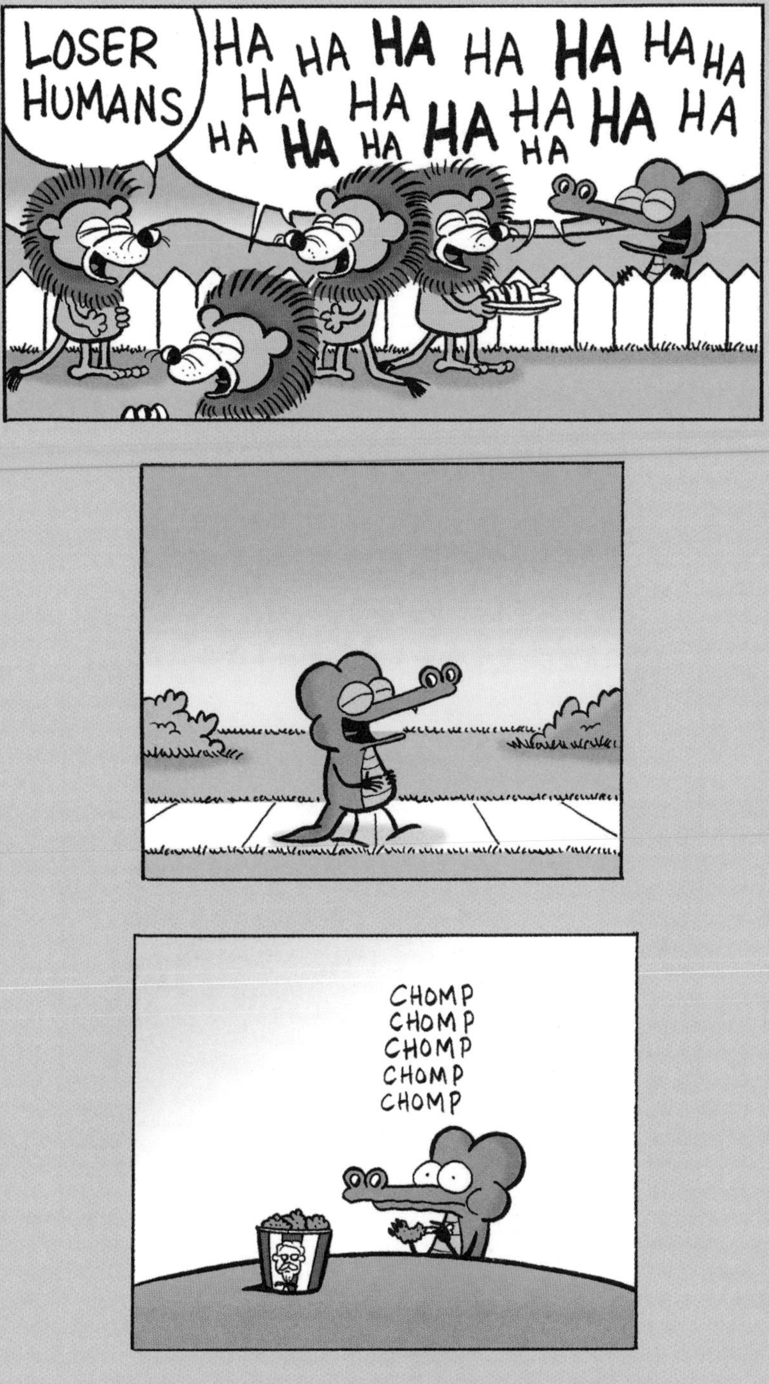
LOSER HUMANS
HA HA HA HA HA HA HA
HA HA
HA HA HA HA HA HA HA HA
CHOMP
CHOMP
CHOMP
CHOMP
CHOMP

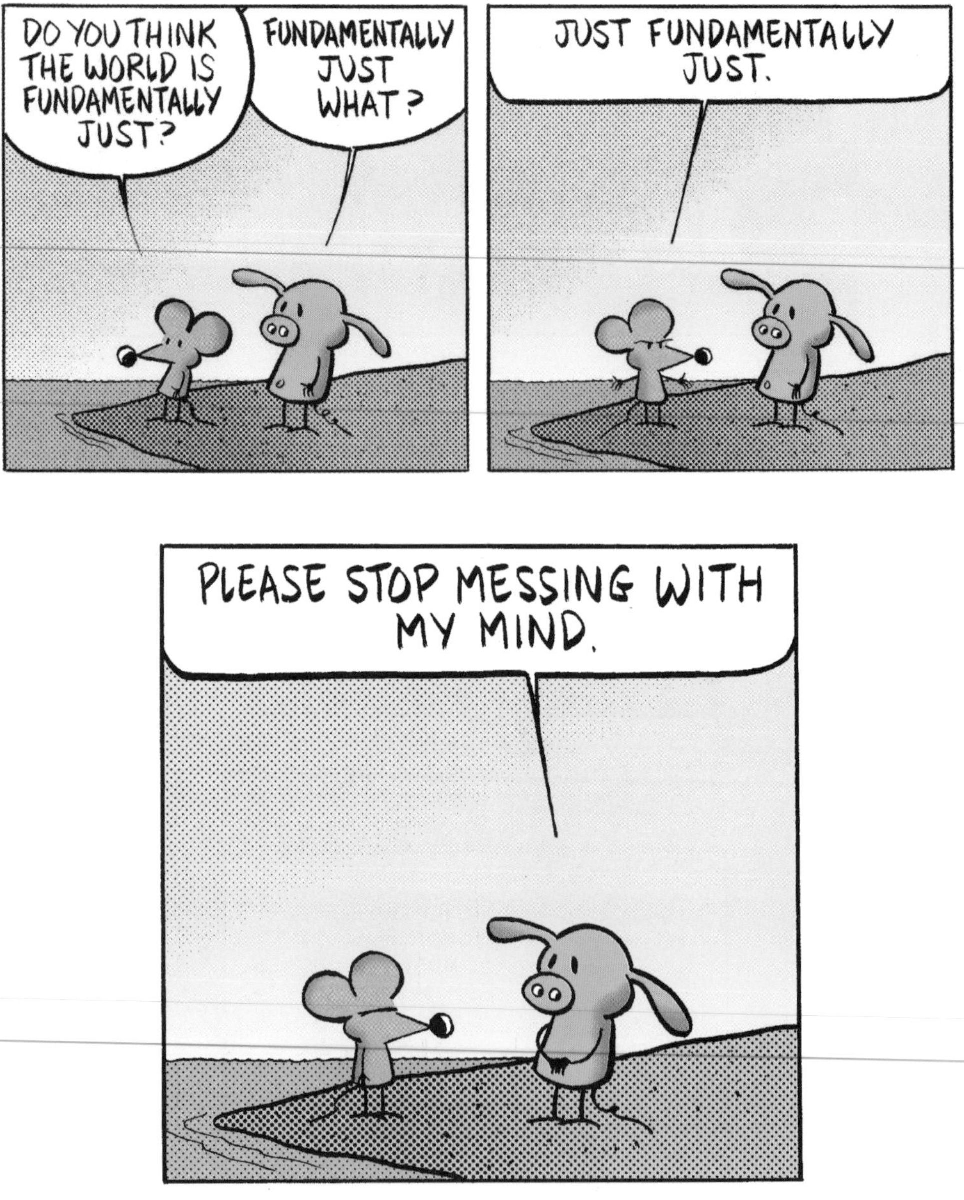
DO YOU THINK THE WORLD IS FUNDAMENTALLY JUST?
FUNDAMENTALLY JUST WHAT?
JUST FUNDAMENTALLY JUST.
PLEASE STOP MESSING WITH MY MIND.

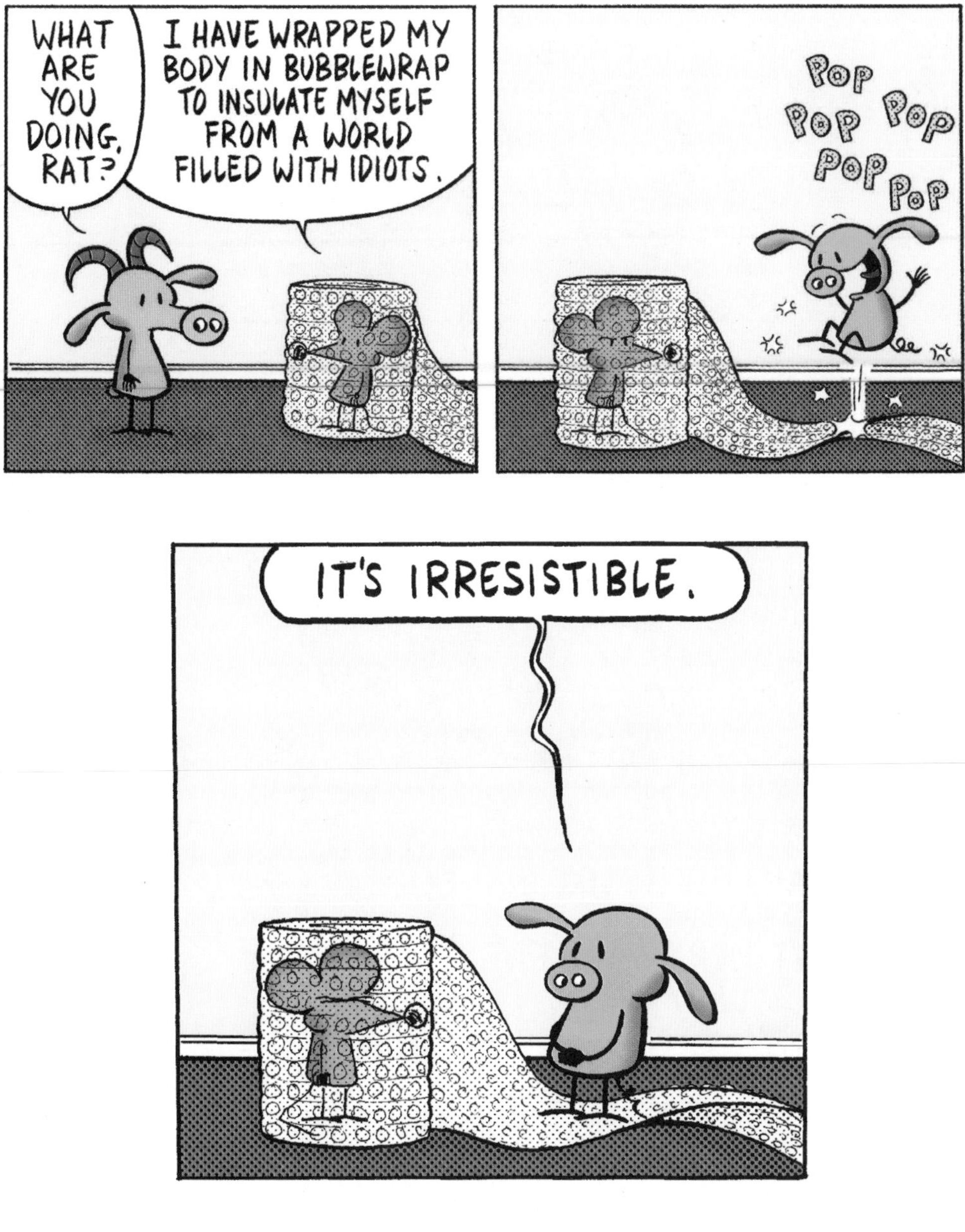
WHAT ARE YOU DOING, RAT?
I HAVE WRAPPED MY BODY IN BUBBLEWRAP TO INSULATE MYSELF FROM A WORLD FILLED WITH IDIOTS.
POP POP POP POP POP
IT'S IRRESISTIBLE.

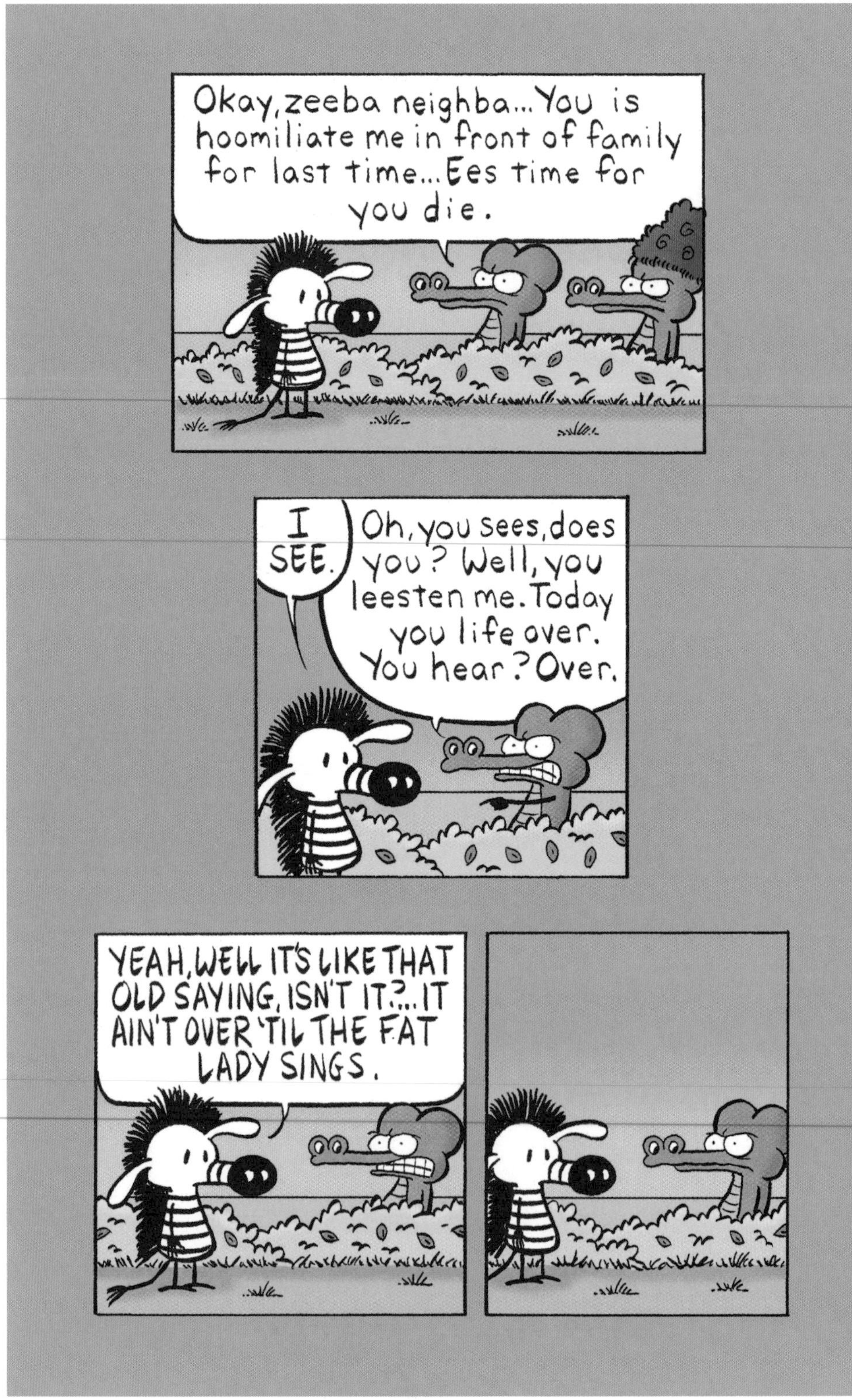
Okay, zeeba neighba... You is hoomiliate me in front of family for last time... Ees time for you die.
I SEE.
Oh, you sees, does you? Well, you leesten me. Today you life over. You hear? Over.
YEAH, WELL IT'S LIKE THAT OLD SAYING, ISN'T IT?... IT AIN'T OVER 'TIL THE FAT LADY SINGS.

WHAT ARE YOU WAITING FOR, LARRY? ARE YOU JUST GONNA LET HIM TAUNT YOU LIKE THAT?!
Me was hoping you know a few tunes.
Mebbe not.

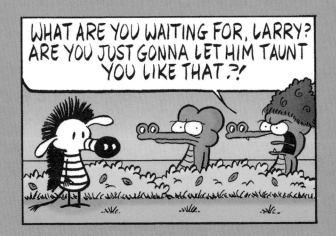

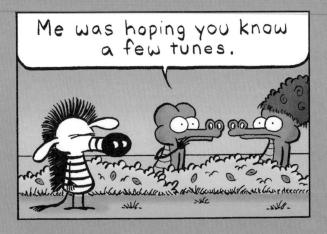

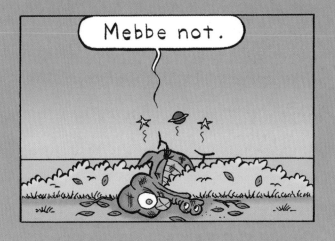

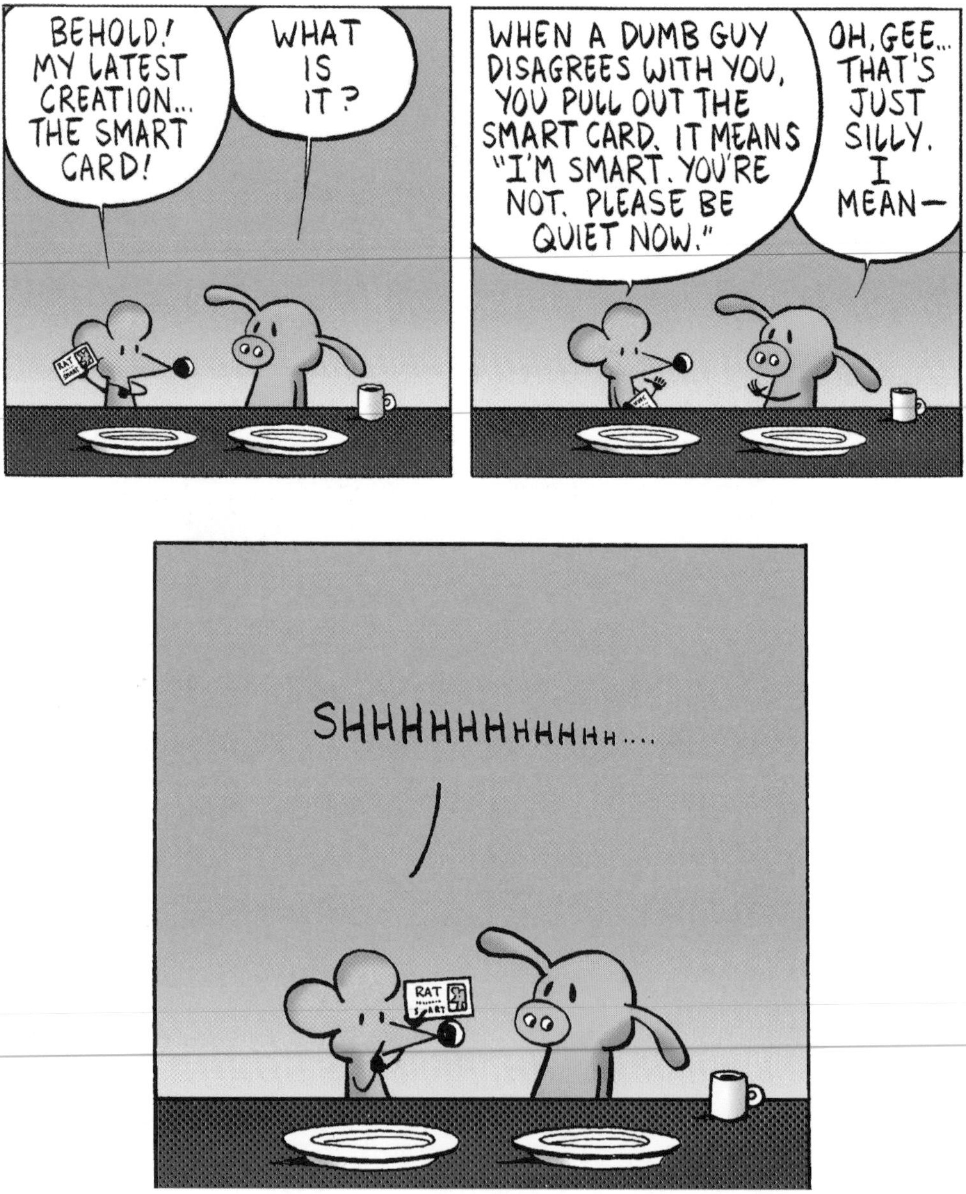
BEHOLD! MY LATEST CREATION... THE SMART CARD!
WHAT IS IT?
WHEN A DUMB GUY DISAGREES WITH YOU, YOU PULL OUT THE SMART CARD. IT MEANS "I'M SMART. YOU'RE NOT. PLEASE BE QUIET NOW."
OH, GEE... THAT'S JUST SILLY. I MEAN—
SHHHHHHHHHHH....

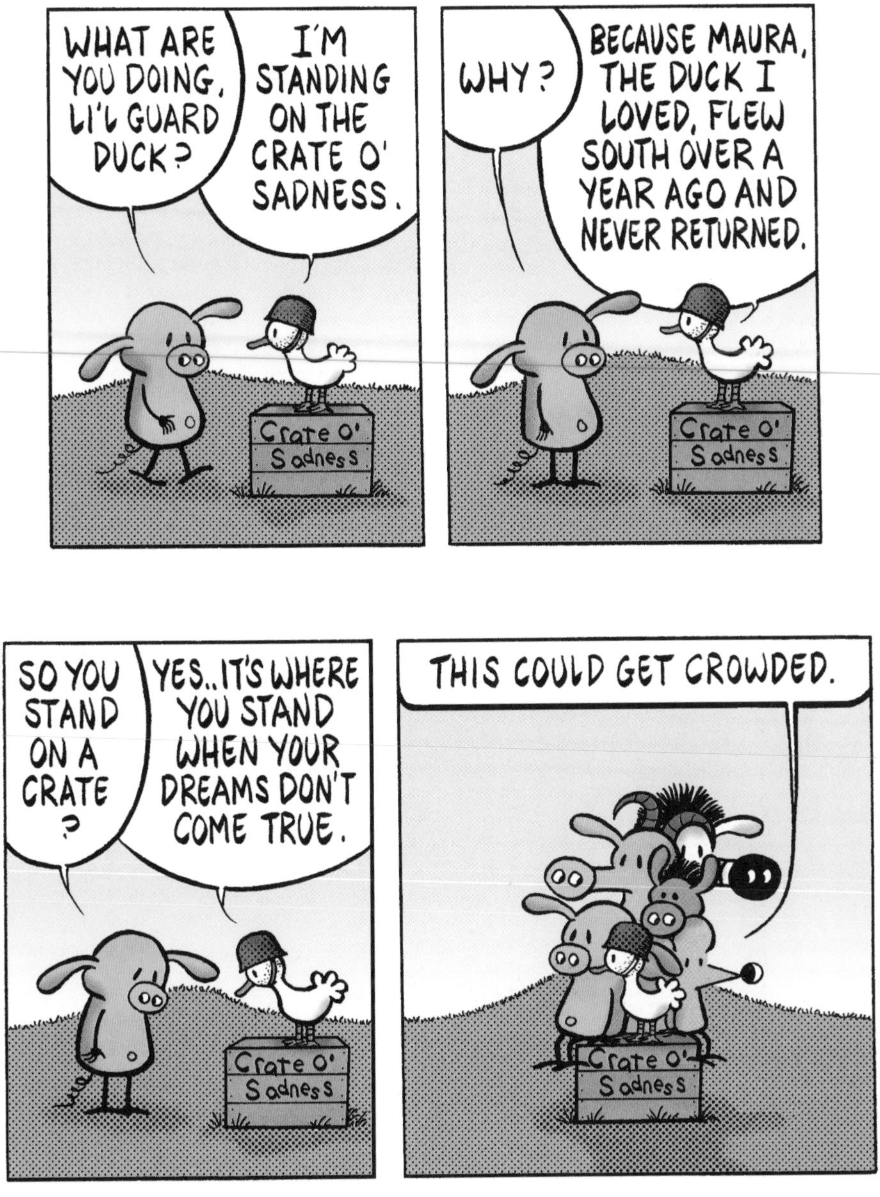
WHAT ARE YOU DOING, LI'L GUARD DUCK?
I'M STANDING ON THE CRATE O' SADNESS.
Crate O' Sadness
WHY?
BECAUSE MAURA, THE DUCK I LOVED, FLEW SOUTH OVER A YEAR AGO AND NEVER RETURNED.
Crate O' Sadness
SO YOU STAND ON A CRATE?
YES..IT'S WHERE YOU STAND WHEN YOUR DREAMS DON'T COME TRUE.
Crate O' Sadness
THIS COULD GET CROWDED.
Crate O' Sadness

Zeeba neighba! Me is fall down! Break leg! Help!
FAT CHANCE.. THE SECOND I DID THAT, YOUR BUDDY LARRY WOULD JUMP OUT OF THAT BUSH AND KILL ME.
Ohh, dat not true, Meester Zeeba.
LISTEN. YOUR PAL LARRY HAS THE MIND OF A LITTLE KID.. ALL I HAVE TO DO IS CALL OUT HIS NAME AND HE'LL POP OUT... WATCH...
COME OUT OF THAT BUSH LARRY!

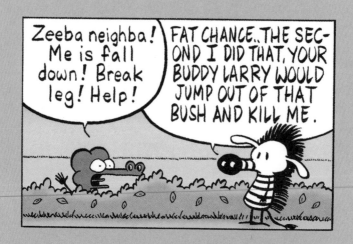

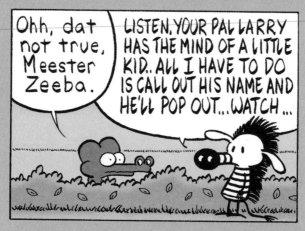

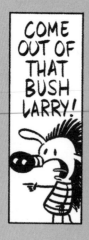

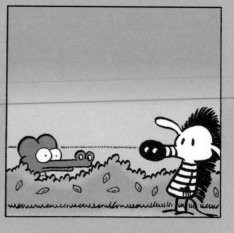

Ooooh...You so smart, Meester Zeeba.. HAHAHA See, what me tell yous? No Larry.
SIMON SAYS COME OUT OF THAT BUSH, LARRY!
Simon says you beeg fat idiot, Larry.
Simon no say dat, Bob.

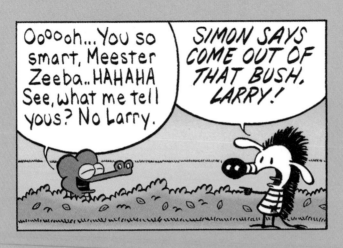

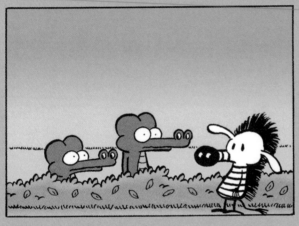

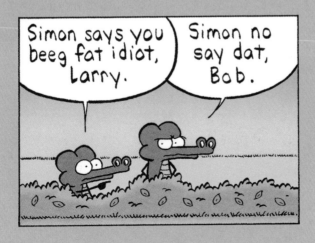

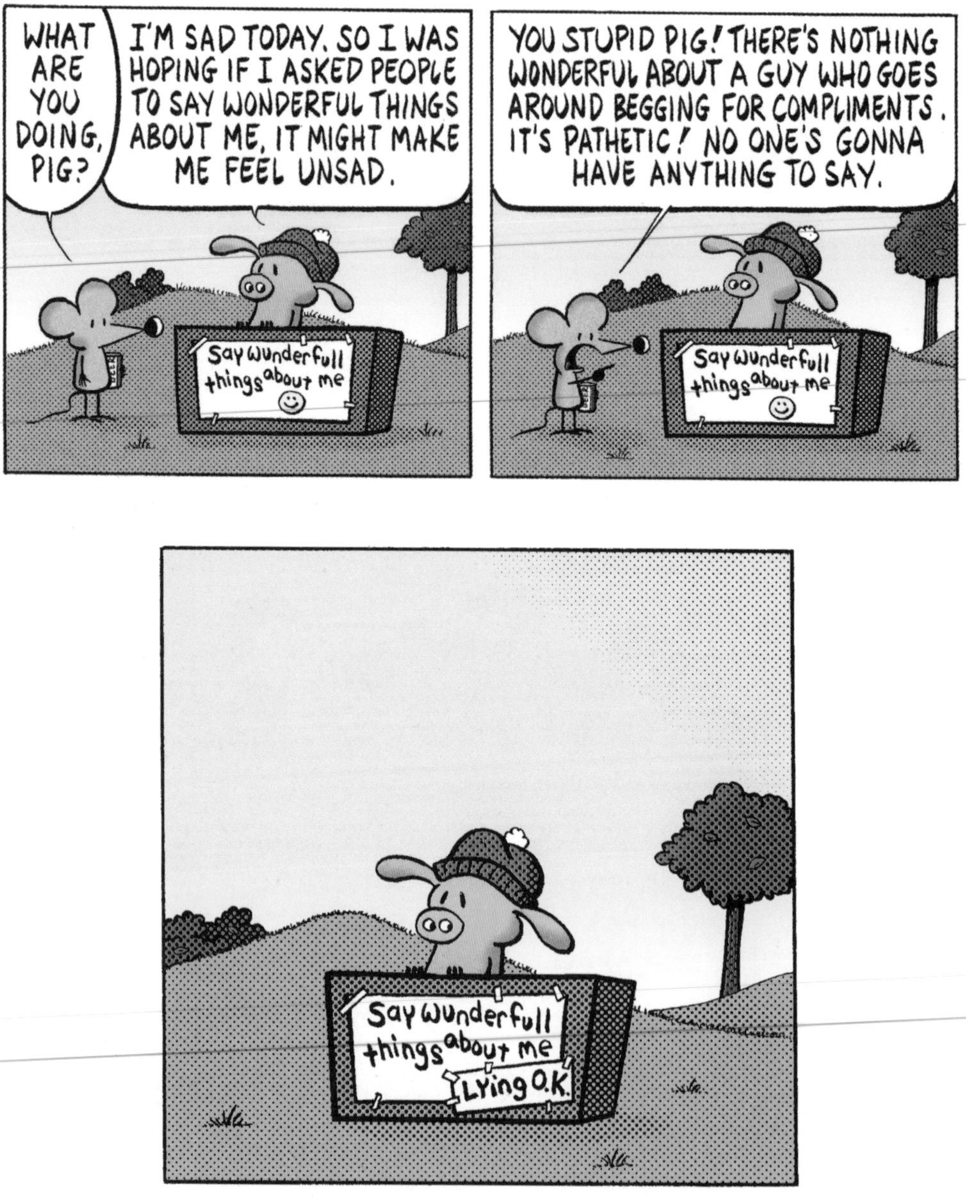
WHAT ARE YOU DOING, PIG?
I'M SAD TODAY. SO I WAS HOPING IF I ASKED PEOPLE TO SAY WONDERFUL THINGS ABOUT ME, IT MIGHT MAKE ME FEEL UNSAD.
Say wunderfull things about me
YOU STUPID PIG! THERE'S NOTHING WONDERFUL ABOUT A GUY WHO GOES AROUND BEGGING FOR COMPLIMENTS. IT'S PATHETIC! NO ONE'S GONNA HAVE ANYTHING TO SAY.
Say wunderfull things about me
Say wunderfull things about me
Lying O.K.

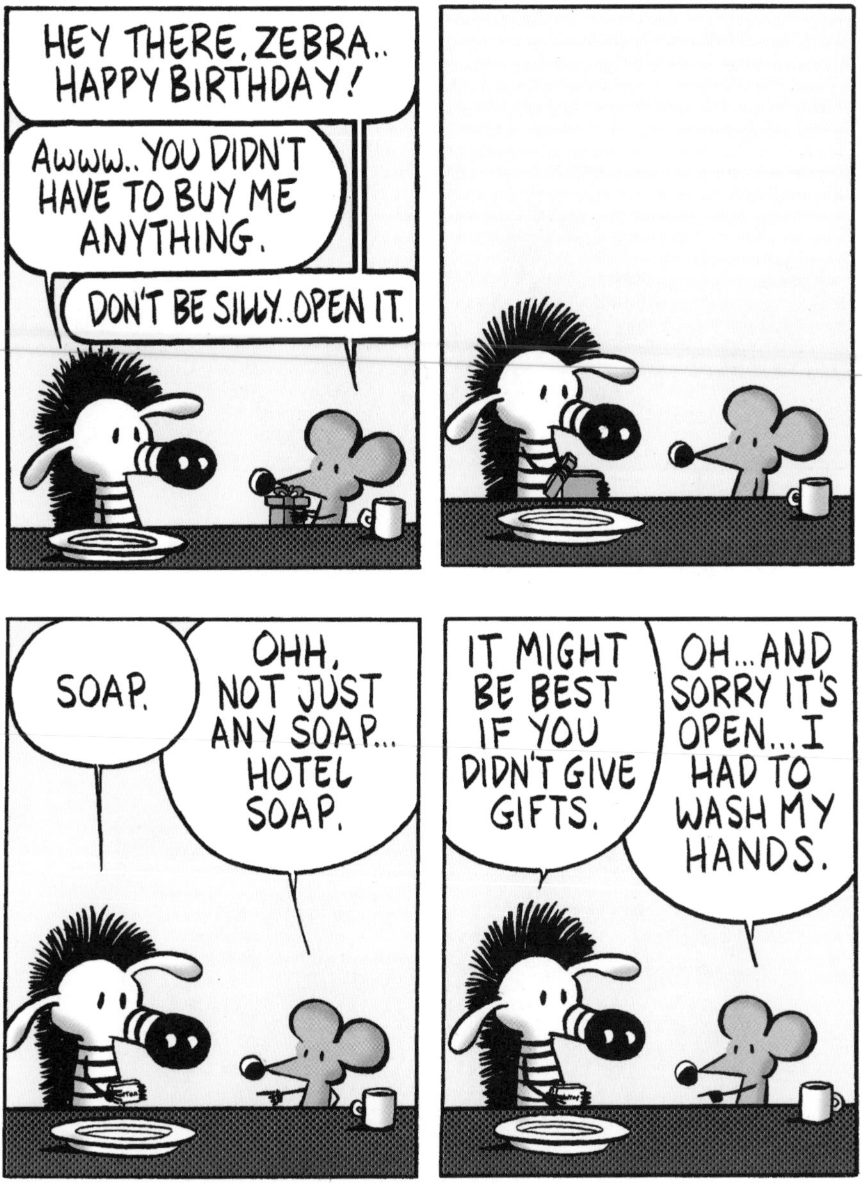
HEY THERE, ZEBRA.. HAPPY BIRTHDAY!
AWWW.. YOU DIDN'T HAVE TO BUY ME ANYTHING.
DON'T BE SILLY..OPEN IT.
SOAP.
OHH, NOT JUST ANY SOAP... HOTEL SOAP.
IT MIGHT BE BEST IF YOU DIDN'T GIVE GIFTS.
OH...AND SORRY IT'S OPEN...I HAD TO WASH MY HANDS.

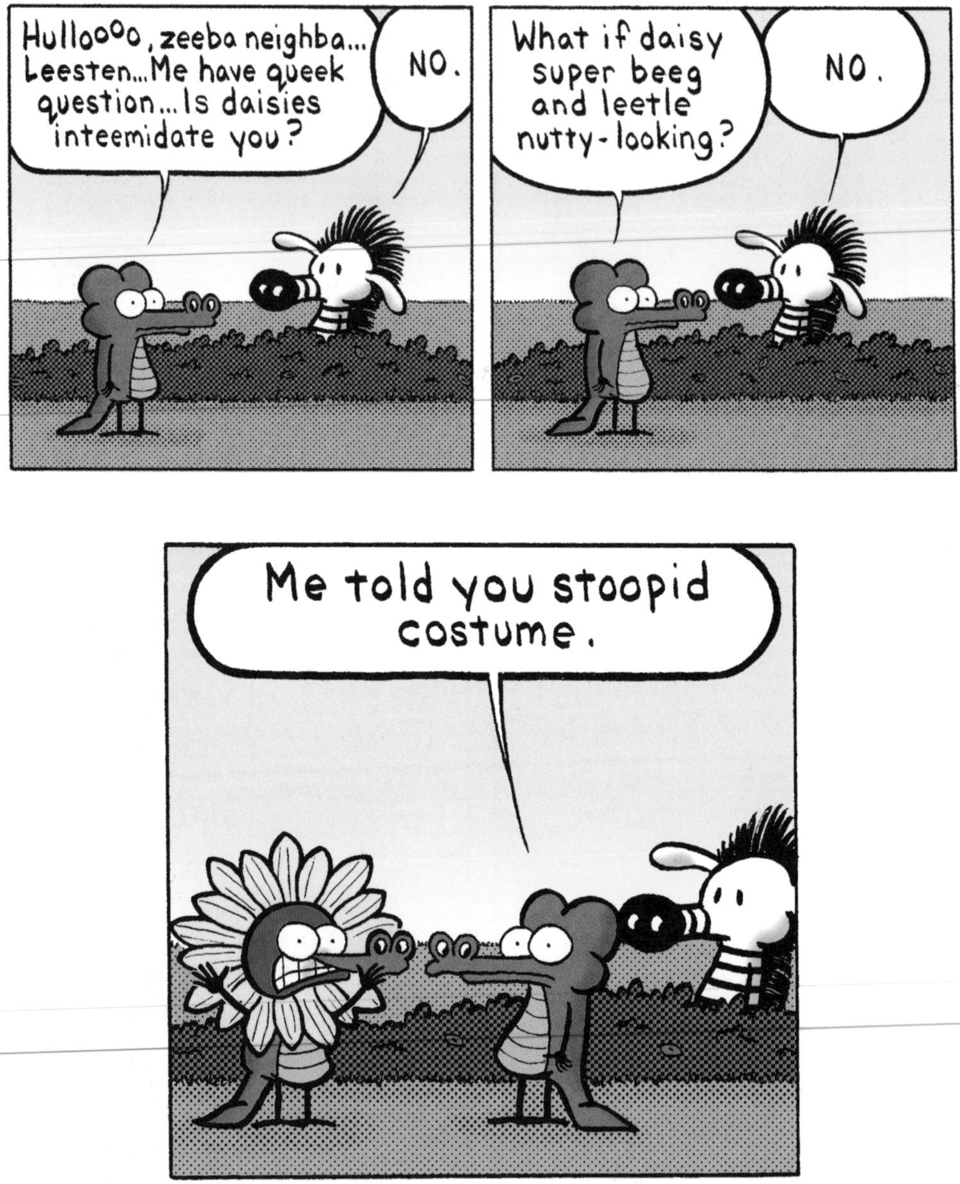
Hulloooo, zeeba neighba... Leesten...Me have queek question... Is daisies inteemidate you?
NO.
What if daisy super beeg and leetle nutty-looking?
NO.
Me told you stoopid costume.

HELLO, SIR... I'M HY, FROM HY AND HY'S FUNERAL HOME.. HAVE YOU BY CHANCE A DECEASED RELATIVE IN NEED OF OUR BURIAL SERVICES?

FORGET IT. YOU'RE HYENAS... EVERYONE KNOWS YOU EAT DEAD THINGS.

PLEASE, SIR... THAT'S QUITE INSULTING. WE'RE NOT LIKE THOSE OTHER HYENAS.

WELL, YOU MIGHT WANT TO CHAT WITH YOUR PARTNER THERE...

NICE GOING, HY.

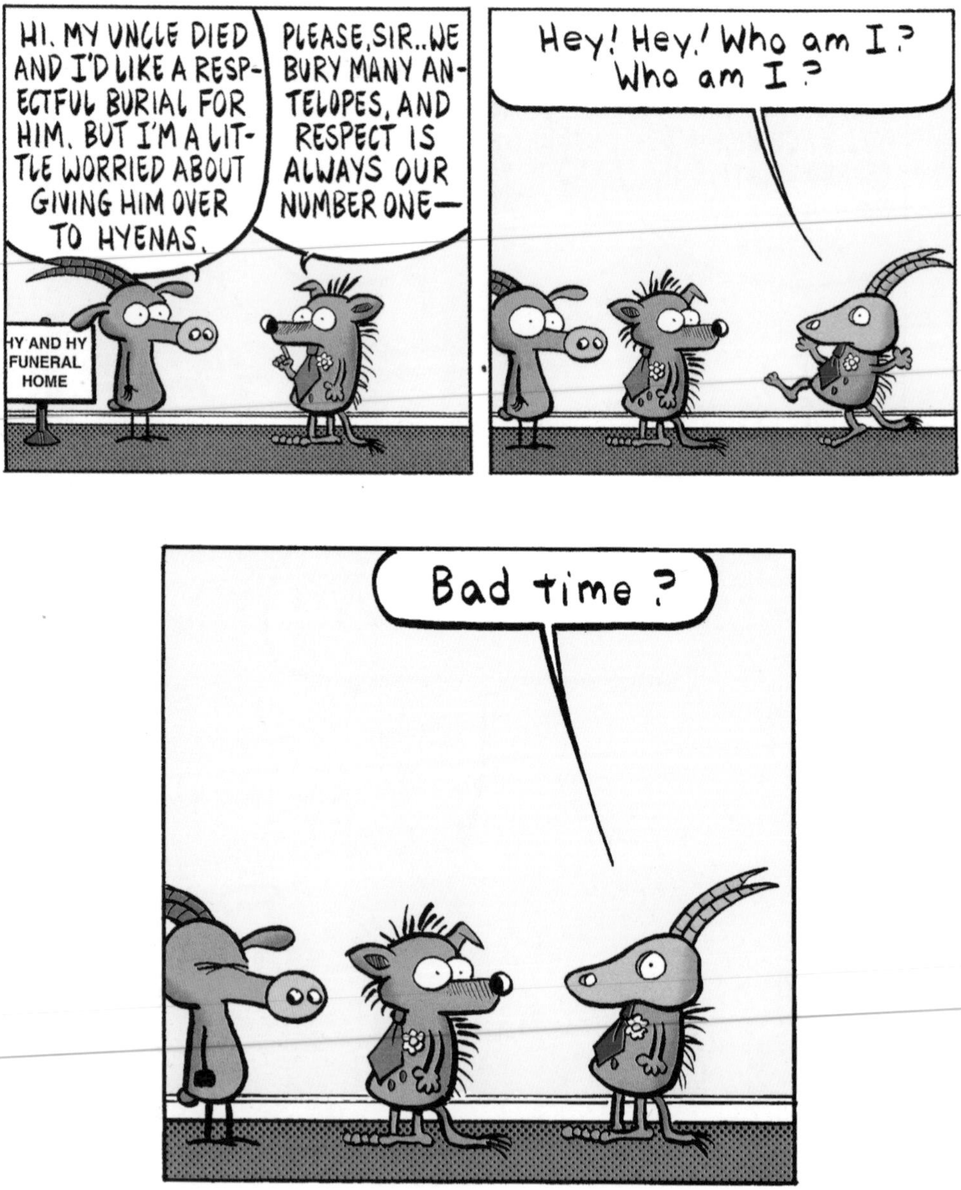
HY AND HY FUNERAL HOME
HI. MY UNCLE DIED AND I'D LIKE A RESPECTFUL BURIAL FOR HIM. BUT I'M A LITTLE WORRIED ABOUT GIVING HIM OVER TO HYENAS.
PLEASE, SIR.. WE BURY MANY ANTELOPES, AND RESPECT IS ALWAYS OUR NUMBER ONE—
Hey! Hey! Who am I? Who am I?
Bad time?

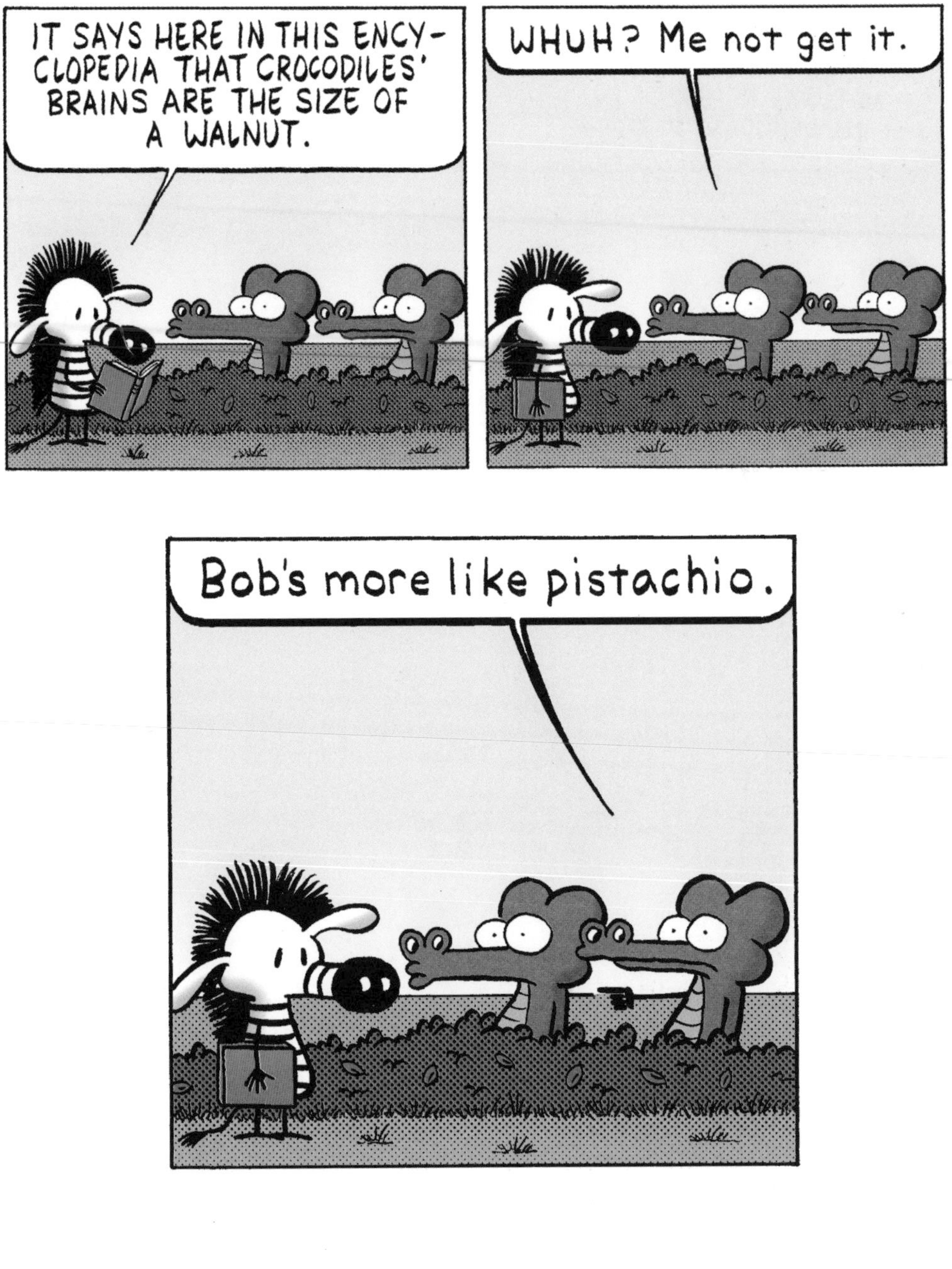
IT SAYS HERE IN THIS ENCY-CLOPEDIA THAT CROCODILES' BRAINS ARE THE SIZE OF A WALNUT.
WHUH? Me not get it.
Bob's more like pistachio.

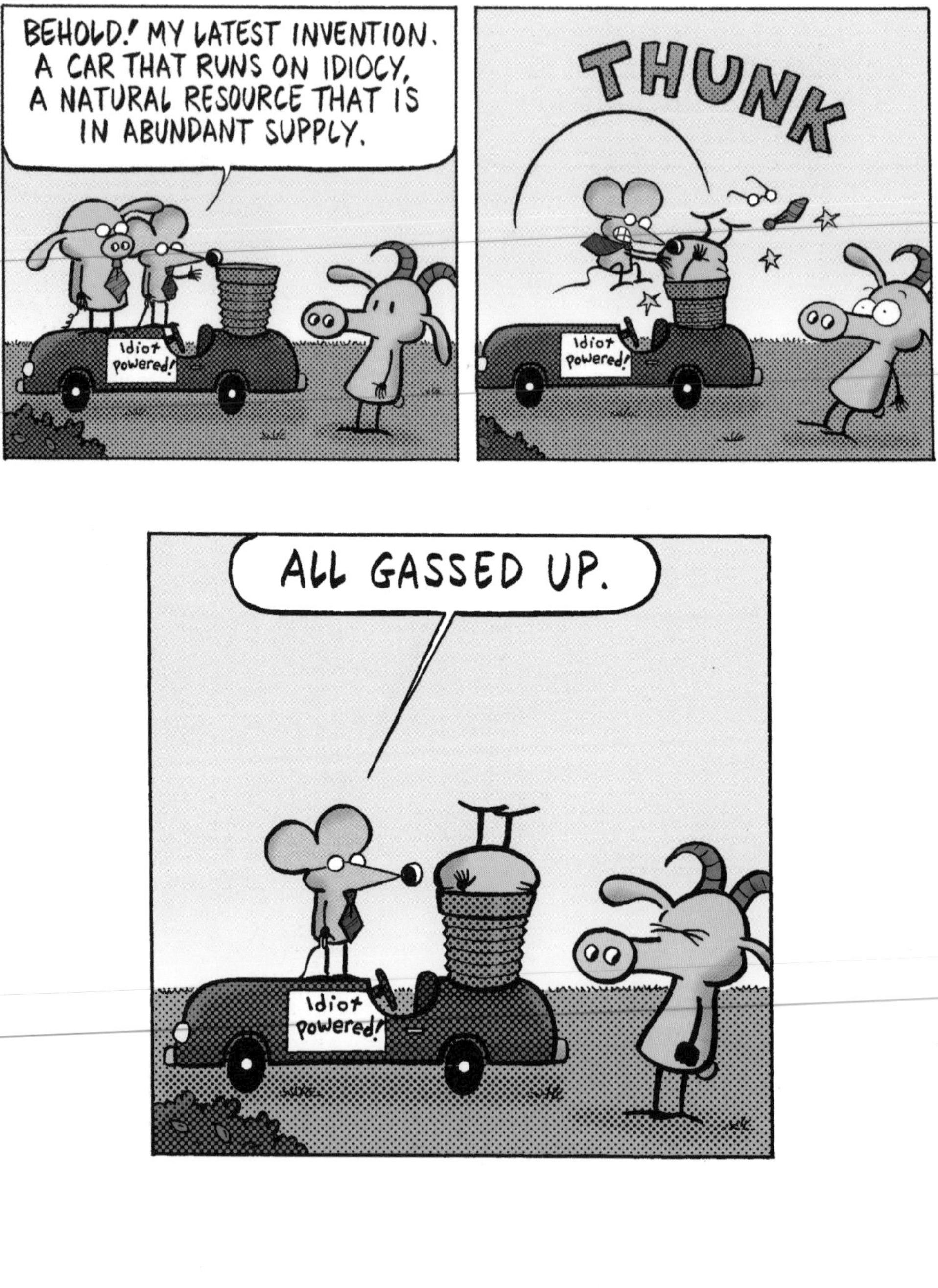
BEHOLD! MY LATEST INVENTION. A CAR THAT RUNS ON IDIOCY, A NATURAL RESOURCE THAT IS IN ABUNDANT SUPPLY.
Idiot Powered!
THUNK
Idiot Powered!
ALL GASSED UP.
Idiot Powered!

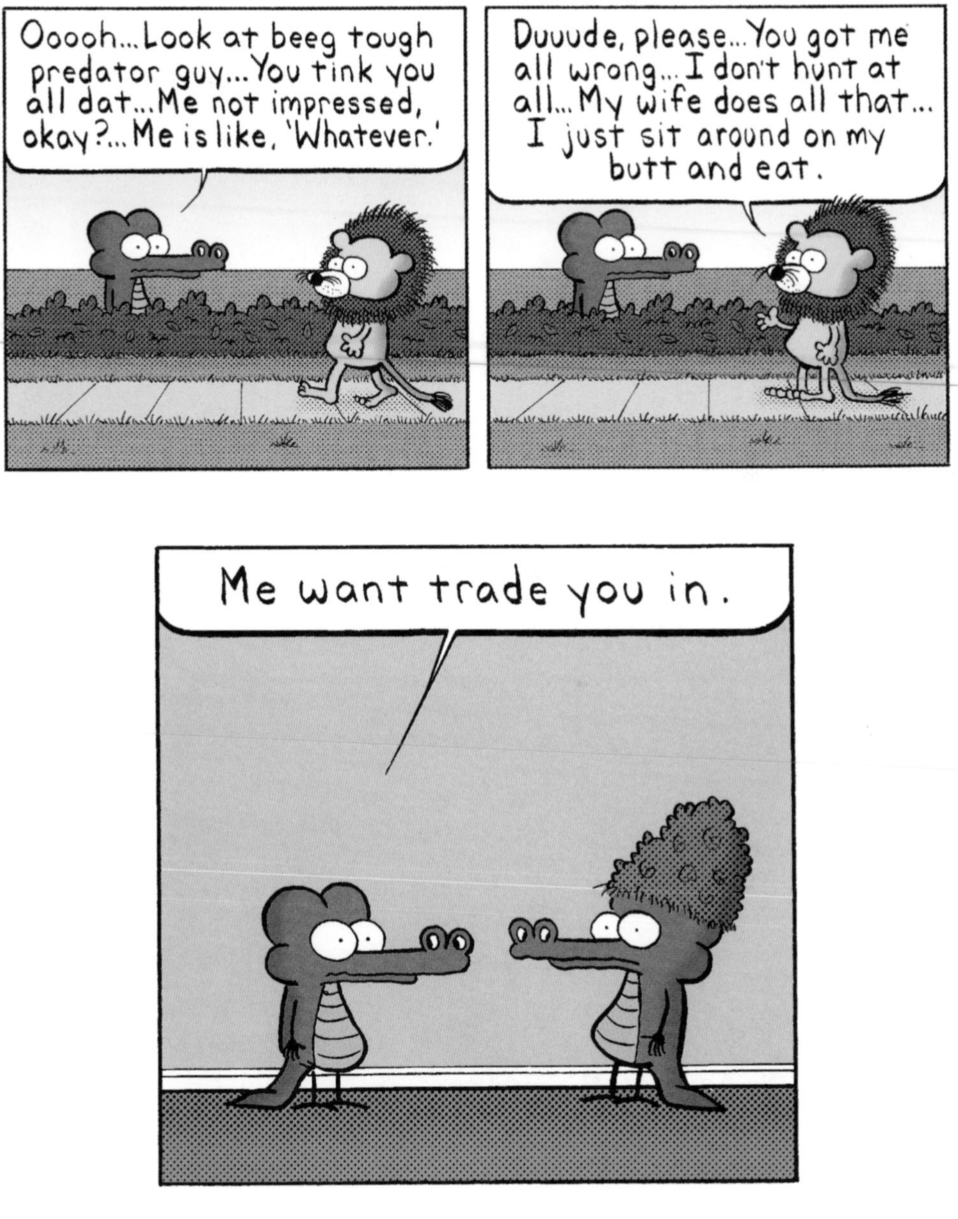
Ooooh... Look at beeg tough predator guy... You tink you all dat... Me not impressed, okay?... Me is like, 'Whatever.'
Duuude, please... You got me all wrong... I don't hunt at all... My wife does all that... I just sit around on my butt and eat.
Me want trade you in.

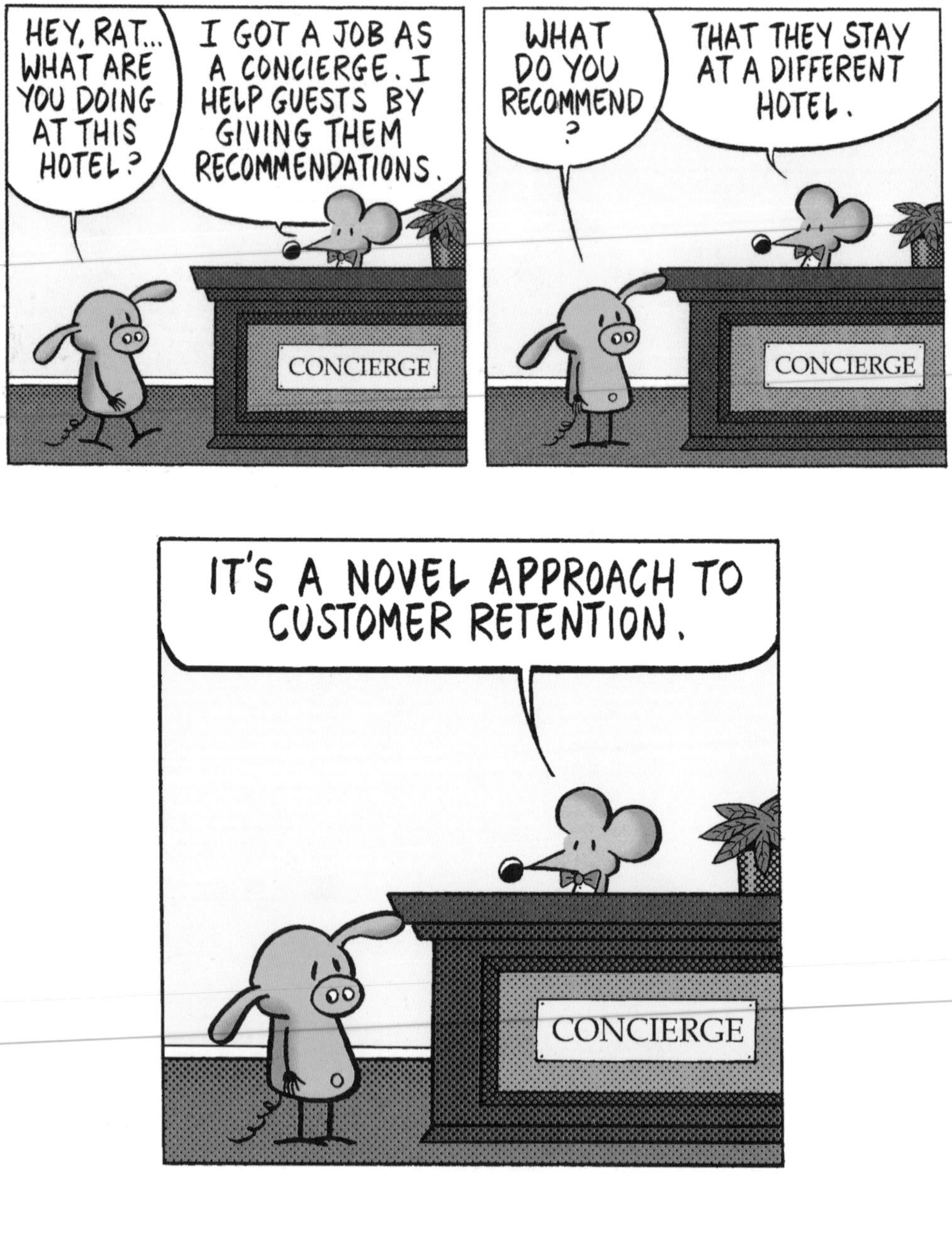
HEY, RAT... WHAT ARE YOU DOING AT THIS HOTEL?
I GOT A JOB AS A CONCIERGE. I HELP GUESTS BY GIVING THEM RECOMMENDATIONS.
CONCIERGE
WHAT DO YOU RECOMMEND?
THAT THEY STAY AT A DIFFERENT HOTEL.
CONCIERGE
IT'S A NOVEL APPROACH TO CUSTOMER RETENTION.
CONCIERGE

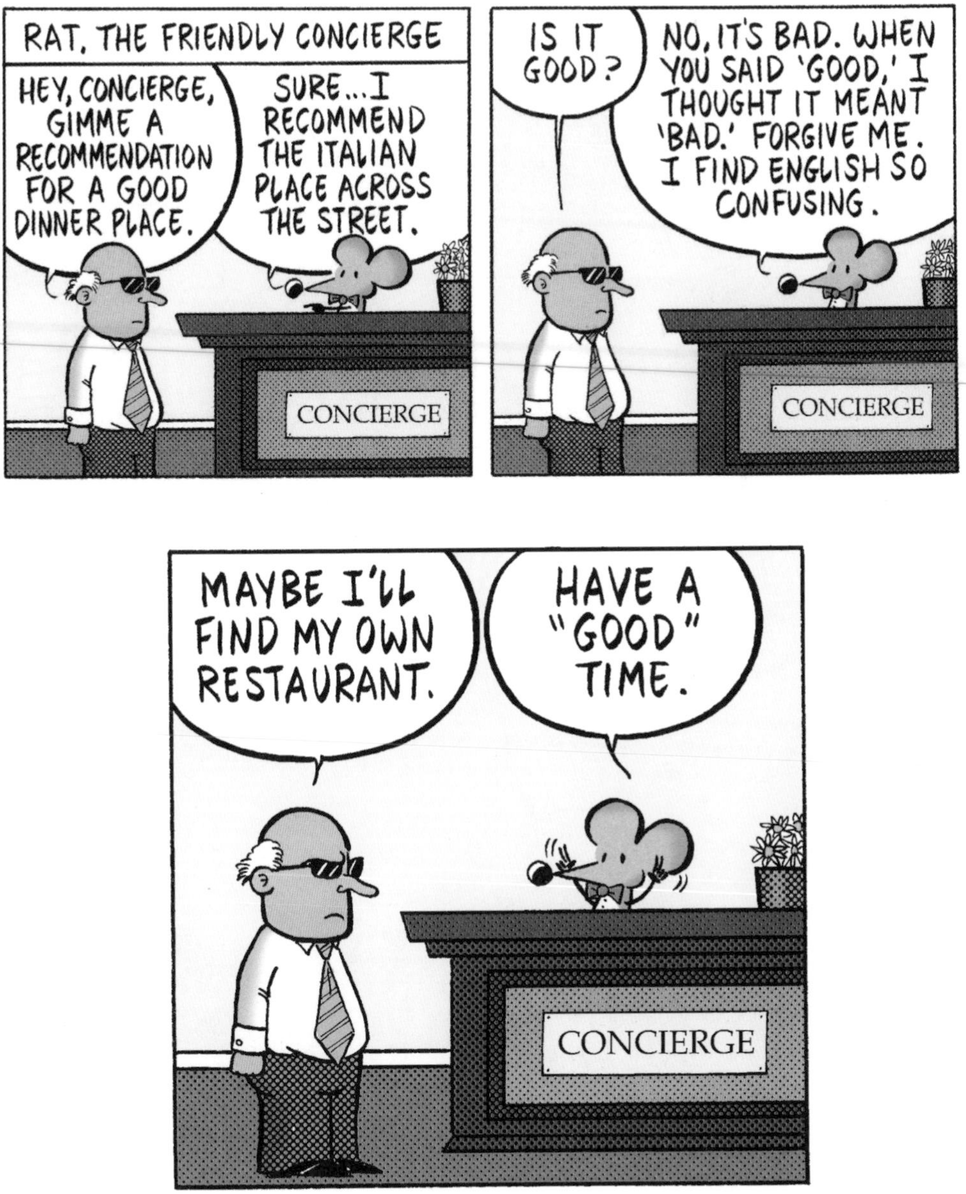
RAT, THE FRIENDLY CONCIERGE
HEY, CONCIERGE, GIMME A RECOMMENDATION FOR A GOOD DINNER PLACE.
SURE...I RECOMMEND THE ITALIAN PLACE ACROSS THE STREET.
CONCIERGE
IS IT GOOD?
NO, IT'S BAD. WHEN YOU SAID 'GOOD,' I THOUGHT IT MEANT 'BAD.' FORGIVE ME. I FIND ENGLISH SO CONFUSING.
CONCIERGE
MAYBE I'LL FIND MY OWN RESTAURANT.
HAVE A "GOOD" TIME.
CONCIERGE

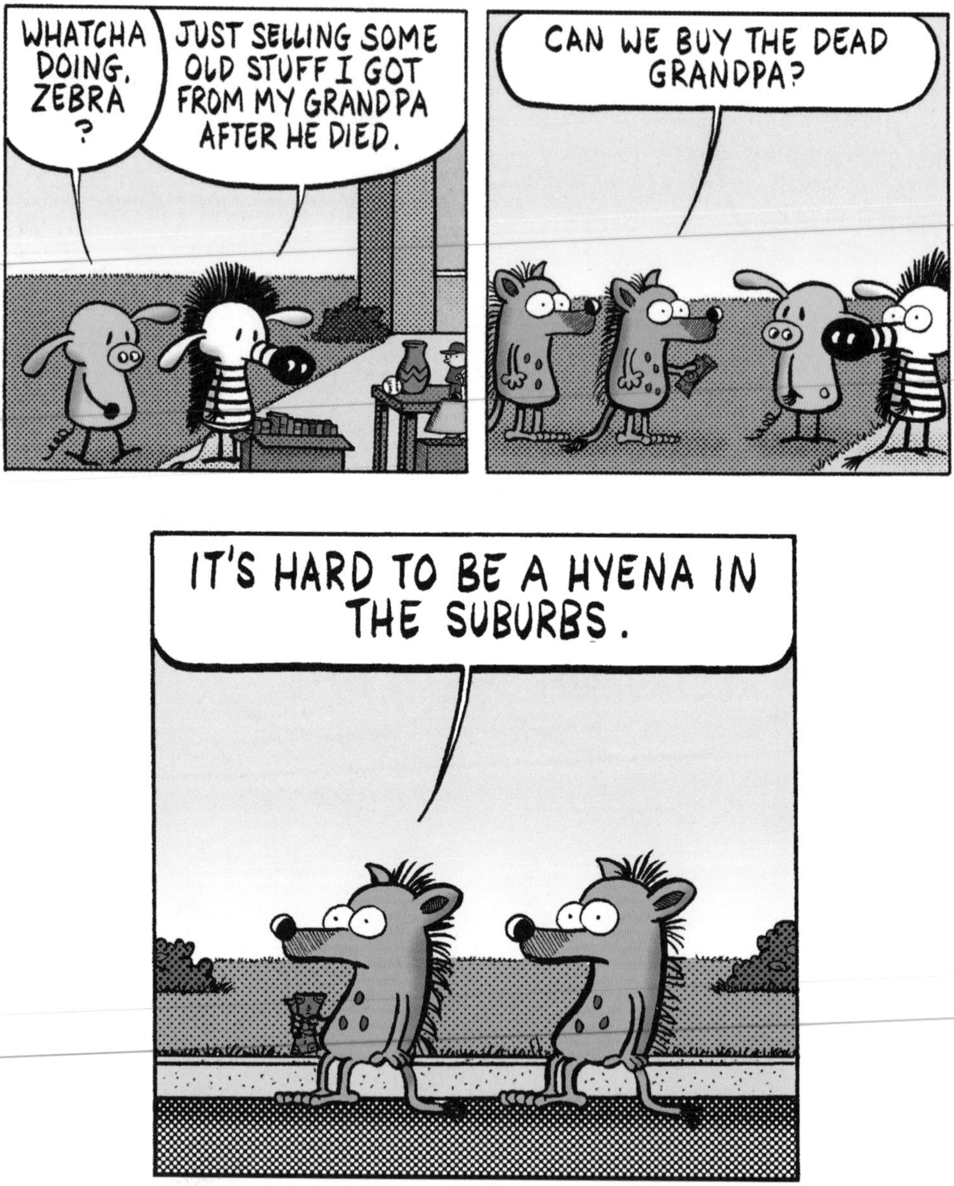
WHATCHA DOING, ZEBRA ?
JUST SELLING SOME OLD STUFF I GOT FROM MY GRANDPA AFTER HE DIED.
CAN WE BUY THE DEAD GRANDPA?
IT'S HARD TO BE A HYENA IN THE SUBURBS.

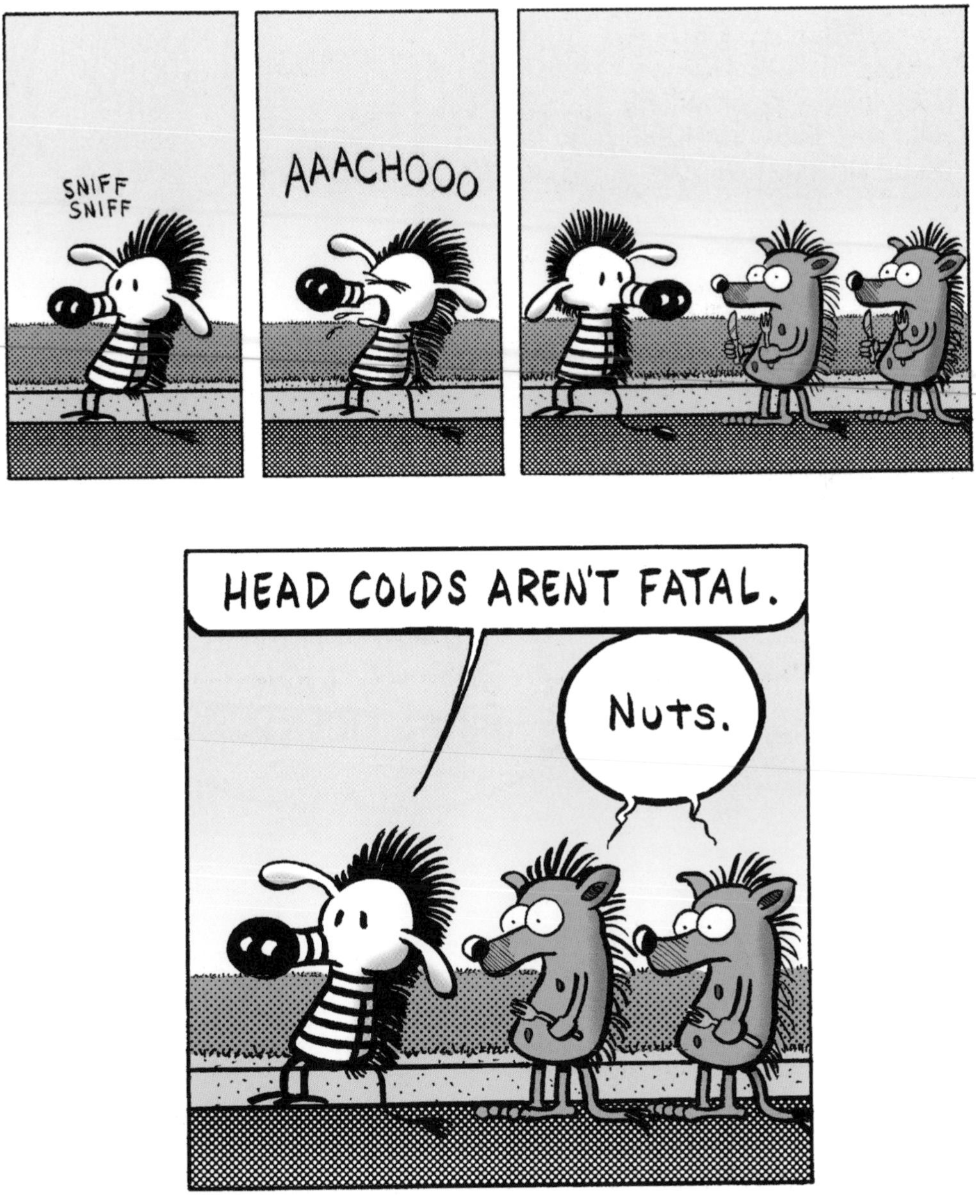
SNIFF SNIFF
AAACHOOO
HEAD COLDS AREN'T FATAL.
Nuts.

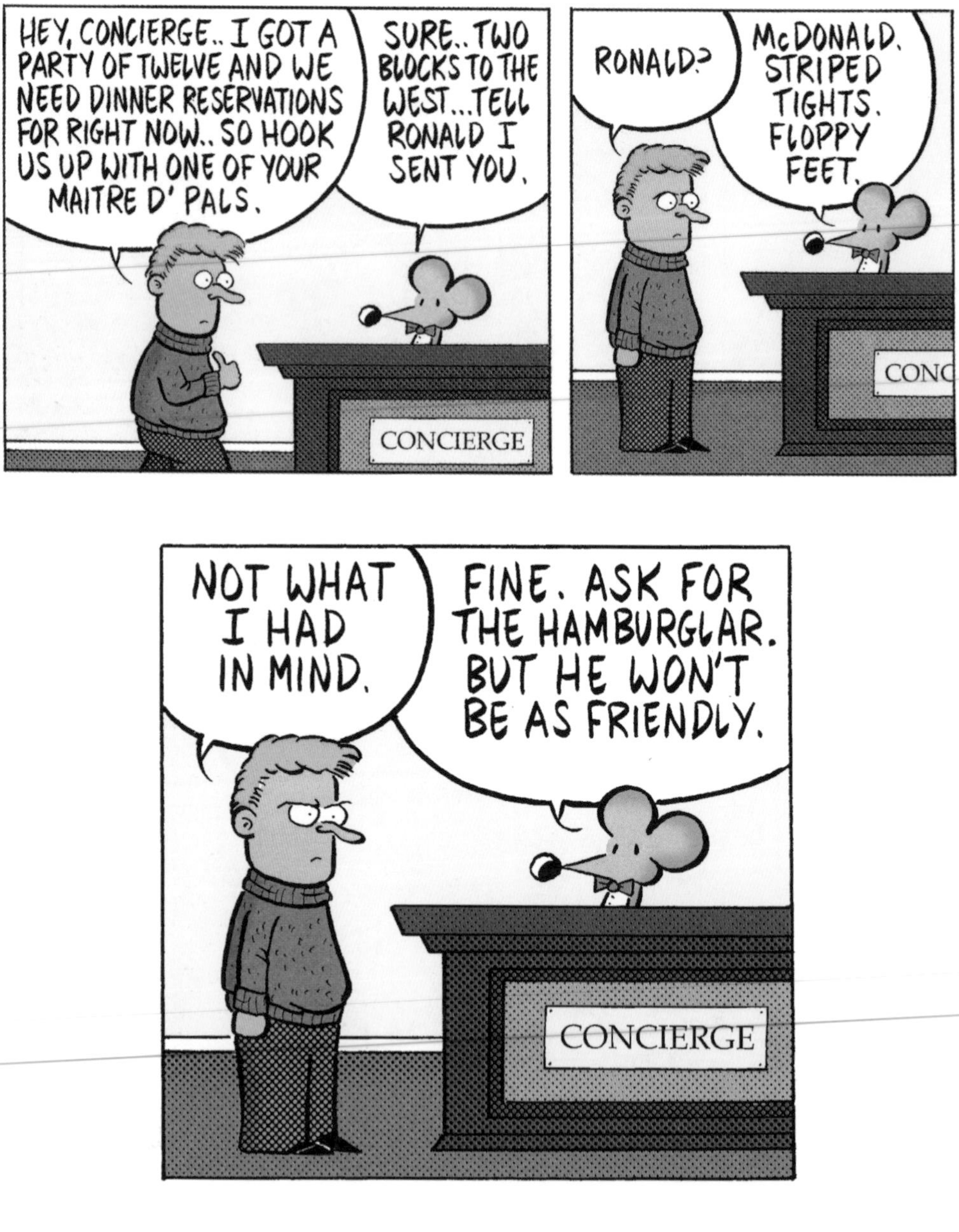
HEY, CONCIERGE.. I GOT A PARTY OF TWELVE AND WE NEED DINNER RESERVATIONS FOR RIGHT NOW.. SO HOOK US UP WITH ONE OF YOUR MAITRE D' PALS.
SURE.. TWO BLOCKS TO THE WEST...TELL RONALD I SENT YOU.
CONCIERGE
RONALD?
McDONALD. STRIPED TIGHTS. FLOPPY FEET.
CONC
NOT WHAT I HAD IN MIND.
FINE. ASK FOR THE HAMBURGLAR. BUT HE WON'T BE AS FRIENDLY.
CONCIERGE

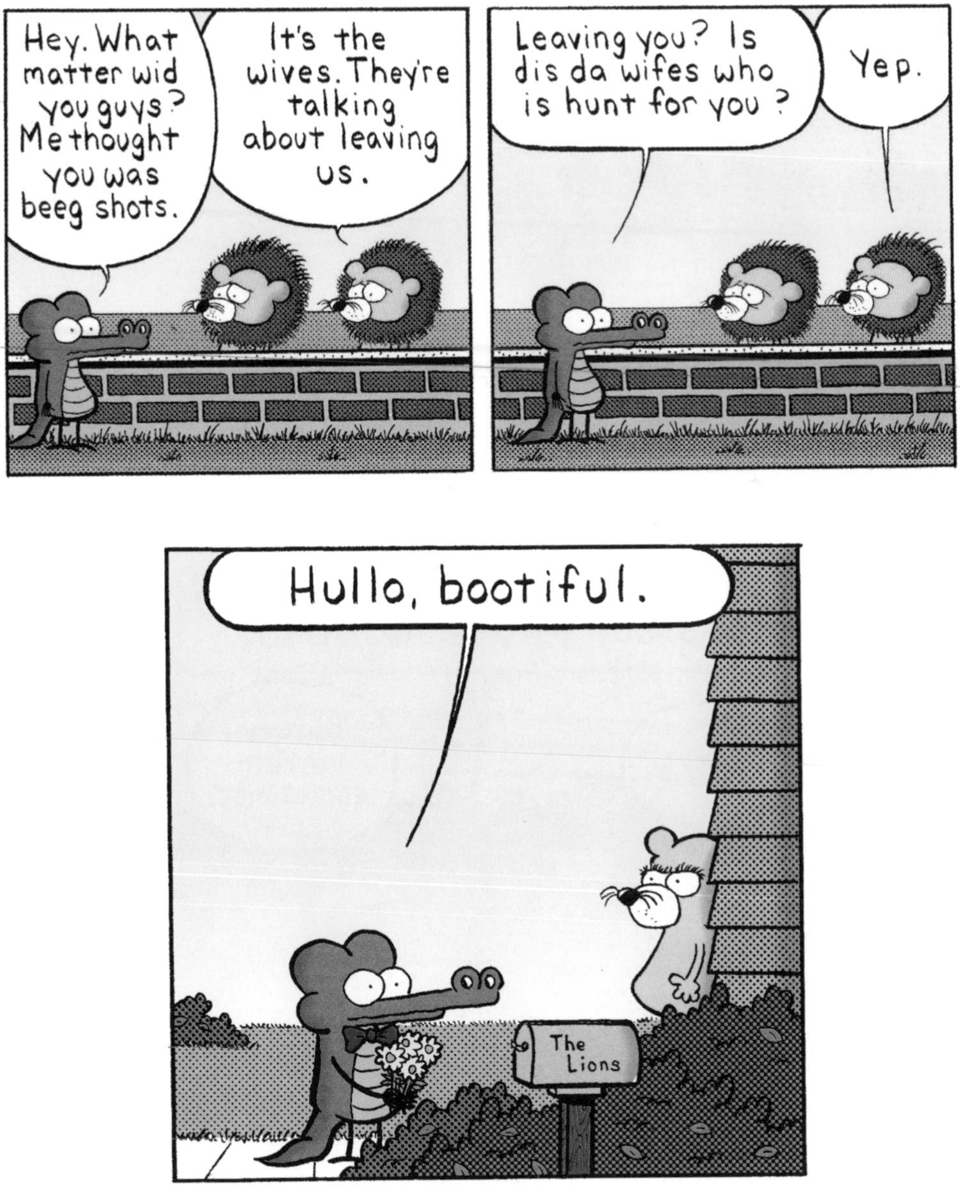
Hey. What matter wid you guys? Me thought you was beeg shots.
It's the wives. They're talking about leaving us.
Leaving you? Is dis da wifes who is hunt for you?
Yep.
Hullo, bootiful.
The Lions

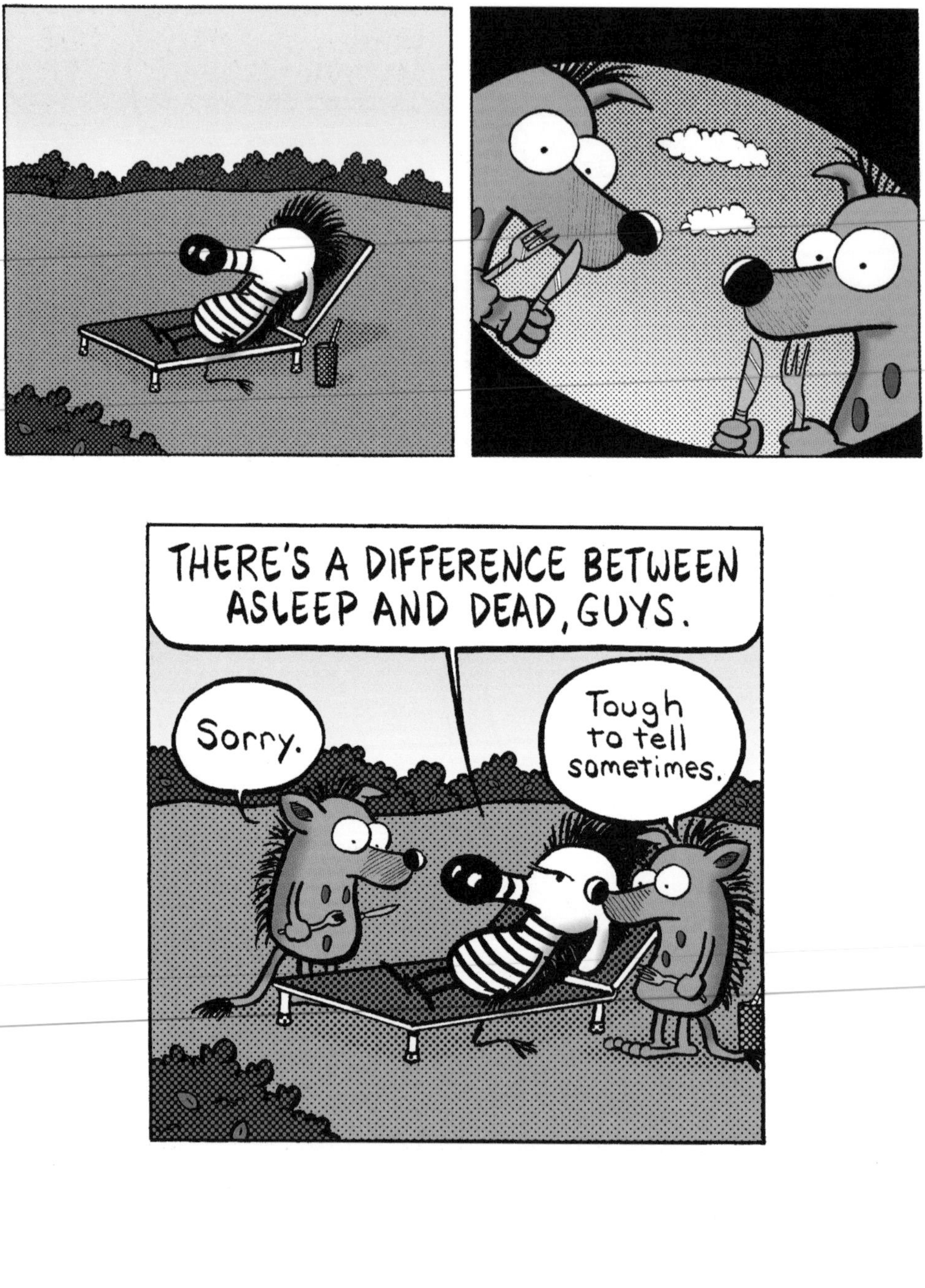
THERE'S A DIFFERENCE BETWEEN ASLEEP AND DEAD, GUYS.
Sorry.
Tough to tell sometimes.

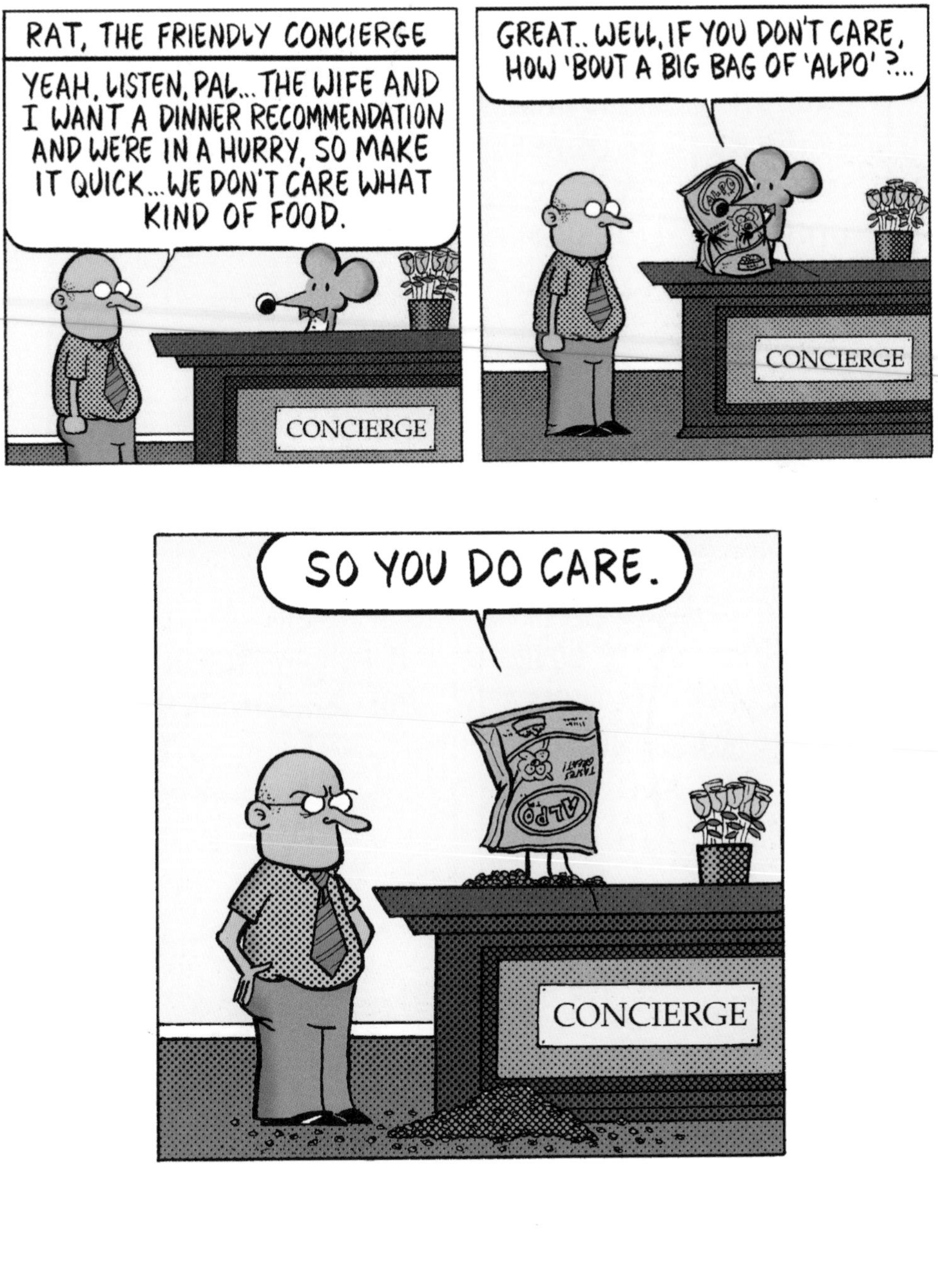
RAT, THE FRIENDLY CONCIERGE
YEAH, LISTEN, PAL... THE WIFE AND I WANT A DINNER RECOMMENDATION AND WE'RE IN A HURRY, SO MAKE IT QUICK... WE DON'T CARE WHAT KIND OF FOOD.
CONCIERGE
GREAT.. WELL, IF YOU DON'T CARE, HOW 'BOUT A BIG BAG OF 'ALPO' ?...
CONCIERGE
SO YOU DO CARE.
ALPO
TASTES GREAT!
CONCIERGE

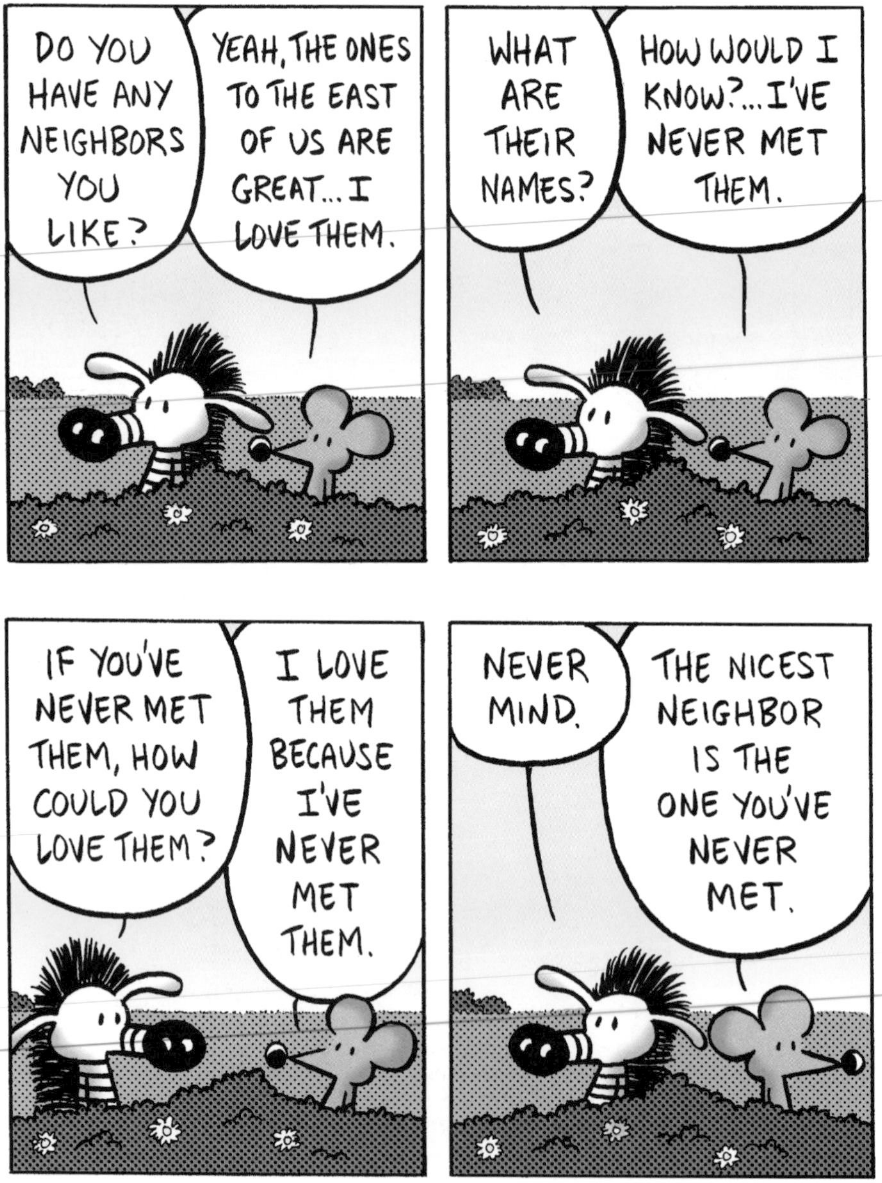
DO YOU HAVE ANY NEIGHBORS YOU LIKE?
YEAH, THE ONES TO THE EAST OF US ARE GREAT... I LOVE THEM.
WHAT ARE THEIR NAMES?
HOW WOULD I KNOW?... I'VE NEVER MET THEM.
IF YOU'VE NEVER MET THEM, HOW COULD YOU LOVE THEM?
I LOVE THEM BECAUSE I'VE NEVER MET THEM.
NEVER MIND.
THE NICEST NEIGHBOR IS THE ONE YOU'VE NEVER MET.

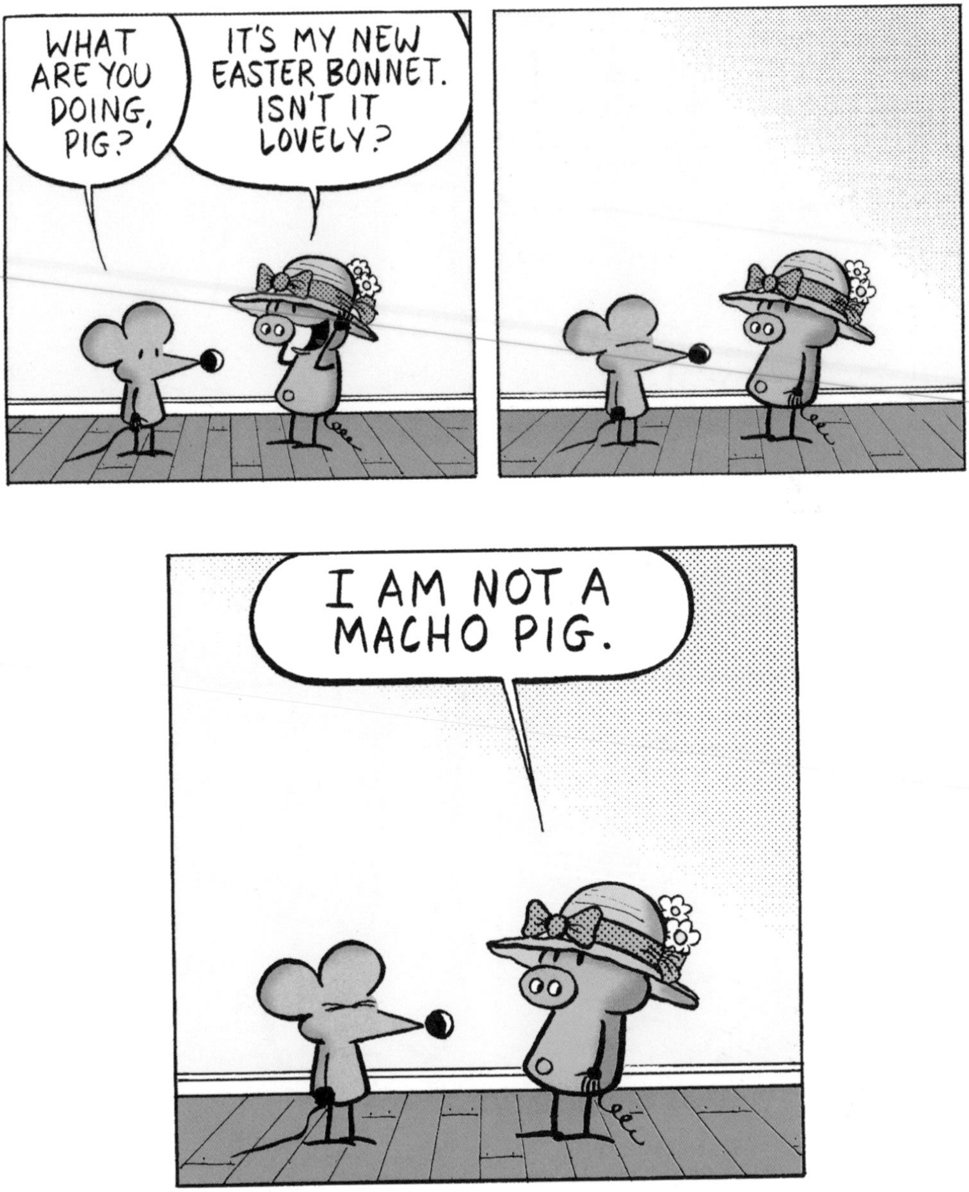
WHAT ARE YOU DOING, PIG?
IT'S MY NEW EASTER BONNET. ISN'T IT LOVELY?
I AM NOT A MACHO PIG.

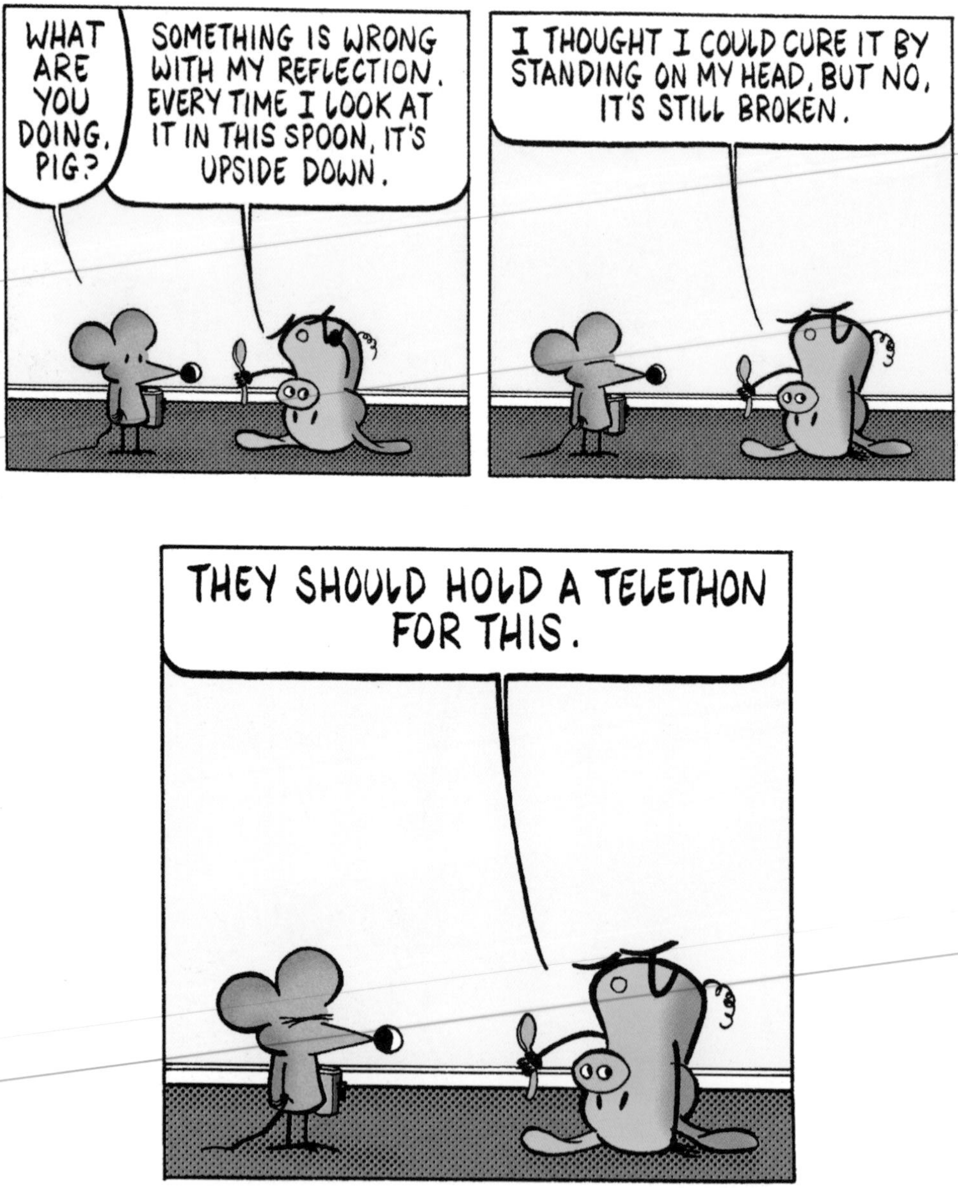
WHAT ARE YOU DOING, PIG?
SOMETHING IS WRONG WITH MY REFLECTION. EVERY TIME I LOOK AT IT IN THIS SPOON, IT'S UPSIDE DOWN.
I THOUGHT I COULD CURE IT BY STANDING ON MY HEAD, BUT NO, IT'S STILL BROKEN.
THEY SHOULD HOLD A TELETHON FOR THIS.

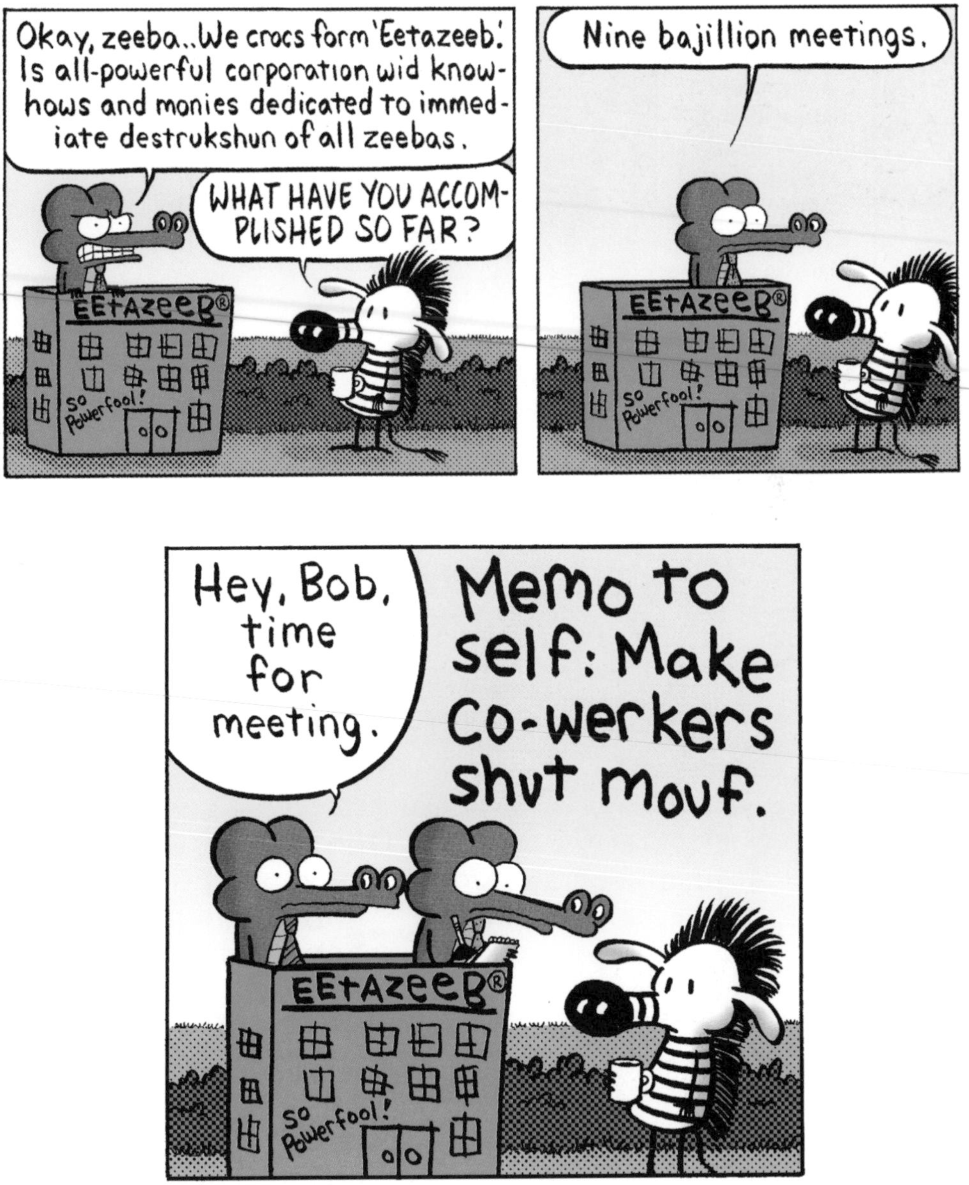
Okay, zeeba..We crocs form 'Eetazeeb.' Is all-powerful corporation wid know-hows and monies dedicated to immed-iate destrukshun of all zeebas.
WHAT HAVE YOU ACCOM-PLISHED SO FAR?
EEtAzeeB®
so Powerfool!
Nine bajillion meetings.
EEtAzeeB®
so Powerfool!
Hey, Bob, time for meeting.
Memo to self: Make co-werkers shut mouf.
EEtAzeeB®
so Powerfool!

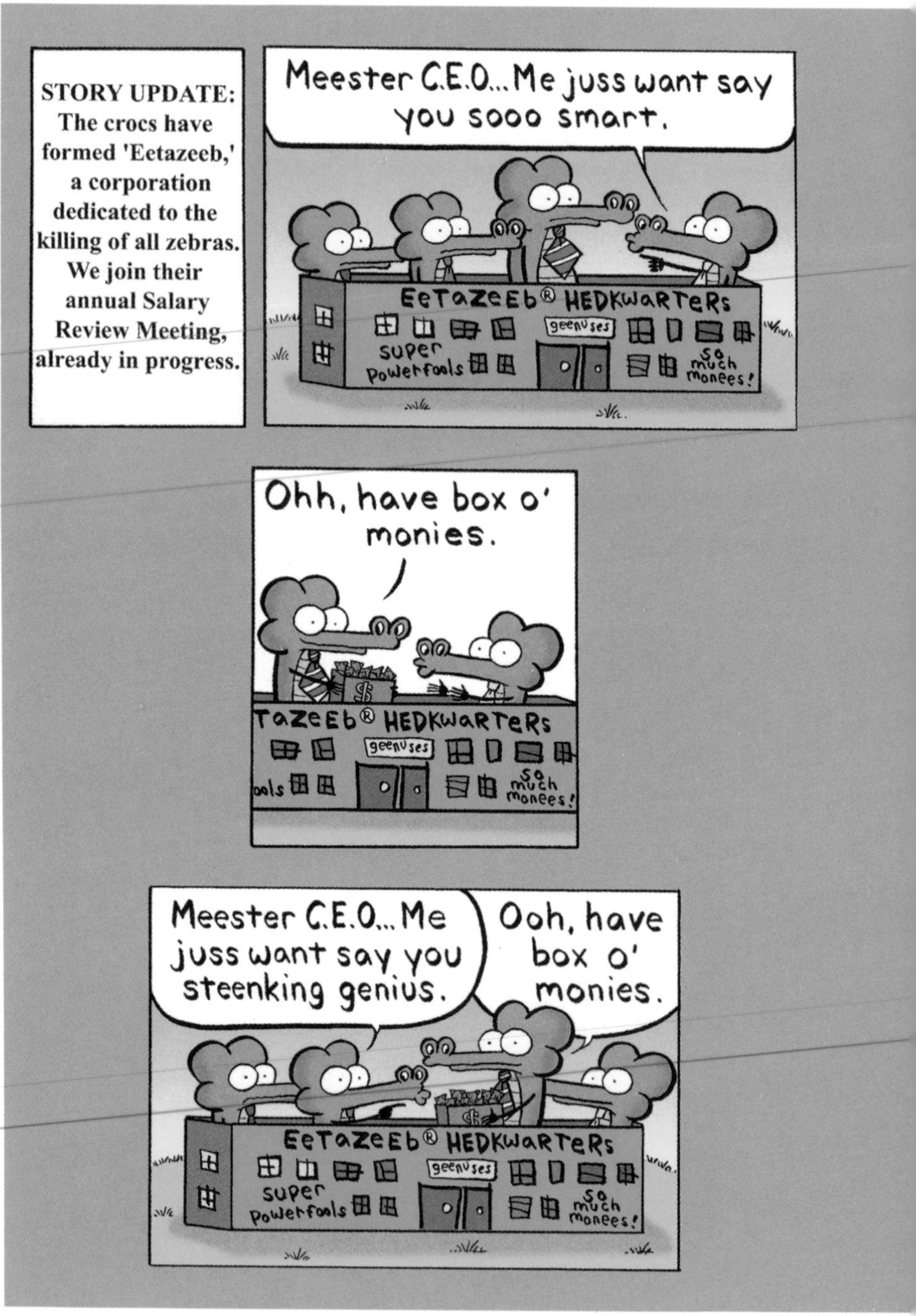
STORY UPDATE: The crocs have formed 'Eetazeeb,' a corporation dedicated to the killing of all zebras. We join their annual Salary Review Meeting, already in progress.
Meester C.E.O... Me juss want say you sooo smart.
EeTazeEb® HEDKWaRTeRs
geenUses
super powerfools
so much monees!
Ohh, have box o' monies.
TazeEb® HEDKWaRTeRs
geenUses
ools
so much monees!
Meester C.E.O... Me juss want say you steenking genius.
Ooh, have box o' monies.
EeTazeEb® HEDKWaRTeRs
geenUses
super powerfools
so much monees!

Meester C.E.O.... No you see? Deese is booty kissers. Dey juss say for monies.
EeTazeEb® HEDKWARTERS
geenuses
super Powerfools
so much monees!
And dat tie sooo bootiful.
Ohh, have *two* box o' monies.

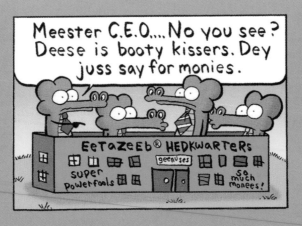

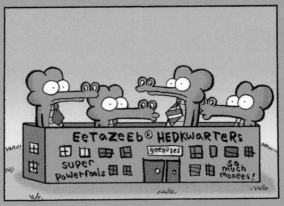

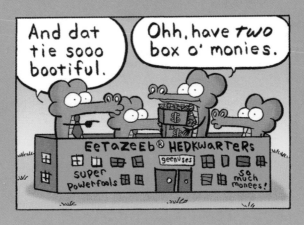

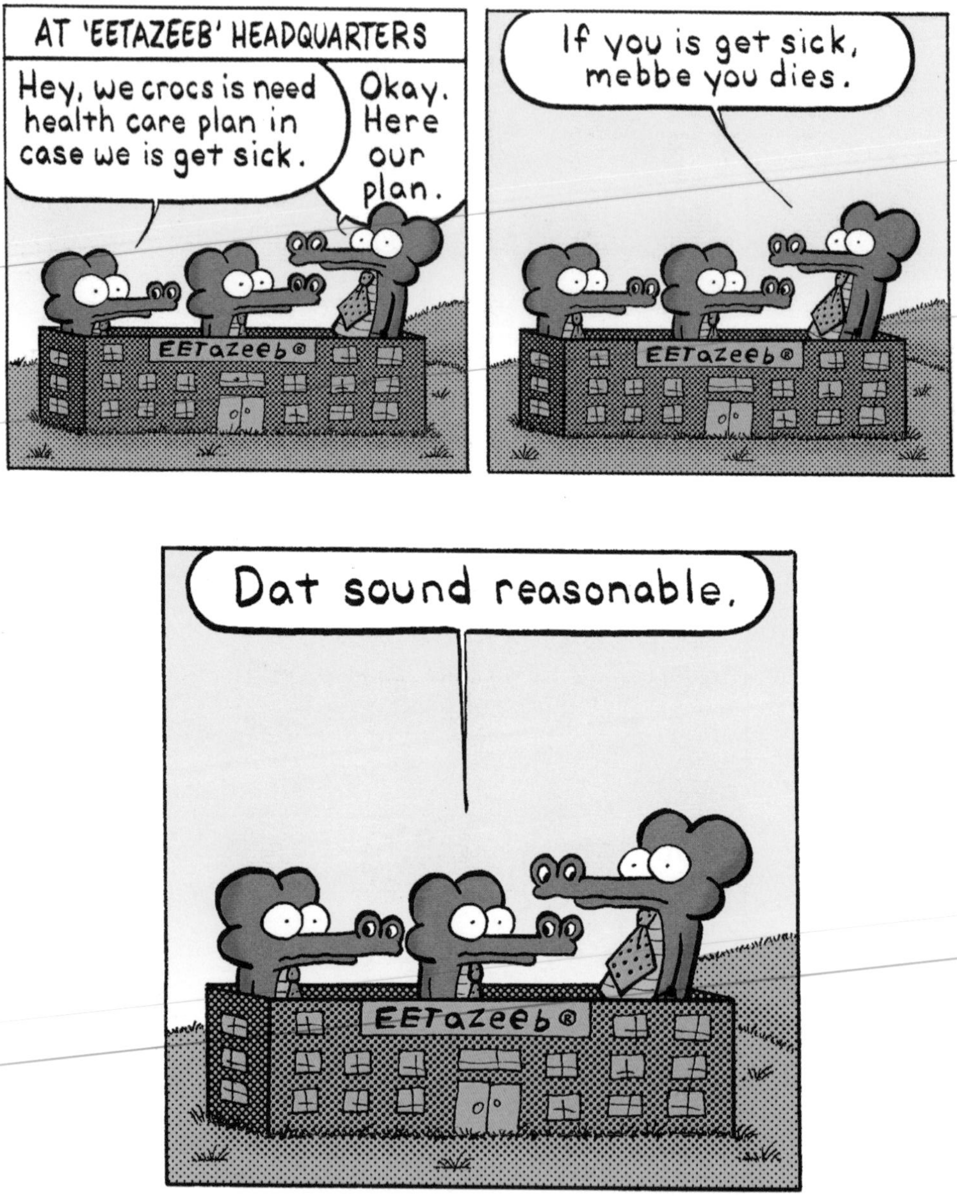
AT 'EETAZEEB' HEADQUARTERS
Hey, we crocs is need health care plan in case we is get sick.
Okay. Here our plan.
EETazeeb®
If you is get sick, mebbe you dies.
EETazeeb®
Dat sound reasonable.
EETazeeb®

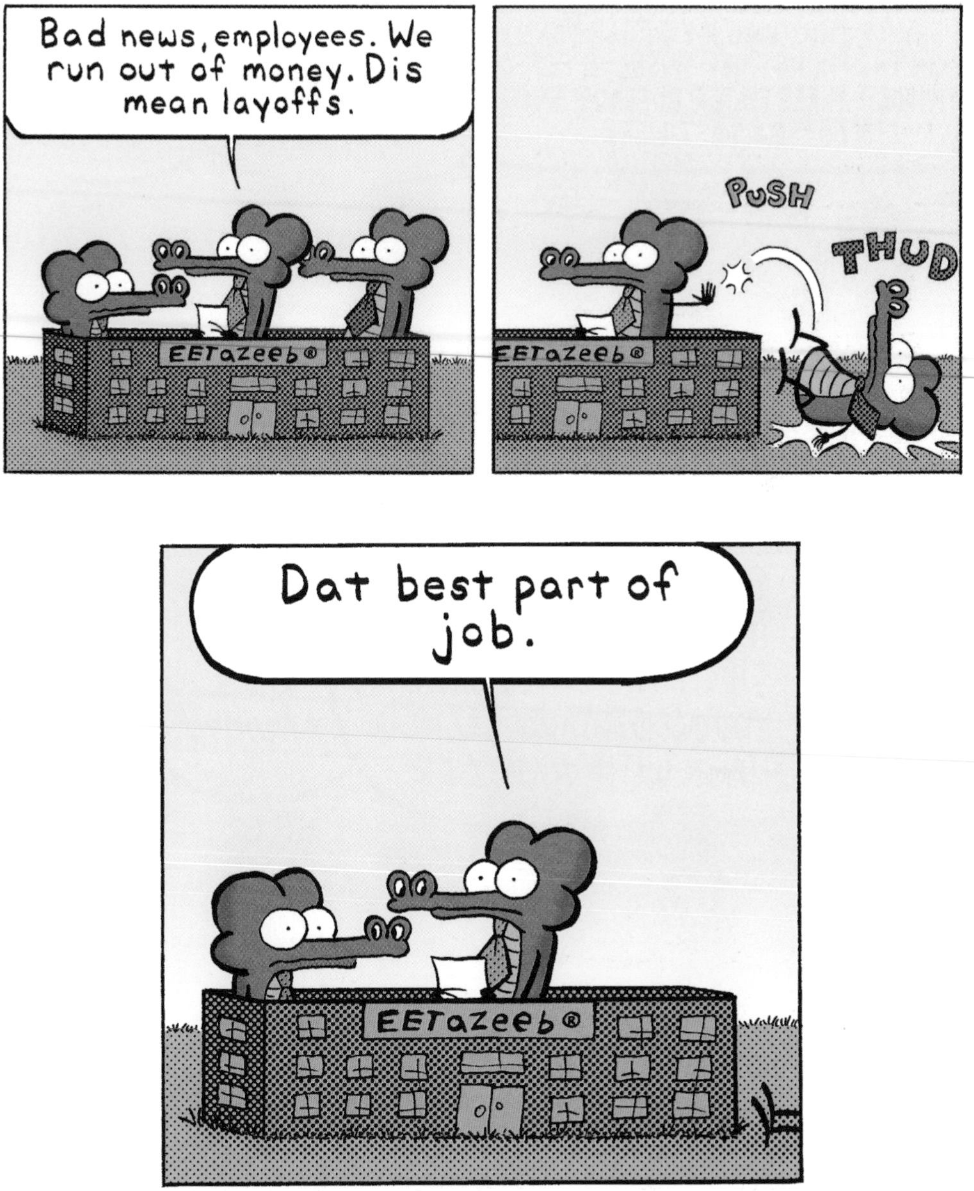
Bad news, employees. We run out of money. Dis mean layoffs.
EETazeeb®
PUSH
THUD
EETazeeb®
Dat best part of job.
EETazeeb®

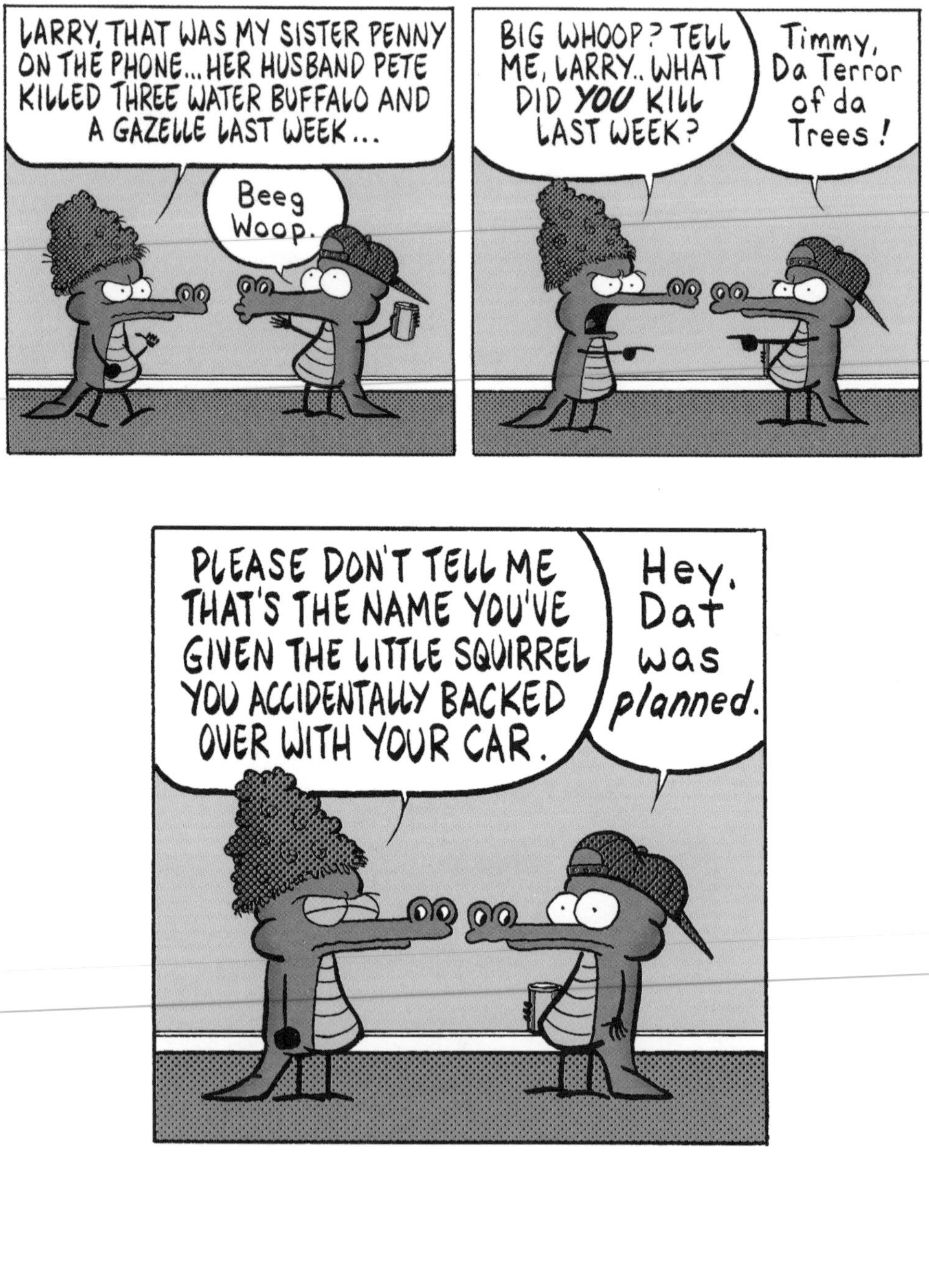
LARRY, THAT WAS MY SISTER PENNY ON THE PHONE... HER HUSBAND PETE KILLED THREE WATER BUFFALO AND A GAZELLE LAST WEEK...
Beeg Woop.
BIG WHOOP? TELL ME, LARRY.. WHAT DID YOU KILL LAST WEEK?
Timmy, Da Terror of da Trees!
PLEASE DON'T TELL ME THAT'S THE NAME YOU'VE GIVEN THE LITTLE SQUIRREL YOU ACCIDENTALLY BACKED OVER WITH YOUR CAR.
Hey. Dat was planned.

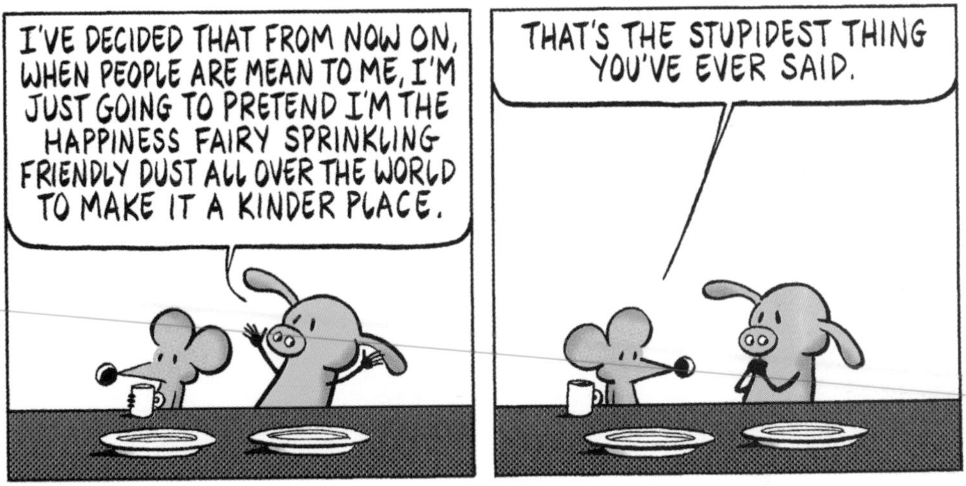
I'VE DECIDED THAT FROM NOW ON, WHEN PEOPLE ARE MEAN TO ME, I'M JUST GOING TO PRETEND I'M THE HAPPINESS FAIRY SPRINKLING FRIENDLY DUST ALL OVER THE WORLD TO MAKE IT A KINDER PLACE.
THAT'S THE STUPIDEST THING YOU'VE EVER SAID.

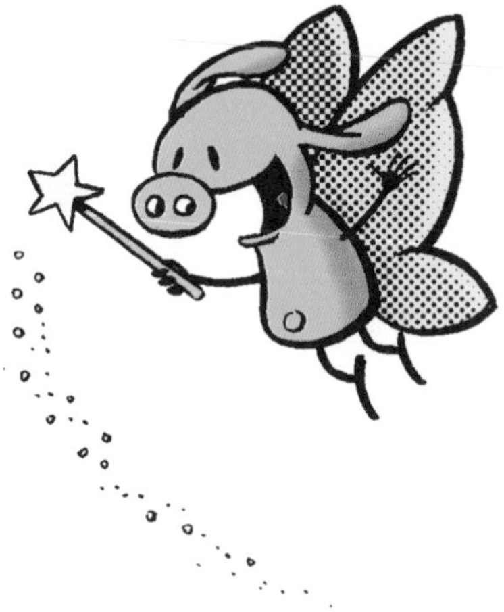

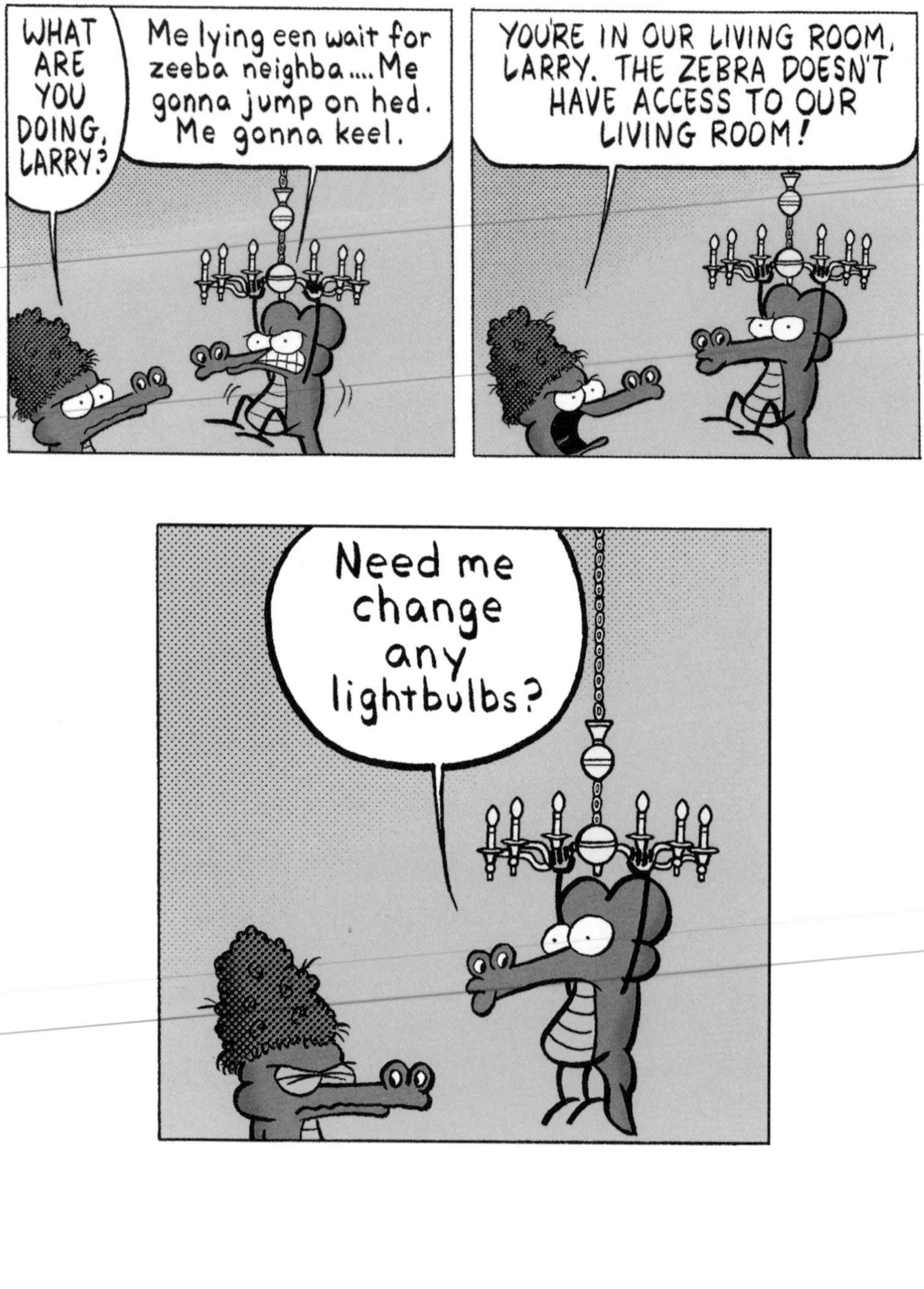
WHAT ARE YOU DOING, LARRY?
Me lying een wait for zeeba neighba....Me gonna jump on hed. Me gonna keel.
YOU'RE IN OUR LIVING ROOM, LARRY. THE ZEBRA DOESN'T HAVE ACCESS TO OUR LIVING ROOM!
Need me change any lightbulbs?

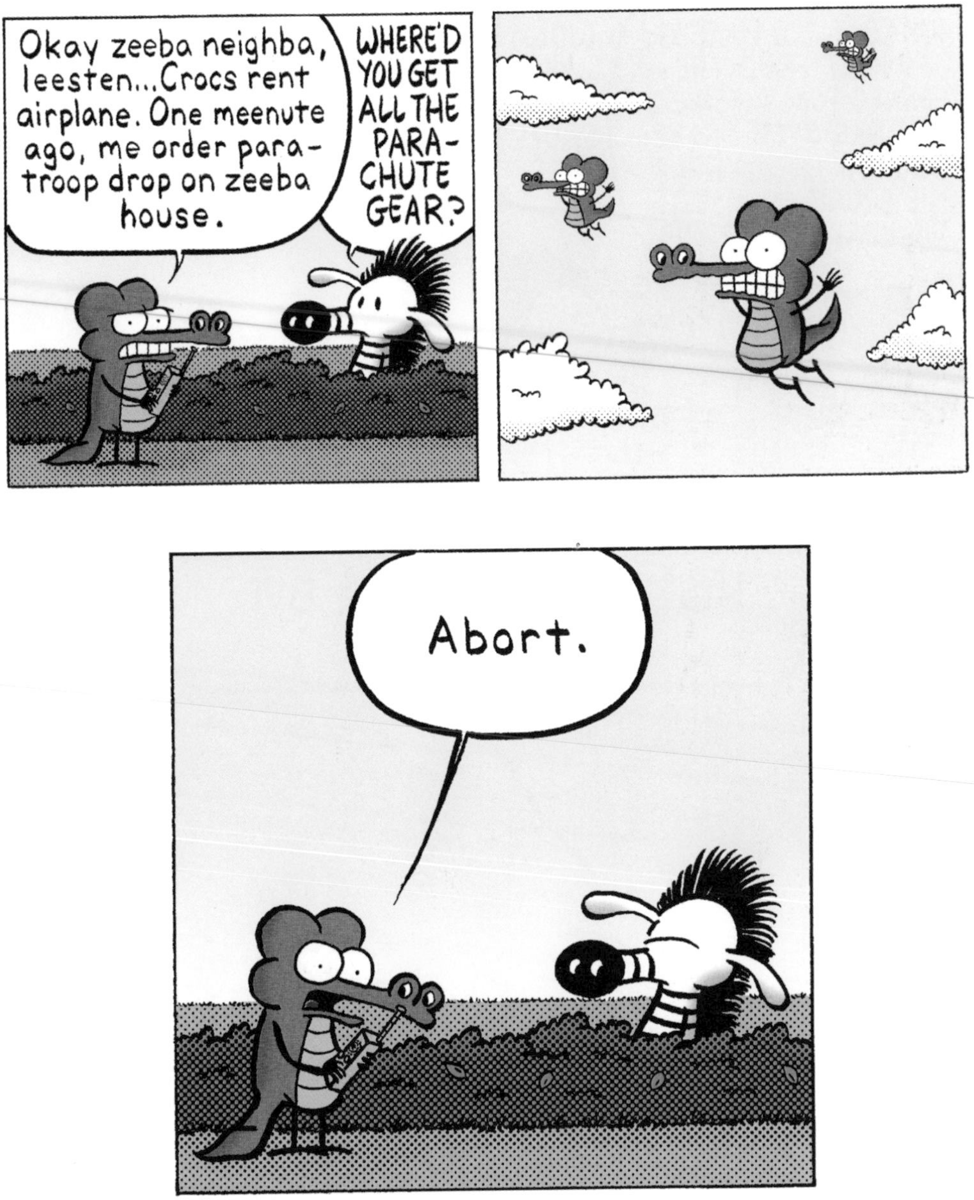
Okay zeeba neighba, leesten...Crocs rent airplane. One meenute ago, me order para-troop drop on zeeba house.
WHERE'D YOU GET ALL THE PARA-CHUTE GEAR?
Abort.

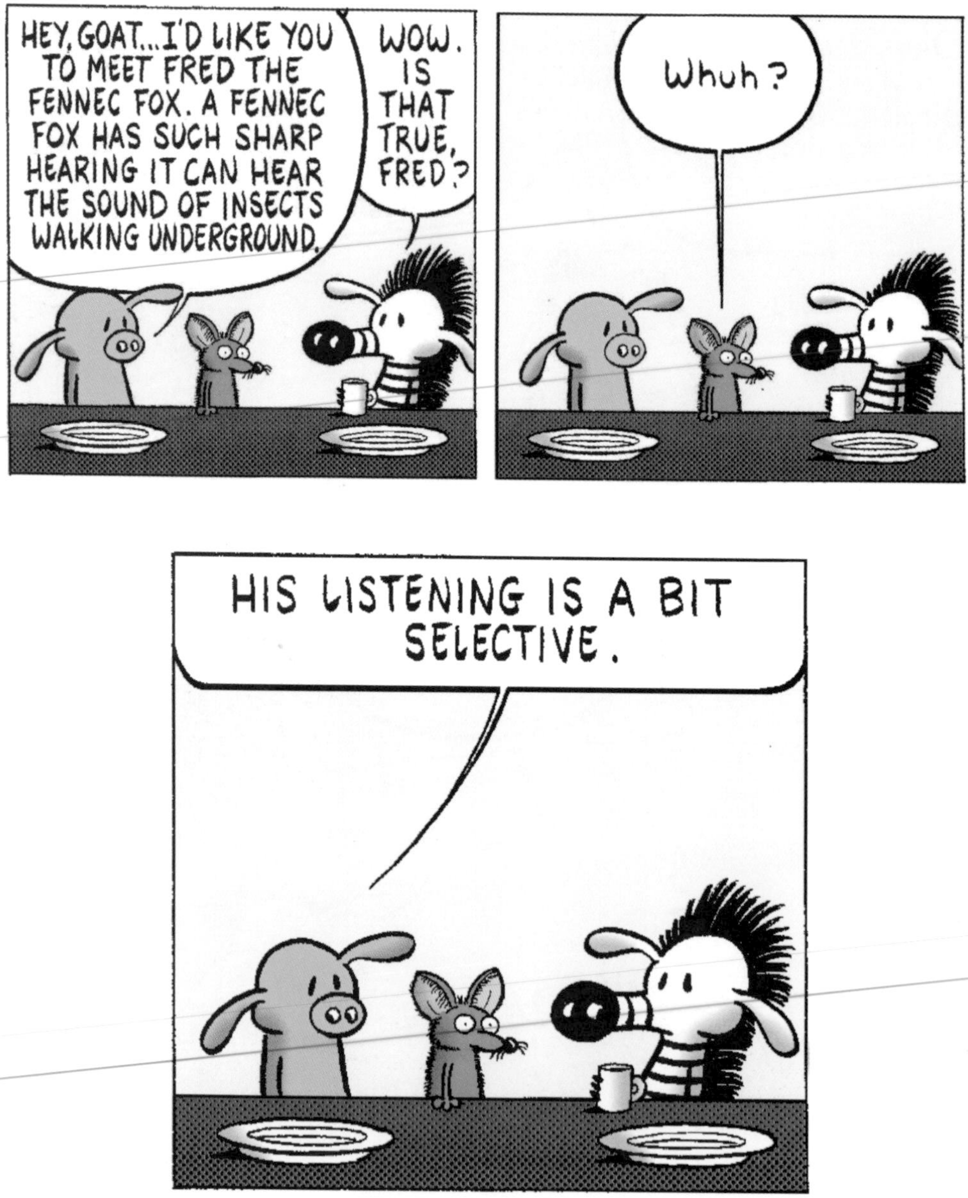
HEY, GOAT... I'D LIKE YOU TO MEET FRED THE FENNEC FOX. A FENNEC FOX HAS SUCH SHARP HEARING IT CAN HEAR THE SOUND OF INSECTS WALKING UNDERGROUND.
WOW. IS THAT TRUE, FRED?
Whuh?
HIS LISTENING IS A BIT SELECTIVE.

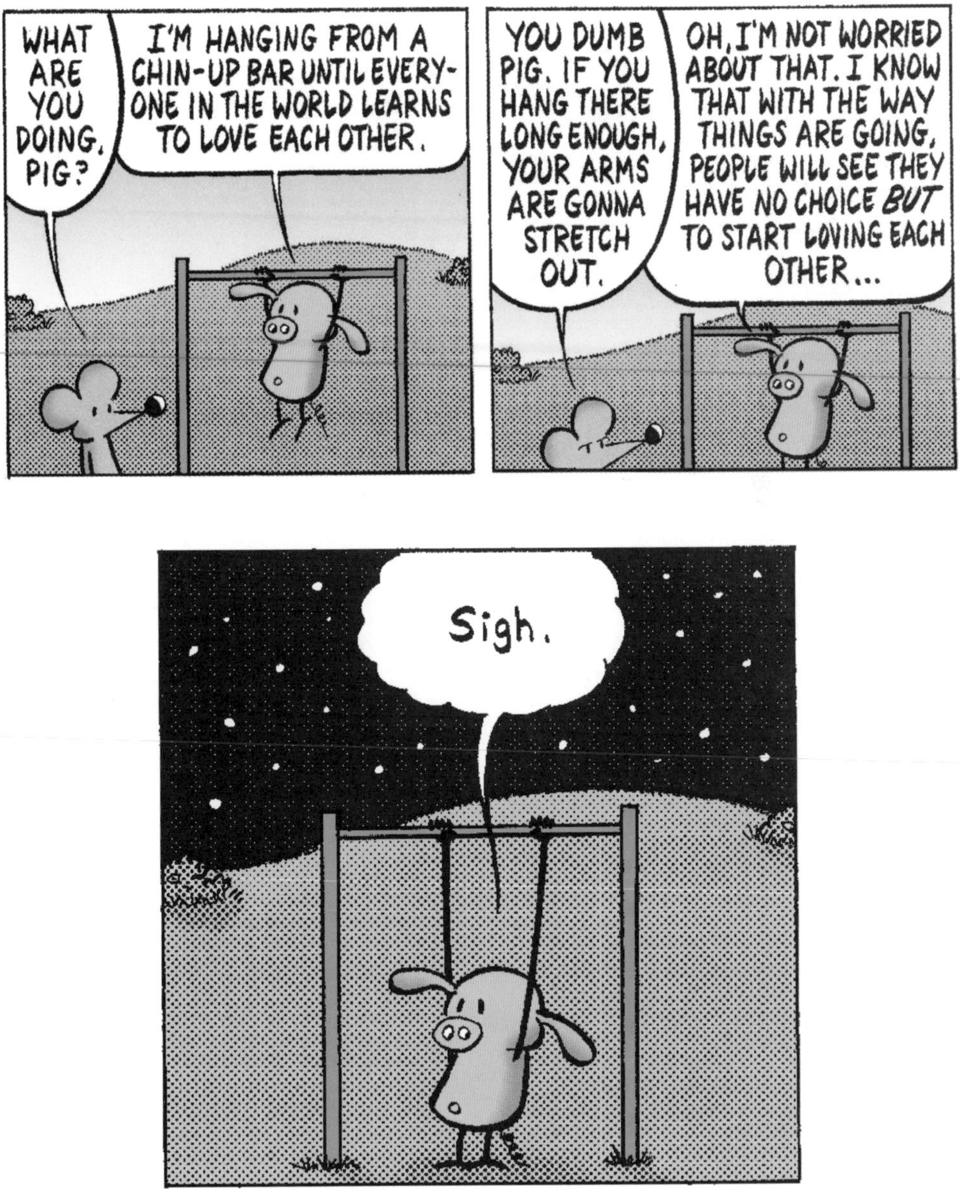
WHAT ARE YOU DOING, PIG?
I'M HANGING FROM A CHIN-UP BAR UNTIL EVERYONE IN THE WORLD LEARNS TO LOVE EACH OTHER.
YOU DUMB PIG. IF YOU HANG THERE LONG ENOUGH, YOUR ARMS ARE GONNA STRETCH OUT.
OH, I'M NOT WORRIED ABOUT THAT. I KNOW THAT WITH THE WAY THINGS ARE GOING, PEOPLE WILL SEE THEY HAVE NO CHOICE *BUT* TO START LOVING EACH OTHER...
Sigh.

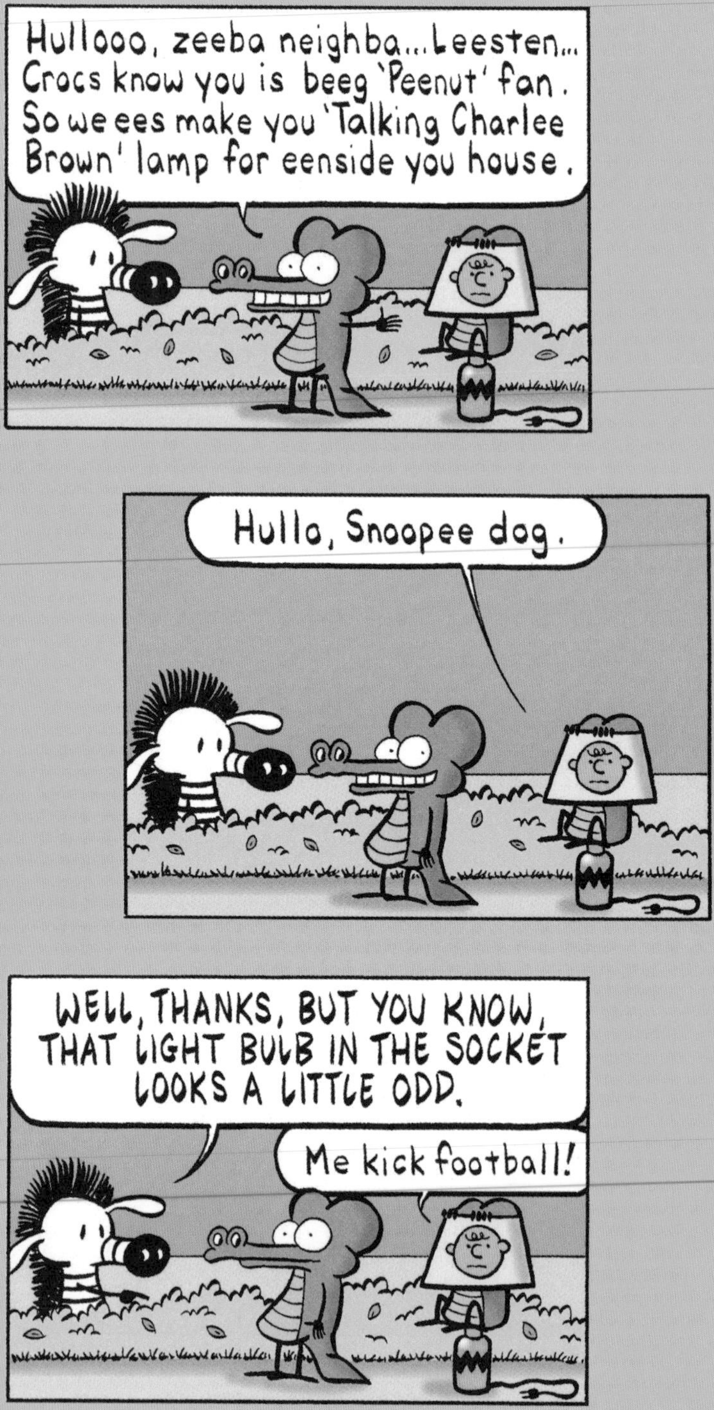
Hullooo, zeeba neighba...Leesten... Crocs know you is beeg 'Peenut' fan. So we ees make you 'Talking Charlee Brown' lamp for eenside you house.
Hullo, Snoopee dog.
WELL, THANKS, BUT YOU KNOW, THAT LIGHT BULB IN THE SOCKET LOOKS A LITTLE ODD.
Me kick football!

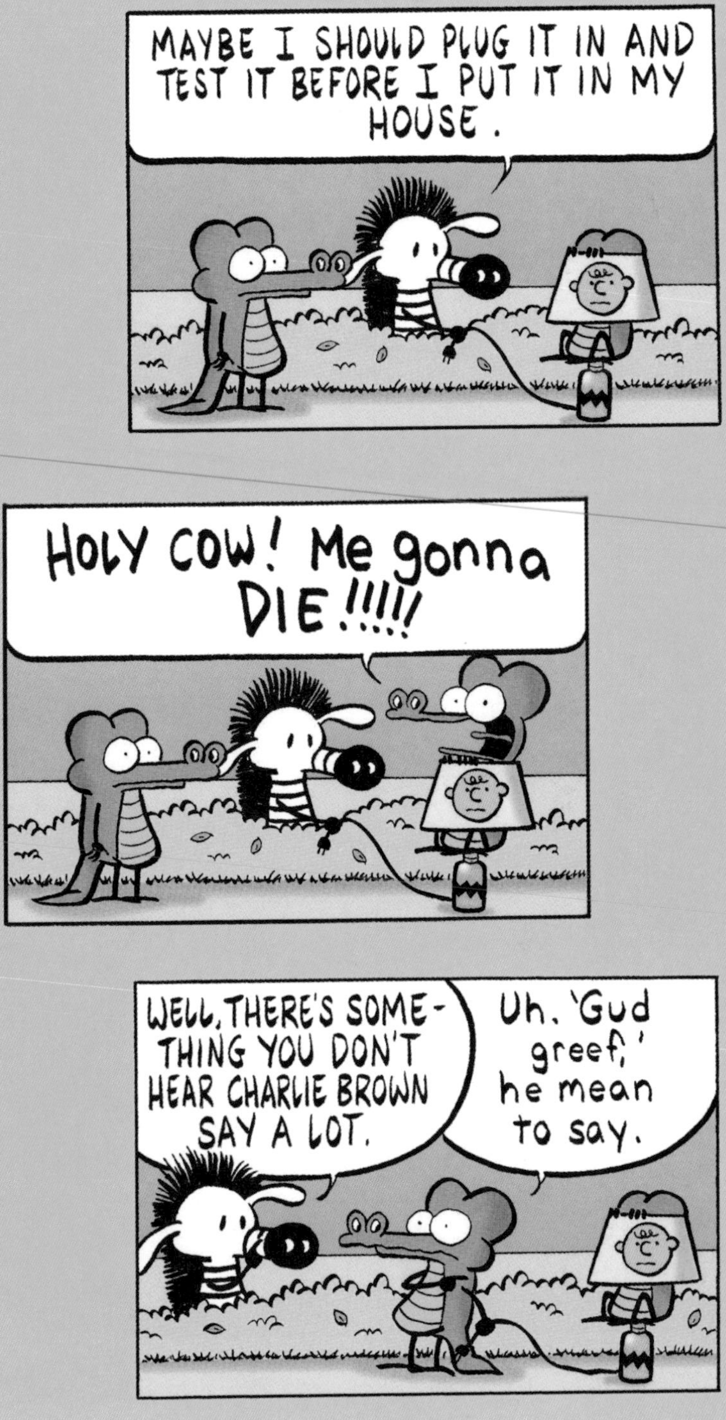
MAYBE I SHOULD PLUG IT IN AND TEST IT BEFORE I PUT IT IN MY HOUSE.
HOLY COW! Me gonna DIE!!!!!
WELL, THERE'S SOMETHING YOU DON'T HEAR CHARLIE BROWN SAY A LOT.
Uh. 'Gud greef,' he mean to say.

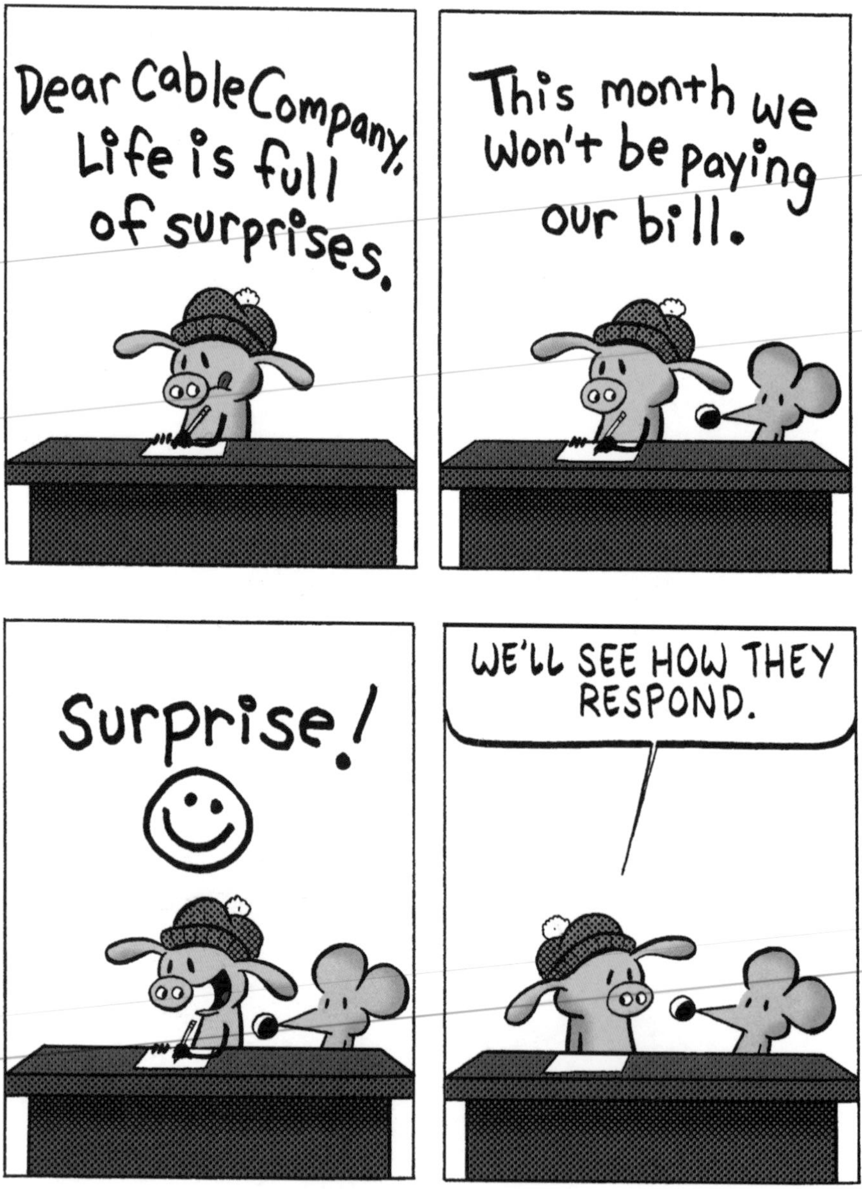
Dear Cable Company,
Life is full of surprises.
This month we won't be paying our bill.
Surprise!
WE'LL SEE HOW THEY RESPOND.

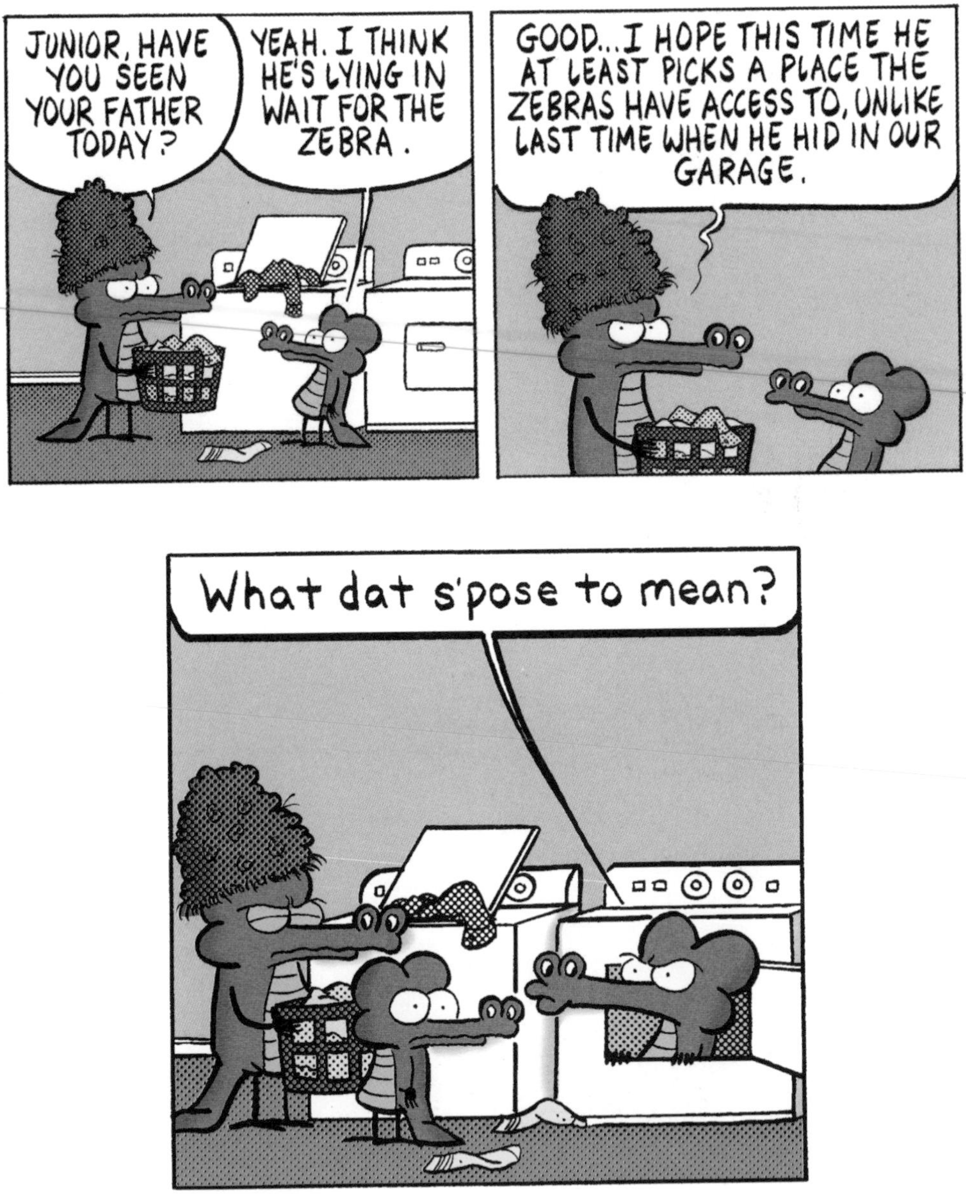
JUNIOR, HAVE YOU SEEN YOUR FATHER TODAY?
YEAH. I THINK HE'S LYING IN WAIT FOR THE ZEBRA.
GOOD...I HOPE THIS TIME HE AT LEAST PICKS A PLACE THE ZEBRAS HAVE ACCESS TO, UNLIKE LAST TIME WHEN HE HID IN OUR GARAGE.
What dat s'pose to mean?

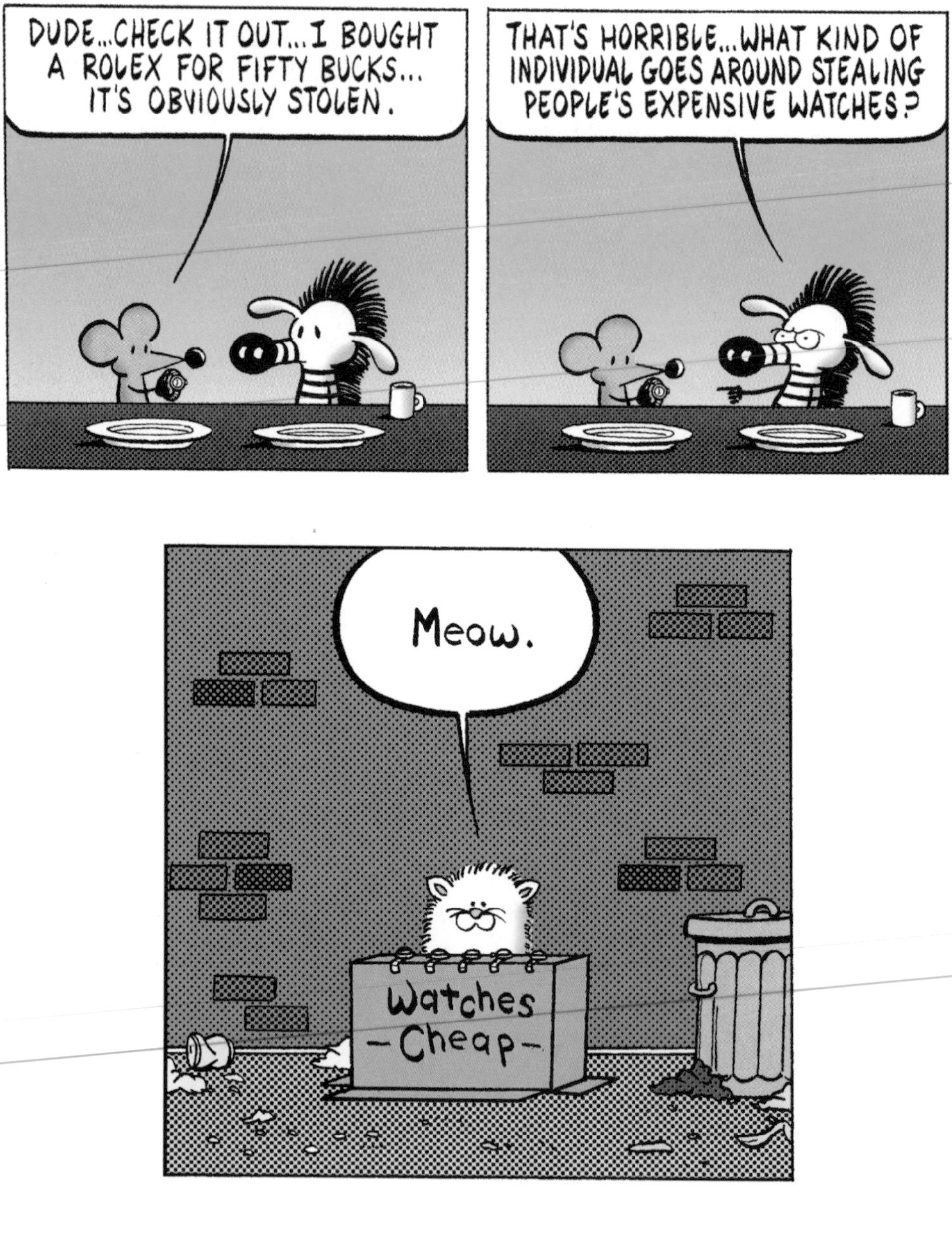
DUDE...CHECK IT OUT...I BOUGHT A ROLEX FOR FIFTY BUCKS... IT'S OBVIOUSLY STOLEN.
THAT'S HORRIBLE...WHAT KIND OF INDIVIDUAL GOES AROUND STEALING PEOPLE'S EXPENSIVE WATCHES?
Meow.
Watches
-Cheap-

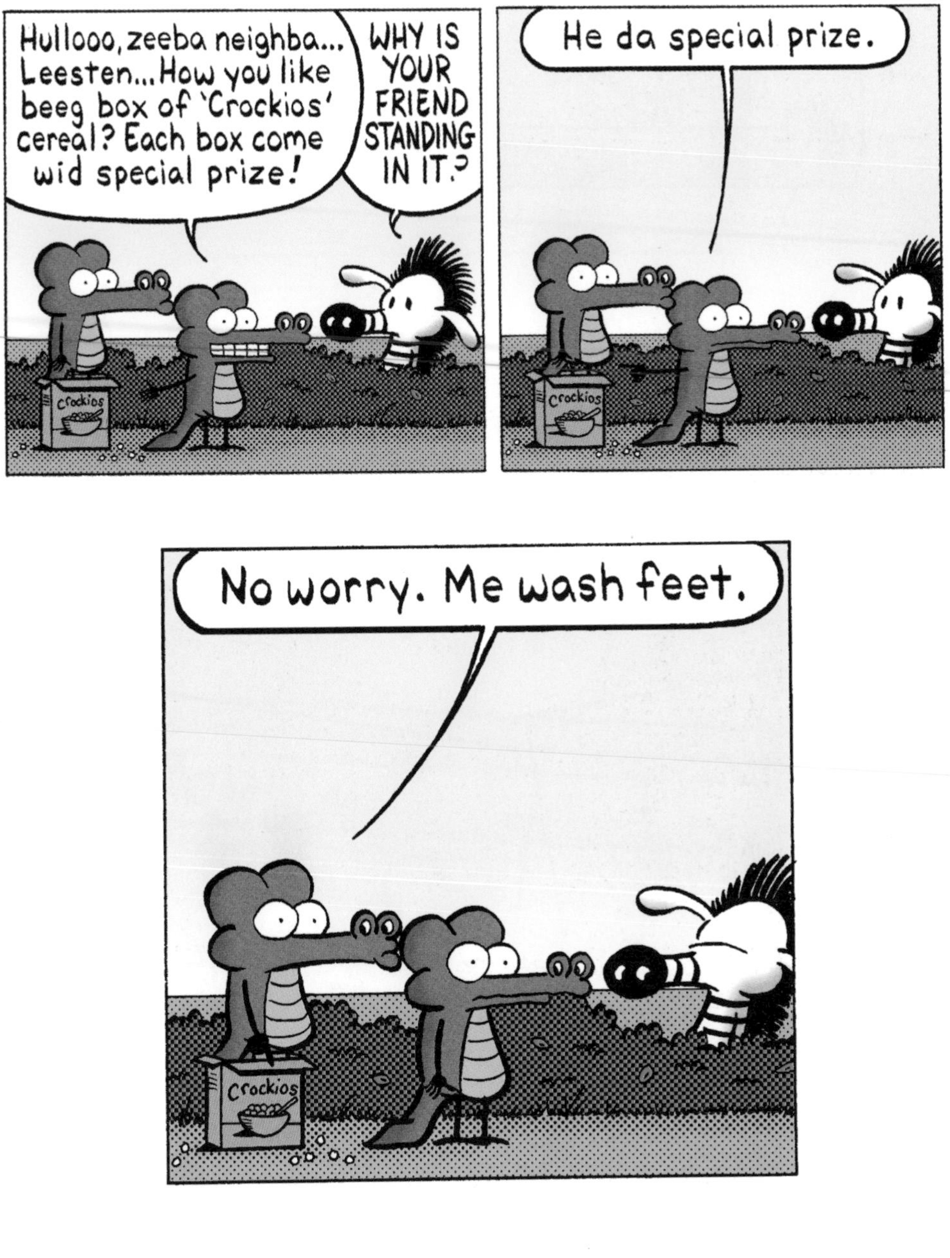
Hullooo, zeeba neighba... Leesten... How you like beeg box of 'Crockios' cereal? Each box come wid special prize!
WHY IS YOUR FRIEND STANDING IN IT?
He da special prize.
No worry. Me wash feet.
Crockios

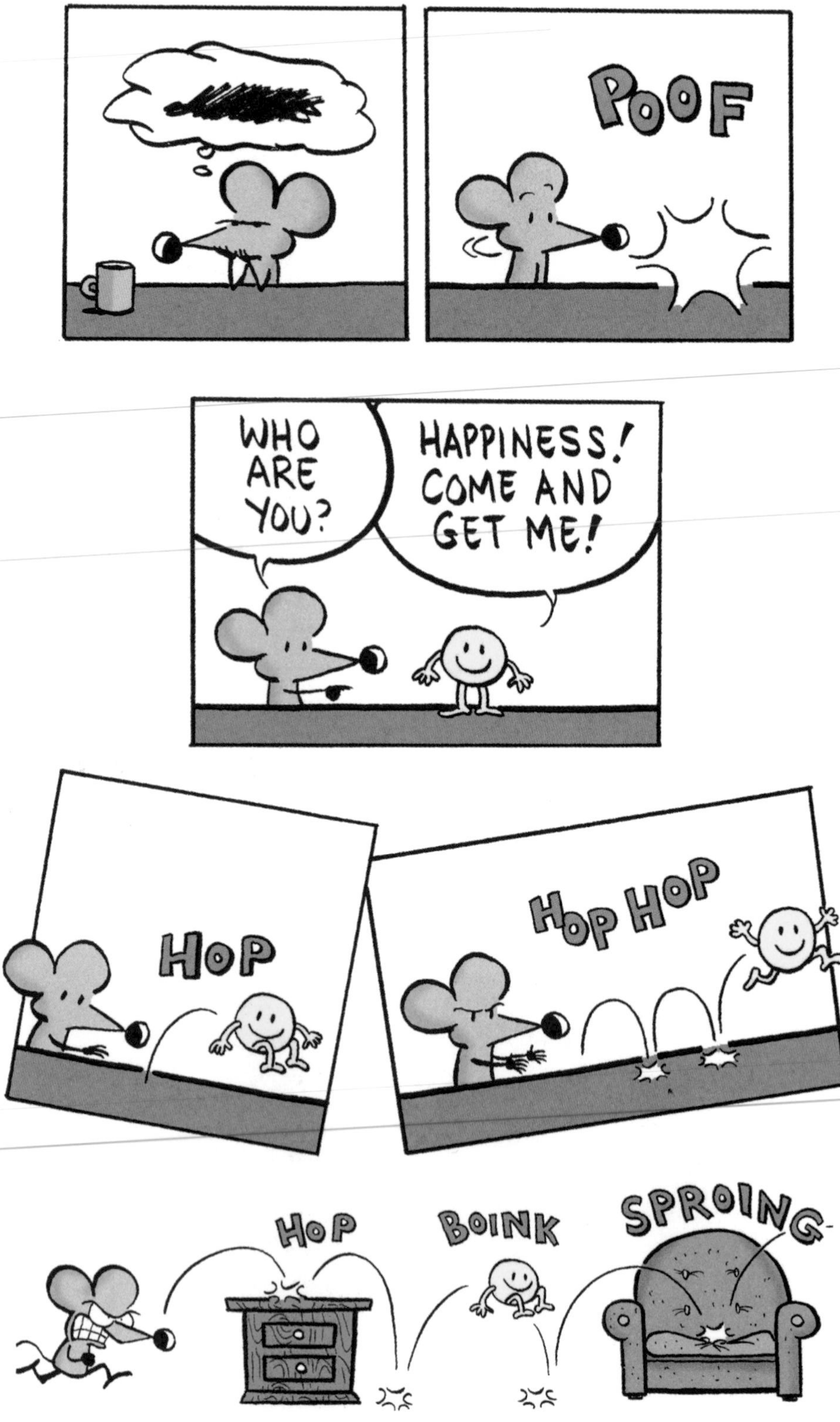
POOF
WHO ARE YOU?
HAPPINESS! COME AND GET ME!
HOP
HOP HOP
HOP
BOINK
SPROING

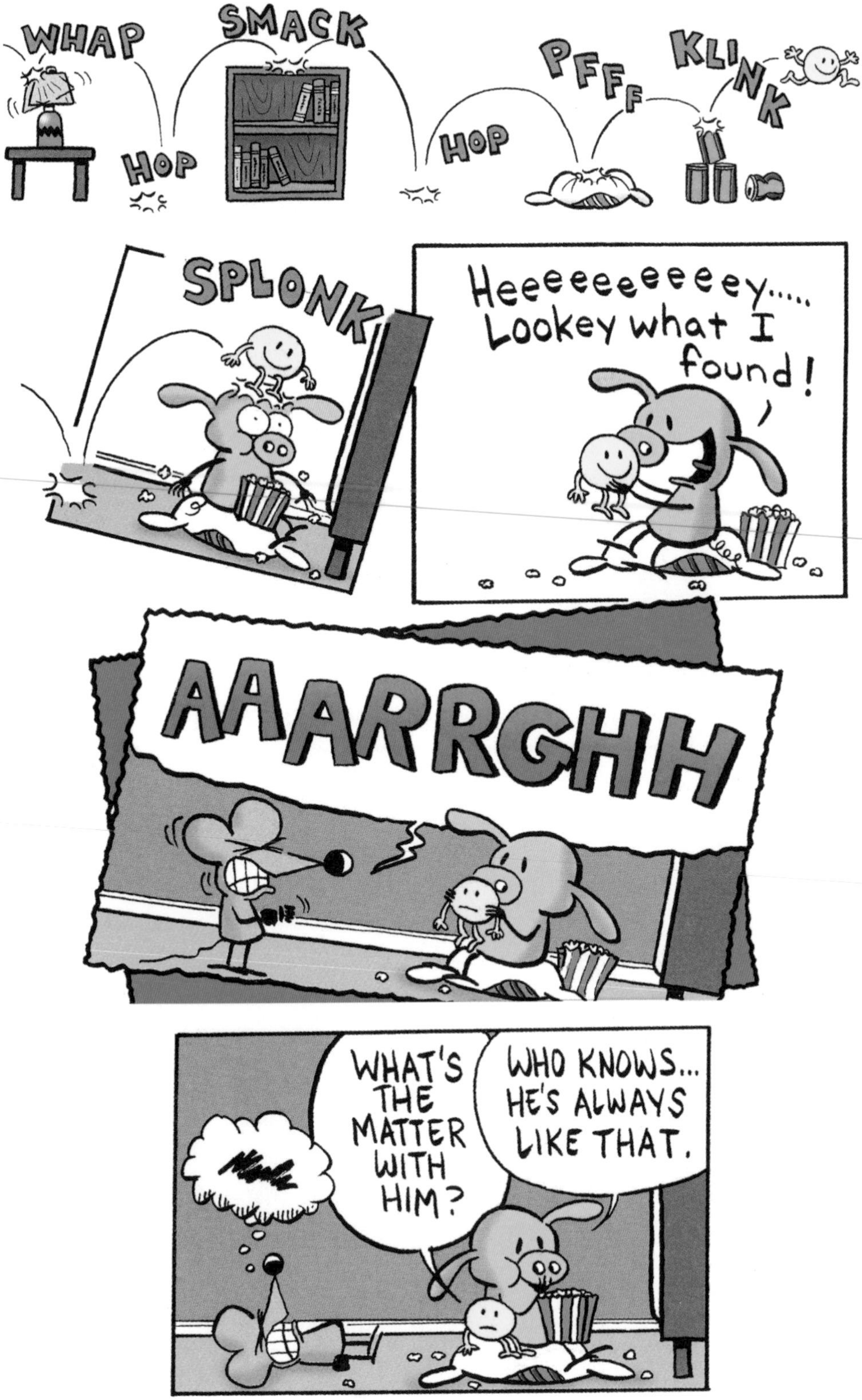
WHAP
HOP
SMACK
HOP
PFFFF
KLINK
SPLONK
Heeeeeeeeeey..... Lookey what I found!
AAARRGHH
WHAT'S THE MATTER WITH HIM?
WHO KNOWS... HE'S ALWAYS LIKE THAT.

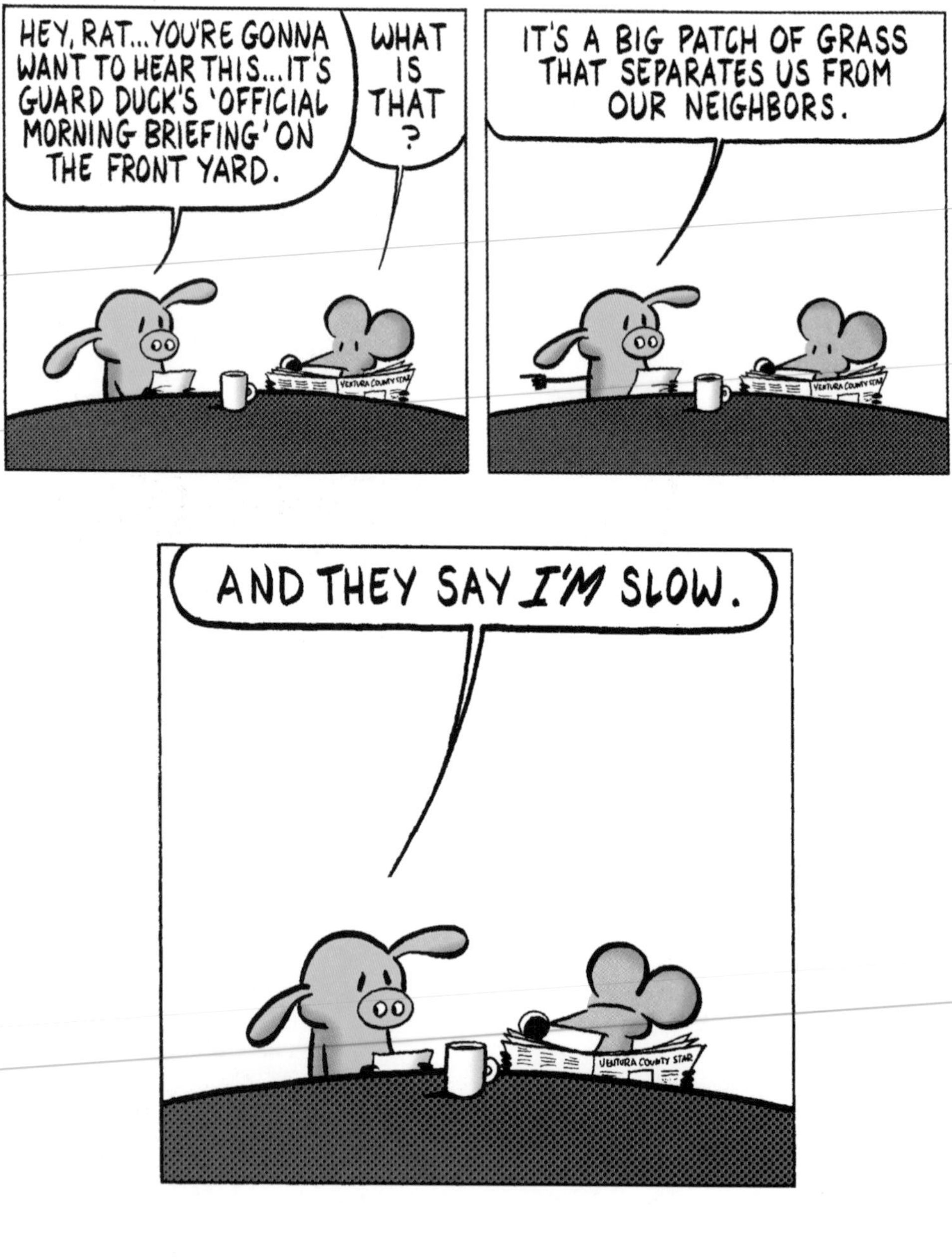
HEY, RAT...YOU'RE GONNA WANT TO HEAR THIS...IT'S GUARD DUCK'S 'OFFICIAL MORNING BRIEFING' ON THE FRONT YARD.
WHAT IS THAT ?
VENTURA COUNTY STAR
IT'S A BIG PATCH OF GRASS THAT SEPARATES US FROM OUR NEIGHBORS.
VENTURA COUNTY STAR
AND THEY SAY *I'M* SLOW.
VENTURA COUNTY STAR

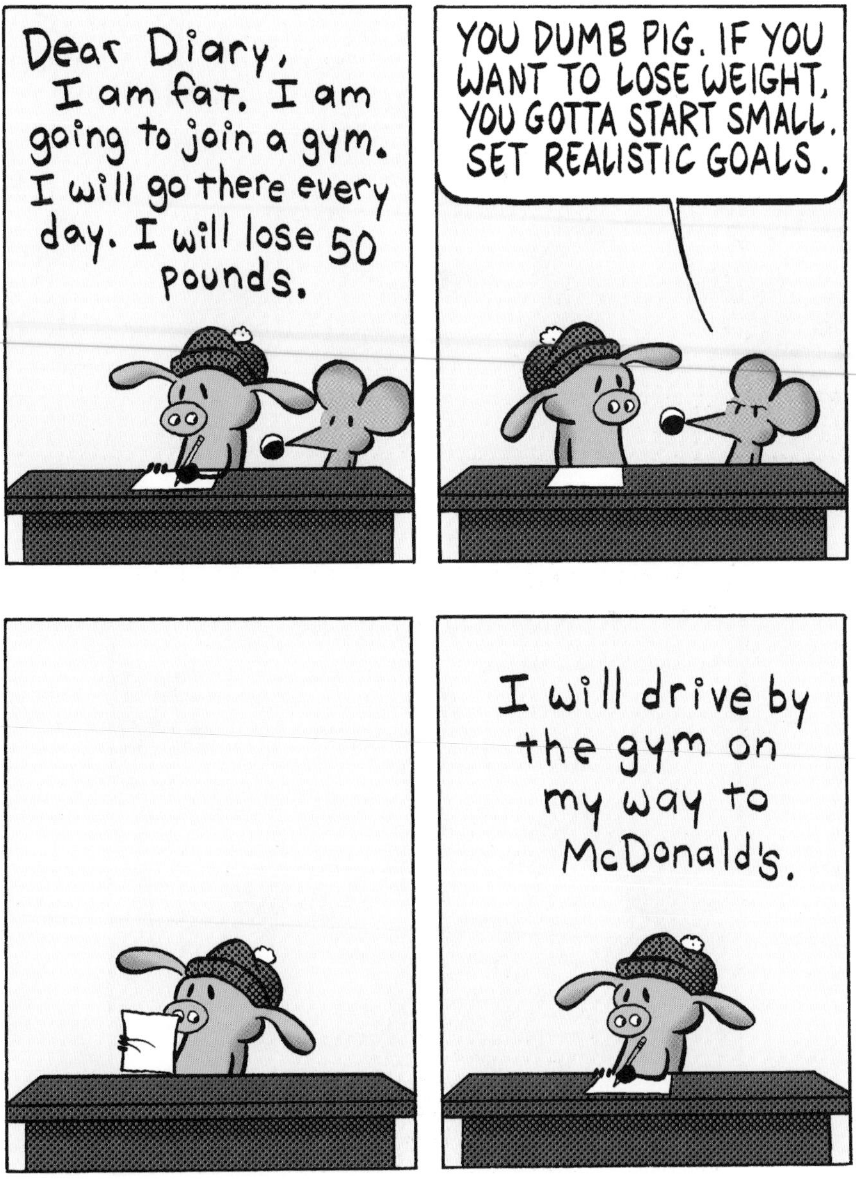
Dear Diary,
I am fat. I am going to join a gym. I will go there every day. I will lose 50 pounds.
YOU DUMB PIG. IF YOU WANT TO LOSE WEIGHT, YOU GOTTA START SMALL. SET REALISTIC GOALS.
I will drive by the gym on my way to McDonald's.

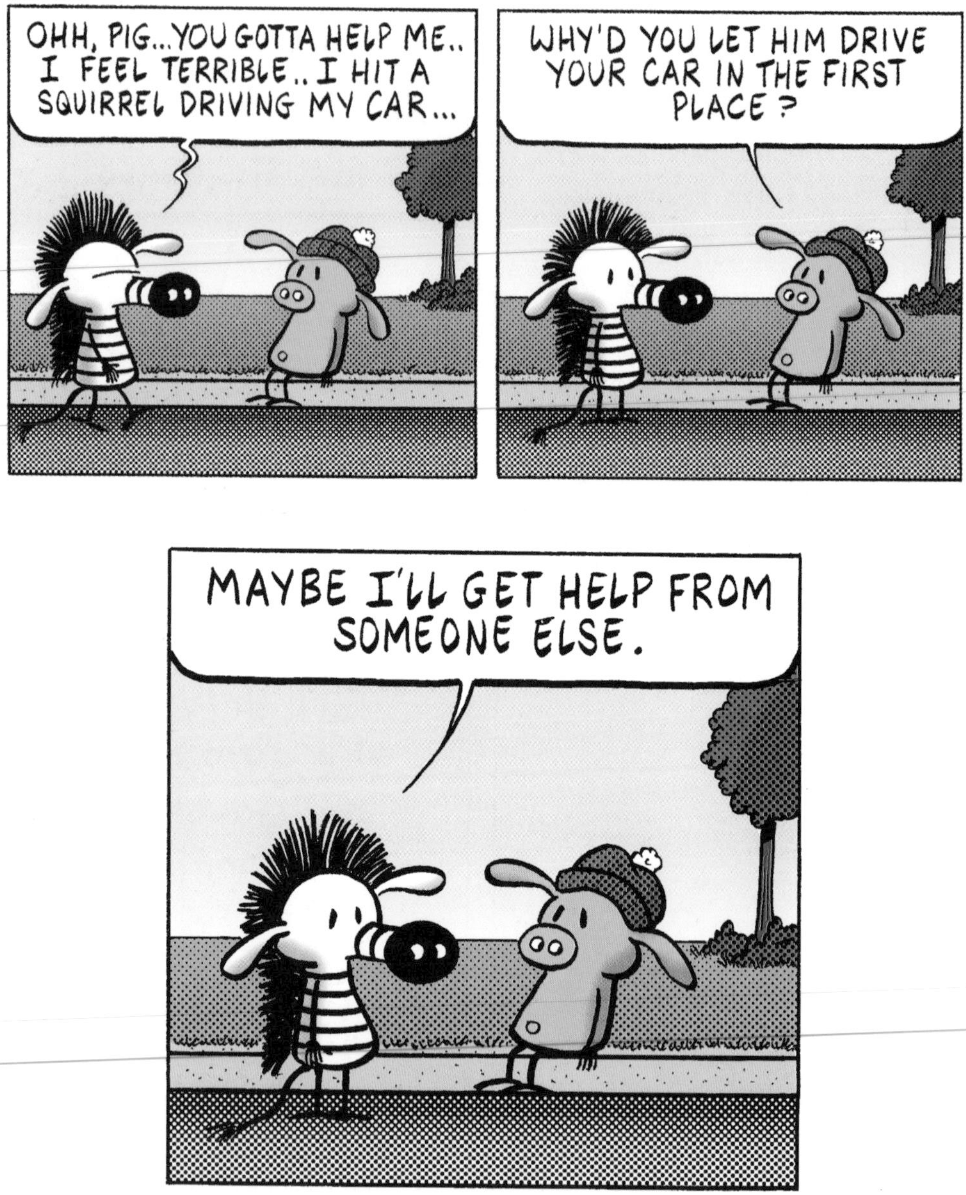
OHH, PIG...YOU GOTTA HELP ME.. I FEEL TERRIBLE.. I HIT A SQUIRREL DRIVING MY CAR...
WHY'D YOU LET HIM DRIVE YOUR CAR IN THE FIRST PLACE?
MAYBE I'LL GET HELP FROM SOMEONE ELSE.

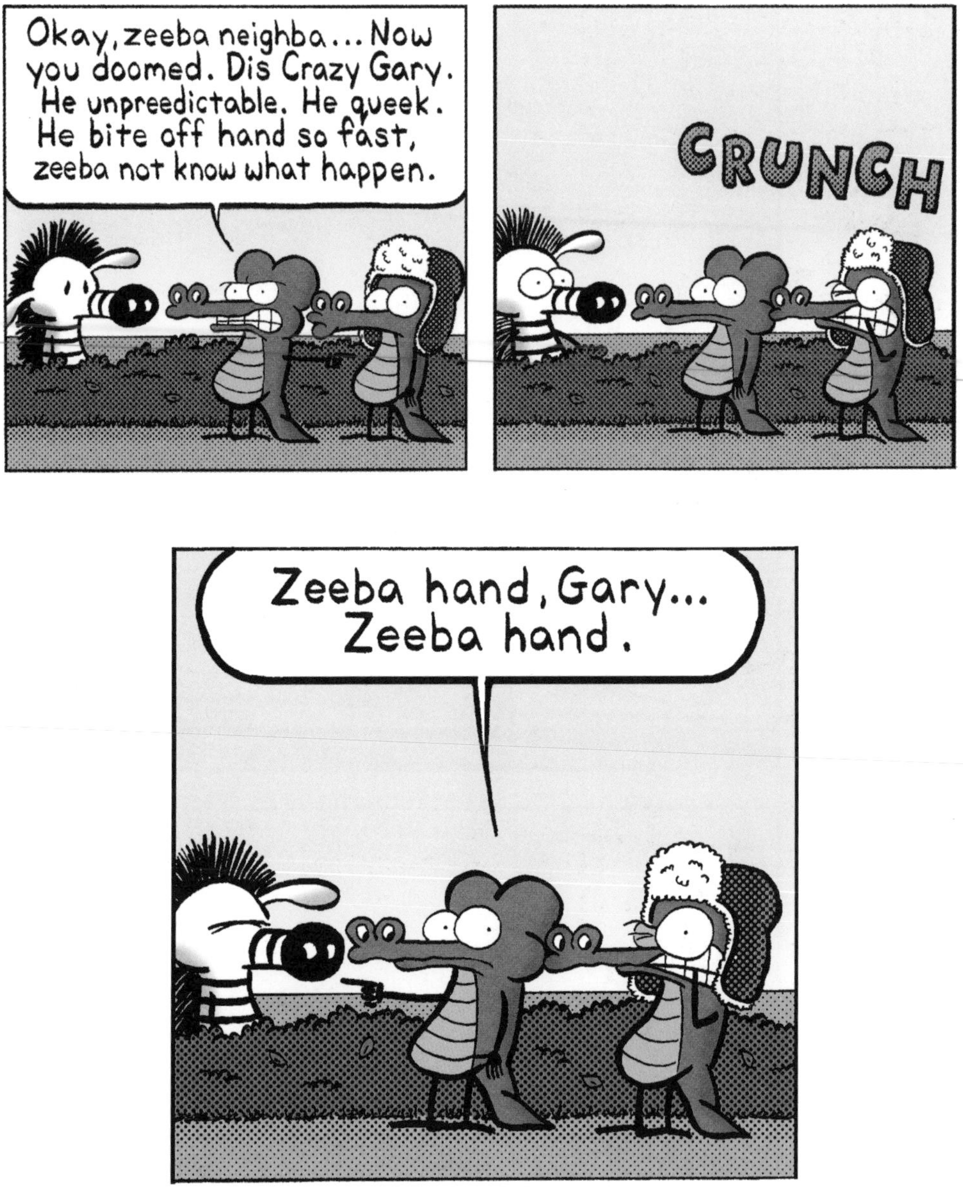
Okay, zeeba neighba... Now you doomed. Dis Crazy Gary. He unpreedictable. He queek. He bite off hand so fast, zeeba not know what happen.
CRUNCH
Zeeba hand, Gary... Zeeba hand.

WHAT'S THE MATTER WITH YOU?
COMPUTER PROBLEMS. I'M TICKED BECAUSE I HAVEN'T BEEN ABLE TO POST ON MY BLOG TODAY.

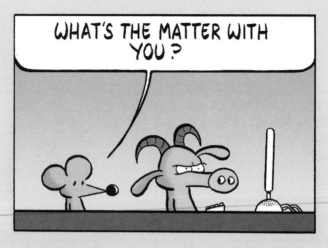

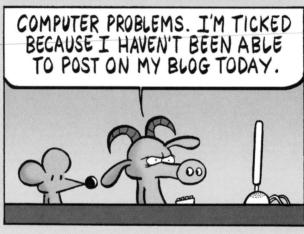

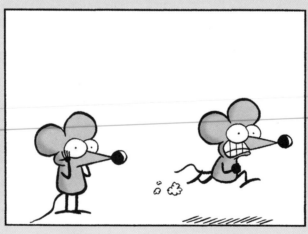

AND YET SOMEHOW THE WORLD GOES ON.
LEAVE.

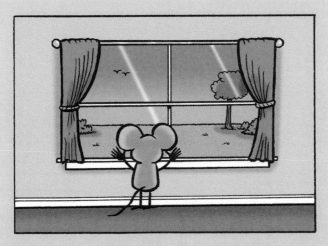

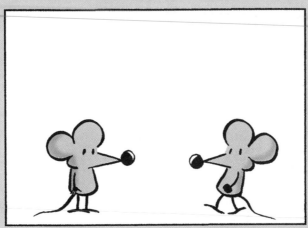

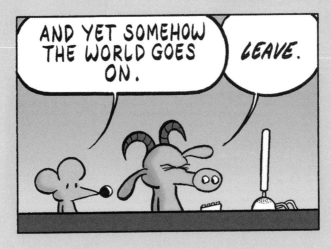

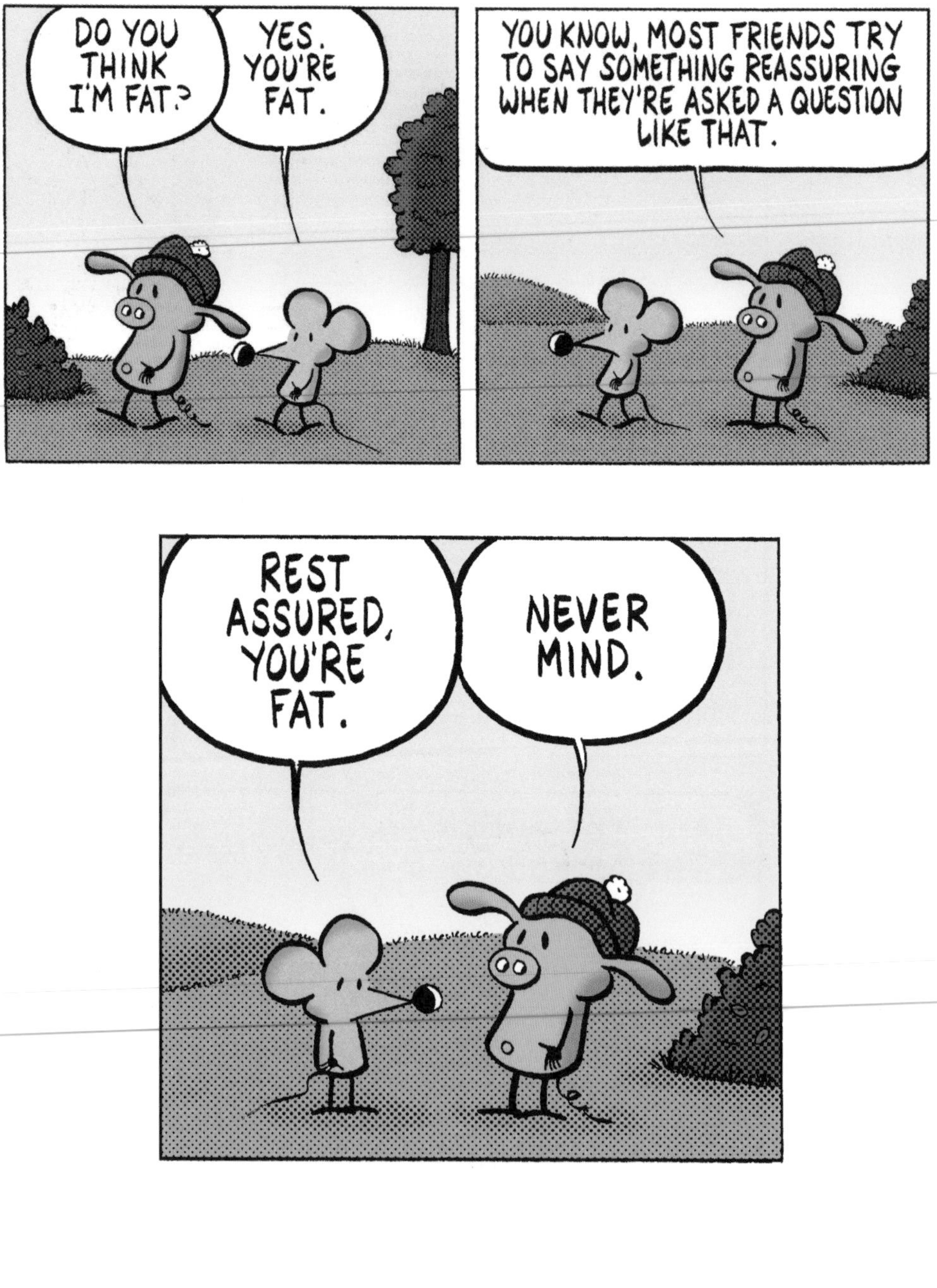
DO YOU THINK I'M FAT?
YES. YOU'RE FAT.
YOU KNOW, MOST FRIENDS TRY TO SAY SOMETHING REASSURING WHEN THEY'RE ASKED A QUESTION LIKE THAT.
REST ASSURED, YOU'RE FAT.
NEVER MIND.

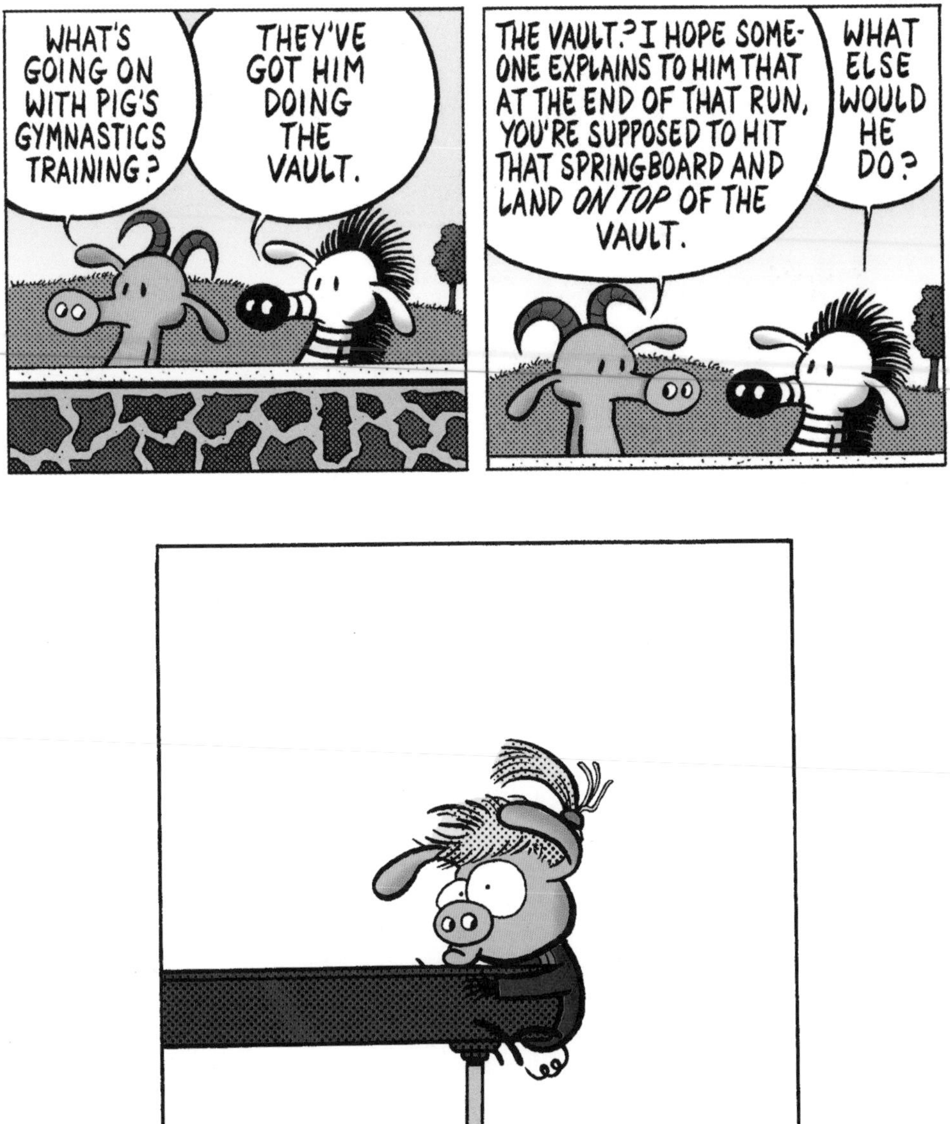
WHAT'S GOING ON WITH PIG'S GYMNASTICS TRAINING?
THEY'VE GOT HIM DOING THE VAULT.
THE VAULT? I HOPE SOMEONE EXPLAINS TO HIM THAT AT THE END OF THAT RUN, YOU'RE SUPPOSED TO HIT THAT SPRINGBOARD AND LAND *ON TOP* OF THE VAULT.
WHAT ELSE WOULD HE DO?

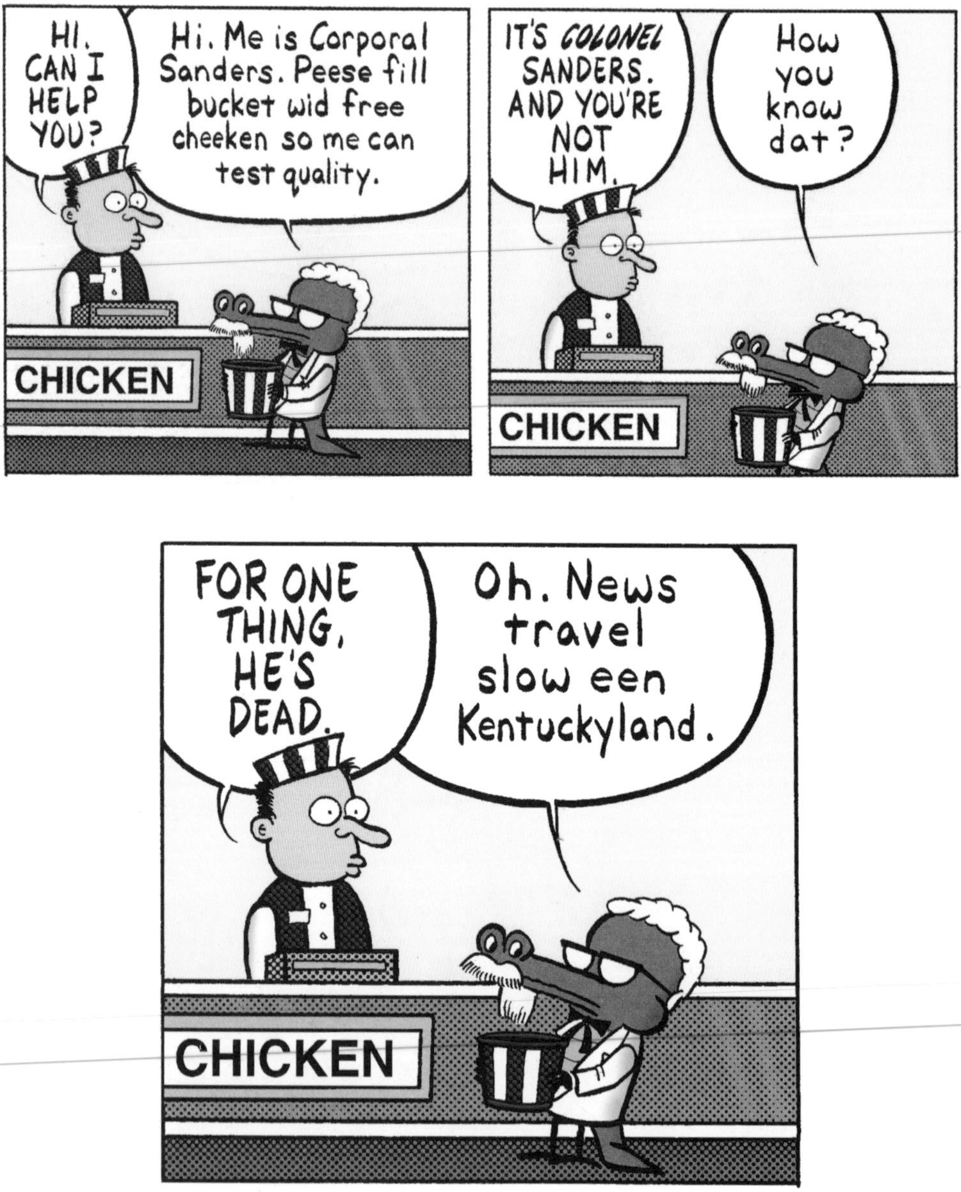
HI. CAN I HELP YOU?
Hi. Me is Corporal Sanders. Peese fill bucket wid free cheeken so me can test quality.
CHICKEN
IT'S COLONEL SANDERS. AND YOU'RE NOT HIM.
How you know dat?
CHICKEN
FOR ONE THING, HE'S DEAD.
Oh. News travel slow een Kentuckyland.
CHICKEN

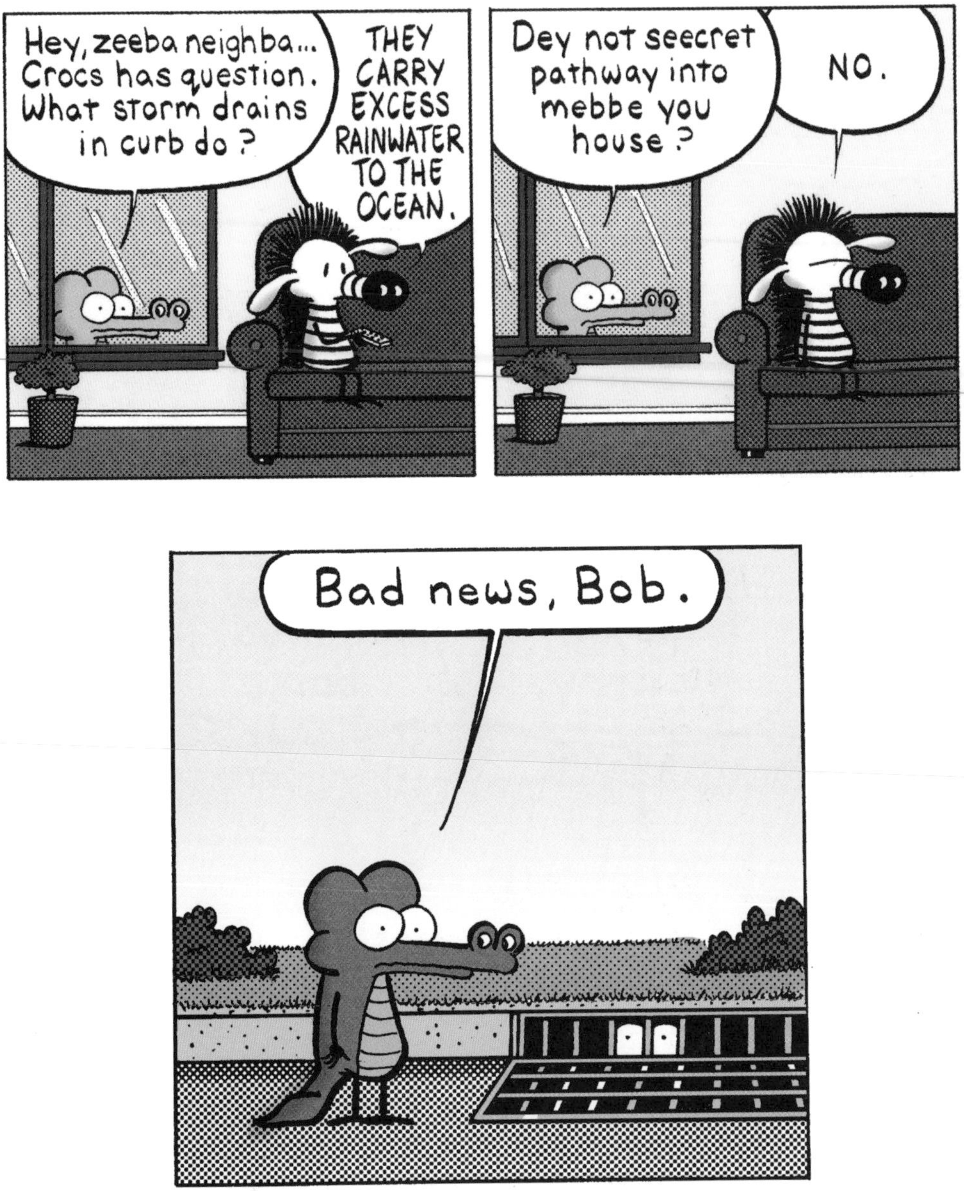
Hey, zeeba neighba... Crocs has question. What storm drains in curb do?
THEY CARRY EXCESS RAINWATER TO THE OCEAN.
Dey not seecret pathway into mebbe you house?
NO.
Bad news, Bob.

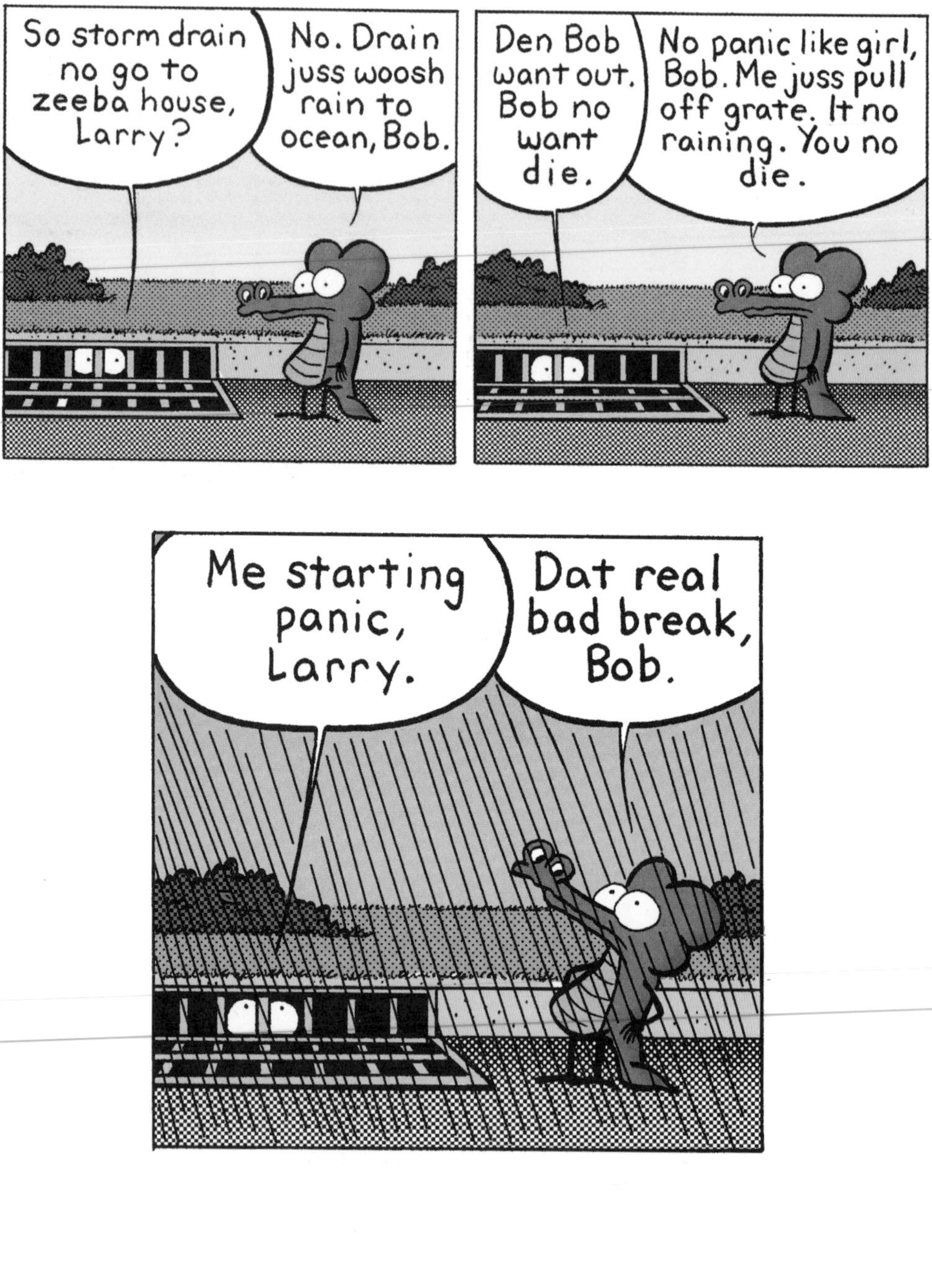
So storm drain no go to zeeba house, Larry?
No. Drain juss woosh rain to ocean, Bob.
Den Bob want out. Bob no want die.
No panic like girl, Bob. Me juss pull off grate. It no raining. You no die.
Me starting panic, Larry.
Dat real bad break, Bob.

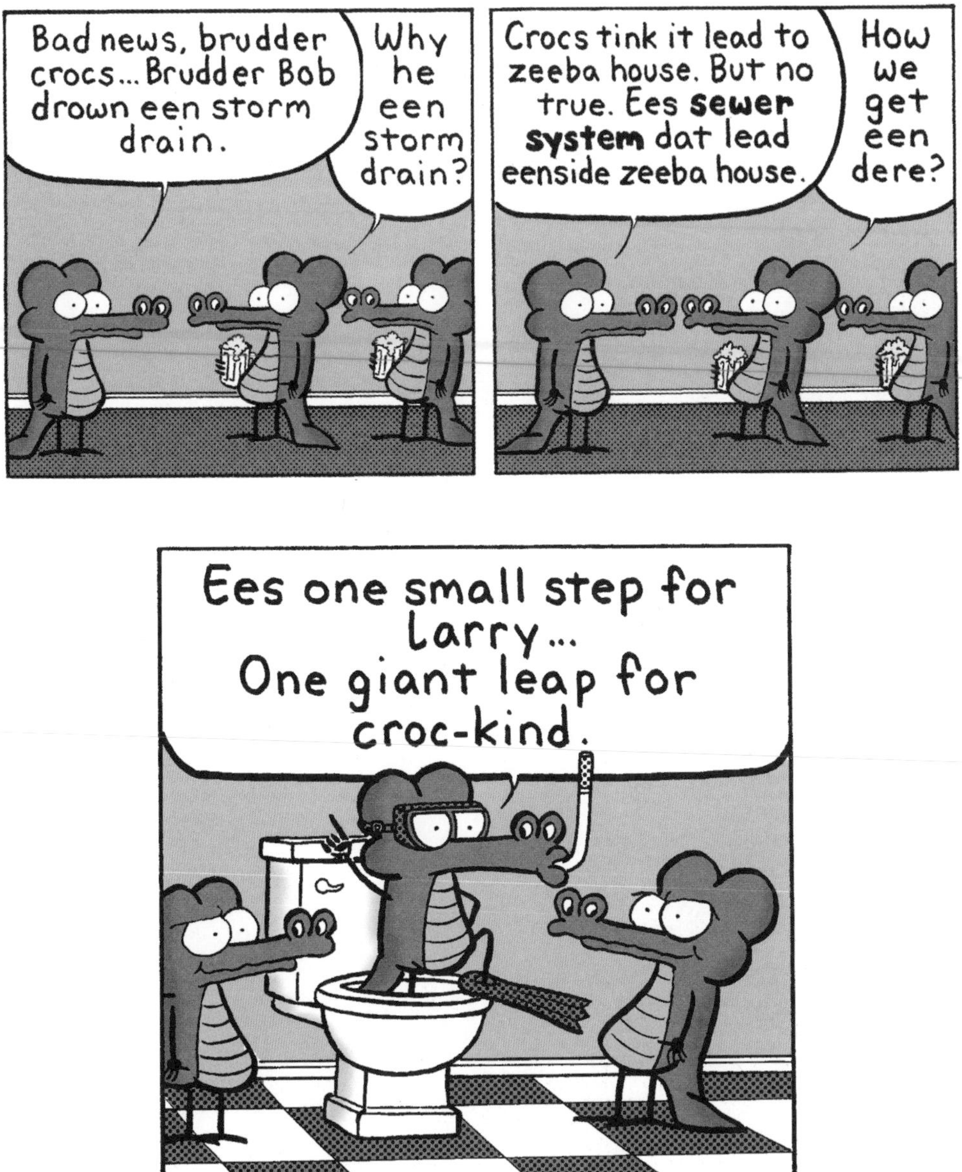
Bad news, brudder crocs... Brudder Bob drown een storm drain.
Why he een storm drain?
Crocs tink it lead to zeeba house. But no true. Ees **sewer system** dat lead eenside zeeba house.
How we get een dere?
Ees one small step for Larry... One giant leap for croc-kind.

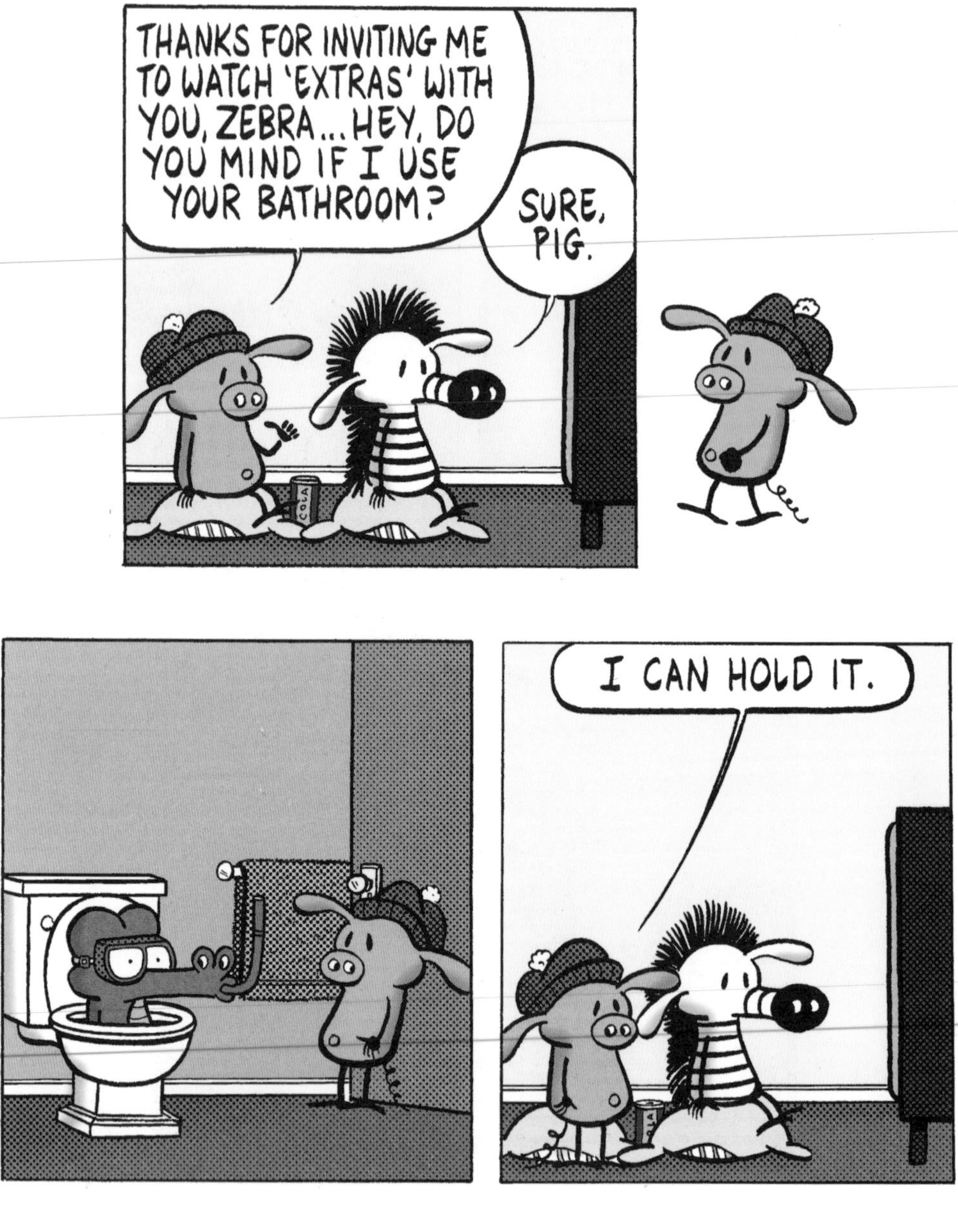
THANKS FOR INVITING ME TO WATCH 'EXTRAS' WITH YOU, ZEBRA... HEY, DO YOU MIND IF I USE YOUR BATHROOM?
SURE, PIG.
I CAN HOLD IT.

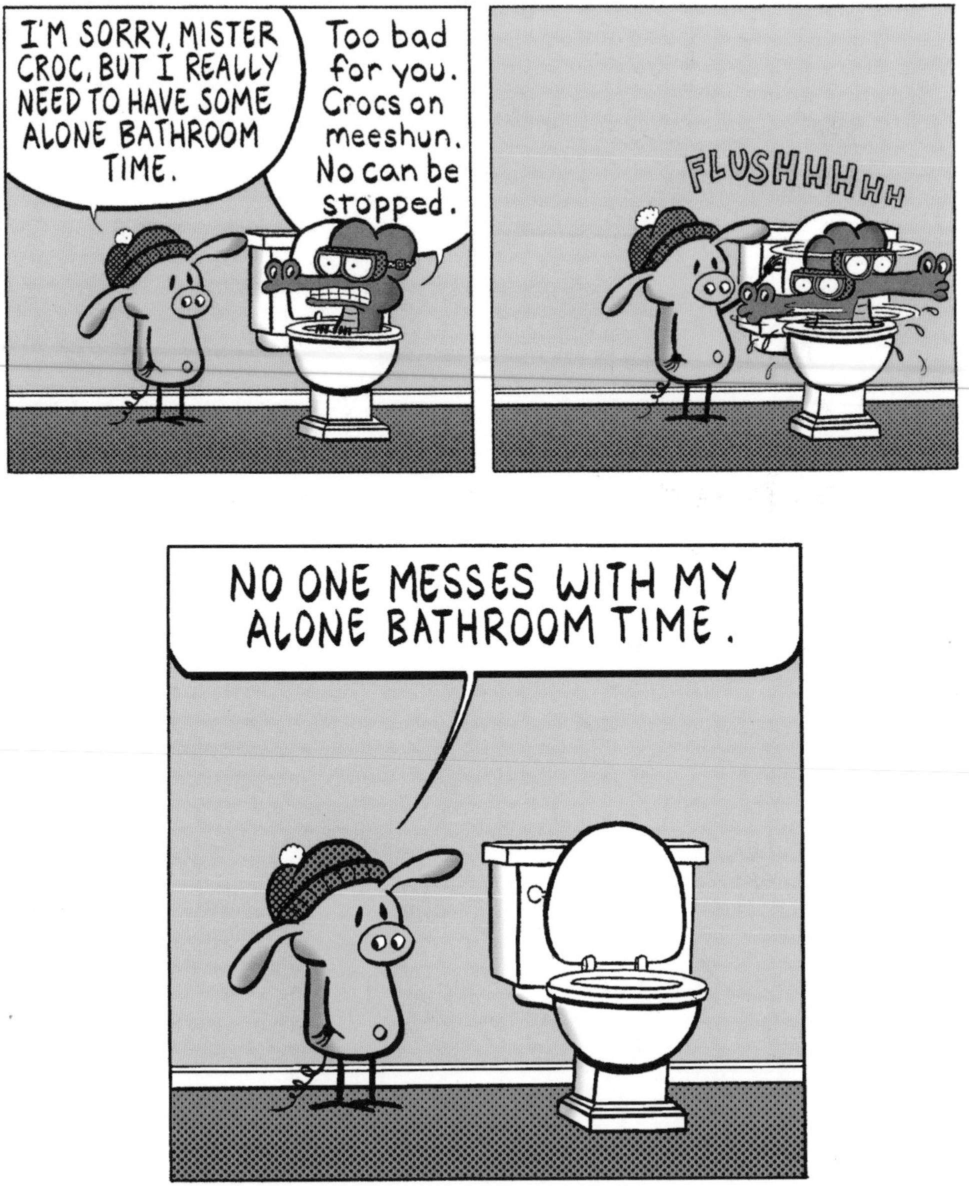
I'M SORRY, MISTER CROC, BUT I REALLY NEED TO HAVE SOME ALONE BATHROOM TIME.
Too bad for you. Crocs on meeshun. No can be stopped.
FLUSHHHHHH
NO ONE MESSES WITH MY ALONE BATHROOM TIME.

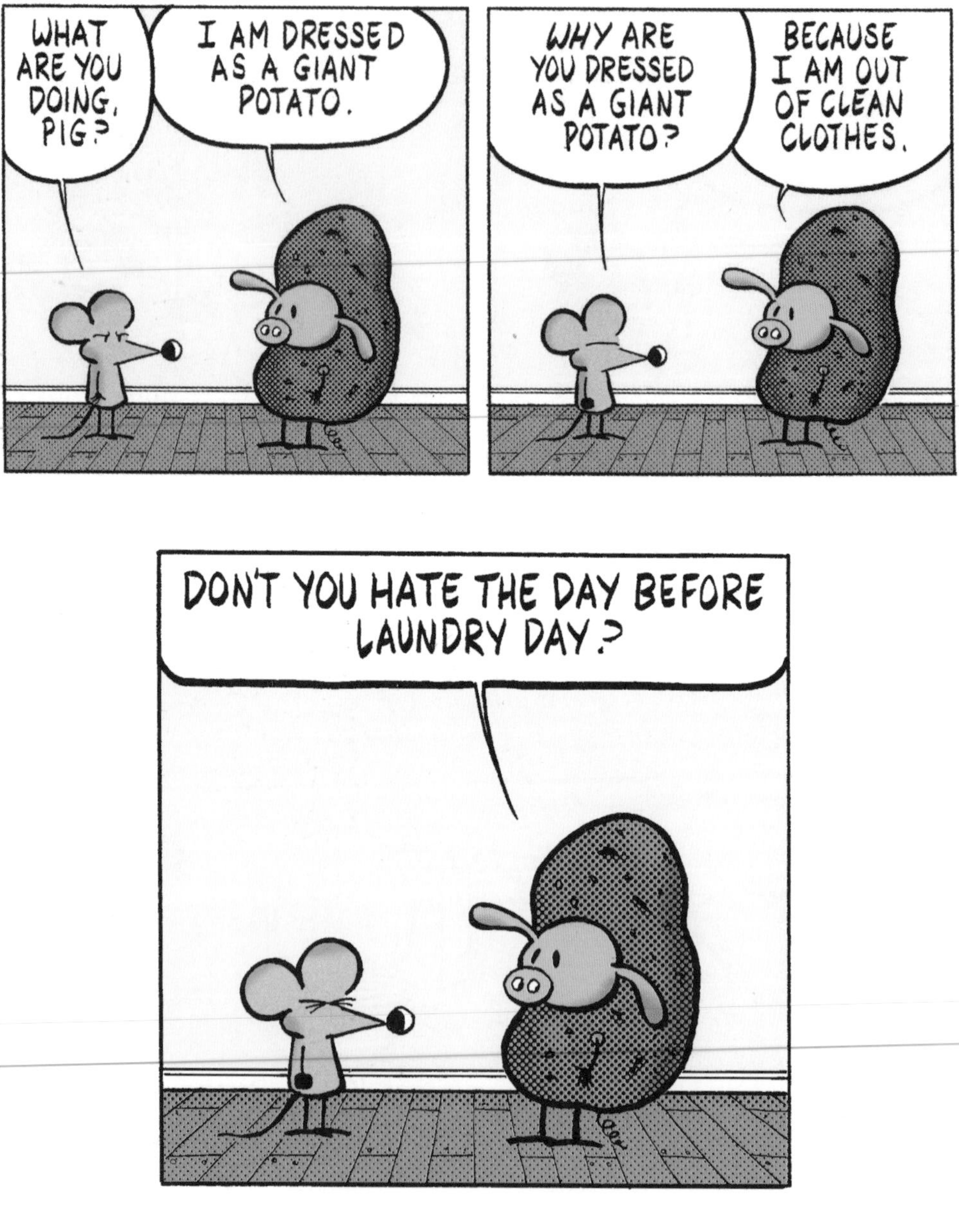
WHAT ARE YOU DOING, PIG?
I AM DRESSED AS A GIANT POTATO.
WHY ARE YOU DRESSED AS A GIANT POTATO?
BECAUSE I AM OUT OF CLEAN CLOTHES.
DON'T YOU HATE THE DAY BEFORE LAUNDRY DAY?

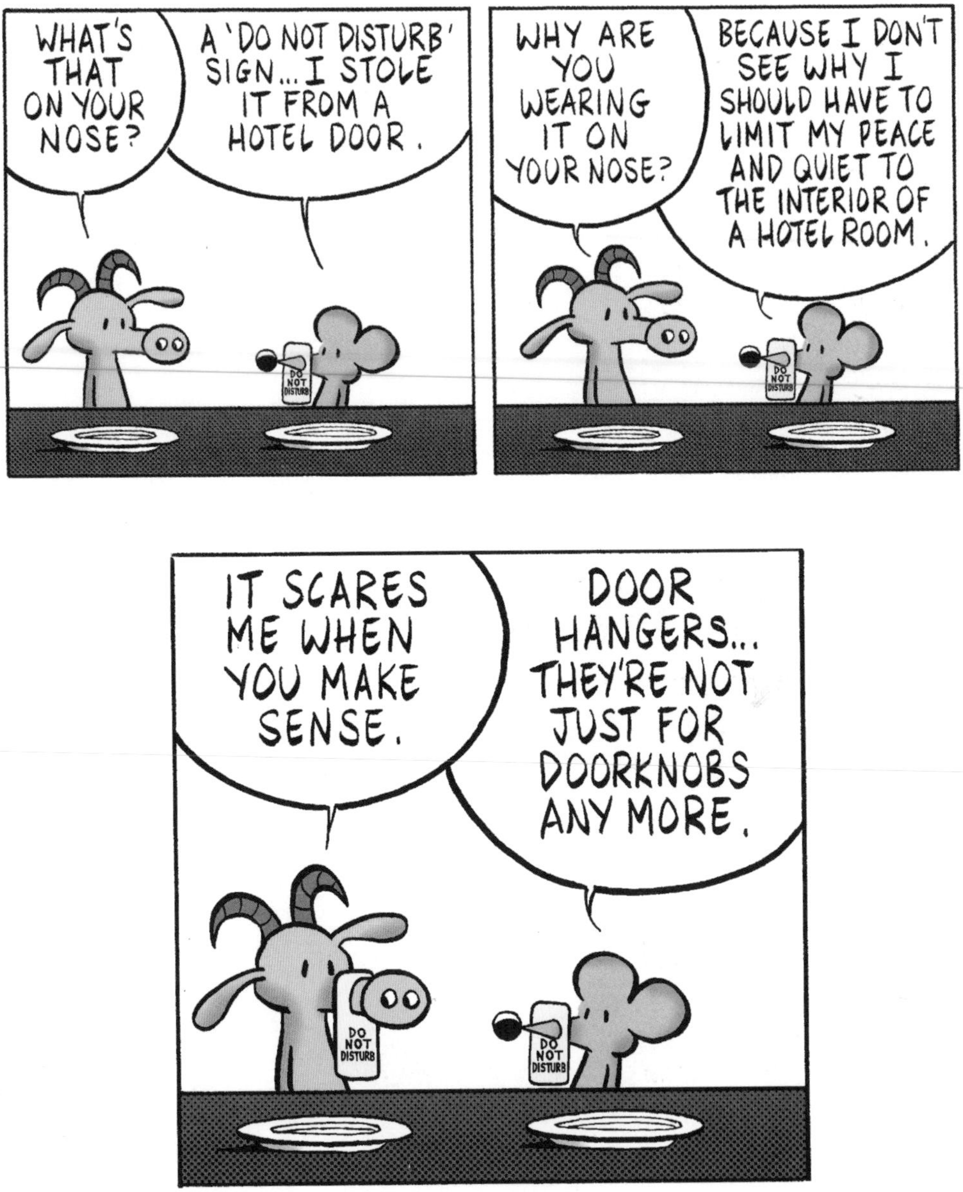
WHAT'S THAT ON YOUR NOSE?
A 'DO NOT DISTURB' SIGN... I STOLE IT FROM A HOTEL DOOR.
DO NOT DISTURB
WHY ARE YOU WEARING IT ON YOUR NOSE?
BECAUSE I DON'T SEE WHY I SHOULD HAVE TO LIMIT MY PEACE AND QUIET TO THE INTERIOR OF A HOTEL ROOM.
DO NOT DISTURB
IT SCARES ME WHEN YOU MAKE SENSE.
DOOR HANGERS... THEY'RE NOT JUST FOR DOORKNOBS ANY MORE.
DO NOT DISTURB
DO NOT DISTURB

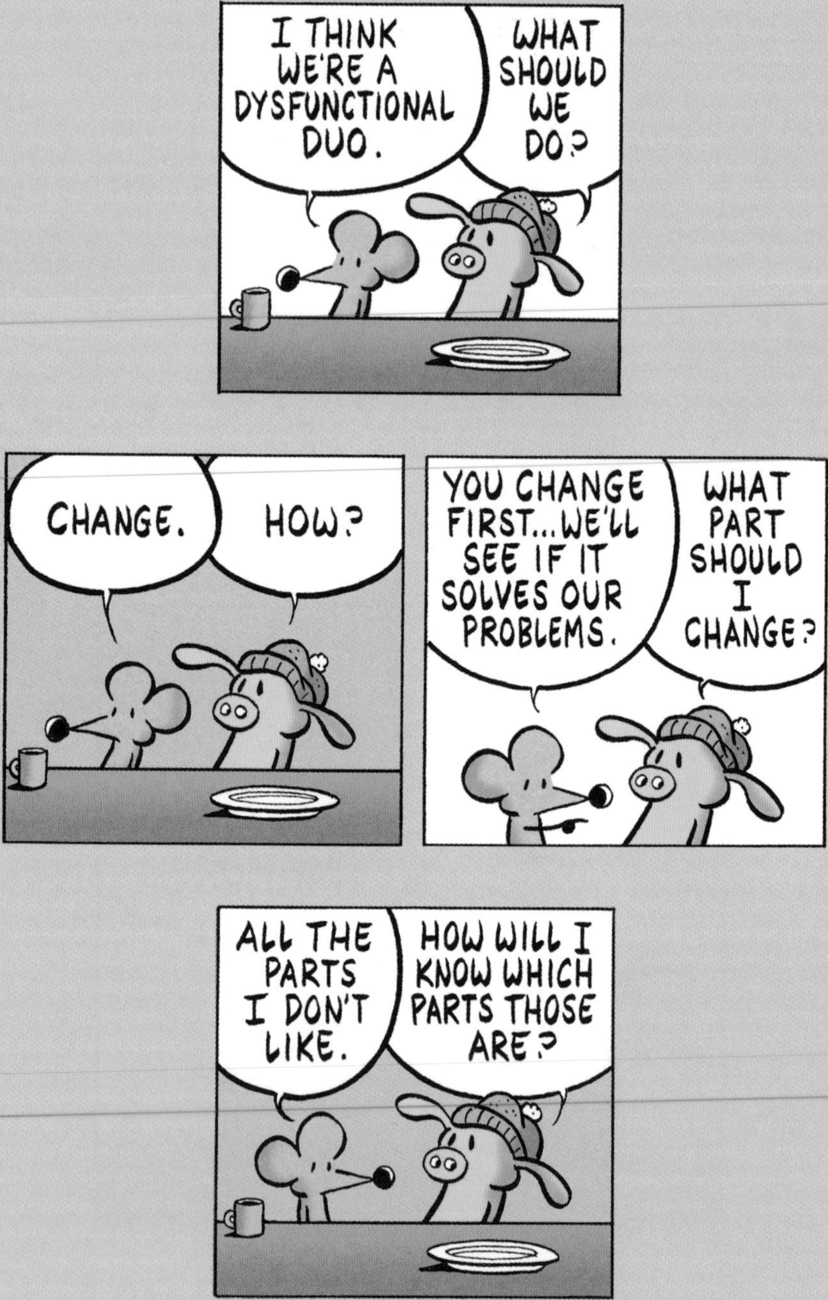
I THINK WE'RE A DYSFUNCTIONAL DUO.
WHAT SHOULD WE DO?
CHANGE.
HOW?
YOU CHANGE FIRST...WE'LL SEE IF IT SOLVES OUR PROBLEMS.
WHAT PART SHOULD I CHANGE?
ALL THE PARTS I DON'T LIKE.
HOW WILL I KNOW WHICH PARTS THOSE ARE?

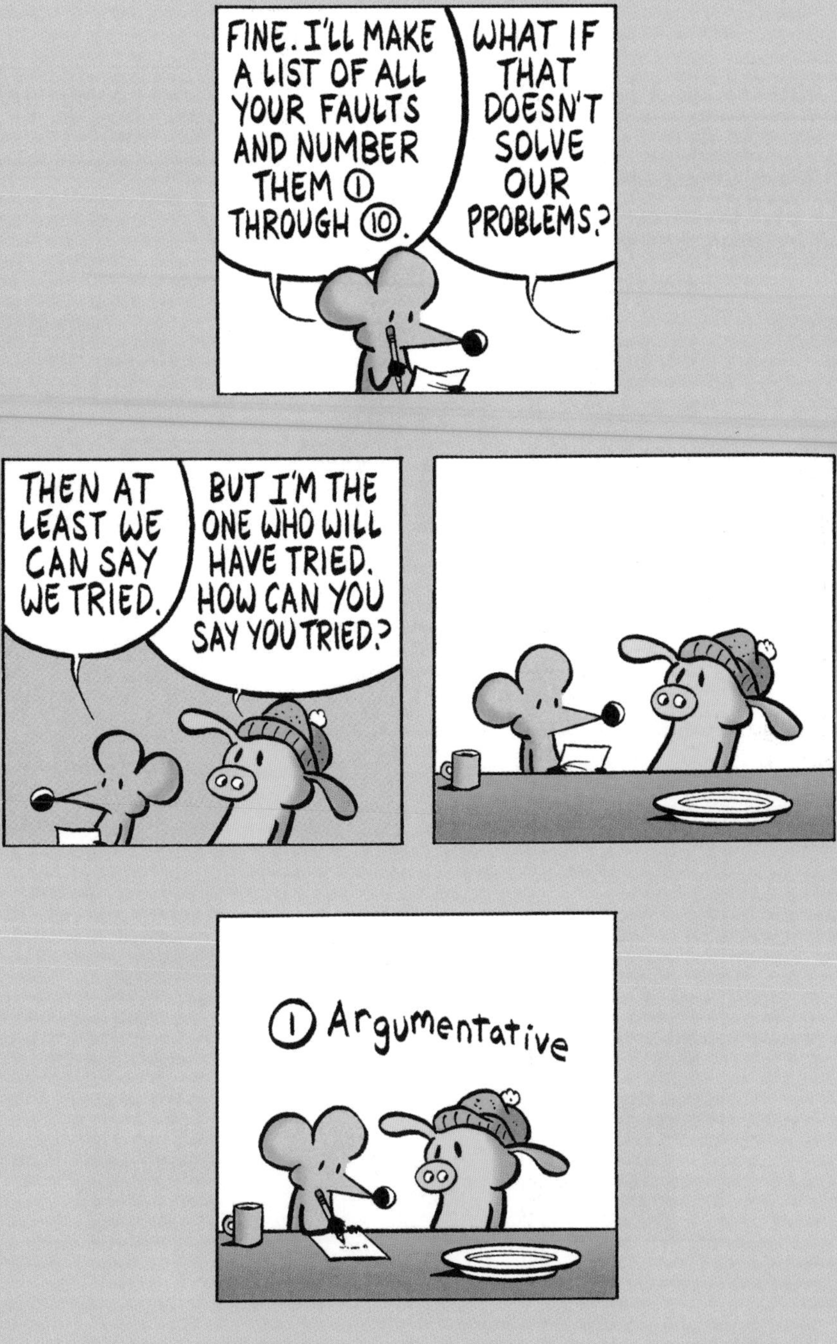
FINE. I'LL MAKE A LIST OF ALL YOUR FAULTS AND NUMBER THEM ① THROUGH ⑩.
WHAT IF THAT DOESN'T SOLVE OUR PROBLEMS?
THEN AT LEAST WE CAN SAY WE TRIED.
BUT I'M THE ONE WHO WILL HAVE TRIED. HOW CAN YOU SAY YOU TRIED?
① Argumentative

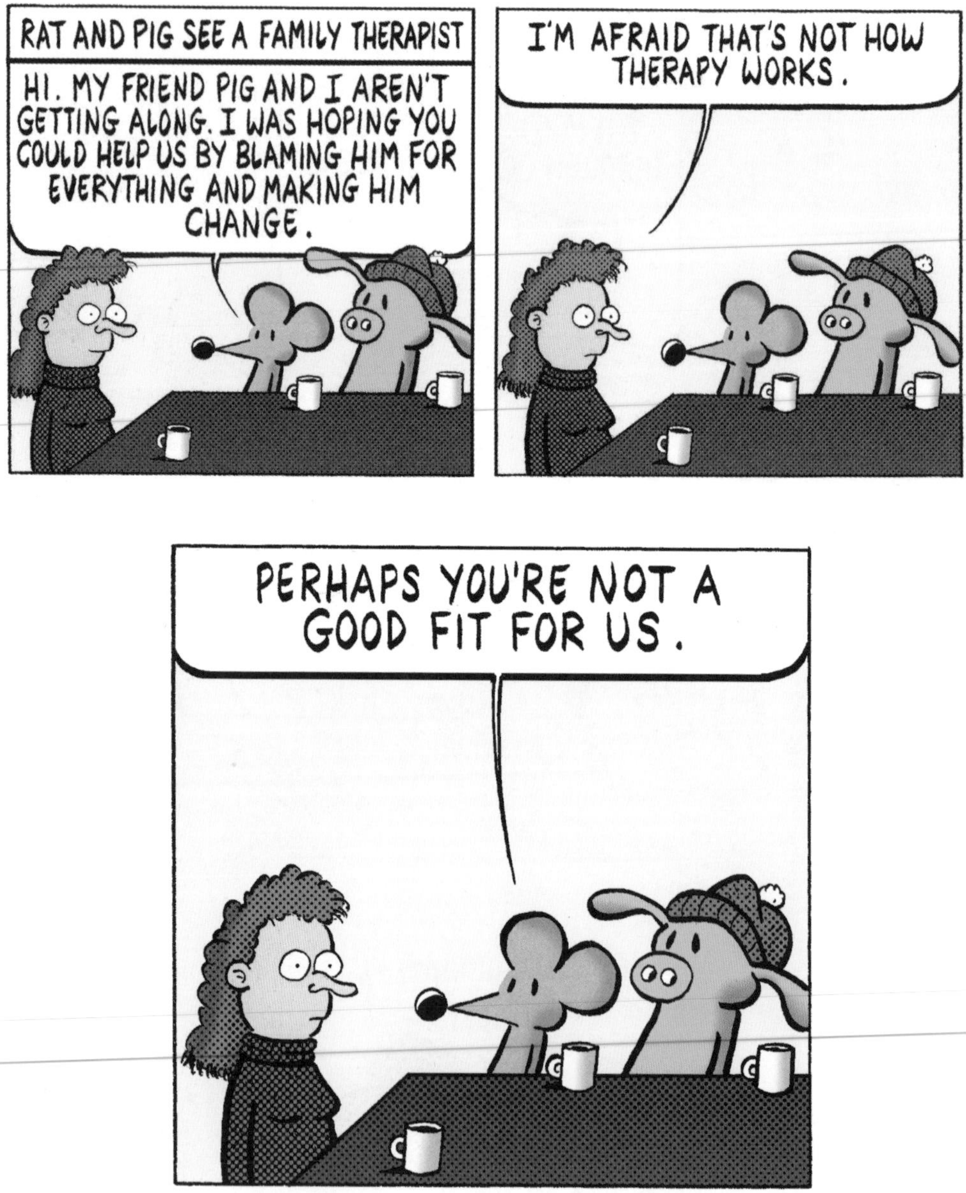
RAT AND PIG SEE A FAMILY THERAPIST
HI. MY FRIEND PIG AND I AREN'T GETTING ALONG. I WAS HOPING YOU COULD HELP US BY BLAMING HIM FOR EVERYTHING AND MAKING HIM CHANGE.
I'M AFRAID THAT'S NOT HOW THERAPY WORKS.
PERHAPS YOU'RE NOT A GOOD FIT FOR US.

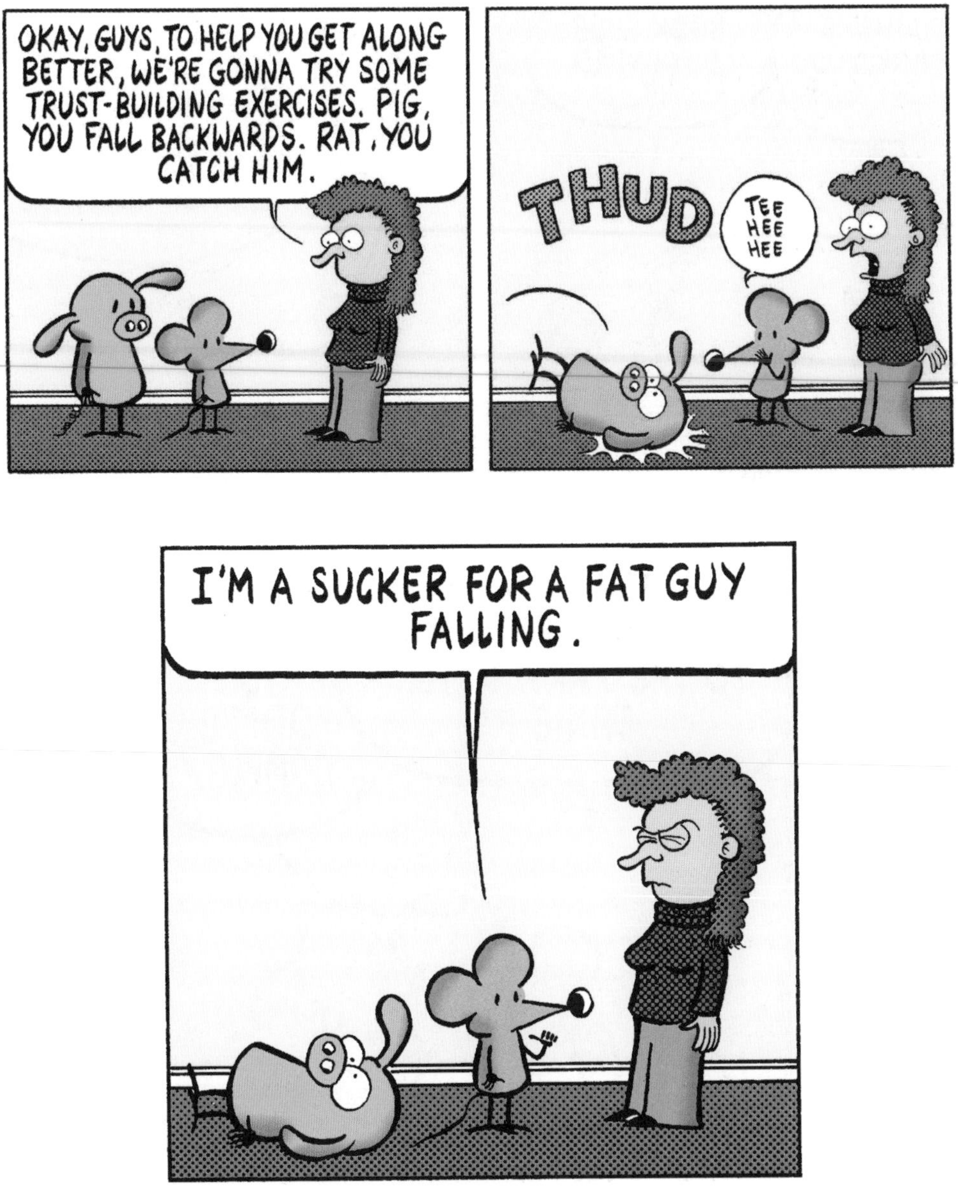
OKAY, GUYS, TO HELP YOU GET ALONG BETTER, WE'RE GONNA TRY SOME TRUST-BUILDING EXERCISES. PIG, YOU FALL BACKWARDS. RAT, YOU CATCH HIM.
THUD
TEE HEE HEE
I'M A SUCKER FOR A FAT GUY FALLING.

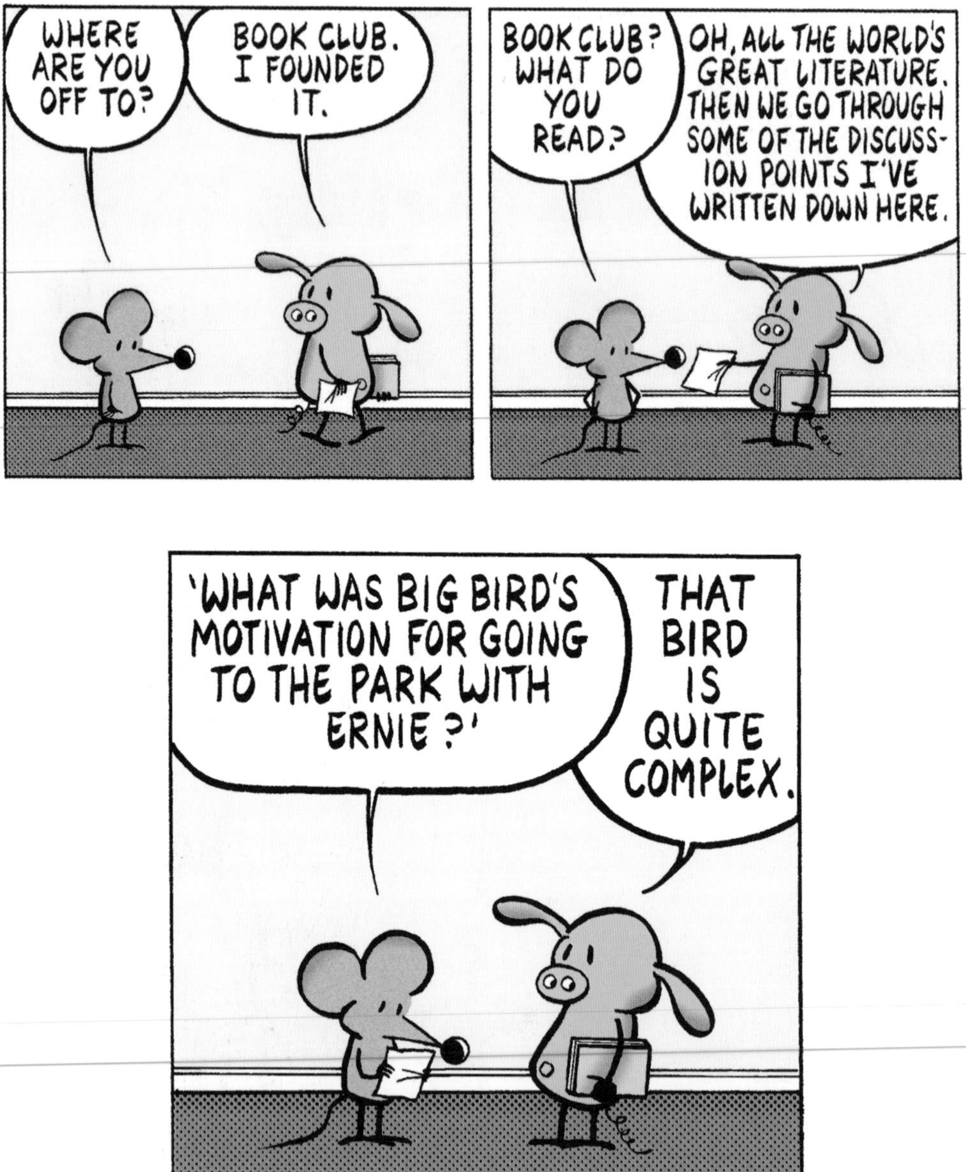
WHERE ARE YOU OFF TO?
BOOK CLUB. I FOUNDED IT.
BOOK CLUB? WHAT DO YOU READ?
OH, ALL THE WORLD'S GREAT LITERATURE. THEN WE GO THROUGH SOME OF THE DISCUSSION POINTS I'VE WRITTEN DOWN HERE.
'WHAT WAS BIG BIRD'S MOTIVATION FOR GOING TO THE PARK WITH ERNIE?'
THAT BIRD IS QUITE COMPLEX.

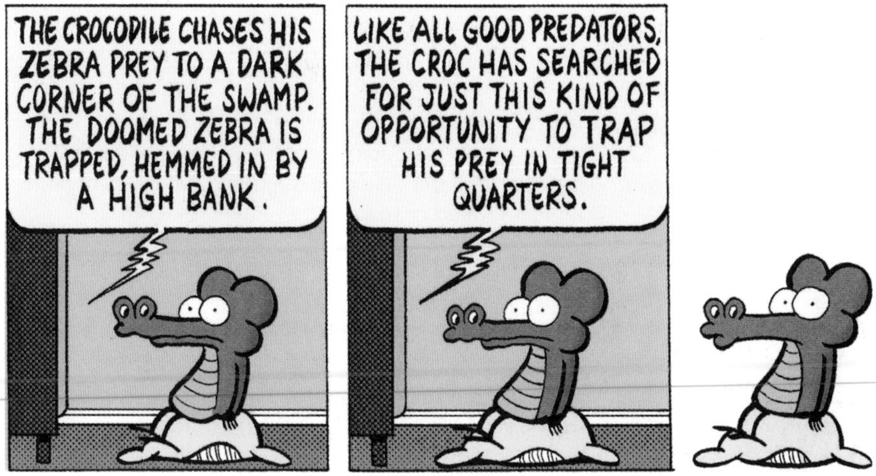
THE CROCODILE CHASES HIS ZEBRA PREY TO A DARK CORNER OF THE SWAMP. THE DOOMED ZEBRA IS TRAPPED, HEMMED IN BY A HIGH BANK.
LIKE ALL GOOD PREDATORS, THE CROC HAS SEARCHED FOR JUST THIS KIND OF OPPORTUNITY TO TRAP HIS PREY IN TIGHT QUARTERS.

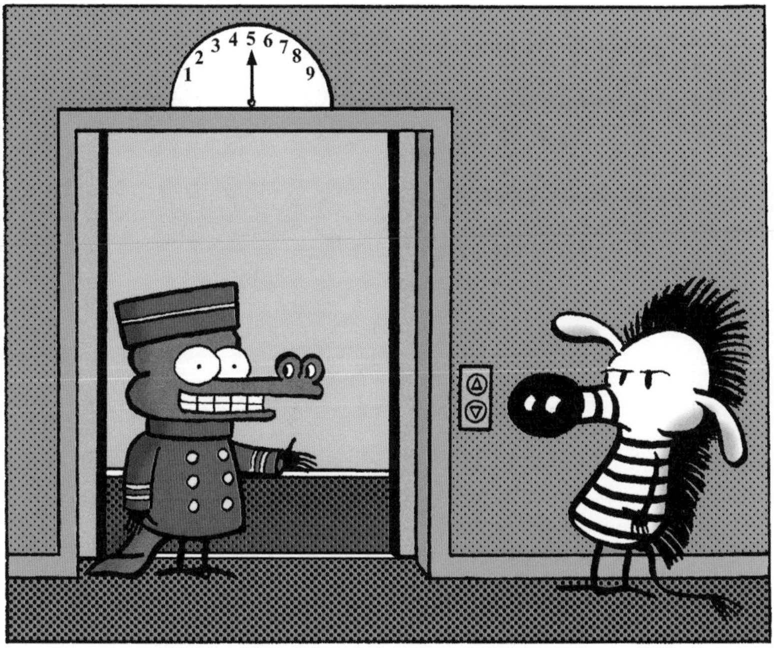

Andrews McMeel Publishing, LLC
an Andrews McMeel Universal company
1130 Walnut Street, Kansas City, Missouri 64106

www.andrewsmcmeel.com

14 15 16 17 18 SDB 10 9 8 7 6 5 4 3 2 1

ISBN: 978-1-4494-3636-0

Library of Congress Control Number: 2013957201

Pearls Before Swine can be viewed on the Internet at www.pearlscomic.com.

Made by:
Shenzen Donnelley Printing Company Ltd.
Address and location of manufacturer:
No. 47, Wuhe Nan Road, Bantian Ind. Zone,
Shenzhen China, 518129
1st Printing – 4/14/14

ATTENTION: SCHOOLS AND BUSINESSES

Andrews McMeel books are available at quantity discounts with bulk purchase for educational, business, or sales promotional use. For information, please e-mail the Andrews McMeel Publishing Special Sales Department:
specialsales@amuniversal.com

Be sure to check out the first *Pearls Before Swine* AMP! Comics for Kids book and others at ampkids.com.

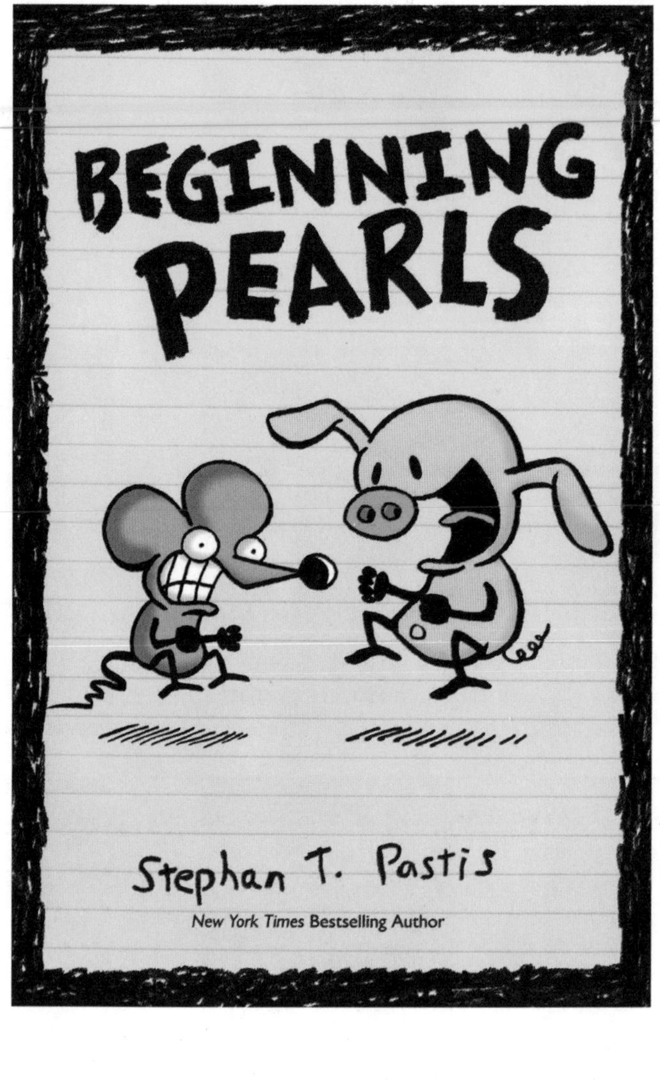
BEGINNING PEARLS
Stephan T. Pastis
New York Times Bestselling Author

Check out these and other books at ampkids.com

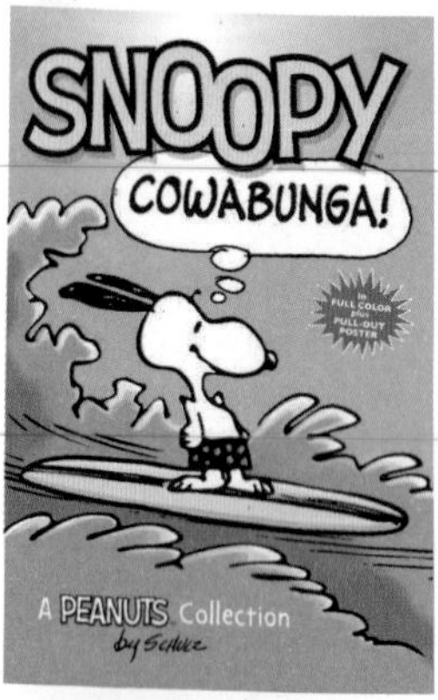
SNOOPY
COWABUNGA!
A PEANUTS Collection
by Schulz

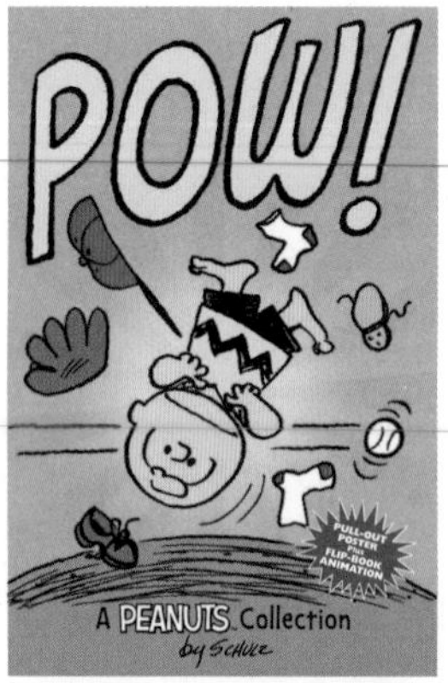
POW!
A PEANUTS Collection
by Schulz

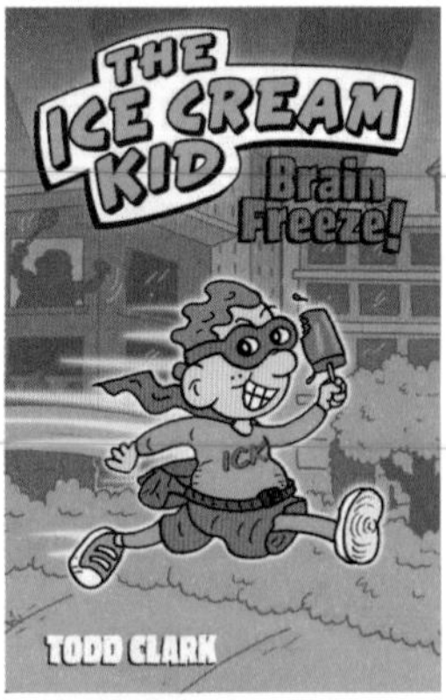
THE ICE CREAM KID
Brain Freeze!
TODD CLARK

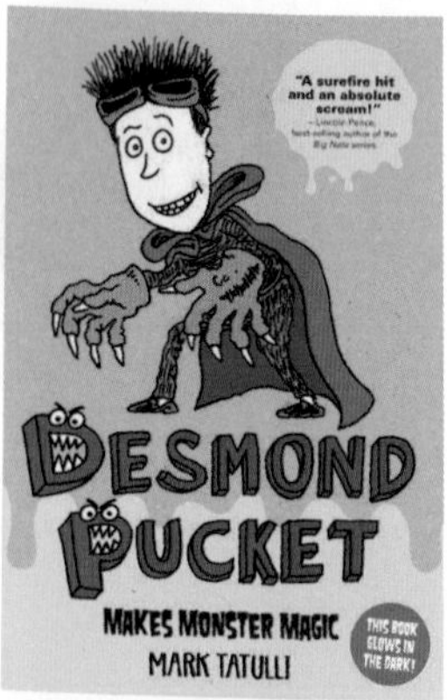
"A surefire hit and an absolute scream!"
DESMOND PUCKET
MAKES MONSTER MAGIC
MARK TATULLI
THIS BOOK GLOWS IN THE DARK!

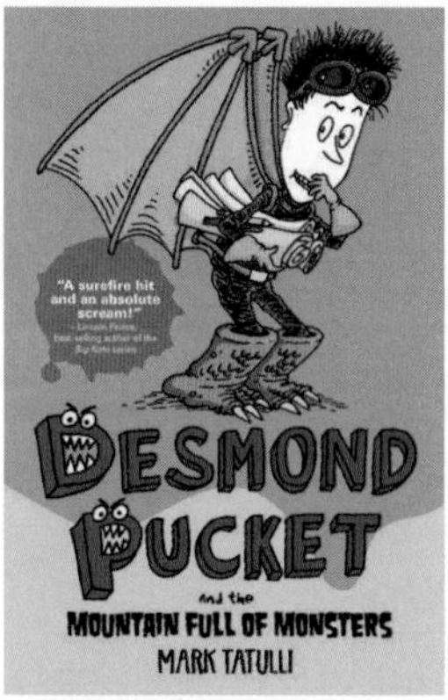
"A surefire hit and an absolute scream!"
DESMOND PUCKET
and the
MOUNTAIN FULL OF MONSTERS
MARK TATULLI

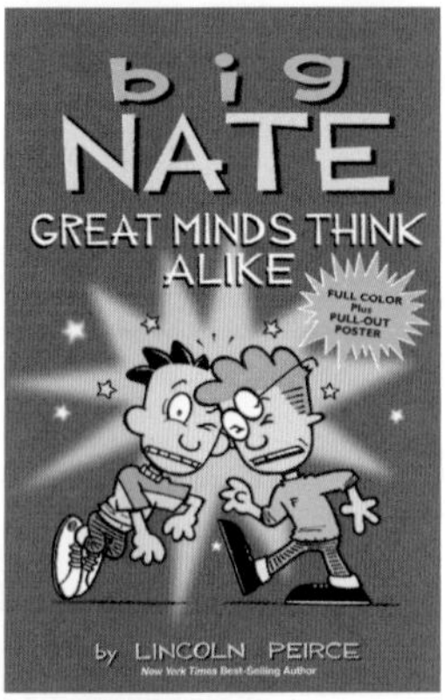
big NATE
GREAT MINDS THINK ALIKE
FULL COLOR Plus FULL-OUT POSTER
by LINCOLN PEIRCE

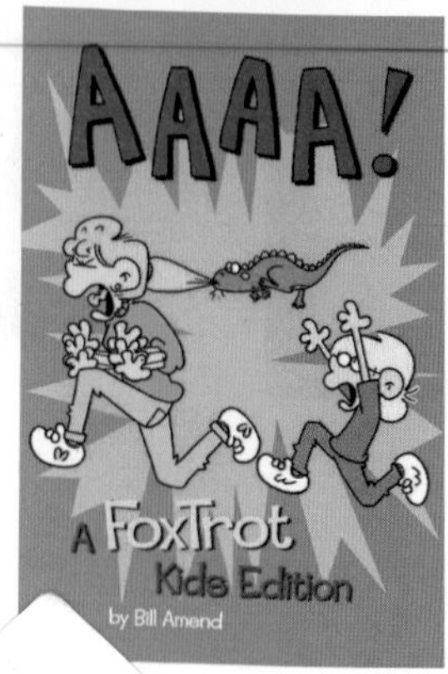
AAAA!
A FoxTrot Kids Edition
by Bill Amend

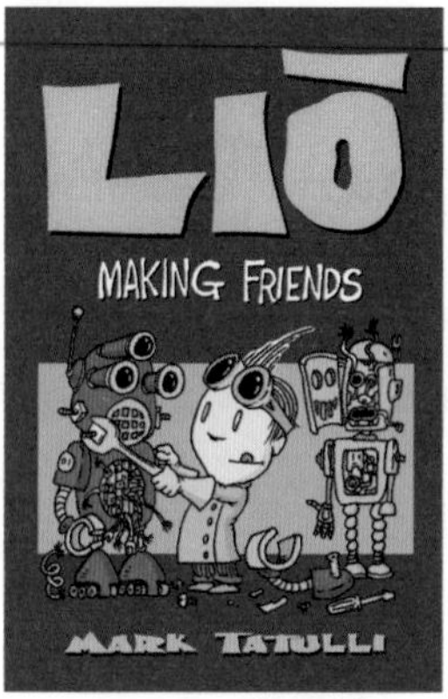
LIO
MAKING FRIENDS
MARK TATULLI

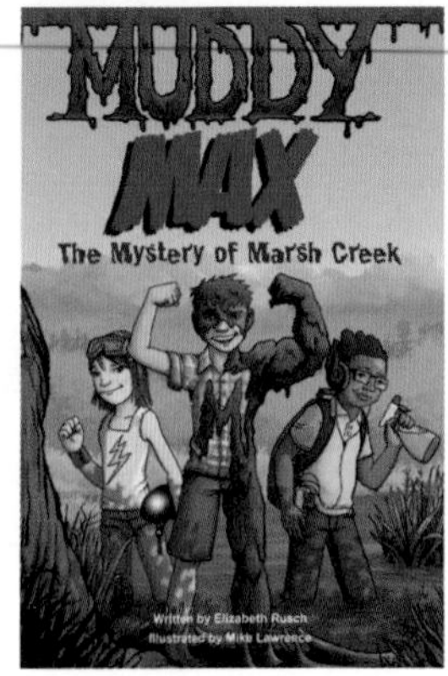
MUDDY MAX
The Mystery of Marsh Creek

Also available:
Teaching and activity guides for each title.
P! Comics for Kids books make reading FUN!

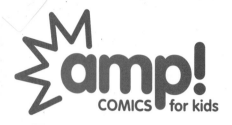